RED GROW THE ROSES

Janine Ashbless

T0318072

This novel is entirely a work of fiction.
The names, characters and incidents portrayed in it are the work of the author's imagination. Any resemblance to actual persons, living or dead, events or localities is entirely coincidental.

Mischief
An imprint of HarperCollins*Publishers*
77–85 Fulham Palace Road,
Hammersmith, London W6 8JB

www.mischiefbooks.com

A Paperback Original 2013

First published in Great Britain in ebook format by HarperCollins*Publishers* 2012

Copyright © Janine Ashbless 2013

Janine Ashbless asserts the moral right to be identified as the author of this work

A catalogue record for this book is available from the British Library

ISBN-13: 978 0 00 753331 2

Automatically produced by Atomik ePublisher from Easypress

All rights reserved. No part of this publication may be reproduced, stored in a retrieval system, or transmitted, in any form or by any means, electronic, mechanical, photocopying, recording or otherwise, without the prior permission of the publishers.

Prologue

I'll sing you Ten-O,
Green grow the rushes-O!
What is your Ten-O?
Ten for the Ten Commandments:
Nine for the Nine Bright Shiners:
Eight for the April Rainers:
Seven for the Seven Stars in the Sky:
Six for the Six Proud Walkers:
Five for the Symbols at your Door:
Four for the Gospel Makers:
Three, Three the Rivals:
Two, Two the Lily-White Boys, clothèd all in green-O.
One is One and all alone
And ever more shall be so.

(Folk song)

There is a City. Maybe you live there: eight million people do. Maybe you've visited it. Maybe you've only heard of it. It's an ancient place, founded by the Romans on a marshy floodplain watered by a great tidal river. Its foundations go deep into the sucking mud of history. But these days its population is young, its faces diverse. More than three hundred languages are spoken in its schools and malls and streets. Proud new buildings are hatched among the husks of ancient architecture.

There is only one person left who still remembers the rushes and the bog myrtle and the wild ducks in what is now the heart of the City. And she is not a living person, not in any real sense.

Come to the City. Take photos of the famous landmarks on your cell phone. Shop for designer clothes and tourist tat. Walk the frantic streets of the theatre district at night. What will you see, there in the neon dark? Is that shadow behind you someone following? Is that reflection in a plate-glass window horribly distorted, or horribly accurate? Are those eyes that watch from the night even human? They must be, surely. He looks like a man – though his eyes reflect the dimmest of lights in crimson circles.

Maybe you'll be lucky. Maybe he's not human. Maybe he'll take you in his arms and you'll feel his strength – a strength that makes it impossible to fight him, even if you did want to. But you've already lost the will to resist, that moment when he looked into your eyes and showed you all his hunger and his promise. You knew then. You knew, quite suddenly, that this is what you are for – what we are all for – with our warm beating hearts and our aching sexual needs.

We are for them.

He'll hold you like a lover. You'll feel his breath on your throat and think to yourself: it's so cold! His fingers will be cold too – cold on your puckering nipples, chill as they slide between your legs and inside you. Perhaps he'll rip your clothes as he works them off; his nails are sharper than they look. No matter: it's not as if you'll have much use for them afterwards. His hard cock will seem startlingly cold, as cold as glass chilled in ice-water, as it presses into you. You'll feel your body yielding to him just as eagerly as your will did, all your hot secret places opening to his gelid insistence. Then he'll enter you, and your flesh will be impaled inexorably on that brutal length. For a moment he might only fuck you. He'll wait for your cries, thrilling to the noises that burst from your throat as he rides you. It's not for your sake but for his, since anticipation sharpens his pleasure. When his teeth first shear through your flesh the pain will make you panic – but only for a second. After that there will be no more pain, only desire. His and yours, as you feed ravenously upon each other, frantic to be filled.

In the morning they will find you limp and drained, the splashes of your spilt blood scattered on you and about you like fallen rose petals.

There are no rushes growing around here any more. But in this City there are always roses.

1: Ten for the Ten Commandments

Sophie met the vampire while speed-dating.

There were twenty numbers printed on the paper, each with a tick-box next to it. So far Sophie had ticked two, slightly reluctantly, and she wasn't all that sure about Number Eight: he'd had an annoying laugh that ended in a snort each time. It was a good thing, she told herself, that this wasn't a professional event, just a charity do put on by their regular bar in aid of some cancer relief charity. She and Netta had only paid a tenner each to enter.

And oh, boy, are we getting our money's worth, she thought, suppressing the urge to giggle.

'I've got a classic MG that I'm doing up myself in my garage,' said Number Nineteen hopefully. 'I've just had the new front wing sprayed British Racing Green.'

This meant nothing at all to Sophie. She stole a glance sideways at Netta, perched just like her on a high barstool at one of those teeny little round tables you could never quite fit all your glasses on, her legs crossed, her foot twitching sharply as she listened to a beaky-nosed man talk. They had five minutes with each guy and this time it had turned out to be four minutes and fifty seconds longer than she needed to decide No. 'Really?' Sophie said.

Luckily, that was the moment the host by the bar picked up the wineglass he was using as a signal and tapped it with his pen. As the ringing died away all the men at the tables stood and started to move on.

Last one, thought Sophie.

'It was nice meeting you,' said Number Nineteen with gallant desperation.

'And you,' she said cheerily. No call to be rude, was there? He wasn't going to be getting a tick though. He wasn't going to be getting hold of her name or her e-mail address.

She was still looking down at her slip of paper in despair when the last of her 'dates' sat down in front of her, saying, 'Hi.'

'Hi.' Then, looking up, Sophie thought: Oh ... wow.

Maybe this was going to be worth doing after all. Number Twenty was easily the best-looking man of the evening. He was one of those scruffy stubbly dark-blond types with hair and skin sun-kissed to nearly the same colour, and rather thick eyebrows. She liked that outdoorsy look. His athletic build was well displayed by a white T-shirt. He grinned at her, an open easy grin. 'You having fun?'

I am now, she thought, but said out loud, 'It's ... different. I've never tried speed-dating before.' What lovely eyes he had, she noted: brown, but flecked with gold. All the patter honed by repetition over the evening suddenly deserted her and she realised she was staring. To cover her unexpected awkwardness she took a sip of her vodka and orange, then berated herself inwardly for wasting time.

'So.' He put his hands on the table. Blunt hands with clean square nails, and a silver thumb-ring on the right. 'Tell me about yourself.'

OK, so he wasn't exactly bursting with originality either. It gave Sophie a little confidence back. 'I work at an art gallery in town,' she said. 'A commercial one, not high art or anything – and I'm just an assistant – but I want to run my own gallery one day. I like hanging out with friends and going out on the town ...' She ground to a halt as she realised she was being obvious and dull. 'What about you?'

He just sat and looked at her with his face almost alight, like he was full of sunshine. She could imagine him climbing a mountain or white-water-rafting or hitchhiking around Asia. 'Me?'

'You. You're supposed to say something interesting,' she reminded him.

'Oh. All right then. I'm a vampire.'

She had, she thought, never met anyone who looked less like a vampire. 'As chat-up lines go,' she said, a little acid now, 'that's better than "I'm a serial killer." But, you know, a bit worse than "I'm a big *Star Trek* fan."'

'Ouch.'

'You could try it in the Fox and Grapes though. They have a Goth Night on a Wednesday, I think.'

'I'll remember that.' His brow furrowed humbly, but he grinned.

'And to be honest,' she said pointing at him, 'even if I wanted to be impressed, that's just not vampire at all.'

'What?'

'Your teeth. Unconvincing. Where's the fangs?'

'Retractable.'

'Really?' She was actually enjoying herself now. He didn't seem at all put off by her sarcasm.

'Of course. Otherwise we'd be lisping and drooling all over the place.'

'Oh, *right.*'

'Hold on. I'll just ...' He pursed his lips and wrinkled his nose back and forth as if something were stuck in his teeth. Then he peeled back his lips and opened his mouth. He had fangs this time: translucent as Chinese rice porcelain, sharp as thorns.

'OK,' she admitted. 'That's quite impressive. And ... different.'

He shut his mouth and flashed his eyebrows in a smile, vindicated.

'Did you show that to all the girls?' Sophie turned to the table at her right. 'Hey, Netta, did you get a look at these?'

Netta looked startled to be interrupted. 'At what?'

But when Sophie glanced back, Number Twenty was gone. 'I ... uh ...'

Gone. Completely gone. Sophie's eyes searched the room. There were plenty of people in buying drinks, apart from those engaged in the speed-dating, but none of them looked like him. Sophie bit her lip. She didn't understand where he could have disappeared to; she had barely looked away from him. She supposed that if he'd leapt up and hand-sprung backwards he could have jumped over the bar itself in time, but that was a bit too Ninja-like to be actually believable. She got up from her stool anyway, and walked over to the bar to check for herself. He wasn't hiding down among the glasses and the plastic crates.

'Weird,' she said.

It was another three minutes before the last round of the speed-dating was over. They were the longest, most awkward three minutes of her life, but at last the chime was sounded and all the couples broke up and she was able to make a beeline for Netta.

'Did you see where he went?'

'Who?'

'The guy with me. Number Twenty ... well, he would have been your Number Nineteen. The really good-looking one.'

Netta frowned. 'Really good-looking? You sure?'

'Oh, come on! Blondish, white shirt ... nice *teeth*.' She was even more confused now.

'Uh, no.' Netta looked down at her tick-sheet. 'I didn't mark him down anyway. I can't really remember him, to be honest. There were so many guys, I suppose, Sophie: you just stop noticing after a while.'

Sophie passed her hand over her face. 'Can we get out of here?' It was the state of her own mind that was worrying her, but she tried to hide it. 'I'm scared the one with the bad breath is going to try and carry on our chat.'

'You're not going to hand your sheet in?'

The piece of paper had grown damp in her hand, she realised. She crumpled it up. 'No. I didn't fancy any of them, really.'

Netta sighed. 'Me neither.'

They made their way to the door – and there he was, Number Twenty, bathed in the magenta strip-light of the Bar Trattoria sign, chatting amiably to the bouncer. His eye fell on Sophie. 'Hey there. You going before I can buy you a drink? I'm Ben, by the way.'

She blinked. Face to face with him once more, she couldn't believe there was anything weird about him. Not that the teeth thing had actually worried her: she'd assumed that was just a trick of some sort. 'Um. We thought we'd head out somewhere else.'

He glanced questioningly at Netta, who looked very pleased indeed. Plump and pretty, she always made the most of her capacious cleavage and now Sophie saw her swing it into action, turning those orbs on Ben like twin lamps, in the hope of dazzling him.

'I'm Netta. Short for Agnetha – my mum was a big ABBA fan.' She giggled. 'We work at the same place, Sophie and me.'

'Ah ... the art gallery?'

'That's right.'

'Well, can I buy you both a drink then?'

'I don't see why not.'

Sophie shrugged and nodded, pushing any lingering disquiet aside.

'You want to go to a club?' suggested Ben. 'How about the Rose Garden? We could skip the queue: I know the guys on the door.'

'Sounds good,' said Netta.

'Yeah,' Sophie agreed. The Rose Garden was expensive and she'd never been there.

He held the glass door open for them both and followed them out on to the street. Netta took the chance to catch Sophie's eye and mouth '*Hot*!' at her. Sophie wanted to ask her if she remembered him from the speed-dating line-up now, but she didn't have the chance.

He didn't let them down at the Rose Garden either, marching them straight up to the bouncers and inside, after a nod and an exchange of greetings. He made sure he paid too, and bought the drinks at the bar, slipping an arm round each of their shoulders as he stood between them and ordered, encouraging them to choose the fanciest cocktails they could find on the bar menu. The dancefloor wasn't yet packed as it was relatively early in the evening, so there was plenty of space for the three of them to go on and dance together. He was a good mover, Sophie noted, though his eyes only really lit up when they played a remix of some jangling 60s hit by a group she was too young to be able even to picture. He flirted with both of them, paying each equal attention and obviously enjoying their company, wriggling up against Netta with a cheeky twinkle during a dirty song, dancing away insouciantly a moment later with an ironic wink at Sophie. Every move he made proclaimed: 'I'm having fun and I'll take the fun as far as you like but I'm not after anything heavy.' His grin gleamed under the UV light, but his teeth were completely normal. Well, Hollywood normal.

Taking a break, they retired to a quieter corner to rest their feet for a few minutes. Netta went off to the toilet then. Normally Sophie would have gone with her, but they had a fresh batch of drinks on the table before them by this point and she wasn't going to be so naive as to leave them unguarded, not with the stories you heard these days. Ben seemed nice, right, but ... they didn't know him. Not yet. You had to be careful, didn't you? So she sat and they made light talk and that was when Ben kissed her, leaning in and brushing his lips softly to her own.

All the noise of the club seemed to fade to nothing.

Oh, thought Sophie in the sudden silence inside her head: Oh, I like this. She was flushed and warm from the dancing; his lips felt cool, yet the flicker of his tongue-tip hinted at a deeper heat. She could taste the tang of the lager he'd been drinking. His stubble was softer than she'd expected on her skin as his mouth moved over hers, swallowing her breath. And oh, his hands – one arm around her, smoothly, like she might startle: the other now on her knee, his fingertips the lightest of caresses, not at all intrusive even as they slid up the inside of her thigh, over the lace patterns of her black tights. His cool fingers sketched pointillist pictures of sensation on her skin as they played over the tiny holes in the lace, and Sophie felt a sly seep of moisture within her, a secretly avid response to his touch. And how she wished she'd worn stockings now, as he reached the hem of her skirt.

Ben's tongue was in her mouth now, smooth as cream liqueur and just as sweet. Not boorish, not greedy. She wondered what it would feel like between her pussy lips and, catching herself at that thought, she squirmed beneath his hand and broke the kiss with a little gasp. His teeth caught her lower lip, gently, and she froze.

He let her go. He looked, with a faint but pointed smile, down at his hand on her thigh, as if surprised to find it there. She looked down too and they both watched as her legs eased apart to grant him narrow passage between thighs barely illuminated by the distant flicker of the dancefloor lights. Slowly his hand disappeared under her skirt, following that warm cleft. His cold fingers tickled their way, like water running underground, to the mound of her sex. His nail caught on the threads as he flicked it, quite accurately, over the hidden spot where her clit burned – and Sophie nearly left her seat, trying in vain to mask the spasm of her arousal. Ben scraped his finger up and down on the coarse weave, and smiled as he looked into her eyes. Sophie couldn't grin; her mouth went slack instead as he played with her, her eyes glazing over.

Then he stopped and sat back, without haste. Sophie shook herself from her trance and realised that that faint bloom of light had been the door of the Ladies opening and closing, that Netta was on her way back over to their table. For cover she lifted her cocktail to her lips and sipped from the glass, crossing her thighs. There was a bubble of heat between them that glowed as she squeezed her legs together.

'This might be a flash place but they've still run out of hand-towels in the loo,' announced Netta cheerily as she sat down.

Ben casually rubbed his fingertips together and lifted them to his face as if inhaling the bouquet; the gesture was smooth and almost unnoticeable. 'Hey, it's always best when the girls are a little ... damp.' The weak joke made Netta squeal and pretend to slap him and he played along.

'My turn then,' said Sophie, rising. She'd had more to drink than she thought, it occurred to her as she staggered slightly. Or maybe it was just that her legs were wobbly.

'Careful, love.' Ben placed a hand lightly on her thigh to steady her. It didn't help.

In the ladies' toilet there was chill-out music playing and a row of mirrors a mile long for the customers to examine their make-up in. Sophie larded on another layer of lip-gloss and stared at her reflection, wondering if Ben was making a pass at Netta while she was away. She wouldn't put it past him; he seemed the sort to try anything and his flirting was aimed in every direction. A critical examination of her reflection didn't make her feel too bad, though. She was slimmer than Netta at least, though she'd never manage to match those fabulous tits. With a slight frown she undid the top button on her dress and tucked the cloth down to reveal more of the valley between her own, imagining Ben's head nuzzling between them, his tongue lapping at the silky skin of her breasts. Even the thought made her wetter. God, he'd turned her on. She wanted more of that. She hadn't particularly come out to get laid tonight – she didn't count herself as *that* sort of girl – but now that it was looking like a possibility her pulse was running faster. She didn't want Netta to snatch him from under her nose – and Netta was so much brassier than her and more likely to get what she wanted.

Maybe Ben was hoping to pull both of them, she thought suddenly. In the mirror her reflection blushed and her eyes snapped. 'Oh,' she mouthed with her bright fresh lipstick. That sort of implied he had a place of his own, if he was planning anything that elaborate. She'd never done it before but the novelty had a certain trashy sort of appeal – and she and Netta were good enough friends that it might work. They'd seen each other undress often enough, and talked about sex without any restraint. She wouldn't be embarrassed in front of Netta.

It could be fun. Ben looked like, no matter what, he would be fun.

Making up her mind, Sophie returned to the toilet cubicle and pulled the skirt of her dress up so she could grab the top of her floral lace tights. It was a warm end-of-summer night after all. She could go barelegged.

By the time she left the Ladies she was wearing nothing beneath that short skirt at all.

Back at the table, she wasn't surprised to see that Netta was sitting up close to Ben's side and that his arm was resting down the back of the padded bench behind her shoulders. Nor was she surprised at his cheeky smile. But his words weren't what she'd expected: 'I was telling Netta here that I have a friend who's an artist. A really good one. Sculpture mostly. You want to see his work?'

'Now?'

'What – don't you mix work and pleasure?'

'I just ... well ... it's pretty late.'

'Oh, he'll be in his studio. He likes to work late. It's not far, if you want to take a look. And he's ... a really interesting bloke. You'll like him. He'd like to meet you two, I'm sure.'

Oh, thought Sophie: that's how it is, then. He was pulling on his friend's behalf too. She tried not to consider whether she was disappointed or not.

It wasn't actually all that late by the time they emerged from the Rose Garden; not that late if you were out on the lash on a Saturday night, that is: late for everyone else. Bars and takeaways were doing a booming trade but the only vehicles on the streets were taxis and buses and police vans. Ben slipped an arm around each of them.

'Ooh,' said Netta: 'you're cold.' She was right, thought Sophie: he wasn't icy, but there was none of the heat she'd been expecting from his body. That white cotton T-shirt might as well have been draped over a mannequin's torso: toned and unyielding and cool.

'Yeah, I am. I need you two to keep me warm.'

Netta giggled and pressed herself up against him in a hug that only looked innocent.

So Ben walked through the night streets with them flanking him, his arms around their shoulders, their arms about his hard waist. He steered well clear of loud and dangerous-looking revellers, but kept to the lighted main roads as if to reassure them. And he kept up a stream of chatter all the way, all about Warhol and Lichtenstein and other names Sophie knew she should have paid more attention to on her art-history induction course, until they crossed under a flyover and followed the road in a curve and there were suddenly trees and a big black building looming over them. A church. It stood in a little island in a whirlpool of main roads and it wasn't floodlit like some of the city-centre churches. Victorian Gothic in style, its stones were black with soot dating back to the Industrial Revolution and it was close-grown with big dingy sycamores.

'Here we are,' said Ben, suddenly grabbing their hands and skipping them across the road under the nose of a taxi. They reached the pavement beneath a white streetlamp that made the building beyond look even more shadowed.

'A church?' asked Netta, pulling out of his hand. She wrinkled her nose. 'It looks derelict.'

'It's an artists' centre now. Naylor's studio's inside – see the light?'

They peered into the gloom, and Sophie was relieved to see that there was a glow high up in one of the tall stained-glass windows – though it barely showed through the encrustation of soot and the thick protective wire lattice over the exterior of the glass.

'Looks spooky,' muttered Sophie.

'Looks like a place for freaks to hang out,' Netta grumbled.

'Aw,' he mocked softly. 'Are the little girls scared?'

Netta cast him a sharp glance. 'Hey – how old are you?' she asked. It sounded like a change of subject but Sophie knew where she was coming from. She'd assumed all along that Ben was their own age or thereabouts: mid-twenties at most. That's how he'd looked under the indoor lights. But out here under the harsh white light of the streetlamp he looked suddenly older. It wasn't wrinkles; he didn't look wrinkled. It was something less definable, something about the way the shadows fell or the look in his eye as he derided their squeamishness. Something about his eyes, for sure – as he turned his face down to them he looked almost blind for a second.

'How old do you think I am, love?'

'Thirty? Thirty-five?' Netta was being deliberately nasty, trying to get a reaction; Sophie could hear it in her voice. But Ben didn't reply. He just smiled, and it was a different sort of smile to the others he'd used upon them. Secretive and coldly amused.

Netta readjusted her bag on her shoulder. 'It's getting late,' she said in a hard voice. 'You know, I think I'm going to go back. My mum's coming over to visit tomorrow and I need to get up early to clean the flat.'

Sophie was surprised and dismayed. So, their hot date had turned out to be a bit of a cradle-snatcher – but did it really matter how old he was, when he was this fit? Wasn't Netta over-reacting?

'Don't you want to meet Naylor?' he asked.

'Maybe some other time.'

'You'd like him, I promise.'

'Like I said, it's late.' Netta looked sharply at Sophie. 'You coming then?'

'I think I'll stay.' She saw the spark of shock and outrage in Netta's eyes, the look that said: You can't stay on your own. You stick with your girl friends whatever. That's the rules.

'Sophie!'

'You go home if you like,' said Sophie, nettled. She wasn't letting an opportunity like this pass. 'I want to see these sculptures.'

Ben folded his arms, counting himself out of the discussion. For a moment the two girls glared at each other. Sophie could hear the unvoiced accusation: On your own?

'Suit yourself,' said Netta with a sniff. 'See you Monday.' Unspoken was the sneer: Don't come crying to me if it goes wrong. With an irate bounce in her step she marched away up the street, toward the neon glow of a Chinese takeaway sign and the taxi rank beyond. Sophie watched her go, then turned to Ben, who was waiting with eyebrows raised.

'Sorry about that.'

'Why be sorry?' He took her arm and slipped his hand in hers. 'Now I get to enjoy the undiluted pleasure of your company.'

Sophie's pulse jumped, and she felt her sex clench in anticipation.

He led her into the churchyard, under the black shadows of the trees, and took her not to the front porch but around the north side of the building. The gravestone slabs had long been cleared away but a few table-tombs remained, and there in near-darkness he backed her up against a cold gritstone box and kissed her, harder this time.

Harder, deeper, hungrier.

Sophie slid her arms around his neck and ground her thighs against his, feeling for the telltale bulge of his erection. And oh yes, there it was – his cock hardening in response to her heat, her softness, her willingness. He put his hands on her waist and lifted her to sit on the tomb-top, and she opened her legs so he could stand between them, pressing up against her. Her skirt rode up, stretched tight across the very tops of her thighs. He took her left breast and squeezed it to the rhythm of his kisses, making her groan into his mouth. The sound seemed to galvanise him and he trapped her nipple between forefinger and thumb, twisting it until she squeaked again.

She'd never fucked in a churchyard before, she thought. It was exciting, in an old-fashioned way. His cock had clear definition now under the fabric of his trousers, and he was pressing right up against the mound of her sex, and she wondered if he'd realised yet she wasn't wearing any knickers or whether his own clothing had fooled him. She wrapped her legs about his muscular ass. Her head started to swim; he seemed to have no intention of coming up for air.

Gasping, she broke from his lips. He laughed low in his throat.

'God, girl: you're hot, aren't you?'

'Uh-huh.' She was seething with heat. She nibbled at his lips, finding them by feeling his face, and heard the hiss of breath between his teeth. He abandoned her breasts to push both hands up her smooth thighs, questing all the way to the top, finding the rucked-up skirt and then her soft, shaven, plump-lipped sex, a fashionable landing strip of hair the only veil to its nakedness. His thumbs plunged into the wet, twin divers, and she writhed with pleasure.

'Oh, let me guess what you want,' he whispered. It made her giggle.

'I'll give you three guesses.'

'Really? One,' he growled, massaging her clit with both thumbs. She arched her back, speechless. 'Two,' he continued, parting the folds of her sex and opening her wide with those thumbs, then working the rest of his fingers into the hot oil she was leaking, getting them good and slick, opening her up. 'Three,' he concluded, entering her with three fingers at once, his right wrist locked like a weapon, the muscles of his forearm tense as he pushed those fingers in deep, right past all those thick knuckles until he was holding her by her pussy, his thumb in possession of her clit – then out, then in again. His fingers were blunt and determined and brooked no refusal. Sophie jerked her hips and squealed and writhed, raking his skin with her nails. He pinned her with his other arm, pulling her hard against him. 'Did I guess right?'

'Mm,' she nodded frantically, her lips bruising themselves on his hard jaw. She wanted his cock even more, but his fingers certainly had the right idea.

'Then guess what I want, love.'

'You want to fuck me,' she whispered.

He chuckled – that dark low rumble again, deep in his throat. Lingeringly he withdrew his hand, enjoying her little whimper of loss. 'Let's go see my friend,' he whispered, confounding her.

'What? Now?'

'We walked all this way.'

'Oh … can't we … first …'

'Don't be impatient. Everything comes to those who wait, love.' He tickled her clit teasingly, then slipped from her embrace, secure in the knowledge that she would follow. Sophie slid off the stone feeling like there was a hollow void inside her, and sure that Ben was getting off on her discomfort. She tugged her skirt back down over her thighs and brushed specks of lichen off her behind. She couldn't care less about Ben's friend or his artwork now, to be honest, but she wanted his cock so badly she would have followed him almost anywhere.

'Ready?' He took her hand and led her off, surefooted even in the darkness. He led her to a small door in the north wall, one so low he had to stoop under the arch. It was unlocked, and a light burned in the room beyond.

Sophie knew almost nothing about church architecture; she was expecting them to emerge into the main body of the building among the pews. She'd expected gloom and age. She wasn't expecting a small room full of shelves and cupboards, or a set of unpainted plywood stairs that took them up into the roofspace. There was a strong smell of new plaster and paint.

'I knew you were lying,' she said, trying to be sparky, as Ben led her up. Her thighs felt sticky.

'What?' He frowned back at her.

'About the vampire thing. You wouldn't be able to walk on consecrated ground.'

He turned away again. 'This was deconsecrated in the nineteen-nineties.'

They came out into a big white space – almost the whole of the interior of the church roof – illuminated by a few floor lamps. Every surface was painted white. There were pale human figures dotted about the place, on dustsheet islands spattered in paint, but none of them moved. Only one was animate: a slim figure crouching over and dabbing at one of the sculptures with a brush.

'Hello, Naylor.'

The young man stood. He moved with great fluidity and, though Sophie's spike heels made a terrible racket on the wooden floor, his bare ones made no sound at all. He was standing in front of them almost before Sophie, transfixed by his grace, had grasped that he was moving at all.

'Ben. Hi.' He smiled at Sophie, not even bothering to hide the fact he was checking out her tits, her hips, her legs. 'You're a pretty one.'

'Sophie,' she said weakly.

He was breathtaking. Slight, not tall, with sharp cheekbones and slanted, narrow eyes that turned out to be a wild pale green when they caught the light. A full lower lip gave him an incongruous pout. He was startlingly pale. Black hair flopped over those eyes, partly veiling the finely angled brows but not the wicked glint beneath them. There was a grace about his narrow hips and wiry limbs that seemed almost dangerous, as if he were poised in readiness for something. Something swift and ruthless, she thought; something never regretted. He looked younger than Ben and considerably more slender, but there was nothing weak about him at all.

He folded his arms, having looked her over.

'I can smell pussy,' he said, gazing into her eyes, the corner of his mouth hooked in a smile.

'Yeah ... it's all over my hands, I'm afraid,' Ben answered, as she started and flushed.

'You been taking her out for a trial lap, you dirty beggar?'

'Just warming the engine.'

'Huh. You want a beer, Sophie?'

The abrupt switches in conversation stunned her a little, and she barely managed to nod and squeak an affirmation. Ben had been right: she did like Naylor. He looked like bad news – but wasn't that always more fun in a man? She had a clear idea where this was going, she thought, and she didn't object – but a little Dutch courage wouldn't hurt. She'd never been with two guys at once. It excited her a lot more than the thought of her and Netta and Ben. It scared her quite a lot more too.

Naylor retreated to a cool-box that stood near one wall, near a pile of dustsheets. She watched as he groped inside for three bottles of beer, then prised the caps off against the angle of the lid with three casual flicks.

'Sophie works at an art gallery,' said Ben.

'Is that so?'

'Just Yardley's,' she answered, her voice husky.

'What do you think of my stuff, then?' he asked, indicating the sculptures with a twist of his head.

Politely she turned to look them over. A standing figure nearby appeared to be a resin cast of a naked woman, her skin the stippled grey of poplar bark, her nipples black knots. But her eyes were only holes and from behind she was hollow, the bark curled and flaked at the edge, her insides cobwebbed. Sophie swallowed. How was she supposed to judge real art? Yardley's didn't cater to the high-concept end of the market, just to people who liked a nice picture and wanted something that would match the wallpaper. Sophie worked selling the products of conveyor-belt artists. There was the one who painted nice autumnal landscapes, and the one who did portraits of cheeky 1930s urchins, and the one who did the red canal perspectives ... Nothing like this. What did she know?

She moved to the next sculpture, a heap of reclining naked women. Their skin had the texture of sand and their sleeping faces were peaceful and beautiful – but once again they were hollow, this time from the ribs to the hips, their abdomens smooth white concavities.

'It's good,' she said. 'Powerful.'

'You think?' Naylor was at her shoulder, though she hadn't heard him approach. She turned a little abruptly, and he slipped a cold bottle into her hand. 'Cheers.'

'Cheers.' He was standing unsettlingly close, almost touching her.

Naylor tilted his own bottle to his mouth. Sophie glanced at the label, but it was some Continental brew she'd never heard of. She took a sip of her beer, all too aware that both men were taking a very personal interest in watching the neck of the bottle ease between her lips. She felt self-conscious: she'd never been the focus of such undisguised greed. She normally was the sort of girl that men could take or leave; rarely without some sort of masculine action in her life, yet never the centre of any drama. Procrastinating, she glanced away at the room again.

'Is that one of yours?' she asked, peering at something a bit different: two large wooden boards mounted on a wall that part-divided the roof-space. They were covered in black and gilt lettering that was hard to decipher.

Naylor snorted. 'Nah. Fixtures and fittings, doll. This was a church, remember.'

'Oh. Yeah.' She could make out some of the words now: Thou shalt not ...

'The Ten Commandments. Not that anyone takes any bleeding notice of any of them these days. "Remember the Sabbath and keep it holy," eh? "Thou shalt not covet." The country would fall apart.'

'There's still one left,' said Ben, stepping in closer and running his fingers down Sophie's spine. '"Thou shalt not kill."'

Naylor sniggered. 'Yeah, well. Our Good Shepherd is still keen on that one, that's true.' He jerked his head. 'You like the beer, dollface? Is it to your taste?'

Sophie opened her mouth but didn't manage to reply, because on the word 'taste' he dipped his hand beneath the hem of her skirt and touched the neck of his bottle to the juncture of her thighs. The glass was chilly and she staggered a little; instantly Ben was behind her, steadying her – and making sure she couldn't retreat. Sophie's mouth went to an O shape as round as the mouth of the bottle that was pressing the mound of her sex – and then nudging to the split there, and the swollen petals that were so puffy with arousal. For a moment she resisted his entry and then Ben slipped his arms round her from behind, cupping her breasts and tipping her weight back against him, and at the same time Naylor changed angle and thrust the bottle between her thighs and then up, into the furrow of her pussy, sliding the bottle-mouth back and forth, cold and frictionless as only lubricated glass can be.

Sophie gasped. She felt the little round mouth embrace her

clit momentarily, like a kiss. Then it dived back again, into her molten flesh and then – changing angle again – up into the wet clench of her hole. He ran the bottle up into her all the way to its shoulders, watching her face all the time. Then he pulled it out. Milky streaks patterned the brown glass. He licked the bottle, swirling his tongue right around the rim, and sucked the glass.

'Only two things taste better than beer,' said he softly. 'And one of them's hot wet cunt.' He took her own bottle out of her limp hand. Sophie sagged back into Ben's embrace as he pinched and played with both her nipples through the thin layers of her clothes. She could feel his hardening cock, crushed against the soft jut of her bum and struggling to rise.

'Nice tits, love,' he breathed in her ear.

'You're up for this, aren't you?' Naylor asked, dipping the neck of his bottle into the cleft of her cleavage and rubbing the glass suggestively from swell to swell of her breasts. His lips were parted and shiny. 'You're game for it, I can tell.'

'Mm,' she whimpered, nodding.

'Told you you'd get everything you wanted, love,' Ben said hoarsely. 'Everything and more.' He nuzzled at her ear and took the lobe between his lips, nipping softly.

'Ben ...'

Her head seemed to swim. Naylor had set the beers aside and was stripping off his clothes now. He shed his T-shirt and kicked his trousers off, revealing a slim smooth body, the only visible hair a black nest at his crotch that climbed in a narrow line to his navel. His beautiful smooth cock was already stiffly erect and nodding in the free air: it had a slight curve back toward his stomach and looked almost out of proportion to his delicate frame, so engorged was it. He stroked it like it was a hunting-dog waiting to be unleashed, as he stalked back to her and looked down into her face.

'This is what you were hoping for, wasn't it, doll?' he asked, taking her hand and rubbing it over his cock. It seemed to pulse against her, its sticky mouth kissing her palm. 'A bit of fun?'

Sophie nodded.

'It's going to get a bit messy.' His gaze lifted to Ben over her shoulder. 'Clothes off, I guess.'

They stripped her of everything: the purse hanging from her shoulder, the cherry-coloured dress from the boutique she couldn't really afford on her wage, the lacy bra she'd bought only last week. All but her high-heeled shoes. Everything was tossed aside in a heap. Her boobs bounced free as Ben whipped the bra off and her nipples stiffened in the cool air of the church. She didn't seem to be required to do anything but accept their hands and the liberties they took groping her as they pulled at her clothes, playing with her tits and ass and pussy, pinching slyly between caresses until she squirmed. Ben pushed her into Naylor's grasp as he wrenched off his own clothes, clearly impatient now. She caught a flash of his body, golden fuzz marching up his stomach and down his legs, before another shove landed her back in his embrace. He caught her wrists and pulled them to the small of her back, guiding her hands to the vertical staff of his cock.

'Hold this,' he said: 'That's right.' Then his own hands went back round her, holding her under the jaw and around her waist.

She wasn't quite sure she liked that. Without the use of her hands to fend anyone off, she felt strangely vulnerable, and she whimpered when Naylor patted her breasts back and forth with stinging force.

'I'm sorry,' he said; 'does that hurt? Kiss it better.' Falling to a crouch he caught her right nipple in his lips and sucked it long and slow and expertly. Pleasure crackled through her nerves, and she squeezed Ben's cock hard in her hands. But it lasted all too brief a moment before Naylor lifted his mouth away and grinned. She saw his teeth, cruelly pointed fangs, just before he stooped back down on her breast and sank them in.

It wouldn't be quite true to say she was surprised, not really. She'd known, after all, from the beginning; she'd just avoided thinking about it. But she tried to scream anyway, except that Ben's broad hand clamped over her mouth and the sound was trapped in her heaving chest. There was no outlet for the pain, the searing hot cut of his fangs puncturing her skin.

Then the pain was gone, and something entirely different took its place. Sophie, pinned and thrashing, took a long time to grasp what it was, as it flowed through her right breast like melted sugar fizzing in every capillary – like worms of sparkling fire – like a hundred tiny meteors circling the burning sun of her nipple. She stopped fighting and sagged back against Ben, only half-aware that her hands were still clenched, sweating, around his erect cock, that Naylor was nursing on her tit, his throat working as he swallowed.

Slowly, Ben slid his grip from her mouth to her lower jaw so that she could breath. She whimpered, 'Oh fuck, oh fuck,' her panic now swamped in the glorious sensation of the suckling, but horror making her pant.

'"Oh Fuck No" or "Oh Fuck Yes"?' murmured Ben. 'Sounds like an "Oh Fuck Yes" to me, love.' Lifting her left arm he sank his teeth into the fleshy bulge of her bicep.

Again – a white flash of pain, a wave of coruscating pleasure.

Then Naylor stopped feeding and lifted his mouth. There was surprisingly little mess on her breast, only two puckered puncture marks over her enflamed and aching nipple, each filled with a little ruby bead. No blood ran. But when Naylor licked his lips his tongue was red and wet.

'Oh, please,' she moaned. All her will seemed to have faded away as the wild chemistry of their saliva ran riot in her body tissues. Her right breast pulsed with the hungry need for Naylor to latch on again and her left breast ached to join it, even though her stomach recoiled from what it meant that their mouths were that colour.

'You like that?' he asked with a mocking scarlet smile.

'It feels ... nice,' she whispered. She felt drunk with shock and her voice broke on the last word into a strange giggle she had no control over.

'You do like it, don't you?' He nuzzled against her, grinning. 'Naughty girl.' His fingers slipped up between her thighs and paddled in the ooze of her sex juices. 'Dirty fucking little girl.'

'Look at this,' chuckled Ben, brushing her turgid right nipple with his thumb; it was as swollen as if it'd been stung by a bee, and so sensitive that she gasped. 'Just bursting with juicy goodness, aren't you, love?'

'Want another kiss, don't you?' Naylor lapped teasingly at her breast. 'Let's try something a bit different, heh?' Then he sat back on his heels, took her thighs in his hands and spread them, lifting one to drape over his shoulder. He and Ben took her weight easily, as she was pulled on to the kneeling man's mouth and he buried his face in her crotch.

'Oh!' she wailed reflexively, as his tongue broke the split of her sex, as he lapped and sucked at the juices welling there. She tried half-heartedly to struggle but her body wasn't co-operating, and even if it had done the two men were far too strong. For a long moment the sensation of his mouth was just one of simple pleasure and she stopped twisting altogether. That was when he bit down, and his fangs pierced the mound of her pubis either side of her clit. She spasmed once – and that was the last time, the last vestige of any resistance that night, because the bite was all ecstasy. Pleasure took no prisoners. Naylor sucked and she burned, and soon she was coming into his mouth, blood and juices together, and Ben was biting at the back of her neck and her shoulders, feeding greedily, the stabs of his teeth no longer even painful as her climax turned everything to gold. She thrashed wildly in their embrace, crying out. Naylor's eyes flashed with triumph. And she couldn't stop coming, even after the first burst was over – he kept sucking and she kept rolling down the waves of orgasm, each lifting her to the crest of the next. She couldn't even draw breath.

'Jeez,' said Ben, gasping. 'Give her a rest, Naylor!'

Naylor dropped her. The deprivation was instant and vertiginous: she felt like the sun had been torn from the sky. He stood up and faced her, lifting her and crushing her against Ben's torso as if the other man were a wall, and then he pressed into her and lifted her thighs apart and thrust his cock up into her pussy and began to fuck, fiercely. His face was knotted into a mask of concentration, his eyes narrowed, his lips tight over his monstrous teeth. Sophie's inflamed sex responded with gratitude to the impaling pressure of his cock inside her, to the battering he was giving her clit, to the pressure from behind as well as before. She began to groan with each thrust, the air forced from her lungs. Ben helped by slipping his hands under her thighs and holding her up, splayed, for Naylor's easier access, and she could feel Ben's cock under her ass-cheeks, rubbing along the spread cleft of her behind as the two men sandwiched her and pummelled her between them.

Naylor slipped a hand round the back of Ben's neck for better purchase.

Taking his cock only momentarily stilled the burning itch of Sophie's clit. Her body was already primed and charged, orgasm throbbing just below the skin and ready to burst out under pressure, so she came first. For all the two men's fierce lust she hit orgasm before Naylor did, and her screams sent him over the edge, pumping into her. She felt the gush – she'd never *felt* ejaculation before, not inside her – and it was cold, even colder than their sweatless inhuman skin. Then Ben bit her again, on the angle of her shoulder and neck, and that rolled her into orgasm and lifted her again, burning like the sun. She nearly passed out.

'Fuck, that's sharp,' whispered Ben.

His ejaculation spent, Naylor stepped away and left Ben to lower her to her knees and let her fall slowly backward, her legs tumbling apart in disarray. Sophie's head was swimming, and in the afterwash of her orgasm she felt faint. Too stunned to support herself, she hung limply at the full extension of her arms from wrists which were gripped easily in Ben's off hand, and her head rolled back as black and red circles bloomed behind her half-closed eyes. His flexed arm didn't even tremble. He took his stiff cock in his right hand and began to tug with the determined motions of a man who knows he's ready to unload.

'Open wide, love.'

Sophie parted her lips and in seconds his spunk jetted out to splash on her – the first squirts on her breasts, the final couple on her face. They kissed her skin like drips of melted ice cream. When she licked it off her lips she found he tasted like fresh-turned earth, with a metallic, coppery tang.

They'll stop now, she thought weakly. They'll have finished with me.

They didn't. They hadn't.

Ben's erection didn't even flag. He lifted her and flopped her forward on to her belly, then took her hips and pulled her ass up as he crouched over her. His teeth pierced the downy globes of her bum, first one side then the other, then he spread her cheeks and munched down on the hole of her ass, each bite a torment and then a beatification, each drawing no more than a single sucked mouthful of her blood. Sophie, her face lolling on the whitewashed floorboards, spasmed at each bite and tried to lift her head, but her arms felt as limp as dishcloths and she could hardly bring them up and plant her palms against the floor. As Ben stood, lifting her, and braced his thighs in a straddle so that he could slip his cock into her burning slot, she could do nothing but hang doubled-up from his grasp, spine and legs limp. It took Naylor sliding beneath her and pushing her up with one casual hand to lift her to even a horizontal position. And as Ben powered into her from behind, Naylor lapped at her dangling breasts once more.

'Ah!' gasped Sophie, as his mouth moved over the tingling ice-water splashes that Ben had left on her skin. Naylor laughed a low throaty laugh and bit her over and over again from below, Ben's semen and her blood melting together on his tongue.

Both men laughed as she wailed and came once more.

The physically strenuous aspects of their recreation were easy for them: effortless. She was no heavier than a rag doll in their arms, and no more capable of rebellion. Her body drove them crazy, her blood intoxicating them so that they fucked her over and over again, as playful and heartless as young lions. Each time she came to climax they both bit her and drank, tasting the spike of her orgasm in her blood. Nor were they restricted, it seemed, in the number of their own orgasms, and in exchange for what they drank from her they washed her in copious outpourings of their own fluids. She took cock like she'd never taken cock before, until she felt like she was an empty sack they were trying to fill, until she was streaked and smeared and musky with come, her hair dishevelled, her make-up smeared.

They never fucked her mouth though.

At the end they carried her to the pile of dustsheets and snuggled up around her, all three of them on their sides, their arms a languid tangle. She liked that: they felt warm now and she was cold, washed in a dark sea. Ben embraced her from the front, his cock wedged up her pussy, while Naylor impaled her ass from behind for the third or fourth time. It didn't hurt: nothing hurt any more. Every inch of her body was numbly replete from their bites. Together they rocked her in slow luxurious rhythm as they fastened their teeth in her shoulders and sucked slow and long. Sophie felt herself falling toward sleep, the room spinning about her as consciousness ebbed. She tried to speak, though her mouth was dry and she had no idea what she wanted to say, only that she was possessed by a strange sense of regret, not even dismay, only the faintest sense that she was unravelling, her soul frayed to loose red threads that would never be whole again. But only a dry croak escaped her lips as she dissolved into unconsciousness.

* * *

'Whoa,' said Ben, unfastening his mouth. His eyes were dark with repletion. He squirmed out from Sophie's limp embrace and looked down at her. 'Better stop.'

Naylor rolled away on to his back and squinted at her, sucking his teeth. 'Let's just finish her off,' he grunted. 'The dregs taste the best; you know that.'

Ben sat up on his haunches. His body was speckled and streaked with dark drops and he absently licked at a smear down the inside of his forearm. 'Do you want to piss Reynauld off?' he asked sweetly.

'Well, now that you suggest it,' answered Naylor with a switchblade grin, 'that would be a bonus.' He sat up though, and scratched at the little spills that had dried on his smooth chest. Ben snorted.

'I'll go drop her off on the embankment, shall I?'

Naylor waved a hand. 'Don't worry about it. I've finished here.'

'What about these?' Ben looked around at the pieces of sculpture. 'They're good.'

'Estelle's sending somebody to pick them up.'

'Estelle?'

'Yeah. Wants them for one of her clubs, she says. Let her worry about the red tape.'

Ben nodded, then as Naylor stretched and wandered off he walked over to the small pile of Sophie's belongings and rummaged in her purse. First he extracted the bank notes, folding them between his fingers. Then, opening her cell phone, he thumbed the keypad three times and then held it to his ear, ambling about the room and shuffling one-handed into his jeans, hopping as he pulled them up over his legs. 'Ambulance,' he said after a pause.

Naylor necked a beer chaser.

After Ben's first answer the woman's voice on the other end of the phone connection kept talking, but he took no notice. He dropped the squawking phone on the sheets next to Sophie and looked down at her with a little smile. She didn't stir. Pale as marble, she looked like one of Naylor's sculptures. Her eyes were half-closed, showing crescent-moons of sclera. Her lips were blue, her features relaxed and peaceful. If there was no obvious movement of her ribs, the thready pulse at her throat – quite audible to him – attested that she was still alive for the moment. Her whole body was covered in paired puncture marks, everywhere but over the major blood vessels at the neck and the insides of her thighs.

'Thanks, love,' he whispered. 'You were a blast.'

But Sophie heard none of that.

(Ben)

And this is Ben, the golden boy, youngest of the six vampires in the City. Young enough that he can still pass for human and that he can still go out in daylight, though he wears long-sleeved shirts and sunglasses then and keeps to the shade of buildings because direct sunlight stings him. His hair is cut fashionably short and quirky now, and his eyes are warm and direct. His skin is still tanned from the sun that shone in 1967, a year of wild fashion, wilder youth and chemical revolution. The year he died.

You wouldn't know that Ben was different from anyone else, meeting him. Undeath hasn't changed him much, not yet. His demeanour is relaxed and he likes a beer, and in fact it's easiest to bump into him in a bar or a nightclub. Only in sudden strong light might you notice anything, because his eyes are so sensitive that he can see even in total darkness and under bright light the pupils contract to invisible pinholes, leaving his irises blank. But his eyes never were windows to his soul; even in life they were more like silvered mirrors, reflecting the gazer's desire.

As a youth his aims were to have fun and chase tail, and in over forty years as a vampire they've altered remarkably little. His life revolves around sex and food, which are almost always the same thing. For vampires, there's no distinction between thirst and desire. Blood-lust and fuck-lust come as a package, one engendering the other. He's constantly horny, eternally obsessed with pussy. It's one of the things he likes so much about his new life: he never has to stop. There are other advantages: he's become faster and stronger and has keener senses, he heals cuts in minutes, his flab has converted to muscle and even his face has subtly changed, honed to a new beauty – but the buzz of rampant desire, the priapic stiffy that threatens to wear a hole in his pants, the heat that grips him every time he spots a potential target: that's what he really trips on.

Being dead – What's there not to like?

He's vaguely aware that others of his kind are different, that things do change with time, but he doesn't worry about that. Ben is young; still young enough to eat, even. Perhaps only a few mouthfuls a night – pizza and Chinese takeaway mostly, and hold the garlic because in the last couple of decades it's started to turn his stomach – but he's still capable of digesting some solids. That will be the first faculty to go, and he will miss it when it happens. The multiple flavours of life will be lost to him, the spices and the textures. All that will be left will be hot, sweet, infinitely appealing blood.

In a big city like this, a world hub, there's no problem with him taking a different person a night as prey – so long as he doesn't kill them – and enough places to hunt in that his face doesn't become known. Notoriety would be a handicap, and Ben likes to fly below the radar. Bars are the easiest places to pull in: hothouses of exotic painted blooms. There's never a problem if you look like he does, and everyone is awash with alcohol, and they're all young and hot and eager to be plucked. He does a lot of plucking.

You might well meet Ben that way, particularly at night. But he is a seducer by nature rather than a hunter, and he's surprised himself in recent years by discovering a taste for the more difficult target. The plainer girl – not the dull, slack-jawed type who'll do it for a bag of chips or the cheery twinkly one who'll do it for a laugh, but the buttoned-down type. Does that describe you? There are more women of that kind about than people think, though they're invisible to so many eyes. Perhaps he'd find you that way, by daylight, when you're least expecting it. He's taken to haunting university buildings, parks, art galleries, even botanical gardens. He's looking for the girls who wear sweatshirts even in warm weather, the ones who haven't starved themselves or fried themselves orange on a sunbed or bothered to use hair-straighteners for that compulsory sleek look. Sweaters ... Sweaters drive him half crazy with lust. Soft, pale, unfashionable girls. The ones who don't actually believe that a man like him would hit on them. He can smell their defensiveness and the aching eagerness buried beneath.

Is that you?

It's hard work to get past their disbelief. They often think he's taking the piss, that he has a coterie of friends hidden nearby killing themselves laughing as he mocks their naivety with his attentions. Oh, but it's worth it for the first bloom of their sexual scent, the rush of heat and wet, the look in their eyes as they tip from suspicion to hope to surrender.

He's prepared to work for days to get that.

So perhaps he'll find you when you're concentrating on something else entirely. At work maybe – your frustrating, claustrophobic job, the one you took just as that first stepping stone, the one that tides you over until you move on to something really worthwhile. Or perhaps he'll find you in a line at a shop counter, or queuing up to hand in a form in some official waiting room. And he'll catch your eye with his frank, humorous gaze, so warmly that you'll wonder, 'Is it me he's looking at?'

Yes, it'll be you. It'll be hard to believe, but even harder to resist. You might be in a relationship, or you might be resigned to celibacy, but it almost certainly won't make any difference – so long as there is a sexual instinct buried in you, he will bring it out and reel you in. He'll use your own nature against you. He's just too good-looking, too charming, to shrug off, and sexual heat radiates from his cold body like an aura. And you can forget morality or common sense: those things won't save you. They don't ever save anyone. Sex, when it kicks into gear – that raging appetite, that dizzy high of anticipation – trumps everything else. Don't you know that yet?

He can be subtle or he can be pushy, whichever works best in the circumstances. In either case he is persistent. Before you know it, your head will be awhirl and your heart will be beating faster every time you see him. You'll feel a cramping thrill every time he smiles, every time his hand brushes yours, every time he leans in a little closer. You'll wonder what is happening to you. Reflected in his eyes, you'll see yourself as if for the first time: beautiful, desirable and free.

And then, finally, you'll let him cross the line. Because by then you'll want nothing in the world more than the sight of his golden skin, his parted lips, his naked body. By then you will be weak-limbed, dizzy, breathless. Your skin will be running hot and cold chills. Your nipples will be so sensitised that the rub of your own clothing is almost painful. Your sex will be heavy with moisture, like a storm ready to break. When he takes you in his arms it will be like a profound pain has finally found release.

Where do you want him, when he takes you at last? In your apartment, in secret? In the park, under a full moon? Behind the shelves where you work, muffled and frantic and daring? He doesn't mind, so long as he can fuck you. So long as he can have your sex juices and your sweat and your surrender, your cries and your tears of joy. Your bright and racing blood.

It can't be denied that he'll give you a good time. Just hope he doesn't bring Naylor in on it, though.

On his own, Ben is about as harmless as a vampire can be – but Naylor is his weakness. Naylor is the trigger for him going badly wrong, because he turns Ben's simple lust to his more sadistic ends.

It was the itch of Ben's lust that brought him to this city in the first place, when he was still alive and living with his parents in a provincial town and had a job as an apprentice repairman, in those days when they still bothered repairing televisions and radios and kettles. He wanted a chance at the big-city nightlife he'd heard so much about, and he found to his delight that there was plenty of sex available: with the Pill now available, trendy chicks had no excuse to say No. He shacked up in a squat with a girl calling herself Moonbeam who had a seemingly endless supply of pot and LSD and a similarly endless line of parties to go to, parties at which the right people showed up to mingle with the hip young things, or if they didn't they should have and everyone said they had done anyway, the next day. He thought he was in love with her, just a bit, though that didn't stop him sleeping with other girls. And she went with other blokes too, of course. She was the one who introduced him to Naylor.

She said he was this totally amazing guy who hung out with the Stones and had insights into history and eternity like no one else.

Ben ended up in a room draped with Indian-printed cotton and reeking of patchouli, on his knees with his cock down Moonbeam's throat, watching awestruck while this skinny beautiful youth fucked her from behind and she gobbled his dick and made noises like she was seeing Krishna himself. Ben had never shared a girl with another man. He thought it the hottest experience of his life, and he didn't mind even when Naylor began to bite at Moonbeam's back and shoulders, sucking her blood. Admittedly, the pot probably helped with that surprise. And Moonbeam didn't seem to mind either; in fact she seemed to revel in the sensation, climbing to new orgasmic heights. It wasn't long before Ben was finding out for himself what it felt like.

In the whole wide world, there was nothing at all he'd ever known that was as good as the sensation of Naylor sucking his dick. Teeth and tongue. Blood and spunk. People who derided that sort of thing didn't know what the fuck they were talking about. Sometimes, thanks to that magic bite, he walked round with a hard-on all day. Sometimes he woke so drained that his hollow balls just about clanged together.

For a little while the two of them were Naylor's favourites. The vampire fucked them together and separately, whenever he felt like it, without asking any leave and without needing to. All shame and propriety vanished from Ben's life. He'd bend over and spread his ass-cheeks in the middle of a crowded room at the flick of a finger, the crook of an eyebrow. He'd offer his arms and his anus and his cock. He'd ask for nothing in return but the benison of Naylor's razor-edged kiss.

That all stopped when Moonbeam's heart gave out, quietly and without any warning, one night as she lay with her head tilted backward off the edge of the bed with Naylor sucking at her crotch and Ben's cock so far down her throat that she didn't even cry out as she died. The two men buried her body in a patch of wasteland and then Ben threw a tantrum of recrimination and they fought, very briefly and with devastating effect as far as the human one of them was concerned. Naylor must be credited with some impulse of contrition, because he saved Ben from bleeding out by force-feeding the boy his own vampiric blood. That was how Ben was reborn.

In very short order he decided that he hadn't loved Moonbeam that much after all.

He was luckier than he knew: it so happened that Reynauld was away abroad that month, and his conversion was revealed as a fait accompli upon the older vampire's return. Moonbeam's death never came to Reynauld's attention at all and Ben was permitted to stay, so long as he swore loyalty like the others.

Ben doesn't resent Reynauld. But he's still close to Naylor, and that way danger lies. Ben's bad at spotting danger, though: he lives his life – if that's the word – on too much of a high. Ironically, these days he's completely straight, chemically speaking. Psychotropic drugs don't work on vampires. He can't even get drunk – except on blood, of course.

That's all that's left to him now: blood and sex.

2: Nine for the Nine Bright Shiners

'Come on. Oh, God, yes – come on!'

And I do. Like I'm told. Filling her.

Sometimes I feel like all she wants of me is the gush of fluid, that I'm nothing but a donor to her. It's the tiniest bit demoralising. I mean, don't get me wrong; I want this baby as much as Penny does. I'm totally committed to the effort. I've given up coffee and alcohol and even fish, to my dismay – they're supposedly caked in pollutants that depress sperm count – and I've switched to boxer shorts instead of briefs to keep the Boys optimally cool. I take my mineral supplements: zinc and selenium and vitamin C. It's just as important to me as to her.

OK, so if I'm honest it isn't. It couldn't be. It's all she thinks about these days. Sometimes I look at her and wonder how the dance-till-dawn party chick I first met turned into this macrobiotic-organic obsessive with the body honed by swimming and Pilates into a lean, mean, baby-bearing machine. Fitness is considered vital in the mum-to-be, these days, it turns out. No one just gets pregnant and carries on any more; it has to be conducted like a military campaign instead. Not that I object to a toned tum and a firm butt, obviously; it's the look in her eyes that worries me, the way they're like holes going down into a big dark place. Whenever we meet someone with a pushchair she tries to hide it but I see. I can see her hunger.

* * *

I get called away from the table during a dinner the mayor's hosting at his official residence. It's not a particularly formal do, luckily: just a Spanish business delegation and some potential local investors and a couple of members of the European Parliament. Not exactly exciting stuff, but not much potential for messing things up either; they're all happily chowing down so no one's going to miss me for a few minutes. Penny has turned up at the front gate, and security have rung through to me.

'It's all right,' I tell them: 'She's my wife.' And I bring her inside. She's dressed up enough not to look out of place, thankfully, in a little cobalt-blue number I'm rather fond of because of the cutaway back. 'Is anything wrong?' I ask, drawing her into a corner of the hall, under a portrait of Gladstone. There are waiting staff at practically every corner so I keep my voice low. It's odd seeing your wife in a work context. Two halves of my brain are in collision.

'I'm ovulating, Richard.'

I try not to frown, though I'm secretly exasperated. 'Couldn't it wait?'

'Well, you're not planning on coming home tonight, are you?' That's true enough: with the mayoral elections coming up in a fortnight, once the guests are gone we're all likely to be in a strategy meeting until the small hours. I'm going to have to sleep over here or else I'll get back home by taxi somewhere near 4 a.m., at a guess. 'And I have to be up early tomorrow,' she continues, 'to catch the train to my seminar.'

I nod reluctantly. Penny is a freelance consultant for the hotel industry and gives talks all over the country.

She switches tack, from rational argument to tease: 'Bet you can't guess what I'm wearing under this dress.' Her eyes glitter and she moistens her lips with the tip of her tongue. It evokes the first stir of a reaction in the region of my crotch, just as she intends. Tease works.

'All right then.' I look up and down the corridor. The diners will be well into the bottles of Krug by now. And it's not as if I'm the only political adviser the mayor's got to hand. 'Down here.'

I need a room with a lock on the door, which means a guest toilet unfortunately: I pick the one furthest from the dining hall. It's an exceptionally well-appointed toilet of course. It also happens to be occupied, because as I lay my hand on the door I hear a voice within. A man's voice, deep and measured. He's talking to someone, although the other voice is not audible.

'Blast,' I mutter. I might think about heading to another location, except that Penny takes the opportunity to lean against the wall and brush her fingers up my fly, a furtive tickle that deprives me of the will to move anywhere. Her eyes are bright, her breasts plumped up even more than usual to create a mesmerising cleft. 'Careful,' I admonish weakly. 'We need to be discreet.'

'How can we be, when I'm gagging for your cock?' she mouths. I love it when she talks filthy, which she knows, of course. That perfect, preened exterior combined with whorishly low speech makes for a delicious frisson.

Then the door opens. A man comes out, looks at us both,

nods with a faint smile and walks away. I think for a moment that I recognise him but the familiarity is fleeting. Penny's eyes follow him down the corridor. 'Who was that?' she asks with undisguised admiration.

I sigh and steer her into the bathroom. That's certainly one sign she's ovulating: she becomes a rapacious flirt. Another man in my position might not take it so well. 'I don't know him. One of the Spanish group, I should think – they're in the running for a contract on the integrated transport initiative.'

'Well, he knew you.'

'Did he?'

'He called you Richard.'

I blink, nonplussed. I can't recall him saying anything to me at all. I can't actually remember his face right now, come to think of it. He was tall and looked like he might have been Spanish; that's all I recall. 'Did you yank me out of dinner just to talk?' I'm a little brusque, I admit, to cover my confusion. Penny rolls her eyes.

'OK, love.' She stalks over to the sink and drops her handbag while I give the room a once-over glance, just in case the conversation we'd overheard had been taking place live and not over the phone. But the room, though spacious for a toilet and slightly over-furnished – an antique armoire against one wall, a small but fiendishly ornate sofa upholstered in brocade, a huge matching gilded mirror over the marble counter that cups two sinks and a large vase of fresh roses – is empty of all human forms but our own. I push the door-bolt to.

'So what are you wearing?'

'Come and find out.' She smiles at me, heavy-lidded, in the mirror. I walk over behind her, Mr Dick already doing his wake-up stretches under my uncomfortable goddamn boxers.

'Inappropriate Behaviour' while working is strictly forbidden even if it is with one's spouse; there've been more than enough embarrassing headlines in the press about waste-of-money politicians and public employees gadding about when they should be doing something worthy and abstemious. The fact that this could get me into terrible trouble adds a distinct spice to the occasion. Standing behind her, I watch in the mirror as she lifts her hands and rubs lazily at her breasts, slipping the shoulder straps of her dress to reveal more of those delectable twin slopes – so pale they make me think of snow, so smooth I want to ski down them into the ravine between.

'Show me,' I whisper, and my voice is thickening. 'Get them out and play with them.'

With a languorous smile she obeys, scooping each orb from dress and bra to prop them on the rumpled fabric, circling her nipples with her fingertips. The blushing points harden under the attention. I reach round and assist her, tweaking and flicking the stiff nubs until she surrenders them to me with the sigh I know very well. At the same time I press her to the marble slab, my awakening cock nuzzling up against the cushions of her bum. I enjoy watching us in the mirror; it's almost like being in our own movie. I can see my hands looking coarse and dark on her cream-coloured skin, catch every flash and flicker of her eyes as my touch sets off cascades of reactions in her body. At this time of the month she's quick to arouse, already primed. I feel her cheeks squirming back against my pressure. She's ready for it.

'As you were,' I whisper. 'Keep playing with those.' As she takes over again I step back so that I can look at that wriggling ass, at her taut legs and her bunched calves, straining on the spike heels of shoes that exactly match the colour of her dress. Sheer blue stockings complete the ensemble. I lift her skirt, and stare. It must have taken some careful work with a mirror: she's not wearing any panties, but written in blue felt-tip down the last couple of inches of her spine is the neat instruction FUCK, with an arrow pointing down into the crack of her behind. And across her bum cheeks is the broken word CUM SLUT.

Well, that puts lead in my pencil: six inches of solid graphite. My cock bounces out into my hand as I unzip. 'How did you get here?' I ask.

'Black cab.'

'With no knickers on?'

'Uh-huh.'

'It's a very short skirt,' I muse, lifting her right leg right up to open her wide as I seek entry. My stiffy goes in like a hot knife into her butter. 'Do ... hh ... Do you think the taxi-driver noticed?'

'He might have,' Penny gasps. 'He was looking.'

That is enough for me: she knows how to push all my kink buttons. I'm in and I'm thrusting, pushing her forward over the sink, plunging the depths of her lubricious hole. Her four-inch heel skids about on the marble benchtop. I know better than to try and take it slow, or to reach for her clit. She doesn't care about coming, she just wants me to come. That's why she's put so much effort into this. She grips the curve of the sink and shuts her eyes, lips open in an O of sympathy for her impaled sex.

God, she feels good. Tight, yet so welcoming.

And as I pound away, as my whole body clenches toward ejaculation, I look past her face in the mirror and see another behind us both. A woman's. She stands on the upright back of the French settee, her bare toes gripping the gilding and her arms stretched behind her to touch the wall, like a Rolls Royce hood ornament: the Spirit of Ecstasy. I know she can't really be there, that there's no way anyone could be in the room with us. It's an optical illusion conjured by my horny mind as it catches in the fire of orgasm. A wraith-woman moulded from shadows, dressed in only a veil through which her delicate body glows, her hair a cloudy nimbus floating about her head. But that's all I glimpse, because just then my climax shakes me and I'm pumping my cum into my wife's hot cunny, and the whole room goes nova.

When I come back down to myself there's no one but us two in the mirror. And no one else in the room, of course.

Penny fishes a pair of knickers from her handbag almost before I'm out of her, then goes to lie down on her side on the couch. Thirty minutes letting gravity help the little swimmers on their way, that's the rule. She smiles at me when I go over and kiss her temple, but the smile is wan. 'That was lovely,' she says. 'Thank you, Richard.'

It was great, I want to say. Didn't you enjoy it? You don't look like you did. It was great ... but weird. Where in my head had that girl come from?

'You OK, Pen?

'Of course.' I can see it in her eyes, which don't really focus on me. They're like empty wells but at the bottom gleam burning coals: the hope that this time it will take.

Like I say, sometimes it's a bit disheartening.

* * *

Christ, if she actually caught me going on like this she'd kill me. I'm supposed to be 100 per cent supportive. It's not as if I actually have to do that much except get my leg over with clockwork regularity and provide the seed. I'm supposed to enjoy that bit, aren't I? And of course I do. Penny's invested in a whole range of fancy underwear and some kinky little costumes – a French maid, a pirate lass, a naughty nurse – so that my co-operation can be guaranteed. I'm getting more sex now than in years. Every other day throughout her cycle, to be precise, with a week off when the red flag of yet another failure paints her pantyliners: mornings preferred because there's a higher sperm load, and if I'm always in a bit of a rush before work that's not a problem; there's no need to linger and coming back for seconds is not encouraged.

* * *

I'm in a taxi on the way home, thinking about our little assignation as I look out at the deserted streets, and wondering when was the last time we had sex just for the fun of it. I'm not complaining; I've no right to complain. Penny has made it her business to find out everything that turns me on and she applies it with ruthless efficiency and not the tiniest smidgen of shame. She's lifted from me the onus of actually giving her pleasure and made it clear I only need to think about my own orgasm; that's enough to satisfy her. Isn't that what every overworked man wants?

Well, maybe.

And I can't help suspecting that the second that blue cross shows up on the plastic wand, all the feathers and fishnets are going straight in the bin. Luckily Mr Dick isn't much interested in the long view. He just goes 'Stockings? Wow! Count me in!'

The streets slip past with unfamiliar swiftness: small shops and tree-lined avenues. It's the dead time of the night and anything that does close down has done. The entrance to my local Underground station is barred with a metal grille, but the illuminated sign warns me I'm nearly home. I shake myself from my reverie as we pull up outside my apartment block. It's only a year old and it gleams darkly against the sodium glow of the sky. It won an architectural award, did Mavin Wood Towers. It's a nice place to live. They had to cut the wood down to build it, of course.

Then the taxi-driver switches on the interior light and all the cab windows turn to mirrors, and I see her in the reflection. She's in the seat next to me, her feet drawn up on the upholstery: the girl from the bathroom mirror. She's very pretty but completely colourless, like she's been sculpted in ash, and only her eyes look truly real. I jump nearly out of my skin this time, and turn without thinking to swipe at the place she sits. My hand bounces off the empty seat cushion.

'You OK, mate?' The cabby sounds suspicious.

'Uh,' I say. 'Yes.' I shove notes into his hand and don't wait for any change. I'm out of the taxi without another glance at my reflection, and as my feet touch the pavement I suddenly remember the identity of the man who came out of the bathroom. It's like a door opening in my head. Of course I knew him. I'd seen him a number of times around the mayor's office. *Reynauld*.

'Oh, fuck,' I say to myself, suddenly sweating with anxiety. The bastards know how to mess with your head like that. They can do more or less what they like, I gather. I'm not directly involved in liaison, but everyone in city politics knows about them.

I hurry to the front door of the block. It's made of smoked glass and, as I reach for the number-plate to type in my security code, I see that behind my own dark reflection there's a woman standing on the pavement under the streetlight. *The* woman. She's veiled from head to foot, but the light goes straight through the gauze to outline her delicate body. She's not moving, she's just watching me.

With a convulsive movement I yank open the door and pull it to behind me. There's resistance and I feel a frisson of panic, but it's probably only the hydraulic spring. I'm inside and safe.

They can't come inside unless you invite them, isn't that right?

* * *

I'm doing my best to help the process along. I want to be a dad. I mean, I guess I do. I accept it's going to change my life, it just doesn't seem real yet. If it were up to me we'd both just bumble on as usual and leave it all up to chance, so it's a good thing Penny's got her teeth into the matter, I suppose. She always gets her way in the end.

Of course, even Mr Dick can be cussed and rebellious. Certain things are on the Forbidden List now, with the inevitable consequence that I'm constantly thinking about how much I want to do them. Like, no more hand-shandies; I'm not allowed to waste good cum.

How strange is it that masturbation is now an unattainable privilege?

* * *

I step out of the bath and towel myself down as the water drains. Somehow I manage to catch my own eye in the mirror. I've been a bit wary of mirrors since seeing that wraith-woman, but there's been no sign of her since that first night and I'm feeling reasonably secure here. I'm at home for the weekend and it's daylight, even if it is a watery winter light. It was probably all a figment of my imagination anyway, I know. If you're awake and working for twenty hours in a day it's no wonder that you start dreaming on your feet.

The bathroom's tiled and accessorised in black and white and the towels match; my body is the only object in the mirror with any colour to it. I look at myself critically, but I'm pretty pleased, let's face it. I look fit. I've kept the stomach bulge and the man-boobs at bay. I've still got a full head of hair, cut in a style that says 'prime' and not 'middle-aged'. My cock and balls look just fine. I focus on the latter, hanging low in their sling of flesh, a bit struck all of a sudden by the magical potential of their bag of tricks. Whole new lives nestle in those spheres. Million of potential futures. If I was the last man alive I could repopulate the whole country, the whole world, given enough women and enough time to fuck them all. The thought makes Mr Dick swell a little, and I cup my balls encouragingly. 'Come on, Boys,' I whisper, giving them a little squeeze. 'You can do it.'

It's my day off: we've not had sex this morning. And now I want to stroke off, but it's not allowed. I lift my cock away from my scrotum, feeling the slight pull as the damp skin separates. My cock responds to the touch by filling up a little, bobbing free of gravity. I shift my hips, restless. My scrotum is gathering to wrinkles. I want to jack off. Just solo, with no expectations and no consequences. A nice leisurely wank without the weight of Penny's need. But I feel guilty; she wouldn't know, of course, but I'd still be letting her down. I stroke the long curve of flesh and feel the swell surge down to the head. Aw, hell. Now it really is a semi.

'Richard! I'm off!'

Wrapping the black towel about my hips, I exit the bathroom. In the hallway Penny is making last-minute adjustments to her make-up in front of the narrow wall mirror. 'How do I look?' she asks as I approach.

She looks great. She always looks great. Even in her winter clothes she's sexy: she's wearing burning red lipstick and a trenchcoat number that just screams of 40s repression and daring, and patterned stockings under that. Well, they might be tights but I can't help seeing them as stockings. I embrace her from behind, my cock pressing with incorrigible hope into her through layers of towel and clothing. 'You look lovely.'

Penny sighs slightly. 'Save it for later, tiger. I've got a train to catch.' It might be a weekend but she's got an exhibition to attend and a stall to run.

I'll be quick, I want to tell her, but I know better than to argue. It would just upset her schedule. I content myself with a goodbye grope and kiss before seeing her off and locking the front door. Then I look in the mirror, shaking my head at myself with blokish sympathy. I can see the bulge Mr Dick is making under the towel.

I need a wank. I mean I *really* need a wank. It makes me feel irritable and bold. I drop the towel on the laminate beech floorboards and strum my cock with slow, defiant strokes.

You going to show up then, ghost-girl?

Nothing stirs in the reflection behind me. Of course not. It's broad daylight and I'm safe in my own home. I begin to stroke in earnest. God, this is good. My cock is growing stiff and straight and tall, pointing at the glass. My balls are bunching to a fat mass like a fist. I put my hand on the wall and rise up on my toes a little, enjoying the clench of muscles that seems to focus my whole body's attention at my groin.

My eyes are open but I'm not really seeing. Instead I picture Ruth, the grumpy clerical secretary at work. I imagine her walking around as we sit in a focus-group circle, circulating the handouts. She always wears her blonde hair in a chignon and a skirt that is tight on her big thighs: in my fantasy she's wearing seamed stockings too. She gets to my place, walking inside the circle of chairs, and as she turns from me I stick my foot out and trip her up. Down she goes on her hands and knees, files scattered everywhere, her head ending up nearly in my lap. She's so surprised she doesn't even get angry; she just stares at me with her eyes wide and her mouth set in a luscious O. I take advantage of the moment to whip out my thick cock and stuff it between her lips, so deep that for a moment she chokes. I grab her hair and use it to pump her head up and down on my huge length, and after a moment's resistance she crumbles and begins to suck obediently. Everyone else seated round the circle makes gasps of lecherous appreciation; it's such a fine sight and we've all fantasised about what that big surly mouth could do if put to proper use. They're getting out their own cocks too; they mean to follow my example and take their own turns once I've come. And I'm going to come right now. 'Take it,' I grunt, spurting into Ruth's mouth, down her eager, gobbling throat.

All over the mirror.

Afterwards I go into the kitchen and find a J Cloth and some glass cleaner under the sink. But when I get back into the hall there's no spunk on the mirror at all. Not a drop. Just the mothprint of a pair of lips, halfway down the glass as if someone had knelt there and kissed the hard surface. It's almost invisible unless you're looking for something. I spray the smudge and rub hard with the cloth but it's no good: the kiss is on the other side of the glass.

* * *

Worse than the prohibition on beating off is the one that says No Blowjobs – not even as an opening move, because saliva inhibits sperm motility or something. Which is especially cruel as Penny used to give head so good that it'd make my brain melt. I miss that. I fantasise about oral all the time. Even when I'm on the job, I might be humping away on top but I'm imagining sinking my cock between her lips, smearing her high-gloss scarlet lipstick all the way up my shaft, feeling the lap of her agile tongue on all the right places. Or I'll be banging her from behind, those ass-cheeks which appear so neat when she stands looking huge now, uplifted under my hands with that black satin corset cinching her waist, and I'll be thinking about how good it would be to slip into her tight pucker instead and waste all my jizz in the wrong hole. Because that one's way off limits now too.

I fantasise about coming on her breasts. She has fantastic breasts, neither flabby nor flat but a good handful each, still as firm and perky as a younger woman's, with the most beautiful big nipples that go hard as pink icing rosettes when I tease them. The areolae crinkle to the texture of cookies. Remember those Iced Gem biscuits you used to be able to buy? That's what I think of when I'm sucking Penny's nips. They're that sweet. Her skin is the colour of rich cream and there's a scatter of tiny moles or freckles from her left shoulder to her nipple, like the splatter flicked from a paintbrush, like droplets of dark cum already spilt in homage to her beauty. And her breasts are full enough that I can straddle her torso and slip my shaft into the valley between them as I cup and squeeze them together, making a sheath for my length. I remember leisurely tit-wanks that seemed to go on for ever, her tongue lapping the head of my knob as it popped out of the ravine to wink at her. I fantasise about doing that again. About taking myself in hand as my orgasm approaches. About feeling the cum gather in my balls and surge up and out to rain on the uplands of her breasts, obliterating the freckles, painting her creamy skin in my whiter shade of pale.

I want to come on the small of her back, and on her bottom and her thighs. I want to watch my spunk slowly dry on her hot skin and ease away the flakes between my fingers, feeding them between her lips to melt upon her tongue like communion wafers. I want to see her kneel before me one more time, the shiny brown swing of her bobbed hair framing her face, her mouth open like a baby bird begging to be fed, her tongue pink and eager to taste my spilt salt.

I miss her.

* * *

I wake in the middle of the night, or perhaps don't wake at all. The covers are thrown back and I'm sweating, I've been having restless dreams and perhaps this is just another of them. There's a glow emanating from the mirror over Penny's dressing table, the reflection of the bedroom light, but it takes me a moment to realise that our own bulb isn't on. And as I contemplate that, my head still full of sleep, the mirror-ghost appears and, stooping forward, steps out through the frame. Just like the girl in that Japanese horror movie, only without the jerky corpse/insect shuffle; she's consummately graceful in fact. She stands on the dressing table with her bare feet not stirring the myriad bottles of perfume and moisturiser and pigment. Naked.

Naked, except for a veil of gauze that wraps spiralwise

about her body in that way fabric only ever does in paintings, hiding nothing. I can see the tremble of her breasts as she breathes. Then with a light step she lands on the footboard of our bed. There's no bump, no sensation of descending weight. I feel nothing. Thank God, I think: this is a dream.

She looks down at me with a slow, sweet smile. She's beautiful, my mirror-ghost. Almost girlishly delicate, with a hairless sex, but with curves to her hips and breasts that are far from childlike. And the eyes in her piquant face are ancient and knowing, her lips lush with promise. She is a fairy maiden, a nymph risen from some still and secret pool. If only she weren't so pale she'd be astoundingly beautiful, but she's the colour of the Portland Stone statues that grace the pediment of the mayor's residence; not a warm and creamy pallor like Penny's, but a delicate grey. I'm reminded of the allegorical figure of the City who sits with her scales and her portcullis in either hand. Even her eyes are colourless, and her erect nipples are white like quartz pebbles.

Down to her knees she slides, slow as oozing cement, eyes huge and fixed on my uncovered form. I think maybe I should protest. But this is only a dream, nothing to worry about – and if it isn't a dream then I'll have to wake Penny, who sleeps beside me, still muffled under the duvet.

I can't wake Penny. It's too much. She can't be expected to deal with this too.

With softly creeping movements the mirror-girl inches her way up my legs, her lips almost brushing the hair that stands erect on my spooked skin but her shining eyes fixed on me. Her own hair billows around her head like smoke: it's a grey like the rest of her but streaked with rust. I think she must have been a redhead once. The lips in that pointed face are incongruously full, almost swollen. The tongue that laps out between them is the palest shade of pink and as she kneels over my crotch and takes me in her mouth I catch a glimpse, the merest hint only, of teeth.

She's cold. Her mouth is cold. It's like being sucked by a cream dessert, yielding and smooth and sweet. My cock responds to the slick embrace with an instantaneous surge of heat, and I arch my back off the mattress as my whole body goes rigid with shock and pleasure. Then she drops me, letting me ease from between her lips as she withdraws her head – only it takes much longer coming out than going in because it's twice as long now and getting longer by the heartbeat. Her saliva gleams on the ruddy column, giving it a pearlescent sheen. She smiles at me questioningly and bats at the crown of my cock with teasing little licks. My hands are pinned by my sides, too heavy to lift from the sheet.

This has to be a dream.

With a tilt of her head she crouches lower, her mouth opening wide to suck my scrotum. Into that cool cave goes first one bollock and then the other, bathed in her wetness. I am shaking now where I lie, every fibre quivering, and my erect cock points up at my face and nods against my belly with every jerk. But as she releases my balls and licks her way back up its length it rises clear of my supine form, twitching. It doesn't give a stuff about dreams or reality, cold or hot. It just wants her mouth. So she engulfs me, a cool ocean in which my body swims, my mind trailing helplessly behind like a plastic float. I surrender all control of my limbs and give myself up to her moon-cold kisses until I'm leaping wave after wave of arousal and surging toward the light. When she bites, I barely feel the pain. I feel the pelagic upswell that follows in its wake though: the perfect wave. It drags me down into the deep and everything turns to black.

It was certainly a dream. I wake in the morning with a monumental hard-on and mount Penny almost before she's awake. And she doesn't object, of course, even though it takes me – despite my breathless horniness – nearly for ever to come.

* * *

I've been having these lurid fantasies, sleeping and waking, for months now. It's a case of what you can't have, that's what you want. And what I want is sex that hasn't a thing to do with procreation. It's become an obsession. I used to be so pedestrian in my fantasies, I'd imagine what it would be like to fuck newspaper models and pretty Australian soap starlets and that girl in the canteen I never spoke to. Now I catch myself in crazy musings. There's a big Catholic church with a convent attached to it down the end of our road: I've screwed Penny while picturing myself standing on the altar, cock in hand, jerking off an impossible spunk-shower over the upturned, outraged faces of the nuns kneeling before me. There's a public garden where, if it's a quiet day at work, I take my packed lunch to eat; there are often students there sketching the statues and the plants because there's an art college on the boundary road, and for some reason a lot of them seem to be Italian or Spanish. I find myself eyeing them up, fantasising about having three or four of those cool, aloof girls on their knees before me, their sleek hair swept behind their shoulders as they take it in turns to suck my cock, squabbling delightfully when one gets too greedy and holds centre-stage too long.

Christ. I'm turning into a real horn-dog.

Maybe the more sex you get, the more you want.

* * *

I come out of the rather fancy town house and stand on the top step with the computer printout in my hand, feeling sick. When I look down at the paper the figures blur and dance, meaningless. It's a good thing the doctor explained the results to me.

A good thing ... Oh, God.

I went to a private clinic for the semen analysis, keeping it quiet, not telling Penny. I just wanted to be sure it wasn't me that was holding us back. Well, now I know. Low sperm count, and those that are there have something wrong with them. Stunted tails, I gather from the doctor's sympathetic words, that cause them to swim in fitful spirals instead of straight ahead.

Fuck fuck fuck. What's going to happen when Penny finds out? Because she will: eventually she'll have us both down our local GP, demanding medical check-ups and assistance. It only counts as infertility if you've been trying for two years, but she's going to lose patience sooner rather than later.

How's she going to react when she finds out it's me, that I'm the one letting her down?

I stumble to the car and drive all the way home without the slightest awareness of my surroundings. It's only when I'm in the big basement car park under Mavin Wood Towers, reversing into my parking space, that I register anything outside my own head, and then I nearly accelerate into the bloody wall because the mirror-girl is back, sitting behind me, bisecting the rear window and visible in my rear-view mirror. 'Ah God *fuck*!' I shriek, slamming the horn by mistake. The cacophony in the concrete undercroft is horrible. I'm out of the car in a flat second, staring in at the back seat – but no one's visible, of course. She was only there in the reflection.

I feel sort of foolish then, and ashamed of my cowardice, and pissed off. I look round to see if anyone's witnessed my panic, but the parking area is deserted.

I make myself take the elevator up to the twelfth floor, not the stairs. The interior of that little box is lined with smoked mirror-glass, but I grit my teeth and step inside. I refuse to be afraid of her. What has she done, after all, but crawl out of my dreams and bestow her cool kiss? Does she even exist outside my head? Should I be afraid of that? Resolutely I turn my back on the mirrored wall and stare at the numbers over the door.

Halfway up, between the sixth and seventh floors, the lift slows to a halt and the lights dim. I shut my eyes. I'm sweating: I can feel the cold trickle inching down my spine toward the cleft of my ass. My shoulder blades bump lightly against the glass and under my suit jacket I feel my skin crawl.

Something brushes my thigh and the front of my trousers. I look down to see a slim, naked arm draped about my hips, the pale hand stroking my crotch and searching for my fly. Her nails are long and just a little too pointed.

Oh, hell.

My eyes flick upwards. There's a camera in one of the corners, of course. It won't get the best angle, but if it's still working – and I've no way of telling that – it'll see enough. The thought of being filmed on CCTV while an unseen woman opens my flies and pulls out my cock is too uncomfortable. I turn my back to the lens and face the mirror.

She's kneeling there beyond the glass, and her hand juts from its surface as if from peaty water in a still pool. I can imagine that easily: there's something about her that makes me think of Celtic twilight and ladies of the lake. But she's perfectly conversant with the uses of buttons and zips, I find; popping one and pulling down the other, reaching beneath to the cotton that's sticking to my skin, finding her way to my over-eager cock and my useless balls.

And my only response is to hold my waistband so my trousers don't fall down. Because all of a sudden those balls don't feel so useless. She doesn't care if my sperm can't swim straight; she just wants to feel the hot spurt of my cream over her cold tongue.

She just wants to suck me.

I lay my forehead on the cool glass. I can see her smooth inhuman face swimming toward me through the depths of the smoky glass, breaking the surface, lifting out from the mirror. Her hair is sleeked behind her as if wet and gravity are drawing it down. Her pale lips part, spreading for the ruddy blunt bell end of my erection. Cold: cold like moor water. The hair rises on the nape of my neck and my scrotum contracts with a heave, but the chill is nothing compared to the slick caress of her mouth.

And I'm so fucking grateful. I could drown in gratitude, if I wasn't going to drown in pleasure first.

* * *

'What's that?' Penny asks, pointing at my chest. I pull my dressing gown over hastily to hide the paired dimples of the puncture wounds.

'Dunno. Just insect bites, I think.' I feel groggy, hungover.

'The mayor's residence has bedbugs, does it?'

'You'd be amazed. Old building, you know. There're all sorts of dirty old corners.'

'Ew. Don't go bringing anything home with you, that's all.'

Too late, I think. I pour my third cup of tea since staggering out of bed.

'Are you going into work then?'

I ought to. Not that there's anything to do, because it's the election today. Far too late for him or me or anyone else to affect the vote, but we've got to be seen to be around. 'Later,' I mumble. 'We're going to be up most of the night waiting for the results to come in.'

'Well, I've got to get going.' She heads off to the bathroom to finish her morning ablutions. I'm so dull-witted that I don't immediately notice that she doesn't come back. I just sit there nursing my cup of tea and staring at the cloudy sky through the window. Picturing a face as pale and luminous as those clouds. When I rise from the breakfast bar the apartment feels eerily still. I wander down the corridor and tap on the bathroom door.

'You still in there?'

There's a soft noise: a sob. My heart sinks. Opening the door I find Penny sitting on the edge of the bath. She lifts her face and tries to smile, but her mouth is all over the place and all the blinking she's doing doesn't hide how wet her eyes are.

'My period's come on.'

'Oh, love,' I whisper.

'I thought this time ... I was late ... I really thought ...' She stops talking and clenches down. 'Doesn't matter,' she grits out. 'Not to worry. We keep trying.'

And all I can do is hug her and rub the stiff angles of her shoulders and wish helplessly that there's something I could do to make her happy. And hate myself.

From the corner of my eye I see pale shadows shift in the bathroom mirror. I press Penny closer to my chest and shield her face, not wanting her to see the girl in the glass – and certainly not that look of possessive avarice burning in those pale eyes.

* * *

The mayor loses the election. It's no landslide, but by shortly after midnight enough of the ballot boxes are in and counted that we've got a clear picture of the results. It's not going to be made public until tomorrow, of course, but a silence falls over those of us gathered in City Hall as the phones ring and the same message is relayed from ward after ward. It's always harder for the sitting candidate to win, of course, and we're not entirely surprised.

I leave the scrum of officials and PR men and activists and head upstairs, wanting to be on my own. The top floor has a famously good 360-degree view of the City from its conference suite: this isn't the mayor's gracious official residence but a modern oblate high-rise that squats on the north bank of the river, an architect's wet dream of steel and glass. The windows run floor to ceiling on the top storey. I stand in the unlit room, looking out over a landscape as darkly glittering and beautiful as the bottom of the sea, the outlines of water and stone picked out only by the phosphorescent glow of individual lights, the sky as opaque and starless as if it's a mile of water pressing down upon us. The creep of car headlights brings to mind the gleam of bottom-feeding crustacea.

I feel the numb ache of defeat in every fibre of my body. In days I'll be out of a job. Perhaps it's a good thing I've not been able to give Penny a child; we're going to need her income. Hah. There's cold comfort for you. I'm a failure, let's face it. Unable to do my job and sway the pendulum of political opinion, unable to provide for my family, unable even to father a baby – that simplest of biological functions. Isn't the most primal and basic goal of all life to replicate itself? Isn't that what we're designed for? Even microbes can reproduce, but not me.

My cell phone rings, making me quiver. It's Penny. I don't take the call. As silence returns I move over to the room's environmental control panel next to the elevator, and turn on the lights.

Instantly the night outside vanishes, the windows becoming mirrors.

She's there, waiting for me. I'm cerebrally intrigued to see that she's only reflected in one of the angled panes, even though I'm visible in several. Her long hair is fox-red now, after days of feeding from me. There is even a hint of colour in her cheeks.

Gracefully, almost idly, she circles my reflection and, as I watch, begins to dance. It's strange to see her brushing up against me, draping her arms about my neck, rubbing her rear into my crotch – all without me being able to feel a thing. The tease is entirely visual. Each flick of her hips makes the blood surge in my veins. Each jiggle of her breasts makes my need grow. But I feel oddly discomfited in the midst of my fascination, as if I'm jealous of my own reflection. I move my hands, trying to interact with her dance, and she laughs silently as my mirrored self moves too, clumsily encircling her undulating hips. Turning in my arms she grasps the front of my shirt and tears it open.

My real shirt, the one on my material body, remains unscathed. The one in the reflection is shredded and my chest revealed. The look of confusion on my face is comic. She's mocking me, I suspect – mocking my desire to rationalise, at any rate. She rakes her nails across my bare skin and my reflection bleeds, yet I feel nothing. She shreds my trousers – effortlessly; her nails must be sharp as knives – and squirms her pert little rump against me.

'Come here,' I say hoarsely. 'Come on out.'

Her eyes lift and meet mine, looking straight out from the glass, her lips forming a smile so wanton that it makes my cock stiffen all on its own. Then she abandons my reflected self and walks out from the mirrored room into the material one. Her feet make no sound on the carpet, of course, but I feel the caress of the cold air that surrounds her. I take a deep breath as she closes on me, lays a slender hand on my breastbone, and then pushes me backwards on to the table and climbs on top.

This time I hear the fabric of my shirt tear.

* * *

She tastes like that Chinese tea: lapsang souchong, that's the one. Slightly smoky, slightly tannic. Cold.

Eat me, I beg. Eat me up. Take me down to that dark place and let me never come back.

* * *

When the elevator door opens I'm lying supine on the polished conference table, speckled with love-bites, and she's kneeling over me. She's framing my head with her straddled thighs and grinding her pubic mound down over my face, but I'm not exactly applying myself to the job. Traumatic pleasure has got me pinned, capable of nothing more than groans.

She's got her teeth buried deep in my balls and she's sucking hard, and that's about all my mind is capable of grasping right now.

Until Penny steps out of the lift.

I look up from between the mirror-girl's white thighs as my world cracks like a dropped glass. 'It's not what it looks like' – isn't that what I'm supposed to say, caught *in flagrante* like that? That's the cliché. Try and talk your way out of this: Mr Dick is standing at full mast, angled as a gnomon over my belly. 'It's not what it looks like, darling: I'm not really fucking her.'

The mirror-girl makes the point far better than I ever could, lifting her face from my punctured balls and stiff cock to snarl at Penny, showing a red mask that's all savage teeth.

'Richard?' Pen takes an unsteady pace forward, dropping her handbag.

Light as a cat, the mirror-girl springs off me and the two women stare.

'That's … That's my husband.' Penny sounds aghast.

The mirror-girl doesn't reply. I've never heard her speak. She snatches my wrist and pulls me up from the table, heading for the window. She's strong, but I'm so weak I can't keep my legs under me. I've lost too much blood, I think, as the floor shoots up to meet me and my shoulder is wrenched at an unnatural angle. Blue-black explosions of colour flare behind my eyes. My knees burn on the carpet as she tows me. I see her bound through the pane of glass and my arm follows, tight in her grasp.

It's like jelly; gelid but yielding. My hand sinks into the pane and it doesn't appear on the outside of the glass where the walkway is, waving over the city landscape, but only in the reflected room. With a jerk she drags me through up to my shoulder. For the first time I try to resist, though not wholeheartedly.

A warm hand grabs my other wrist, drawing it out behind me. Penny. It's Penny, holding me back.

The mirror-girl pulls again, much stronger, and my head is wrenched through to the other side. For a moment, strung between both worlds, I see what the reflection looks like from within. I see what *she* looks like in her own world.

I scream, but I know Penny can't hear me any more. The warm hand is nearly pulling my left arm off: the cold one is wrenching at my right. I shut my eyes and haul backwards as hard as I can, twisting my wrist in the mirror-ghost's grasp. Her fingers feel as thin and hard as bone.

Then she lets go. It's so abrupt it has to be deliberate: I pitch over backwards and the glass shatters to tiny cubes, letting in a ferocious blast of night air. Every light on the observation floor goes out as I tumble into Penny's arms. It's freezing cold. She gasps my name over and over, and we crawl together over the crunching safety glass toward the lift. We end up crouched together by the wall, and she takes my head in her hands and presses her cheek against mine, trembling.

'Pen. Oh, thank God.'

'I came ... I came to see if you were OK.' Her skin feels hot and even though I'm dizzy and shaking I wrap my arms around her, craving that warmth. The tears running down my face – hers or mine – burn my cheeks.

For a moment the memory of what lies beyond the mirror fills my head, and then I push it away, burying my face in my wife's warm scent.

This is terrible. I've still, despite everything, got an erection that could stand for Parliament. My balls seethe, swollen and tight with the urge to erupt and shed – well, I can't even guess: the mirror-ghost has drained me dry and I ought to be shrivelled and flaccid but I'm not, I'm burning with arousal. Pulling Penny further up on to my lap I kiss her fervently and push her skirt up her thighs. She makes an incoherent noise that might be protest, but she kisses me back and clings to my neck. My fingers find the edge of her panties, and I pull at them, sharply, my hands clumsy and quivering. Her gusset is thick with the sanitary pad that I wrench aside. Then I pull her up and over my stiffy, impaling her slippery depths.

'Richard!'

'Please,' I groan, my dry lips mumbling her in the half-dark, my breath coming hard and bitter. 'Please, Pen.' I have to: I have to slake this torturing tumescence. All my cum's been drained already but I need to go again. Right now.

'Oh, God.'

'Please. Yes. Oh, yes.'

Grunting, sweating, clumsy – we slither together, frantic now. Penny's thighs rise and fall and I grip her hips with desperate strength. She's gasping. I'm nearly weeping with the need for release, because I can't possibly come again, not now.

But somehow I do. Riding a long white streak of pain I flood her, pulse after pulse.

* * *

And now Penny is pregnant. When she couldn't have been fertile. When I had nothing left to give her, from testes inflamed with poison.

Now I'm really scared.

(Roisin)

And this is Roisin, the mirror-ghost. She is the oldest of the vampires in the City: so very old that she hardly remembers her first life, so old that only her name remains to her. Her history has dissolved in the murk of years, her ambitions and personality washed away by the tide of time. She has forgotten almost everything. Her body too has surrendered its identity, even its reality. It has become as tenuous and fragmented as her mind.

Matter is no longer material. The material is no matter. She is on her way to becoming a ghost, or a god.

She remembers only how to love. The thirst for love still drives her. She doesn't feed casually, not like Ben or Naylor, Reynauld or Estelle. She doesn't choose a different lover every night then abandon them disbelieving and distraught before morning. When Roisin feeds, it is with passion. She falls for her lovers with the swift, heart-clutching imperative of romantic fervour. She becomes obsessed and will woo a new flame for weeks, lavishing her kisses upon them alone. She shadows and protects them, keeping them close, shutting the world with all its dangers and horrors away, spinning a cocoon of love to cradle them.

And she will be gentle as she eats you. Tender as her lips wrap about your warm flesh and seek the throbbing pulse. She will mourn you with exquisite sorrow when you leave her bereft.

Fear her love.

Roisin will come to you out of a silvered glass. Be not too vain, or the white lady may spy you and want you for her own. Under the moonlight, she will stoop to kiss your flesh with her pale lips and fill you with her cold fire. In silent places she approaches, her presence marked only by the faintest whisper, a stir of chill air not strong enough to break the cobwebs spun on an autumn night. Her skin is whiter than porcelain, her lips full, her breasts small and soft, her eyes an empty void aching to be filled with the sight of you. She needs. She is the embodiment of need.

She is beautiful, and she will break your heart.

It's hard to say what it is that attracts her in the first place: a look in someone's eye, perhaps; a particular indefinable scent of skin or the sound of a racing pulse. It's the indescribable chemistry of passion: a mystery. Perhaps she sees or tastes in them a faint echo of her first love. And yet every time she is betrayed; that is her tragedy. Her lovers grow wizened and ungrateful, dull as clods of earth where once they were brimming with life, and unresponsive to either pain or pleasure. Just as swiftly as she falls for them she inevitably finds herself one night, without warning, perplexed and frustrated and indifferent, and she turns away in search of new succour for her empty and aching heart.

And she forgets.

Once outside of the fierce focused light of her love, the living are too ephemeral to make any impression on her memory. Roisin has lived so many years, seen so many faces, that mortals are like transient patterns formed by mud swirled in water. She finds comfort in places she knows, but even places change. Meadows are suddenly covered in swathes of housing, trees grow to giants and then vanish in the blink of an eye, skylines rise and fall like a tide. She clings to those people whose immortality – if not their permanence – makes them more than passing shadows, to Reynauld and Naylor in particular. They are the anchors of her disintegrating life. They are beacons in the fog.

The present washes over her, too ephemeral to grasp. The past decays. She recalls … What? Fragments only.

The smell of the wild briar roses after which she was named.

A lead-weighted spindle hanging from her fingers, twisting flax to thread.

The seep of bog water into leather shoes stuffed with fleece to cushion her numb toes. Hands heavy on her arms, marching her too fast through the puddles, the mud splashing up under her woollen skirt all over her bare legs.

Long-handled, Y-shaped lengths of wood. They pushed her underwater, face down, pinning her limbs to the muddy bed. The water looked yellow as piss from below, and bubbles of air rose like golden balls from her open lips.

She remembers love. It was love that destroyed her and love that kept her alive through death. She'd loved someone, though she can't remember who – or what. Just the ferocious, all-consuming passion of his embrace; the terror and the ecstasy. Only that it made everyone afraid. That they'd met in darkness, though she cannot recall whether it was once or many times, and that dogs had been howling.

Some things still prick her memory at odd moments, recalling briefly that first raw passion – strange things, like the lift of a white dog's muzzle, or the feel of leaf mould under her nails, or the smell of wet and sweating horses.

The first, fresh, coppery taste of blood.

They staked her in the swamp because they were afraid of the one she loved. All winter she lay there, while the ice thickened over her head and in the tissues of her body. Nothing lived in that acid water: no fish or insect gnawed at her cold flesh. Nothing moved except the occasional bubble of gas ascending to the surface. Then when the spring thawed her out she rose from the mud, thrust aside the stakes and went home. Looking for love, hot and red.

She became legend, but even legends are forgotten.

Water is a gate to the Otherworld: that's ingrained in the psyche of those who live in this country. Roisin's people would break weapons in half and throw them in to propitiate the powers that lurked below, and even now the people make coin-offerings for reasons they can't articulate. A creature of that Otherworld, Roisin didn't dig herself a grave, not even when the sun became a torment to her. She returned to the water. It was a part of her death and it pervades her unlife too.

Roisin is not urban by nature. It took centuries for her to become reconciled to the City, and even here in the heart of the metropolis she haunted those places that felt familiar to her: canals and duckponds, by and large. She would rest in pellucid calm far beneath the silver surface of one body of water or another, while overhead barges eclipsed the light or toy boats fled the wind. In the shadow of river bridges and inside tunnels she would lie motionless just below the surface, and those who spotted her would edge closer for a look and then flee in terror. Sometimes she would snatch a duck by its paddling legs and then people would start and ask themselves: Was that a pike? It'd have to be a bloody big pike to take a drake like that.

Sometimes she'd take a child. They find water so alluring and drown so swiftly.

Beware the depths beneath the still surface. The water may be shallow but the reflection is infinite.

Still water is the only reflective plane in nature, but in time human ingenuity created new gates into the Otherworld, using glass backed with silver nitrate. At first people knew the dangers and would cover mirrors at night or when there was a death in the house, fearing quite rightly what they might see within. But it is the nature of humans to forget even the wisest precautions. Roisin retreated into the mirror world when she found she could live on one side of the glass or the other at will – and that behind the glass the sunlight did not touch her.

Behind the glass is a golden gloaming; waving weed, skin textureless and yellow. A thousand drifting speckles of darkness suspended in the haze. There are things in here that never come to the surface. If it were not for her need for love, she would drift through the labyrinthine passages of the Otherworld and never come up.

Cover your mirrors. Never look into one after dark.

Roisin was already an inhabitant of the City when Reynauld arrived from France. Younger than her, he wooed her with some caution. But his wariness was wasted effort; Roisin has no interest after all these centuries in anything so complex as temporal power. She hardly noticed when he demarcated his territory. They are still lovers, upon occasion, but their mutual heat is chilled by an instinctive tristesse: she is reminded by him of the vitality she has lost, and he sees in her what they all must become.

Reynauld grants Roisin more latitude than any other vampire in his domain. It is even possible she recognises this, though it is hard to truly say what awareness still flits through her empty mind.

In another century she will be nothing but a chill in the air, a persistent feeling of being watched, a rumour attached to some particular building or location: Bad things happen here. Pets go missing. There are cot-deaths: too many of them. People go a bit, you know; mad. There are stories …

Mirror, mirror, on the wall.

3: Eight for the April Rainers

The railway line had been taken up years ago but the bridge over the River Lea remained, its dignified Victorian ironwork acned with graffiti tags. Rubbish and leaf mould had accumulated on the span, deep enough to support the growth of elder bushes and a few spindly birches whose newly unfurled leaves drooped now in the rain. It had been raining most of the night and all this morning, and even before Lilla reached the bridge her clothes were soaked through. She paid it no attention.

The bridge was closed off at each end, of course, with heavy chain-link gates, but the fans of iron spikes that were supposed to stop kids climbing along the outside of the girders were rusted and broken, and in some cases had been hacksawed off. It was enough to give her room to swing herself round the safety barrier, the skirt of her black coat flapping and sodden. Kidskin gloves – an eBay purchase – gave her some grip on the chilly metal, though she scowled at the marks left on them once she'd found her footing again: rust and dirt and pigeon shit.

She kept to the side of the bridge as she worked her way along, setting her feet over a main girder. She didn't want to fall into the river below. Not yet, anyway. Not until the right moment.

From the centre of the span she could see down the river toward the plastics factory, and to both banks. To the left, from where she'd come, the flat land was occupied by an industrial estate and beyond that the bulwarks of high-rise flats. This wasn't a fashionable part of the city. To the right the line of the dead railway skirted a brick wall; a very old brick wall with no windows that encompassed a triangular piece of land between the track and the river. Inside the wall was a large building with a jumbled roofline and tall chimneys, built of the same small greyish bricks. It looked like a prison. In fact it had long ago been the Stratford Fields Lunatic Asylum, and nowadays the front door bore a small brass plate inscribed 'Wakefield Specialist Roses Ltd'. Lilla knew all this. Her research had been very thorough.

Right now, defying the overcast sky, there was a dull bloom of light in the high window of Wakefield Roses. It was almost the only sign of life in the wet and dreary landscape. Lilla forced herself to look away from it, down at the river. The water looked grey-green and filthy; the drop made her feel sick. She slipped under an iron strut and inched out on to a protruding beam. Her little cross-laced boots gave her almost no purchase and her velvet coat felt heavy, like it was pulling her to the water. She knew she must be very obvious to anyone watching: a black flag flying from the grey beams. Cowardice fluttered in her belly but she swallowed it down.

For a long while she hesitated.

Better this way, if there was no alternative. Better death than being cast out as *nothing*. Betrayal coated her insides; she could feel its tarry blackness eating at her throat and stomach. She'd wanted to love him, for ever and ever. His cold expression as he'd dismissed her was burned into her memory, his disdain turning her blood to acid. In the cold April wind tears prickled at her eyes.

Crouching, she found an eye-hole in the beam and slid her fingers into it. Then she eased her weight to her knees, wriggled – and dropped to hang from that hand, her boot-heels kicking over the centre of the river. She grabbed on tight with the other hand too and then, as panic surged through her veins, screamed. She screamed until her lungs were empty. Then she just clung on, while the pain grew unbearable in her shoulders and her wrists, while her fingers slipped on the rusted metal.

And then, just as she thought, Too late, a hand closed over her wrist and wrenched her into the air. She caught a glimpse of a man's pale face before she was crushed against his torso, and as he lurched back into the safety of the bridge's iron beams she burst into sobs. The tears were real, the relief genuine and overwhelming. She'd been rescued.

The stranger didn't set her down: it was obvious that she wouldn't be able to stand. He cradled her to him, wet clothes plastered about her limbs, and she buried her face in his chest as he walked. Lilla felt herself swimming in and out of consciousness as the blood squeezed back into her wrenched arms, but she didn't care now. It was all like a dream. Dimly she heard metal protesting as a gate was forced wide. She heard a latch fall. She heard feet pacing across wooden floorboards, and then up stairs, and then muffled on a carpeted floor. Finally he stooped, and she was laid out on what felt like a hard couch. Her gloves were peeled off before her hands were vigorously chafed.

'Lie still,' said a male voice as she tried to force her fluttering eyelids open. 'Just relax.' But as he moved away she won the battle and brought the room around her slowly into focus. Dim pools of light created shadows that clung to secrets. It was particularly hard to make sense of the scenery because it was so very cluttered: furniture everywhere. Pictures in gilt frames crammed on to every inch of the walls. Pot plants, a piano, ranks of porcelain ornaments, a tiger-skin rug that looked threadbare but authentic. Oil lamps burning on the velvet-draped tables. All very Victorian.

Then her rescuer came back with a small crystal glass in his hand, and he looked threadbare and Victorian too, in the style of a Romantic poet. He even wore a frock coat of some sort – its colour an indefinable faded murk, gone to splits at the elbows, the cuffs frayed. The cravat wound about his high collar was growing ragged, his waistcoat was down to the warp and his trousers were creased. But his face was strikingly attractive, even framed as it was by long greying hair: his pale-blue eyes were both haunting and haunted and he had the rumpled, eccentrically handsome features of a Shakespearean actor. And he took himself just as seriously, it seemed. 'Drink this, for your health's sake,' he told her, helping her to sit up. It was sherry, Lilla discovered as she took an obedient sip. She had to force herself not to spit it out – she hated sherry, especially the sweet stuff.

'Thank you,' she whispered, and burst into tears as the strain found release at last. He rescued the glass from her grasp and as she pitched forward against him he laid a hand lightly on her hair and stroked it.

'There, there: you're safe now.'

'I'm sorry!' she wailed. 'Oh, I'm so sorry!'

'Don't worry. Don't worry.' He rocked her ever so slightly.

'I've got you all wet!'

'It's nothing.'

Choking down her sobs, she sat up. She knew the mascara she'd applied so thickly that morning would be tracked down her cheeks and she tugged at the bright blonde tresses of her hair, trying to make them look less dishevelled and succeeding not one whit. The man was studying her, his brows knotted.

'Now why were you on that bridge? Don't you realise how dangerous it was?'

Lilla lowered her eyes and looked up at him through her wet lashes. His face was set in a look of sympathetic concern, but his gaze was drifting all over her: throat and breasts and hands and back to her throat. Possibly he wasn't even aware of it. Her heart juddered, quickening. 'That was the point,' she answered with a tremulous smile.

'My poor girl …' His voice was low and pleasant despite being so weirdly formal: a voice made to whisper in maidenly ears and make suggestions to turn their owners pink. 'Is it that bad?'

She covered her mouth with her hand, unable to answer.

'A man?'

'My boyfriend. He threw me out.' The words were inadequate to express her feeling of betrayal, but the wobble in her voice and the quiver of her lip made up for them a little.

'Are you … in trouble?'

'Not in that way.' She shuddered. 'I'm cold.'

He glanced apologetically at the fireplace which, behind its guardian chinoiserie brass lions and its polished grate, was empty. 'I'm sorry, I haven't lit a fire in months …'

Lilla thrust her hands into his, searching for warmth, but they were as icy as her own. He jumped a little at the contact, and his eyes widened. 'Please light it,' she whispered: she really was shaking now, the waves of trembling rippling across her shoulders. 'I'm freezing here.'

He frowned. 'The boiler is on in the rose house. Do you think you could make it there?'

Lilla didn't want to move but nodded, but then when she tried to rise her legs gave way and she sagged against him. He caught her deftly, as chivalrous as he had been on the bridge, and hefted her into his arms like a bride with a muttered 'Oops-a-daisy'. Though he wasn't a broadly built man her weight seemed like nothing to him. She looked up with wide eyes and parted lips, responding instinctively to his strength.

'Do I know you, young lady? Have we met?'

Oh, thought Lilla: no one had called her 'young lady' since junior school. And then it had always been a term of disapproval. 'I don't know. Have we?'

'What's your name?'

'Lillabet.'

He shook his head and carried her out of the room.

'What's yours?'

The corridor walls were stone, the plaster stained and bulging with damp, the floor beneath his feet bare boards that creaked alarmingly. Lilla caught glimpses of doors opening on to small empty rooms with barred windows. He hesitated before answering her. 'Robert Wakefield.'

'Wakefield's Roses?' she asked, snuggling up ever so slightly against him, pretending an ease she didn't feel. She hadn't relaxed in days, had barely even slept, her skin crawling restlessly at the touch of her clothes. His clothes, old as they were, smelled a little dusty, and that was all. 'Is that you, Mr Wakefield?' She thought he would like being addressed as 'Mr' by a young woman and she was right: she saw the slight, proud lift of his chin.

'That's right. We supply flowers right across the country. As you'll see.'

Down through the twisting bowels of that house they passed, through wafts of damp and patches of darkness where there were no windows at all, until they came to a big room which though equally bleak contained the first signs of modernity she'd seen since entering the building: stacked cardboard boxes, rolls of cellophane and labels. Robert walked straight through, his stride and his grip no less easy now for having carried her this far, and shouldered open a large wooden door. He carried her over the threshold and they were outside.

No, not outside. It was a cloister, she thought, like in a monastery, but triangular not square. It was the area enclosed by the complex's forbidding outer walls. Robert paused, giving her time to look around. The whole area was roofed in with glass upon which the rain was drumming, and the glass was supported by the most elaborate wrought-iron frame held up by white-painted iron columns. All around them sounded the chuckle of water being channelled away down drainpipes. It was also warmer here; not quite a hothouse warmth, but after the dank chill of the building it seemed almost muggy. Growing under the glass were ranks and ranks of rosebushes in full leaf, their buds as full and crimson as pouting lips, the air fragrant with their scent.

With a shift of her weight Lilla indicated that she wanted to try and stand, and Robert left her slip down and set her feet on the floor. The paths between the rose-beds were of soft flaked bark, mounded so deep that she felt like she was standing on cushions. She filled her lungs with the perfumed air.

'Roses! – in April?'

He acknowledged her surprise with a tilt of his head. 'A unique variety, grown only here. It's a talent of mine.' He smiled thinly. 'A gift, you might say.' From his pocket he produced a hooked pruning knife, a gesture which made gooseflesh prickle Lilla's forearms. 'Green fingers.'

She turned slowly on her heel to scan the glasshouse. 'It's amazing.'

'This land used to be all marsh once. Sour grass and reeds and rushes, rough grazing in the summer and duck-hunting in the winter.' The way he said it, so melancholy, sounded as if he remembered it personally and she gave him a searching look. 'They built this place out here because it was isolated in those days. It was a private asylum,' he explained.

'For madmen?'

'For the better class of madmen. This area was the exercise yard, where the patients could take the air in safety.' He shrugged. 'Then they built the railway along the embankment and the City grew out eastward to surround this place, and the land was drained and the river tamed. And I bought the building because ... because here I could grow my roses.'

'May I?' she asked, indicating the bushes.

'Please, be my guest.'

Still a little unsteady, she walked a few paces to the nearest bush. It stood as tall as she did, the young leaves bright green and the older ones so dark they were almost black. The blooms, mostly still in bud, were a deep vibrant crimson but with a black stain at the base of each petal, and when she bent to sniff one that was half-open she inhaled not the strong musky perfume associated with red roses – a reek that always made her think of bathroom air-freshener – but a wild and spicy scent that reminded her of patchouli and caraway and melted muscovado sugar.

'They're beautiful.' They were almost perfect, in fact; not one overblown or misshapen flower head or discoloured leaf. The blossoms were borne on tall straight stems, and the only flaw seemed to be that these were clad in wicked-looking red-tinted thorns. 'What's the variety?'

'Rosa "Sanguine Heart".' He went to a nearby bush and cut a flower on a long stem.

'And what does "sanguine" mean?'

There was the slightest of pauses. 'Optimistic,' he answered, with such inapposite chill that she bit her lip, not wanting the tension in her breast to burst out as laughter. 'They've won RHS awards, if you know anything about that sort of thing.'

'Sorry, no.' Rubbing her arms, she returned to his side.

'Would you care for one?' He offered her the rose, its dark-red petals so charged with colour that it seemed to throb. 'Be careful of the thorns. They have to be cut off before shipping.'

She smiled up at him, taking the stem with care. 'Can I sit near the boiler?'

'Of course.' He offered his arm and she fell in beside him as he walked her through the mass of plants. Under his worn sleeve the limb was hard with muscle, but the fingers he rested on her wrist were long and delicate. She imagined those hands trailing drifts of cobweb finer than lace and the unexpected image made her shiver. She pressed closer to his arm to reassure herself of his solidity and felt him respond with an intake of breath.

'What's this?' In the centre of the strange garden was a stone sarcophagus, knee-high, with a slate slab for a cover. There were lines of script carved into the stone. Robert didn't reply. 'Is it a grave? Why've you got a grave in your garden, Mr Wakefield?'

'This way, Lillabet.' He tried to lead her past but she dragged from his arm enough to read the inscription: no name or date but a verse of poetry.

From too much love of living,
From hope and fear set free,
We thank with brief thanksgiving
Whatever gods may be
That no life lives for ever,
That dead men rise up never;
That even the weariest river
Winds somewhere safe to sea.

'Swinburne,' she said. She'd had to set a Swinburne poem to music for one of her college projects and she recognised the rhythmic cadences and the bleak sentiment.

The tight line of Robert's lips relaxed. 'Yes. A fine poet, much underestimated in the modern age.'

'Is it a grave?'

'Not yet. There's no one in it at the moment, anyway.'

'Is it yours?'

'I imagine you think I'm morbid,' said Robert, sounding a little uneasy. 'But it doesn't hurt to be prepared in advance.'

'You sound like you're looking forward to it. In the poem, I mean.'

'Do I?' He looked away.

Lilla gave him a conspiratorial smile. 'You're a bit of a goth, aren't you, Mr Wakefield? The clothes and everything?'

He frowned. 'A goth? Oh – oh, yes, I see ...'

'Don't worry. I have a lot of goth friends. And I love the clothes.' She indicated her own: a black velvet coat-dress, very fitted to the waist but full below, that buttoned all the way down from the neckline to the hem. It showed off her figure admirably despite displaying not a hint of skin.

'Especially the women's underwear, don't you think?' she added with a sweet grin.

A flush mounted in his pale cheek and he set off again, leading her with a firm grip on her arm. 'Let's get you to the boiler.'

'Oh, yes. I need warming through.'

He stumbled ever so slightly.

'I am grateful, you know, Mr Wakefield. It's so kind of you looking after me like this.'

'Think nothing of it.'

'No one else cares. No one else would have come and saved me the way you did. So quick. So strong.'

'Here we are,' he mumbled. They'd reached the far wall of the cloister, where a great black cast-iron boiler stood. It looked Victorian, with ornate brass dials and levers, but from the quiet hum it was giving off the interior fittings were very modern. Pipes snaked away from it, disappearing into the earth. Robert released her and bent to look intently into the inspection panel, then tap some of the dials. 'It's gas-fired,' he said, clearly trying to focus on the new topic. 'I had it converted. It's on a low setting now we're into spring, but if you stand close it's quite warm.' Straightening up he glanced back at her and his eyes opened wide. 'What are you doing?'

While his attention had been on the boiler, she'd been opening the buttons up the front of her coat – or to be precise, her dress, since she had nothing but underwear on beneath it. The sodden velvet buttons oozed water under her fingertips as she slipped them one by one. 'I have to take it off to dry it out,' she said softly. 'You don't mind, do you?'

He stared. 'What is this?'

Not as dumb as he might seem, she thought: he was starting to guess. That Dickensian scene on the bridge: the rescue of the swooning maiden – now this, her costume. How long would it take him to work it out? 'Haven't you ever seen ladies' underwear before, Mr Wakefield?' Slipping off the long-sleeved dress, she laid the rose coyly across her chest while keeping her expression one of wide-eyed innocence. She was wearing reproduction Victorian-style lingerie: a sleeveless chemise with lace ruffles and pink ribbons about the deep curve of the neckline, long cotton drawers, and underneath them opaque silk stockings gartered above the knees. Over the chemise was a satin corset, laced in matching pink, that narrowed her waist and lifted and cupped her generous breasts. Of course everything was soaked through from the rain: the thin cotton of her top and pantaloons was quite transparent where it clung to her, offering immodest glimpses of her dark gold pubic fleece and her pink nipples which were poking out against the cold fabric like boiled sweets.

'This is quite improper,' he said hoarsely, but his eyes swept up and down her figure.

'But how else am I to warm up?' She walked slowly toward him, dropping the dress, crossing one booted foot carefully in front of the other so that her hips swung with every step. 'Unless you can think of another way?'

His mouth sagged. The front of his trousers stirred as something very improper indeed flexed beneath.

'What about it?' she whispered, standing right in front of him, lifting her mouth. 'Would you like to warm me up, Mr Wakefield?' Softly she laid a hand on his chest, sliding it under the edge of his waistcoat.

His jaw clenched. His hand moved. Without warning he had a hold of the back of her hair and he wrenched her head back, making her gasp at the blossom of pain. 'Don't,' he snarled, his other hand hard on her waist, his fingers digging in despite the boning of the corset. 'I am a gentleman but I cannot be held responsible for my actions, girl, if you provoke me.'

Riding the flare of shock, Lilla felt the explosion of arousal burst, hot and wet, inside her. The rose fell from her fingers. 'That's right,' she breathed; 'that's Victorian values for you. We know all about the "gentlemen" and what they got up to: the brothels, the servants seduced and thrown out on the streets, the hundreds of "respectable" girls throwing themselves from river bridges because they'd been ruined. One in sixteen women in this city making their living by prostitution. Your Swinburne – he had a thing for being whipped, didn't he? Would you like to whip me, Mr Wakefield? Would you like to thrash my pretty white bottom?'

'Be quiet,' he hissed. 'You have no idea of the trouble you're getting yourself into, girl.'

'Oh, I know,' she countered, nearly giggling. 'I know exactly what you are.' Her lips shaped the terrible word that hung between them, though she gave it no sound: vampire. 'I know,' she whispered, 'you're just aching to bite into my cold skin and taste the hot blood beneath.'

For a moment his eyes, which had narrowed to burning slits, widened. Then he wrenched her around and pushed her backward, right off her feet, until she was slammed up against the great black barrel of the boiler, her back arched over its warm curve, and his hand was no longer in her hair but gripping her throat. Blood hammered in her head: she thought for a moment she would pass out.

'That Pre-Raphaelite exhibition at the National Gallery. That's where I've seen you. You were with Reynauld. You're one of his women.'

Lilla licked her lips and struggled for air: he let her breathe with some reluctance. 'I was one of his donors,' she admitted. 'Not any more.' She could feel his newly sprung erection grinding into her. And now she was horribly, helplessly aroused, wet in anticipation of his bite.

Robert grinned, showing fangs, which made her heart thump wildly. 'He threw you out.'

'Yes.' The anger was still there inside her, like a black stain through her lust.

'Why?'

'I upset him. I had the cheek to ask for too much. I wanted him to make me ... like him. Like you.'

He stopped grinning abruptly. 'You did what?'

She met his eyes. 'I want to be a vampire.'

'So you've come here – to me?' The dawning truth was visible in his face: the realisation of the way she'd inveigled her way into his house. Lilla decided that brutal honesty was the best tactic now.

'You're as much use to me as he is.'

He shook his head slightly. 'You could have drowned falling from that bridge, you do realise? What if I hadn't heard you? What if I'd taken no notice?'

'Then I'd be dead.' That prospect seemed unreal to her now that she wasn't hanging over a cold river any more. She twisted her mouth, nearly spitting the words. 'Better that than living like this. I've seen you people and I know what I want. I have as much right as any of –'

'Don't be stupid!' he snarled, but then his next sentence sounded more weary and disgusted than angry. 'You have no rights. Nobody has any *rights*.'

Lilla took a strangled breath. 'I want to live in the night. I want to drink blood. I want to be immortal.'

'Then no wonder he repudiated you. We don't make

more of our own. That's Reynauld's iron rule.'

'That's a lie!'

'What?'

'There are loads of you. Don't fob me off.'

'What do you mean?' he asked softly, but there was nothing soft about the carnivorous teeth hovering inches from her face. His breath was cold. 'There are six of us here. Neither more nor less in many years, by Reynauld's own interdiction.'

'Six Master Vampires, yes, but loads of bloodkinder. Everybody knows that. Haven't you read StakeGirl's blog?'

'I haven't the faintest idea what you're talking about. What in the name of all that is holy is a "blog"?'

That shocked her. For a moment he didn't look like a young man wearing antique clothes, but an old man trapped in a young man's body. 'It's an online diary,' she said weakly. 'On the Internet, you know?'

'Ah. Yes. The Internet – I've heard of that. Well, I don't own a computer. But I assure you ... Master Vampires? Bloodkinder?' He wrung the word out as if it were a filthy dishcloth.

'StakeGirl's a vampire killer.'

'What?'

'She goes around taking out lesser vampires: the bloodkinder. There are dozens of them. She writes it all up and puts it on her blog. She's famous.'

Robert Wakefield blinked, and he let go of her throat and leaned back a little. 'Truly, I swear I would laugh, if it were not so pitiful. There's no such thing as bloodkinder. The last human converted anywhere around here was sometime in the 1960s.'

'But ...' Lilla's mind raced, anxiety seeping in as the threat of violence receded. Robert's expression had slipped from anger to contempt, and she didn't like that. She knew that it would take a miracle for this to be anything but her last chance.

'It is a joke, this blog of yours. Or a work of fiction you've been naive enough to take for fact.'

Lilla stuck her bottom lip out in a pout. 'Make me into a vampire.'

'Have you heard a word I've said?' he growled. 'He's forbidden it.'

'So?' She couldn't keep the desperation out of her voice.

'So?' He was flabbergasted by her obstinacy – or perhaps by her ignorance. 'Have you any idea what he'd do to us?'

'Reynauld wouldn't hurt me. He doesn't hurt girls.'

'Very true. And fortunate for you. But I am not a girl.'

'Oh, I'd noticed that.' Lilla prided herself on her adaptability. Now she reached down and grasped the thick curve of his cock. If he'd had been a living human she'd have felt its heat through the cloth of his trousers, but he was cold as clay. It didn't stop his flesh heaving in response to her touch though, and when she spoke next she dropped her voice to a purr. 'I never met a girl with one of these ... Mr Wakefield. It's so big.'

His eyes darkening, he took her by the shoulders. 'You think you can manipulate me?'

'I think ... that you want to fuck me.' She tugged at the bow at the neck of her chemise, untied the ribbon in one long, sensual pull and without hurrying – there was no hurry, he was fixated on the sight – loosed the cloth to better reveal the luxuriant swell of her breasts and their swollen needy nipples, poking out over the lip of her corset. 'I think that you want to bite my beautiful big tits, Mr Wakefield.'

His eyes were wide now, but his mouth a hard tight line.

'Aren't they lovely?' she whispered. 'Aren't they all big and soft and juicy, just ready for you to stick your face in?'

With a convulsive movement he flung her away from him and she sprawled back on the bark-covered ground, breasts bouncing and the wind knocked from her lungs. Robert took a step forward, looming over her, his fists clenched as if in revulsion – but the bulge in his trousers betrayed him. Lilla raised herself to her elbows, but didn't try to sit up for the moment. This position suited her quite well: her legs had fallen apart and the crotch split in her capacious Victorian drawers was undoubtedly revealing her blonde snatch. And she had a very good view of Robert's erection, which looked like it threatened to split the worn fabric of his tented trousers.

'I don't feed from humans,' he hissed, trembling.

'That's what I heard. I just find it hard to believe.' Rolling on to her knees, she reached out across the bark, to the discarded rose he'd cut for her. 'Nasty sharp thorns these things have got,' she mused, laying the stem across her bare breasts. With a twitch she drew it down, scoring her flesh with half-a-dozen needle-pointed thorns, shuddering as the pain burned through her. Pinpoints of blood rose on her pale skin and swelled, a string of rubies decorating the white flesh and the roseate nipples. 'Ah,' she groaned.

Robert Wakefield seemed to grow taller; his hard-on bulged. She could taste the coppery tang of her victory.

'Tell me, have you ever whipped a girl with your roses, Mr Wakefield?' Lilla began to crawl backwards from him on hands and knees, arse swaying, breasts wobbling. 'Maybe one of your servants? The parlourmaid perhaps? You ever taken a bunch of roses and whipped their tits?' She put on a country accent for her next words, her voice suddenly breathlessly innocent but at the same time teasing: 'Oh, Mr Wakefield, you wouldn't be thinking of doing that to a poor innocent girl? I couldn't bear that, sir – it'll hurt something cruel. You wouldn't want to ruin a helpless maid, would you, sir? You wouldn't want that on your conscience?'

Inhumanly swift, he lunged and grabbed the front of her bodice and yanked her up to slam her against one of the wrought-iron pillars. Eagerly Lilla extended her hands over her head and crossed them at the wrists, thrusting her breasts out so that he might feed. But he didn't, not right away. He looked down at her with a face hollow with hunger, and then he took hold of her long drawers at the waist and snapped the drawstring with one tug of his wrists. He tore the damp, clinging cotton from her thighs to bare her sex, and then he tied her wrists with the twisted strips and secured her to an ornamental bracket high on the pillar, hauling her up on to her toes. She said nothing, breath and words robbed from her by anticipation, lips parted about her shallow breaths.

His face mask-like, his eyes burning, he plunged his cold fingers between her thighs and up inside her, breaching the gates of her sex to take the measure of her heat, the slick of juices, the yielding sucking flex of her tight hole. Lilla writhed on his hand, twisting helplessly with each thrust of his wrist, and he watched her breasts jiggle and bounce, their pink points dewed in red. His teeth were so extended now that his upper lip did not hide them.

'Oh, please,' she gasped.

'Shut up,' he snarled. 'You've said quite enough already.'

Then he walked away.

Lilla's exposed skin seemed to crawl under every tiny movement of the air. The bite-marks of the rose burned. She watched in terror as he cut himself half a dozen long-stemmed roses without even looking at her and methodically stripped off the leaves. The crimson buds seemed to blaze on the tips of the stems as he turned and swished them experimentally.

Oh, God, thought Lilla, her mouth dry and her pussy running wet. The dread and the desire for pain were part of her wiring as a vampire's donor: for the icy stab of the incision followed by the rush of the bite itself, the magical whatever-it-was in their saliva that made being fed upon even better for the victim than for the devourer. She craved being eaten almost as much as she wanted to eat, and far more viscerally. Her whole body was inflamed with arousal now at the sight of a few droplets of her blood, with the anticipation of hurt. Reynauld himself had never whipped her – the bastard had such a poker up his arse that he would never stoop to indulging such a kink – but she wasn't new to the pleasure of pain. She knew how well her body responded to a good spanking or to the bite of a crop, and roses were just a new variation on an old theme.

When Robert Wakefield came back he had eight stems bunched in his hand. He took his stance on her right and used his left hand to push her head back, gripping her jaw and part-covering her mouth. Then he brought the whip flat across her breasts with a loud and stinging slap. Lilla convulsed, feeling the pain stab her with scores of tiny teeth. He struck again and again – not hard, but then he didn't need to because the thorns did all the work for him, biting and tugging at her skin. She began to shriek, because she needed to and because she knew he wanted to hear it too, her screams breaking the seal of his cold fingers. Her whole body writhed and jerked, utterly helpless but cold no longer, burning now and wet with perspiration.

After a dozen blows he stopped, breathing hard. He kept her head forced back so that she couldn't see what sort of mess he'd made of her, but she could feel something damp trickling down between her tits and she didn't know if it was sweat or blood. Stopping, he licked her breasts, his tongue cold and smooth and leaving a wake of prickling pleasure as he lapped and sucked. Even his tongue, for God's sake, she thought, as he stirred her nipples and their buds burst into what felt like multi-petalled blooms of ecstasy, making her groan.

'Bite me,' she begged. 'Please. Bite me.'

He lifted his head to glare into her face, his mouth and chin smeared. But it was punishment she read in those pale eyes. He lifted his flail again and struck at her – this time harder, and across the tops of her thighs and her sex. Rosebuds broke, the petals falling. Lilla screamed. Each blow felt like sparks of fire landing on her skin; each sent a jolt through her sex straight to the nub of her swollen clit, stoking its own heat. Pain made pleasure. As the whipping continued, her legs, which had kicked out in protest and tried to escape the first blows, grew stiffer and began to tilt her pelvis forward, that whole area of her body transforming into a zone of arousal. Even those slashes which scored her legs and lower belly seemed to add to the accumulating wave of need. Her squeals of shock became staccato cries urging him on, and as the measured slaps he dealt her became crueller and swifter she broke down suddenly into heaving thrashing orgasm, drinking the pain that was no pain, nearly pulling her arms from their sockets. Robert Wakefield paused, watching her intently as she spiralled down from her orgasm.

She curled a lip. 'Bite me. Bite me, you fucker.'

'You need to learn some manners,' he snarled. Reaching up over her head he tore her bonds apart and then pulled her forward, right off her feet, throwing her down on hands and knees in the soft bark at his feet. She stared dumbly at the shredded cuffs around her wrists that were the remnants of her knickers, lying between his cracked leather boots. He grabbed the corset at the small of her back and hoicked her arse up, then he stood deliberately on her wrists, one foot on each. Lilla bit her lip and burrowed her wrists into the soft path to ease the pressure: she was pinned to the ground now. He didn't want her escaping. He was going to hurt her some more.

And oh, he did. He laid into her upraised bum with the bunch of roses, sparing her not at all this time, painting her buttocks green and crimson as he thrashed her, striping the backs of her thighs. The stems couldn't take it for long, cracking and snapping off and turning to shredded string in his grip, the last remaining flowers pulped while all the time Lilla squealed, exhilaration mixed with her anguish, her backside dancing from side to side in panic. When the last stem fell apart he threw the ruined stubs aside and paused. She gasped into the loose bark, her mouth coated with dust. There was a moment's respite as he fumbled at his trousers, a movement she was only dimly aware of, and then he stepped round behind her and bore down on her stinging, burning rear, shoving his cock deep into her hole. She was wet with readiness, her soil well prepared for the root he was planting in her. He took her with four or five ruthless thrusts and she felt her core gather and clench.

'There now!' he gasped – though whether to her or himself she couldn't tell – and thrust to the hilt as he bit her shoulder just by the nape of her neck. The pain was like lightning, the pleasure that followed as deafening as a clap of thunder. Lilla began to come as the jolt coursed down her spine; she was peripherally aware that he was coming too, a cold flood, shuddering into her as he gnawed.

The rolls of thunder rumbled through every part of her body, wave after wave, as he fed on, his hunger fierce. By the time he was slaked enough to lift his face, her shoulder felt numb and the tears of release that had escaped her had dried to stickiness on her cheeks.

'Make me a vampire,' she moaned, 'and we can do this for ever.'

He sat up, pulling out from her sex but slipping his fingers back in where his cock had been. She heard him swallow and clear his throat. 'This is what you think it means to be a vampire?' he asked, his voice still thick with lust and rage. 'This is your hope of eternity?'

'Fuck yes.'

Lifting her by her pussy for a moment, he licked at the torn skin of her buttocks. His fingers withdrew on a slick of her juices and his own seed and he scooped the slippery mess further up the crack of her arse. Two fingers, closely pressed, found the aperture of her anus and, twisting, pushed into it. He didn't ask permission or persuade her flesh gently: he just opened her up. Lilla moaned in her throat, forcing herself to ignore the instinctive spasm of panic at his invasion and to relax. She was glad for the soft ground under her knees as she spread her thighs wider, the pursed mouth of her arse unfurling like the petals of a rose as she bore down.

There was a tiny grunt of satisfaction from behind her. His cock slithered in the trough of her pussy, rooting greedily. Fingers slid out again. Then – there – that was the head of his cock: hard and cool and polished as wood, as the handle of a trowel, pressing in on the ring of muscle that had tried so quickly to tighten again. It shouldered its way in, implacable, overcoming all resistance, until the glans was resting just within her.

Sweat gathered in the hollow of her back.

'I used to be a painter, you know,' he whispered. Adjusting his knees and hands, he sought a better angle. 'Understand: I was good. Driven, talented, inspired. The Royal Academy accepted me at twenty. My classical scenes hung in the best galleries, the most discerning households. I was sought after.' With a shift of his weight he bore in on her, his cock sliding past the portal of her arsehole and into the hot depths beyond, filling her up. God, but he felt so much thicker in her butt than in her pussy – and cold as stone. She imagined his unseen cock the colour of marble. She was sensitive to every tiny movement in there. Her sweating hands clawed at the bark and her pulse hammered in her ears.

'Then I became ... what I am now.' He started to thrust, not hard just yet, each stroke ruminative and punctuated by the rhythm of his words. 'And I lost my talent. Oh, I can still paint. Technically ... I have improved. But it's worthless. No vision. No muse. These days, all I do ... is tend my roses. And fuck trollops ... up the arse.'

His thrusts were threatening now. Lilla closed her eyes tight. She loved being shafted in the butt, but it was no less of an ordeal than being whipped. That was what she liked about it.

'Look around you, Lillabet. How many great buildings were designed by vampires? How many symphonies have they created? How many poems? How many paintings ... or new schools of art? Shall I tell you? None. All those years ... and nothing to show. Nothing new. Inspiration comes only ... to those who live brief lives.'

'I was never going to write a great symphony,' she groaned. 'I just want to live for ever.'

'We're parasites. A dead end.'

'You're perfect.'

'Fool.' He added a savage thrust.

'Bite me!' She pawed at her face in frustration. 'Make me into one of you!'

'You stupid girl!' he snarled, riding her hard now, nipping at the back of her neck and between her shoulder blades. Safe places, as she knew: despite his aggression he was still a gentleman. The first precursor of a new orgasm humped and flexed in Lilla's pelvis and she let rip with a gabbled string of words.

'You have to! You have to! Turn me, you fucking bastard!'

He began to roar wordlessly, his pounding brutal. She started to claw at her own throat, gouging at the skin with her nails. 'Bite my throat, you cunt!' she screamed. 'You fucking coward! It's what you want! It's what you really want!'

He grabbed her hair and wrenched her neck over. There was blood under her nails now, though she barely felt the hurt. 'Yes!' she cried as he fell on her, grabbing for her throat, his teeth slicing into the flesh, fire and light and everything her body craved exploding through her.

And a hot gush over her fingers.

'Save me!' she choked, triumphant, blossoms of blue and black flame clustering at the corners of her vision. 'You have to save me!' He clamped down hard over the wound and she felt the indescribable bliss of his kiss as the fireworks exploded and fell, smothering the world in darkness.

* * *

He crawled away afterwards, retching, his stomach a boiling cauldron. Fifteen years he'd managed – fifteen years without giving way to the shame of his base urges. Fifteen years of animal blood and black-market plasma and soy products. All alone. Fifteen years of self-respect, bitterly won. And now this. Now this.

He hadn't meant to. He hadn't. It had been a mistake. If she hadn't torn at her own throat like that …

There'd been far too much blood for him to drink once he'd sliced her jugular, no matter how eagerly he'd gulped it down. Too much damage for the wound to seal itself too. Most of the hot liquor had gone to waste and was soaking away, invisible, into the red-brown bark chippings.

Wakefield wiped at his face, utterly ineffectively. His hands were crooked into claws and trembled wildly, and his head buzzed. Dizzy and with limbs aching, he twitched with the desire for escape. As the hothouse spun around him he pitched over sideways into the dirt, but he didn't want to lie there and rest; far from it. He felt like running. Like bursting out of the stone confines of the building and running through the wet streets and never coming back.

I'm just not accustomed to it, he told himself, huddling up in a crouch, clasping his arms about his knees. He rocked himself back and forth, trying to soothe the demon within. I've fallen off the wagon and now it's rolling right over me. That stupid stupid *selfish* girl …

Turning his head, he looked over at Lillabet's still body.

She'd been convinced he would save her a second time. She'd been wrong. Once on the bridge, yes, but not here. Not this way.

He'd felt her die. He'd done nothing.

Shaking, he forced himself to his feet. He'd have to burn these clothes, he thought. He'd have to …

What do I tell Reynauld? Oh, God in Heaven: what do I do?

There was a rosebush with arm's reach and he ran his open palm up a long stem, the thorns raking through his skin but the pain hardly registering. His fist closed over the full flower at the tip, robbing the head of its crimson petals. Four stumbling steps took him to Lillabet's corpse, to look down on her slack and ashen face. For a moment his mouth twisted.

'I am weary of days and hours,' he quoted, so soft a plaint that she might not have heard even if she had been alive; 'Blown buds of barren flowers / Desires and dreams and powers / And everything but sleep.'

Opening his hand, he scattered rose petals as darkly red as a vampire's tears, drifting down gently to lie upon her face.

(Wakefield)

And this is Wakefield, who doesn't feed from humans. Who hides himself away, reluctant to face the turn of the years or his own predatory condition: aching, ashamed and tormented. And hungry. Always hungry. He doesn't even have more than fleeting contact with the staff of his company, for fear of the temptation they proffer. Of necessity, therefore, he is celibate and has to tend to his own sexual needs. His restraint is legendary among vampires, a topic discussed with awe and incomprehension and derision.

You are safe from Wakefield. Unless you enter his lair of your own will. Unless you provoke him. Then, beware his appetites, so cruelly suppressed.

The most sedentary of the City's vampires, he remembers this land before it was built over, when as a youth he would come down with his father to hunt duck, with long-barrelled fowling-pieces over their shoulders and spaniels casting about at their feet. He was always keen on the wide green marshland, and the great wedge of the asylum meant no more to him at that time than a landmark to guide their feet back to the dry track at the end of the day. They are among his fondest memories, those days with his father: the yelp of the dogs, the grey light over the open water, the wet soaking into his tweed coat as he crawled on his belly through the sedges, the comradely walk home with the feathered bodies slung in braces. James Wakefield, owner of a string of drapery and haberdashery emporia, was proud of his son: the first of the line to be born into respectable estate, the first to speak like a gentleman and attend a good school where he learned Latin and was beaten with commendable regularity.

He remembers his father's distress and fury the day he announced he was going to be an artist, that he was submitting paintings to the Royal Academy.

He remembers that autumn in 1857 when, just before dawn and in the middle of a thick fog that tasted of coal dust and made his throat ache, he was crossing a park in the centre of the City and first saw her sitting on a bench, all alone, shawled in white with her long red hair coiled about her shoulders like a cat. Red hair fit to catch the attention of Rossetti himself. He'd stopped at a nearby bench and taken out his sketchbook, pencilling the lines of her delicate, pensive face. She hadn't moved, just sat there in the wreathing yellow mist like a statue. When he'd finished he'd walked away, but as he reached the wrought-iron gates of the park he'd found her somehow there before him, waiting.

'Show me,' she'd murmured, her eyes huge and commanding despite her delicate stature. Then: 'Is this what I look like?'

It was a very fair likeness, he'd told her, flushing.

'Then you'll paint me. Tonight.'

That was not how it was supposed to happen. He didn't

paint after sunset because the light was no good, and he chose his own models – working girls usually, unless he was on commission for a society portrait. His models sometimes made him uncomfortable with their coarse humour and their brash laughter, and he tried to be stern with them and deliberately scorned their sly offers to see to his other needs at the end of a long afternoon's sitting – for a consideration, of course. He laboured under too much dignity to stoop to that, imagining in horror how they might gossip and laugh about him between themselves if he did succumb. But there'd been something about this woman that was almost bewitching, and he'd ended up telling her his studio address and had waited there for her that evening, watching the street. She'd called herself Roisin*; a suitably Celtic name for such a fey and ethereal women, he'd thought. He'd assumed she was a demimondaine, having been seen out with neither escort nor bonnet nor gloves, but she didn't sound or behave like any of the mistresses he'd met. An actress who'd lingered too long in the role of Ophelia, perhaps, he'd mused: many actresses were half-crazy on laudanum and gin. But he already had an idea for using her as a model for the fair maid Elaine, burning up with unrequited ardour for Lancelot.*

She'd tapped at his door without ever appearing on the street below and when he'd admitted her to his studio she'd drifted around it like a ghost. Her clothes were decades out of date, he'd noticed, but the final detail had escaped him until she'd paused in front of an ornate mirror that he'd used as a prop for his version of The Lady of Shalott*. 'I cannot tell what I look like any more,' she'd whispered. 'So you must paint me a portrait.'*

That was when he'd realised that she cast no reflection at all. It had been a long time before his hands had steadied enough for him to pick up the charcoal and begin to sketch.

She'd sat for him for hours that first evening while he roughed out sketches from different angles and decided on the composition that suited best. Not once did she stir, except to blink. Once he'd got the basic outline down on canvas he'd shown her and she'd seemed pleased. As he'd shrunk back into the sofa she'd straddled his lap and kissed him, peeling his clothes open delicately to eat her way down his slim body, all the way to that part of him that stood stiff with fear. She'd been like milk in her pallor, he'd thought, except for that red hair: milk and blood that washed his senses clean away.

For weeks he'd drawn and painted nothing but her: not as Elaine but as Calypso, as La Belle Dame Sans Merci, as Melusine and Medusa. At the same time he'd worked on her portrait, applying every tiny brushstroke as precisely as possible, trying to capture the luminous pallor of her skin, the multitudinous strands of russet and chestnut and copper in her hair, the depths of her dark-blue eyes. In turn Roisin had been obsessed by him, returning to feed every night. He'd grown weak and pale and daily more afraid that she wouldn't leave him time to complete any of the works that burned in his fingertips. One night he had thrust her roughly away as she tried to mouth yet again at a prick that was raw with overuse, shouting that he needed to work, that she had to leave him alone.

She'd killed him and returned him to unlife. Partly out of fury, partly out of desire to give him what he asked for: time. Partly, perhaps, because she feared she would lose him otherwise. And then, while he was still a neonate only weeks into his new existence, she had forgotten him.

He remembers trying to reclaim his life, to pretend that

nothing had changed – and the time his model Clara broke a lamp and cut her hand, and he'd come within a hair's-breadth of rape and murder before he even realised what he was doing. He'd fled, out here, to the asylum. It had been easy to purchase a lease upon a suite of the best rooms whose barred windows looked out upon the wild green sea of the rushes, whose heavy door could be bolted from the outside and never opened. He'd refused to see his father after the first visit and the only things that crossed his threshold went on a tray pushed through the flap in the door. Thirst – an unending burning thirst for warm blood – had pushed him to raving.

He remembers the evening he had a visitor, unannounced. The bolts had grated back to admit a tall man, very well-dressed, with a foreign look to his complexion but perfectly well-spoken. He'd explained his name was Reynauld, that he knew all about Wakefield's condition, and that he was here to help. Wakefield, crouched in a corner as he had been most of the day, banging his forehead dully off the plaster for the faint sense of relief it gave him, had been too stunned to realise what was strange about his visitor.

'Gwendolyn, my dear – would you join us?' he'd said.

The cell door had opened for the second time and a young woman had walked in, bringing Wakefield scrabbling to his feet. He'd dimly judged her a servant of some sort because although her skirts were full she didn't wear a proper crinoline. Her dress was neat and respectable though, her gloves clean, and her large brown eyes had moved to Reynauld with simple, direct trust. When she'd divested herself of her grey bonnet she'd revealed dark hair neatly parted down the centre and drawn back into a bun. But it was only when the scent of her body – that warm, delicious scent part new-baked bread, part sex, part saffron – reached Wakefield and made his mouth run with water, that he'd realised that he hadn't been able to smell Reynauld at all. And though he could faintly hear her heartbeat, it was the only one audible in the room.

'You can't bring her in here,' he'd rasped, choking on fear and hunger and arousal. 'Please. My blood-mania …'

'Lesson One,' Reynauld had answered, unperturbed, signing the girl to sit in an armchair: 'You don't have to harm anyone.'

She'd looked Wakefield full in the face with a faint, complacent smile and slipped the buttons of her fitted woollen jacket. The tiny pearl buttons of the white blouse beneath had followed suit. Under that she was uncorseted and wore no shift: her stunningly big, firm breasts had emerged through the trimming of white lace to reveal for his inspection brown nipples with areolae the size of teacups. For a moment Wakefield had thought that he might actually black out. He'd been faintly aware that he was half-crouched, his erection straining painfully against the fabric of his trousers, his teeth bared in a rictus snarl. If he'd been himself he would have felt utterly ashamed, but as it was the only thing stopping him hurling himself on the girl was the tall cool presence at her side, one hand on her shoulder. There'd been an indefinable something about Reynauld that chilled the hottest appetite.

'Please, do come and feed. Not the throat – never the throat or the insides of the thighs where the arteries are, never on a joint or over a bone. Your bites are self-sealing unless you strike a major blood-vessel. Choose soft tissue. Her breasts will do very well: she will enjoy it greatly. And she does have magnificent breasts, don't you agree?'

They were breathtaking.

Dazed, nearly drooling, Wakefield had stumbled forward to kneel before her and sink his teeth into one of those irresistible orbs. As the blood flooded his mouth he'd lost all sense of himself and his surroundings, his head full of a black rushing wind, his body – even the red-hot column of his cock – lost somewhere far away. He wasn't aware of anything but the delirious pleasure of the warm liquid in his throat.

It is after all the most primal of instincts: to suck.

Then, slowly, as his overwhelming thirst abated, he'd become aware of his surroundings once more. Aware that the girl was shifting beneath him, moaning sweetly, her hips undulating. Distracted, he'd lifted his head, but as she'd cupped and hefted her bosom he switched immediately to the other breast she offered him so eagerly.

'See,' Reynauld had murmured. 'She's more than willing to suckle you.' Pulling up the girl's many layers of petticoats and skirts, he'd revealed for Wakefield her plump stocking-clad leg, then her glossy pubic bush. She'd been wearing no drawers. 'Stroke her quim.'

He'd obeyed, dizzy with shock, easing his fingers into that pelt to find whorled skin and heat and moisture – slippery as marsh-mud, slippery as oil paint – delving into that complex mysterious furrow until she tensed and heaved beneath him, crying out shamelessly in what was obvious even to him as her orgasmic crisis. And he'd tasted it too, in the blood he was sucking from her swollen teat: that first rush of a sharp flavour he was unable to compare to anything else until years later when he first smelled lime zest. The taste of her climax.

As she fell back, gasping and heavy-lidded, he released her breast to look down at her open sex. For the moment his need for blood was slaked and now another appetite demanded satisfaction. 'May I?' he'd asked hoarsely, squeezing the ridge of his trapped erection.

'I think she'd be most disappointed if you didn't,' Reynauld had answered.

So he'd freed his prick and pulled Gwendolyn's unresisting body to the edge of the chair and draped her legs up over his shoulders in order to bring his ram to bear on the portals of her citadel. It was almost the first time he'd ploughed a living woman, and after Roisin she'd felt feverishly hot and padded like a cushion, her wet grip wringing his seed from his bulging scrotum in racking spasms of release. She'd climaxed for a second time too, under his assault, and he'd tasted it as he bit her.

'Remember this,' Reynauld had said as Wakefield slumped to his knees on the rug. 'We must bring them pleasure, not terror. We take what we need, but we ourselves are a gift to the living. Immortal guardians who confer our own blessing, in a balance of mutual joy.'

But Wakefield, despite the erection that thrust up unquelled from his loins, had at that moment been feeling nauseous: the same queasiness he'd felt so often after a model left him alone in the studio and he'd finished masturbating ferociously, spurting all over the costumes they'd worn for the sitting until his balls were empty and his head ringing. It was, he imagined, a spiritual nausea. He didn't believe the wonderful vision of the promised land that Reynauld described.

'Who are you, to try to tell me?' he'd groaned. 'I'd like very much to believe you, but I fear I do not, sir. This thing that I am – whatever that is – it is no blessing, but an offence against God Himself and against Nature.'

'Which leads us,' Reynauld had said with a certain relish,

unbuttoning his own trousers and easing out into view an engorged member of intimidating proportions, 'to Lesson Two.'

* * *

There are habits of mind too deeply ingrained to conquer. In the months that followed, Wakefield had established himself as a divinity among the inmates of the asylum, accepting that much of Reynauld's dictum. He had no desire to leave and took from them only what he required, without causing particular harm. That was when he'd started growing roses in the exercise yard, and under his hand the first unlooked-for bloom of the new variety had emerged. But he never embraced his new state. As the years passed and he grew no older his family ceased to visit. He bore the loss as one he deserved. Even when the asylum closed he did not leave. He remains, venturing out only on special occasions, still trying the best he can to remain an upright gentleman.

See now, and pity him if you like: Wakefield is a fly caught in amber, a man trapped beyond his time; a rose pressed between the pages of an old book, still bearing in its withered petals the remnants of its old colour and a fugitive hint of perfume.

4: Seven for the Seven Stars in the Sky

Jacqueline was marching to war. She counted off her weapons in her mirror while the hired limousine crept through the city streets. Jimmy Choo shoes, silver, five-inch heels: check. Versace evening dress, silver, low-cut and backless but tasteful: check. Diamond necklace that Leon had bought her on their third anniversary, the one that hung above her pushed-up breasts like a cascade of waterdrops about to run down a golden ravine: check. Perfect make-up, pillar-box-red lips and smouldering dark eye shadow: check. Louis Vuitton purse: check.

Divorce papers in the purse: check.

Jacqueline had had enough. Enough of being a trophy wife. Enough of a husband who stayed away from home for a week or more at a time, not telling her where he was. Enough of the jewellery and the goddamn roses he always brought her on his return, as if that made up for anything. Enough of Leon's turned back, rumbling gently as he snored and she stared at the ceiling. Enough of their great big bed where only the miniature schnauzers tussled. Eight years of marriage, she reminded herself, and in the last six months they'd had sex only once.

Leon might look the part – oh, he certainly did, in fact: he was a former rugby international and he'd not let himself go downhill since retirement. A big bluff guy with a broken nose and a head of bristly hair, he still looked more like a jobbing builder than a successful businessman with his own chain of sportswear stores and a column in the Sunday papers, not to mention a lucrative sideline in rental property management. But his sexual interest in her had died off in the last couple of years. Jacqueline might have tolerated a readjustment of their relationship – one couldn't expect the libido of someone in his forties to match that of a younger man, and besides she suspected he might be taking steroids – if there had been something to fill the gap: children, or a passionate hobby in common, or a close social circle. But there was nothing of the sort, and she'd been left to grow bored and frustrated and resentful.

Hadn't Mummy and Daddy warned her that she'd have nothing in common with this man, when she announced her engagement to him? That he was too old, and not the *right sort*? Well, she'd taken no notice of them then, at eighteen. But she knew they'd nod sagely now and murmur, 'Well, darling, you can't say we didn't foresee this.' Knowing that only made the sting of failure worse.

It hadn't always been like this, of course. In the beginning their love-life had been hectic, and even after years of marriage, when they'd carved out their own comfortable but separate social ruts, he'd still been enthusiastic between the sheets. She remembered so much of their time together fondly. The occasion she'd given him a hand-job under his coat at the theatre during a Royal Premiere Performance, his cock a hot sticky bar of opportunism, and he'd had to fake a coughing fit to cover up the groan of his orgasm. The night he'd smuggled her on to the international pitch before the world rugby cup final and fucked her up against the post of the upright, her skirt up around her hips, his trousers round his ankles; they'd left her knickers there for the groundsmen to find in the morning, she recalled. Leon had always had a bit of an exhibitionist thing going, and she'd never minded that. On their last holiday together on their yacht they'd anchored in the Mediterranean just in sight of Mykonos, and under that perfect sky he'd stripped off her bikini and stood her with her hands on the brass rail of the stern and fucked her from behind with consummate appreciation. No one else was there: just the sky and the darkly rocking waves and the sun glinting off the brass and the varnished woodwork, just the smell of salt and sun-cream mingling with the sea tang of her pussy, and the lap of the waves echoing the slap of his thighs and balls on her out-thrust rear.

She'd had no notion then that anything was about to go wrong between them. Was this how it was bound to end? she wondered. Had it been inevitable that he'd tire of her, of the posh blonde bird who'd seemed such a novelty all those years ago? All she knew was that in the last year or so something had changed.

She watched the neon-lit streets crawl past. She wanted out of this humiliating marriage before it was too late: before she lost her own looks, before the tabloid newspapers came falling through the letter-box with the pictures of Leon caught in a Nazi-themed spanking session or some similar degrading honey-trap, and she had to face the paparazzi with the shreds of her dignity wrapped about her and play the hurt-but-unbowed wife to the cheating slimeball.

Because Jacqueline was pretty certain that Leon was up to something.

Convinced at first that he had a mistress – because what else would explain the lost days and the plunge in his sexual appetite at home? – she'd hired a private detective to follow him, but it had turned out to be nothing so simple. When he was away from home, she'd found out, Leon was staying in an apartment he owned in the city centre. His regular haunts consisted of a kick-boxing club and a tae kwon do school, plus a very exclusive private club called the Pleiades which the detective could discover next to nothing about. He'd visit the club, then usually spend a few days at his apartment, staying in and not receiving visitors.

So he'd taken up kick-boxing: a little ambitious at his age, she thought, but not out of character. He was a very physical man. It explained the bruises and the cuts she often saw on him – although since he'd taken to wearing pyjamas she was less familiar now with the state of his body. The club worried her more. All research into its function and clientele seemed to hit a brick wall. As a private club it had of course complete control over whom it allowed as members, and it didn't advertise on the Internet. From his surveillance the detective had only been able to report that the customers were all top end, and always wore evening dress. Hollywood chic was *de rigueur*. But she assumed lap-dancing, at the very least ... and probably something much less palatable. With pole-dancing bars open at lunchtime in the respectable heart of the City, would Leon really go to such lengths for anything that mundane?

Perhaps he had a girlfriend who worked at the club, she thought, twisting the knife in her own guts. Perhaps she was a Thai contortionist who did unbelievable things with ping-pong balls and champagne bottles, or some Polish slut who let men stuff money up her cooz as she lap-danced them to orgasm.

Well, whatever it was, she was determined to know for herself. She would know the truth at last, and to hell with all his evasion. She was going to catch him red-handed in this club of his, and she was going to give him his papers there in front of everyone, and then her lawyer was going to take him to the cleaners.

She'd packed a can of mace into her purse as well, packaged as a body-spray. She wasn't completely reckless.

'We're here, madam,' said the driver, pulling up into a reserved parking bay. Jacqueline lifted her eyes to the narrow black glass door in an anonymous brick wall, and to the small sign over it that read 'Pleiades' and from which shone a cluster of seven blue LEDs.

'Wait until I've gone in and then just circle the block. I shouldn't be more than half an hour. If I'm more than an hour phone my secretary and tell her. Here's the number.' Jacqueline passed over a marked banknote: a fifty. Why be frugal with her husband's money, after all?

Her dress shimmered as she slipped out on to the pavement, its silver catching the blue light from above: it was split to mid-thigh up the left side because she'd always been proud of her legs. She noted a security camera over the door and a discreet buzzer next to it. When she pushed the button the door opened electronically, without a sound, to reveal a man in a polo shirt and grey jacket blocking the way into the dark space beyond. His hands folded before him and the breadth of his shoulders spoke the unmistakable body language of the bouncer.

'Can I help?' he said.

Without a word Jacqueline drew from her purse a white electronic pass card embossed with the Pleiades logo. It was quite genuine: she knew that because she'd stolen it from

Leon's wallet, and had a replica made to take its place. To her dismay the door guard slipped the card into a handheld card reader: she had hoped to get past the first layer of security before having to bluff. His eyebrows rose slightly.

'You're Mr Herrin?'

'I'm Mrs Herrin,' she said, drawing herself up confidently. Attitude was everything.

'That she is,' said a man's voice, and a second bouncer emerged from the dimly-lit porch. 'I did some work for them once.'

Jacqueline took in the new man's face, thanking her stars she had a good memory for people. She did recognise him: while Leon was playing in South Africa and she'd gone to accompany her husband they'd taken a group of bodyguards and this was one of them. He'd even been on safari with her. 'John, isn't it?' she asked pleasantly. 'What a nice surprise. How's it going with you?'

'Not so bad, Mrs Herrin. You here for the big night then?'

The big night? She had no idea what he meant. 'Leon wanted me to be here,' she improvised with a crook of her own eyebrow that might have been read as anticipatory or condescendingly amused, whichever they were expecting to see.

The bouncers exchanged glances.

'Go on then,' John told the other man. 'She's kosher.'

He handed back the pass card and gestured her in. 'You're just in time, I would think.'

'Down the stairs,' called John.

She was glad to have some directions because the corridors inside were very dark, lit only by floor-level emergency lights, and her eyes didn't get used to the gloom fast enough to allow her to pick out the signs on the doors. The stair banister was rough iron, cold under her hand, and from below her feet a hubbub of voices and music echoed faintly up the stairwell. Setting her jaw, she descended step by step – until she turned on a landing and a dark shape loomed up suddenly next to her. Jacqueline nearly jumped out of her skin.

'Shall I take your coat, madam?'

The girl was pale-faced and unsmiling, her breasts tightly constricted in a leather corset and her legs hobbled by a long rubber skirt with buckles and straps pinning her legs closed even at the ankles.

An SM club, Jacqueline was beginning to suspect. Oh, Leon, she thought, what have you been up to? But she shed her cashmere wrap gratefully. It was surprisingly warm down here.

'This way, please.'

The leaking music would have told her that anyway. She pushed through the double doors and found herself in the belly of the Pleiades.

It was still dark in here, but after the stairs it seemed a haven of light. A relatively big room, she thought, filled with low tables and solid leather armchairs – and, against the far wall, a stage which was in fact the only spot brightly lit. On that stage two girls were dancing. So far, so as anticipated. Jacqueline moved to the side of the entrance and looked around her, partly to orient herself, partly in search of Leon. There was a bar, of course. There was a mezzanine floor to one side of the stage, walled off with silvered glass. There was an overhead walkway around the wall of the room and some winching machinery clustered up near the roof which was either industrial or theatrical, she was not sure which: steel cable stretched at several points from ceiling to floor around the stage. Most of the chairs were occupied, and as

Jacqueline made her way slowly barward she realised that although there were some women with the lean moneyed look, and a fair scattering of what Leon called Rolex Girls – 'they cost a fucking fortune, but look great on your arm' – most of the occupants were men. Feeling her antipathy harden she paused to take a better look at the dancers.

How tacky, she said to herself.

It was a sex-show, of course: she'd have been taken aback if it wasn't, to be honest. The only surprise was how restrained it was, and that they were actually making any show of dancing. The taller girl was wearing thigh-boots and a one-piece body of scarlet PVC, and carried a whip of fine red rubber strands. All exactly the same colour, Jacqueline was slightly irritated to recognise, as her own high-gloss lipstick. From between the domme's thighs in an elegant and exaggerated curve rose a strap-on dildo of the same colour and texture, and with this she was menacing the second girl, who wore what looked like a minidress of black fishnet and whose big breasts were displayed by every bounce and twist. Their dance seemed to consist of the girl in red grabbing the other, pressing up against her with lascivious intent, forcing her to bend and accept the red phallus in her mouth, pawing at her breasts and bottom and using the horse-tail whip on both at every opportunity. The blonde victim would suffer these attentions for a while and then fight free, only to be recaptured and subjected to more and worse. The cock might be fake but the penetration was real, her pink slash invaded again and again.

How disgusting, thought Jacqueline, but she carried on watching, unable to avert her gaze. There was something mesmerising about the melodrama: it was all so very bright and pretty and offensive to every better instinct. Jacqueline felt a flush of outraged taste start at her cheeks and seep all the way down to her sex.

'Excuse me, madam. Would you like to place a bet?'

She turned with a start to the waitress who'd materialised at her elbow, another of the young women in fetish getup, like the cloakroom girl. 'Sorry?'

'Would you like to place a bet?' She was carrying an electronic notebook and wearing a money-belt that seemed to be stuffed with bills.

'What are the odds?' Jacqueline improvised.

'The house is giving 2:1 on Herrin.'

She smiled faintly, her mind racing. 'No thank you, not this time.'

At that moment the music faded out and the on-stage entertainment came to an end behind her. There was some applause from the audience and, as the two dancers stood up and sashayed off into the wings, some wolf-whistles, but the enthusiasm wasn't wild.

It's not what they came here for, Jacqueline told herself. There's something more.

'Ladies. Gentlemen.' The voice on the loudspeaker was masculine, but hushed and reverent. 'You've seen both of these men in action earlier tonight. You know what they are capable of. You know only too well the blood, the sweat and the pain that's brought them to this point. Some of you think this should have been your night, your opportunity for glory – but everyone had their chance. In this place there are no excuses. These two men are the best of the best: the strongest, the toughest, the hardest. Men of iron. Which one of them will reach out tonight for the ultimate prize? Which one of them will dare? Ladies and gentlemen – I give you tonight's grand final: Able versus Herrin!'

The machinery overhead began to turn. The cables started to flow. From the floor on three sides of the stage a veil was raised into the air: a veil of steel. It was chain-link fence, and it turned the stage into a cage. Everyone in the audience got to their feet. Some stood on their chairs and tables, but most pushed forward into the centre of the room to cluster about the metal netting.

Oh, hell, thought Jacqueline, frozen to the spot. It's not a sex club; it's a fight club.

She glimpsed two men walking on to the stage from the rear, but that was her last chance as the audience – men all taller than her, and probably about a hundred of them all told – thickened between her and the stage. They were shouting and cheering now, as excited as football fans before a match. She was walled off. For a moment she didn't know whether to retreat and try to climb the furniture or just sit down in shock. Instead she approached the back of the nearest man and tugged at his sleeve.

'Excuse me, please!'

The man turned and she caught a glimpse of a face so swollen over one eye that he must have been nearly blind on that side: dried blood was still caked on one ear. She'd been meaning to explain that it was her husband up there on stage, but she lost all words. Then it turned out that they weren't necessary: he stood to one side and nudged the man in front of him.

One by one, without any demurral or any explanation, the men made way and let her up to the front. Glimpses of their faces revealed that many were bruised and cut themselves. Jacqueline slipped her fingers through the wire mesh and stared.

There were two men up there: a stranger and Leon. The

stranger looked younger and leaner, but they both looked messed up. Leon was wearing the remnant of his evening apparel: dark trousers, a white shirt that was torn and blood-stained, his bow tie hanging loose around his neck. He'd been punched in the nose recently, judging from its shiny swollen look and the blood smeared down his upper lip and chin. Sweat gleamed on his close-cropped scalp; his eyes were fixed on the other man, who was dressed similarly and like him barefoot, but grinned and nodded at the crowd. Leon's hands and wrists were strapped up with white tape; so were his opponent's. No gloves. No head protection. Not even a gum shield.

'You stupid man!' Jacqueline wanted to call out. 'What the hell do you think you're playing at, you stupid stupid man!' But the words didn't have the strength to emerge and battle the roar of masculine approval dinning in her ears. Not just masculine, she realised belatedly: there were quite a few women visible too, pressed up against the mesh like she was and screaming along with the rest of the crowd. It was clearly the privilege of her gender to be at the front. She noted dizzily that despite the affluence of the crowd none of the men looked paunchy or elderly: they all looked like they could take care of themselves to some degree.

The fourth wall was raised now that the combatants were inside, and rubber-clad female staff moved to efficiently secure all the corners. The taut wire made a barrier that solid bodies couldn't escape.

A whistle blew. The fight started.

Both men came in circling, and it was clear they were both trained martial artists. For the first few moments it looked almost like a regular boxing match, as they held up their hands in a guard position and jabbed the air between them.

Then Able aimed a kick at Leon's hip and Leon dodged by perhaps half an inch. He feinted right himself and then lashed out with the other hand in a sneaky jab that connected with his opponent's ribs, staggering him, before following through with another strike.

Ridiculous, thought Jacqueline as she watched them trade kicks and punches: just ridiculous – though she had to admit there was something weirdly hot about Leon stripped down and fighting. So much focus and energy between the two of them, though wasted on their pointless aggression. What the hell were they thinking of, brawling like that? Were they regressing to the schoolyard? Did they think they were being Real Men, battering at each other in that way? But she stopped thinking it was risible when Leon took a blow to the mouth and spat blood – instead she flinched in outrage and screamed his name, her voice drowned in all the others. After that she forgot her scorn, as the primal urge to see her man win surged up like fire in her belly instead.

Back and forth the battle raged, the combatants sometimes on their feet, sometimes crashing off the netting, and sometimes down on the floor, each trying frantically to get a lock on their opponent that would be too painful to break. The smack of flesh on flesh was brutal: knees and elbows as well as fists and feet. They blinked the sweat out of their eyes and wiped the blood from their faces and kept on hitting back, and at moments when they were too stunned or slow to block they just endured the pain of the blows that rained upon them. The other man was quite a bit faster on his feet, but he didn't have the mass to inflict the sort of punishment Leon was meting out. Jacqueline found herself looking for his weaknesses, the openings he left, as if she could will Leon to hit into those gaps. Her hands on the chain-link were wet with perspiration. 'Get him!' she mouthed, frantic, as Able retreated round the cage, Leon lumbering after him like an enraged grizzly bear.

Sweat washed the blood from both their skins; red droplets turned the floodlit air pink as another flurry of blows was launched. It was followed by a clinch, each man gripping the other's slippery flesh and trying to knee him in the torso, then wrestling for a clean hold, scrabbling at each other's heads. It was clear they were both growing tired.

'Hit him!' she shouted, jerking the mesh back and forth.

In the end, Leon won by being able to soak up more damage than the other man: he'd spent a professional career enduring pain and exhaustion, and his stamina and his bigger bulk told when it came down to it. Able took one blow too many, staggered and sat down suddenly. As Leon fell on him, knees in the ribs, he folded and slammed his hand down on the canvas.

'Submission!' roared the loudspeaker. 'We have tonight's winner!'

The crowd cheered and groaned in equal measure and Jacqueline sagged against the wire. The whole bout had taken perhaps five minutes. She was shocked by her own visceral reaction to the violence and to the threat to her husband; and then nearly as shocked by his. Slightly unsteady on his feet, Leon still managed to strut about the stage, arms aloft in triumph, spitting blood and blinking wildly. His sweat-soaked shirt had been ripped open and his broad chest was gleaming as it heaved. He looked twice as large as life. Red marks over his ribs showed where he'd have terrible bruises in a few days, and his face was already swelling into a lumpy moonscape.

Jacqueline found herself taken aback: she'd almost forgotten what a big strong man he was, how broad his shoulders – and how utterly stubborn he could be. The thought made her self-conscious and she averted her face, not wanting him to recognise her. But Leon was beyond recognising anyone right now: he was buzzing on his victory. The crowd roared and he roared right back at them.

The wall at the back dropped again, and Pleiades staff hurried on to the stage. Three of them plucked Able up on to his feet and led him off, while a white-haired man with a microphone came to greet the warrior triumphant, raise his arm and then calm the crowd in the afterwash of their final acclaim.

'To the victor the spoils,' he breathed into the mic. 'What's it going to be, Herrin? Are you going to claim your prize now?'

He gestured and two male attendants dragged a much smaller figure on to the stage. It was the dancer, Jacqueline realised: the blonde in the fishnet dress. She had her wrists tied at the small of her back and was dragged on almost bent double. The MC jerked her to her knees at the front of the stage and pushed her face down, ass up, yanking up the hem to bare her bottom and then planting the sole of his shoe on the back of the girl's neck.

Jacqueline's heart and stomach crashed together.

'Well?' he said.

There were shouts and catcalls but the noise of the crowd was ragged now, no longer the voice of a single beast. They were unsure of Leon, divided among themselves. The girl didn't struggle, though her pale ass swayed from side to side a little. Leon was looking right down at her bare pussy. He must be looking right at the twin bull's-eyes of her cunt and anus, wondering which to aim for. Slowly he reached to his crotch and hefted his package through the material of his trousers. It was obvious he was packing lead there. Then he unzipped his fly. The room was suddenly so quiet that even the rasp of his zipper was audible. Manhandling his cock and balls out from the open fabric, he revealed a full-on erection.

It was so familiar, Jacqueline thought: that little list to the left, the colour and the shape of his pubic thatch, the bulge of his ball-sac, hairy and heavily wrinkled and seamed up the middle. So familiar, but not in this context. Here, it looked mean and threatening and somehow considerably bigger. She was suddenly hot all over, despite the fact that this end of the room was air conditioned. Something uncomfortable seemed to writhe in her sex. Would she – could she – stand and watch him fuck that girl in front of a slavering audience? Was he really going to do it?

Oh, he'd always loved the public stage, hadn't he?

Leon stroked himself lovingly, revelling for one more long moment in his triumph and in the helpless pink snatch presented for his pleasure. Then he lifted his chin.

'What's it going to be?' the MC urged, stepping away from the girl, circling to Leon with the mic. 'Are you going to claim that sweet little cunt?'

'Fuck the slut!' someone shouted from the crowd, but was silenced by others: a rumble of irritation.

Leon gave his hard-on one more preening tug. 'No. I want to see the Boss.'

The crowd went absolutely ape. There was no mistaking their approval. This, thought Jacqueline wildly – this was what they'd come here for tonight. The men behind her surged up against her, bouncing her against the mesh, and she felt her hardened nipples snag on the wire with a sensation of physical shock.

'Herrin! Herrin!' they started chanting.

From the Olympian heights of the mezzanine floor came movement: a glass elevator was descending to the main level of the club. Jacqueline couldn't see the door open because of the crowd, but she saw when the occupant emerged into view from the back of the stage. There was a collective roar, and then everyone went quiet. It was like they were holding their breath.

The Boss was a tall black woman: over six foot in her heels, her hair a 20s-style platinum-blonde bob, with lips painted the oozing red-black of Angeleno plums. She strolled into the open cage with the lithe, swaggering arrogance of a lion-tamer. Jacqueline's glance, once she'd got over her surprise, was critical: the woman was, she thought, only saved from being categorised as wiry by the jut of her breasts and bottom. Both of those were wrapped in a shimmering dress, as white as her hair, that clung to every curve and was slashed in a multitude of places to show slivers of her skin, the satin skirt long enough to trail on the canvas but split to her hips.

Around her hips was tied a pale suede belt with no buckle. The effect was oddly medieval.

That's a wig, Jacqueline thought, trying to find some chink in that aggressive and overwhelming beauty, as if it would make the woman any less unnerving. She looked so completely at ease there, surrounded by those excited men and practically swimming in their testosterone, looking Leon up and down as if he were a horse she'd been asked to judge. Her luscious lips curved in a faint, amused smile. She lifted a hand and signalled off-stage, and staff hurried on with a padded bench – the MC having already made himself scarce by this point, taking the dancer with him. Meanwhile she approached Leon and looked him long and coolly in the eye. His gaze didn't falter, though his chest was rising and falling sharply, all the adrenaline now making him unsteady. He just gripped his erect cock tight in his fist.

'The hero of the hour,' said she. Her silky voice needed no electronic amplification: everyone in the room was hanging on each word. She glanced down at his purple-headed glans with no apparent interest, then drew two fingers down his chest, over his ribs, probing at an enflamed red patch before licking her fingertips to taste his sweat. Leon gritted his teeth. 'Strip,' she ordered, turning on her heel and going over to sit on the bench.

Leon took a deep breath, then pulled off the shredded shirt that clung, transparent, to his shoulders and arms. The Boss crossed one long bare leg over the other, sitting with her back very straight, her attention entirely on him. He dropped his trousers next, kicking them away, and stood with his legs apart, naked.

'Arms out.'

He raised them wide. The stance emphasised the breadth of his chest. He was still a fine-looking man, thought Jacqueline, shot through with pangs of very physical admiration. His erect cock bobbed slightly.

'Turn.'

He turned, showing her the pale flash of his untanned rear, then faced her again. Her smile broadened momentarily.

'Kneel.'

Without a word he went down on his knees. Jacqueline's mouth had gone dry. She hardly believed what she was seeing, unable to reconcile the everyday Leon she knew with the warrior, unable to reconcile the proud warrior with such obedience. Unable to defend to herself her own reaction to the sight.

'Are you hurting, hero?'

He didn't answer. He just jerked his chin in affirmation, keeping it high. She unfurled her long legs and stood again, approaching him. Now that he was on his knees she could look down into his face without effort.

'Think you can take more?'

'Yes,' he croaked, his cock twitching.

Whipping back her hand, she slapped his face hard – hard enough to knock his head sideways. His eyes widened and he blinked fiercely: Jacqueline could almost see the rush of adrenaline through his system as his face went pale, leaving the red imprint of her palm to bloom slowly on his cheek. Jacqueline herself had to grip the wire to hold herself up, so shocked was she.

'You sure, hero?'

'Yes,' he said through set teeth.

She backhanded him on the other cheek: this one drew blood, because she was wearing heavy silver rings. 'Really sure?'

The breath hitched in his throat, but his cock didn't falter. 'Yes.'

The Boss laughed, low and delicious. Then, stepping back, she untied the suede belt from about her hips, looped it round her hand and swished it through the air. Leon clenched his jaw. The lash whipped out and snapped at him, right across both nipples, with a crack like something breaking. His head jerked, but he didn't utter a sound.

'Good,' said she, lifting the belt again.

She whipped him on the chest and the back and the thighs. She whipped his clenched ass-cheeks. She whipped each of his outstretched arms as if trying to pull him down from an invisible cross. She shortened the strap and beat him on the face. She snapped the very tip of the leather across his penis. She was fast and accurate and incredibly strong: she beat him over and over and didn't tire, didn't get sloppy, didn't miss. Not once. Leon began to groan with every strike and roll his eyes, but he didn't protest or lower his arms or flinch. His erection sagged – but only to half-mast. Sweat rolled down his body in rivulets, but she didn't even start to perspire. And Jacqueline's world turned upside down and inside out as she watched, appalled. She didn't recognise this Leon. Her husband was a man who took shit from no one: she didn't understand why he was kneeling there and soaking up the pain and the humiliation like that. What sort of man was he?

Then she looked round the other faces at the wire and knew that they were all that sort of man. They were watching in avid wide-eyed silence, quivering at every blow, every one of them wanting to be up on that stage. Imagining themselves in his place. There was a strange charisma to his suffering: a nobility even. And the women – did they see themselves in the role of the Boss, or were they picturing themselves being punished? She couldn't tell. She just knew that they were pressed to the mesh, mesmerised by the spectacle of her husband's pain. One woman had pulled down the top of her designer gown and thrust her small breasts into the diamond gaps between the wires and was plucking at her big dark nipples. Jacqueline's own body felt like it didn't belong to her, awash with sensation that made no sense, off-balance and trembling, her sex swollen like rising dough despite herself.

At last, when the scarlet welts on Leon's torso had melded into one burning glow, the Boss halted. She took his jaw in her hand and lifted his face, then stooped to as if to kiss him – but she wasn't kissing his lips and his cheeks and his forehead: she was licking him, mouth wide, sucking the salt of his pain and the ooze of the little cuts left by the fight and her own hand, mumbling greedily at every gash and bruise. The whole crowd groaned low at that.

'Can you take more?' she growled, forcing him to look at her. Her eyes were flashing now, her voice suddenly laced with an accent that sounded French. Jacqueline had always thought dominatrices were supposed to be ice-queens: not this one. She was far more fire than ice.

'Yes,' he rasped.

She picked him up. Jacqueline's eyes widened, but she had ceased to balk at anything now; the line between possible and impossible had dissolved in Leon's sweat. The Boss hefted him to his feet one-handed, gripping him under the jaw, and flung him down on his back on the bench where she'd sat before. Then she straddled his belly – her incredible legs taut now and bare to the thigh – and raked her nails down his chest, hard enough to bring blood welling up in breadcrumb trails. She bent to lick her way up each red path from belly to heart, while the audience murmured. Then she opened her mouth wide and sank her teeth into his chest, framing his left nipple. Leon arched and jerked his legs: his cock rose from where it bounced on his thigh and stuck straight up, jabbing the woman in the rump. She lifted her head, eyes feral, and lips now much more red than black. Her own arousal was more subtle than his but equally shameless. Adjusting the fall of white satin at her groin, she pulled his cock to the hidden cleft of her sex and sat back hard, engulfing him.

Jacqueline took a broken breath. She felt with all the envy of memory that cock filling her own hole.

'Give me your hurt, hero,' the Boss crooned, sinking her nails into his skin and making him spasm. 'That's right: give it up. Give it up to me.' She started to rise and fall on his cock, slamming her hips down, and as she rode him – as she *fucked* him, because there was no doubt about who was active and who was recipient here – she dug the nails of one hand into his flesh and struck him with the other, aiming at his face. The heave of her hard round ass over his thighs was dazzling. Little barks of pain escaped Leon's chest with every blow, a mindless animal noise, but he didn't struggle. And she didn't take long: her orgasm was on her swiftly, making her shudder and hiss and lose all rhythm and finally arch her back and nearly fall forward over him.

There's no difference in their reactions, thought Jacqueline. If you're watching, not feeling it, pain looks just like pleasure. You can't tell them apart.

Then with a wrench the Boss was off, standing, and Leon's cock stood bereft, glistening with her moisture. She raised her hand over her head and clicked her fingers, pointing at the ceiling, at the winches and drums of cable. Things began to descend with an electrical hum: a small box on a snaking length of cable; chains; some sort of metal bar with shackles at either end. She took the bar and with swift, practised movements bound Leon's ankles in the shackles, which meant his legs were spread wide and helpless. Then she attached the chains to the bar and, using the remote, raised the chains again. His legs were lifted from the ground, higher than his recumbent body – and then he was pulled up bodily from the bench, swinging with head down, his arms hanging limp over his head. The Boss took up the fallen belt she'd used to thrash him and bound his wrists behind his back. Jacqueline could see that his eyes were wide and glassy, almost unblinking.

What now? she wondered. The audience were waiting for something, shifting restlessly, almost swaying on their feet, pressing forward. The air felt heavy in her lungs; every breath she took was laden with male sweat and the reek of their impatience. She could hear the men on either side of her panting.

Spinning him on his chains the Boss thumbed the control once more, raising him a foot or so, putting them face to face. She kissed his upside-down lips cruelly, more bite than kiss, then dropped him back with a jerk. Her head was on a level with his chest now. She twisted his nipple between her fingers, then stepped in to embrace him and took a big hard bite. No kiss at all in that. For a moment suction hollowed her cheeks, then she pulled back with a wet noise and bit him again, a little further over. A thin trickle of scarlet ran down toward his throat. She worked her way up his body bite by bite, lowering him on his tether to get access. Leon quivered in every fibre, his legs jerking, and a long dark note of suffering tore from his chest.

And this was what the crowd had waited to see: this feeding. They groaned softly with every bite. The guy to Jacqueline's right had his hand on her bum-cheek, someone had his spread fingertips planted in the small of her back, and the one at her left had his flies open and was jacking off. She didn't look. She didn't care. It wasn't personal. She wasn't the focus of their desire because that was the woman up there on stage, the one with the teeth and the thirst; she – Jacqueline – was just a part of the crowd, one of the worshippers, a fragment adrift in a sea of longing and lust. The scent of her arousal was another note in the crowd's scent, the gasps of her breath just some of a thousand thousand whispered prayers. 'Bite him,' they prayed with every breath: 'Bite him; bite him; bite me.'

Then that monstrous goddess reached Leon's cock, which

hung down stiffly against his belly. There was a momentary pause before – at last – she took it in her mouth. Her jaw clenched. Leon roared, thrashing in his bonds, arching backward then banging his head on her thighs and pubis. There was agony in his cry but ecstasy too: broken words shot from his mouth like spittle, a hailstorm of blasphemy and obscene release. Jacqueline felt the crowd surge forward and she was shoved against the wire, hot bodies grinding against her back, the whole audience writhing in sympathy with the hanged man's immolation. A nubbin of curved wire rubbed against Jacqueline's own pubic mound and in a moment she found her own orgasm: not a big earth-shaking one, because she didn't have a cock inside her or a vibe pressed to her clit, but a twisting shameful thrill of pleasure that spread through her whole body in a slow-motion wave, leaving her gushing and aching in its wake. 'Oh, fuck!' she squeaked under her breath, her words echoing Leon's roar.

He kept on groaning even when he ran out of breath for words. He kept groaning even when the Boss let him go and walked away back to the elevator, her eyes heavy-lidded with satisfaction, her beautiful dress no longer white or pristine. His cock was purplish, swollen, still grossly erect, and it pulsed and jerked as he hung there shaking just as if it was ejaculating, even though no emission was visible. He was still coming, Jacqueline realised, appalled. His balls had been sucked dry by that bitch-goddess and he was still coming, empty.

It took him a long time to stop. He was still groaning softly when the staff came to lower him down.

As the crowd unfurled like a poisonous flower releasing its sticky scent of semen and lust and male sweat, individuals drifting away, she wove slightly unsteadily back toward the cloakroom. Moisture slicked her inner thighs. She felt filthy and shamed and excited. There were stains on her designer dress too, stains from other crowd members; she'd actually felt the man on her left splash against the split of her thigh. It didn't matter. She had seen: she had taken part: she had understood. She'd seen her husband with new eyes. Seen him not in relationship to her but most primitively, as a man. A body. An object of desire. She'd got hot and wet for him in a way she hadn't since their earliest years.

And she understood Leon. In a few days he'd be healed up and recovered, and when he came home she'd be waiting for him. She understood him now: his need for pain, his ruthless hyper-masculine urge to test his courage and endurance, the demand of his body to be taken to the very limit. She needed to consider everything, and to be ready.

She still had her purse with her, and the divorce papers inside it. Let them stay there. She had other plans now.

(Estelle)

And this is Estelle: beautiful irresistible Estelle. 'The Boss' is her nom de guerre only in some of the establishments that she owns; she has half-a-dozen different titles and four times as many businesses under her control. She's had time to build up quite a portfolio since the 1920s.

She was born in Mississippi, but she doesn't like to remember that these days and when she's excited or tired her accent slips to French rather than that of her childhood. The eldest of seven daughters, she grew up on a farm her father worked as sharecropper for a white landlord and she spent most of her youth chasing round after her siblings, trying to keep them fed and safe and obedient. Her family were good churchgoing folk and the girls all learned to sing long before they could spell out their alphabets. A few of them could sing really well, Estelle in particular, so they became a regular feature of Sunday meetings, and with the addition of a name – 'The Seven Little Sisters of the Lord's Gracious Mercy' – they began to tour the circuit of country churches and gospel gatherings.

Estelle was sixteen when a visitor from out of state spotted her potential and persuaded her to come to Chicago to try for a singing career. Alcibiades Nash was like no local man she knew: smooth and scented and cultured, full of stories and a knowing humour, he carried himself with an arrogant confidence even around white folk and didn't appear to mind the danger. Yet with her he was always polite, seeming almost awed by her talent. He called her 'Miss' and told her she was beautiful and walked with her after church, describing how much the people up north would love her for her voice and her lovely face. He said she had a glorious future ahead of her, and he took her hand and stroked her palm and wrist with one finger until she was squirming and wide-eyed and half out of her skin with wanting what he had to give. The stranger woke in the young girl feelings stronger and wilder and sweeter than any she'd known before, and she fell for every one of his honeyed words.

Her father and mother, rigidly respectable folk, wouldn't hear of their daughter going into the theatre, so she ran away with Alcibiades Nash.

Estelle grew up fast after that. Fast and bitter. Too proud and ambitious to break, she hardened instead, losing old comforts and finding new consolations. Knowing that the powerless obtain no mercy, she worked hard not to be in any one man's thrall, playing one off against another to find her independence somewhere in the cracks between. It was a risky strategy and she took her share of pain, but she survived and more.

These things are beautiful to Estelle: ruby beads of blood like strung gems on masculine skin; the thickness of a weight-lifter's neck, tendons corded with strain; the gather of sweat at the very base of a man's spine, just at the cleft of his proud butt-cheeks, and the way it hangs and drips from his balls; the smell of his anguish, sharp and bitter on the oozing skin of his crotch; the gasp of agony and surrender as his skin gives between her teeth. Above all she wants to see the look in their eyes that tells her that they need her, that they need the pain she brings.

You will not find Estelle casually, and she will not seek you. You have to be the right sort of person, and you will have to go looking for her, and you will have to bring her the things she desires. Offerings to her divinity.

You will have to earn the right to be her victim.

Unusual among vampires, Estelle is specific about the gender of her donors. For her it's always men; she doesn't touch women. Ask her why, if you dare. She has said, and quite possibly even believes, that it's because of her sisters. She grew up looking after girls, after all: she can't bring herself to prey on them. It's not the whole truth, but she's not introspective.

From Chicago she moved to New York, where – 'tall, tan and terrific' as the management required – she danced and sang in the chorus line before all-white audiences at the Cotton Club, and began her first forays in singing jazz. She has a low, husky voice, does Estelle, and she still likes to sing. Her private collection of original 78s and studio recordings is worthy of a museum.

In 1926 she signed on for a revue tour of France, and

her life changed. To her bemusement, she became exotic overnight: 'Une Princesse d'Afrique', they billed her in the Folies Bergère. From une petite danseuse *she became a well-known singer in the more exclusive clubs and restaurants, and soon she had a number of male admirers only too willing to supplement her wage with extravagant gifts. It was during this time that she developed her stage persona, haughty and merciless, and she grew into that armour like a crab into its shell.*

God, how those sophisticated men loved to play the trembling swain to that sassy, hard-edged chanteuse. To turn the world and its rules upside down in the perfumed sanctuary of her boudoir. To have her slap their faces and mock them and jiggle her dark-nippled breasts before their pleading mouths, flaunting her contempt for them. To have the proud African Princess thrash their flabby white backs and asses until they begged her for mercy, then make them crawl and kiss her beautiful cinnamon feet and bury their faces in the dark curls of her sex. It astonished and delighted her, what they wanted from her. She learned to use the whip and the paddle, the rack and the strap-on dildo, all instruments of a private theatre that earned her far more than the public stage. She learned how much strength and endurance is needed to wield a whip, and how much cunning and invention goes into breaking a man in ways he can't anticipate but wants with all his heart.

It was during this time that she met Reynauld and he fell in love, ignoring the self-imposed rule of centuries – and for the last time. He was not like her other lovers. Charmed as he was by her public persona, he saw beyond it. And there was of course the matter of his being immortal, ageless and terrifying. She could not despise him: not entirely.

It was also at this time when the tuberculosis incipient in her lungs made itself fully known, flying its crimson flag. When she retired suddenly from the stage and fled Paris he tracked her to an exclusive TB sanatorium in Switzerland and offered her the only cure at his command. Coughing blood and fighting for breath, she didn't hesitate to accept.

He took her on a silvery night, under the snowfields of the watchful mountains. He'd fed from her before, of course, but only lightly. This time she had to surrender herself entirely to him, baring her long throat. This time she had to trust to his embrace and let his strength carry her to the edge and beyond.

She hated that, and died hating.

Crossing the dark waters of the Jordan, she found new life on the far shore: eternal life, just as she'd been promised when sitting on those hard pews in the whitewashed church so many years ago, holding her head high in order to catch the breeze from her mother's fan. 'Life in abundance,' as the preacher had roared. She has, she believes, made good use of it. Almost the first thing she did after coming into her power was to return to the States, leaving Reynauld bereft. She spent a year hunting down every person she remembered as having hurt or exploited or slighted her, and took her revenge with consummate thoroughness, Alcibiades Nash first and last. But she didn't stay after that. Mississippi was no longer her home, and at least in France she had status.

She loves the limelight. Don't ever forget that: what she craves is adulation. Adulation ... and blood, of course. She regards both as her due, earned with hard work. She stayed in Paris until the Nazi invasion in 1940. Only then did she seek out Reynauld once more and make her new home in his domain, their relationship strained but mutually acceptable.

She likes power. She likes notoriety, of a certain sort. She likes money because it gives her control, and allies herself with Reynauld because his rule is peaceful, which allows her to make more money and enmesh donors. All those she feeds from are men in the prime of life: big, hard, confident men at the swaggering apex of their prowess. For her, blood isn't enough: she likes to inflict pain. She gets excited beating up on men – especially but not exclusively, in fact, white men. Luckily there are more than enough willing participants for her games, and she's got the self-discipline to make sure she doesn't fall foul of Reynauld's rules even in the extremity of her desire.

They are queuing up, all those men who want her to test their manhood to the limit, who want to make their pain an offering upon her altar. The fight clubs and the BDSM dungeons under her aegis, both gay and straight, are flourishing. The Pleiades is only one of several locations where the secret needs of men are met; and the deepest and darkest human need is to be not simply the one who sacrifices to his god, but the sacrifice itself.

The Seven Little Sisters are commemorated now only as a nightclub sign: the years when she herded and hugged them, slapped and comforted them, a memory coated in nacre. If she ever thinks of those six little girls it is with an uncomfortable twitch of the shoulders and a faint sense of nausea at their tears and their fear and their silliness, their helpless need exposed before a world of hurting and injustice, as unappealing in its nakedness as a hairless baby possum.

This is something even Estelle doesn't know about herself: that it's not entirely lust or vengeance she brings to her cruel games, though both are there in abundance. There's a twisted admiration too. The traits she values – physical strength and courage and independence – she sees in men, so she spares women not out of kindliness but because they're not good enough for her. She wouldn't take well to being told so, but it's decades since she last identified with any gender, ethnicity or species that isn't top of the food-chain.

If she had her real desire, it would be vampires that she fed from.

5: Six for the Six Proud Walkers

The dark of the moon always made me tense.

Reynauld had only four women in with him that evening: he was keeping it brief because he was expecting the others of his kind for their monthly meet. On the night of the new moon the five blood-drinkers were expected to pay homage to their king in the shadows, and it was never a relaxed affair. I was prepared to welcome them at midnight, so while I waited I curled up on the chaise longue in the private bathroom beyond the playroom, ready should he call. I didn't expect him to need anything from me, but I needed to be on hand.

I could have chosen to be inside the room, of course, and join in with the other girls. He'd never said anything to stop me, and sometimes I still did take part, but I had to be in the mood. It's hard at 49 to have to compare one's body to those sleek, pretty young things. I felt self-conscious. I'd always taken care of myself and I'd never put on any weight, even after having Tim. I was trim and fit and not at all unattractive – for my age. Ah, there's the rub. When you used to be truly beautiful it hurts bitterly to lose that edge.

So while I waited outside the bedroom door with my chin in my hand, I could easily picture what was going on within. Four girls tonight. I knew all about them, since it was my job to arrange their arrival and departure. There was the R&B starlet who'd just had her first Top Ten hit, all big-eyed wonder at the world she'd found herself in and suffering from a slightly hyper desire to be liked. Big breasts too, and big bum; the sort you wanted to roll in. Not as pretty as she looked in her videos, but then very few people are, and certainly pretty enough. She was the one I could hear squealing at intervals. I doubted she'd get invited back, not unless she learned to calm down a bit.

Besides the pop star there was a weather girl from breakfast TV, very popular with the nation's dads, very sweet and girl-next-door. And the current Miss Malaysia, who was over here on a publicity tour of some sort and finding out things about Western culture that I doubted she'd ever anticipated. And some girl that he'd picked up at a Home Office reception, a ministerial aide of some sort. She was a bit on the thin side but had big, watchful eyes in which there was no trace of fear. I quite liked the look of her; she had probably been put up to the job by her department, but she might be a keeper.

The weather girl was five months pregnant, her breasts swollen and her belly a ripening curve, and I knew that Reynauld found that utterly charming; he could hear the foetal heartbeat as he fed from her. I remembered what he was like from when I was pregnant with Tim – oh, not by him, of course; vampires don't breed that way. I was married then and had just given up my modelling career and then this man ... oh, this man. This beautiful, beautiful man with the honey skin and the aquiline nose and the eyes that said he wanted to eat you alive and the mouth that promised you would love him for it. All of which was true, of course. I loved him. I loved him so much.

I still did.

Part of me, inside, was still young and that part wished it need never end: the games in his commodious bed; the thoughtless living in the present, like a summer holiday that stretched on for ever. Listening to the muted sounds through the door I knew what I would see if I looked in there. His strong, spare, muscled body riding the waves of their flesh like a long-distance swimmer in a rolling sea. His cock, thick and dark with one prominent vein, webbed and glistening with cum and sex juice, sliding from one pink hole and twitching with impatience as he guided it into another. The shadowed muscles of his thighs and ass flexing as he thrust between their thighs or up against their cushioning bottoms. The clench of his jaw as he nuzzled hard into ripe flesh, splitting that peach-fuzz skin with his teeth and drinking their juices. He never tired. He was never sated.

It's weird. You get used to the assumption that a man has only one shot in him. Not vampires. I don't know what it is – maybe the liquid diet, but I hesitate to apply pseudo-science because science flees the room in the face of some of the things they can do. Vampires, male as well as female, can orgasm over and over, and there never seems to be a night when they're not itching for sex and never an end to the supply of jism; as soon as their balls are empty they're recharged. I couldn't begin to count the number of times Reynauld had fucked me over the last 27 years. I would arrive home, when I still had a home that wasn't this place, with my legs trembling with exhaustion, my well-used bum-hole burning and my pussy swollen and numb.

Nigel didn't cope well with that. What man could? My marriage died but Reynauld kept fucking me and I didn't even surface for air. Not for years and years.

Part of me wished that it could have gone on for ever. Another part of me knew I had to grow up. He'd made his decision that there were to be no more new vampires, and that was that. It was a matter of principle. I was allowed to grow old, and one day he would allow me to die. He'd go on unchanged, immortal, when I was ashes. I still wanted him, but how much longer would he want me?

That's why I'd made some changes. I'd realised I needed to be useful to him in other ways. I learned to know and appreciate the wines he liked in order to be able to manage his cellar. I honed an interest in the kind of music and books he enjoyed so that I could indulge him that way. I started to organise the comings and goings of the house: the other girls, his diary, his purchases, his travel and contacts. I even drove the car when he went out in public. So that's how I became what I was now: PA to a vampire. I liked to think he needed me, though I didn't really know.

I needed him.

He was fucking those girls, while I sat there in my grey skirt and jacket waiting, my own sex wet with neglect. I buried my face in the crook of my arm and thrust my hand between my legs, not to masturbate but to hold myself. Some poor comfort.

You're too old to cry, I told myself. Suck it up. This is the life you chose. This is what it means to love a vampire.

Concentrating on my breathing, I practised the meditation I'd learned in yoga class, emptying my mind. It didn't have quite the intended effect of empty awareness but slowly the wash of self-pity did ebb away, and I came close to dozing off.

'Amanda.' A murmur. A hand stroked my hair, running through the silvery threads of my neat bob. My blonde hair had gone grey early; perhaps a result of my being fed upon too often, perhaps not.

I sat up then, flustered. God – I hadn't expected to hear his feet, he made practically no sound when he moved, but I hadn't even heard the door open. A glance over the back of the chaise and I saw him running water into the sink, stooping to rinse his face and hands. The low light gleamed on his bare back and I stared, struck with aching need. Drying off with a hand towel, he moved to stand by the window. All the windows had big hardwood shutters that sealed out any daylight, but he drew one back to look out. I could see the neon glimmer of the river, the bridge, the embankment buildings: this one we lived in was used in the eighteenth century as a bonding warehouse where goods were unloaded and it's still called The Bonding. From the outside it was all red brick arches, but the vast interior had been converted at phenomenal expense into a private residence. I'd been in charge of some of the redecoration myself.

Here's a tip on interior decoration for vampires: no carpets. But white towels. They like to see fresh bloodstains on the white.

His expression as he looked out was troubled, I thought, not his normal post-coital satisfaction; he seemed intent on some private thought. 'Is everything ready?' he asked as he turned back.

Reynauld was naked. He wasn't shy. I caught my breath, still mesmerised after all these years by his beauty. His build was athletic rather than broad, but every inch of it was muscle and when he was unclothed the muscle made hard angles in all the right places. His legs, his belly and his chest were flecked with dark hair, like someone had taken a fine fibre-tipped pen and inked flow-lines down the sculpted contours of his pectorals and his abs, all the leys finally converging in his crotch. I tried not to look at his cock and nearly succeeded; it was quiescent for once, hanging long and sleek, though because he was circumcised it always had a suggestion of readiness.

'Yes, of course.' I got up, feeling slightly discomfited at having been caught napping, and smoothed my clothes. My outfit looked very formal, almost like a uniform, and that was the point of wearing it tonight. I glanced at my watch. 'You've got about forty minutes before they're due. Do you want to wash?'

He smiled a little. His black, slightly wavy hair was swept back from a high forehead with a widow's peak; you'd think it was starting to recede but it hadn't retreated any further in nearly 1,200 years. 'I don't think so.'

I nodded, understanding. Vampires don't sweat, I'd learned, and have almost no body odour of their own – but they do have a phenomenal sense of smell. Reynauld meant to walk among his fellows stinking of sex and blood. It was a blunt but effective message of dominance. 'Clothes? I've laid out a suit, a dinner jacket ...'

He twitched an eyebrow, amused at the cliché of a vampire in evening attire. I sighed, exasperated.

'There's the leather coat if you prefer.'

'No. I think I'll ... dress myself.'

With a twitch of his hand he summoned the shadows. From out of the cupboards and from the dark places under the furniture they came flowing across the floor towards him, like great swathes of cloth, textureless and insubstantial. They swooped up about his legs, furling him momentarily in layers of black, then settled about his shoulders, taking on the cut of a robe with a deeply split neck, its skirt so vast that it encompassed the room, fading to transparency at the furthest reaches. Only his face, hands and breastbone were bare, but I knew that if I stepped up to him the opaque robe would have no more tactile resistance than a layer of soot. When he moved, every shadow in the chamber moved with him, the darkness drawn to him like filings to a magnet.

That's when I knew that something bad was going down that night. I bit the inside of my lip.

The shadows whispered as they flowed in his wake. He looked down into my face. 'Am I presentable?'

Of course he couldn't check himself in a mirror. His reflection would be nothing but a blur, as if the glass were warped. I reached up a hand to pull a long blonde hair out of his small beard and studied him critically. Dark beard, dark brows, dark eyes, prominent cheekbones. I burned to kiss his lips but I didn't dare. He'd feel warm to the touch now, I knew, because he'd just fed. 'You look fine.'

'You're nervous.'

'Am I?'

'I can hear your heart, remember.'

I looked down, hoping he wouldn't see the yearning in my eyes. He didn't like neediness in his girls. It was one of the reasons I'd stopped joining him in bed so often: I'd been too fond of being bitten and I'd needed to take control of that. 'I'm always nervous on these nights,' said I quite truthfully. 'I don't want you to get hurt.'

A smile escaped his lips on a breath: 'You worry for me, Amanda?' He touched my face, gently, then drew me into his arms to plant a kiss softly on my forehead and then my hair. I was right; his lips were warm. 'How can there be anything to worry about? You'll be there to look after me.'

Not always, thought I. Not for ever.

* * *

I made sure I was downstairs to greet the guests well before midnight, and that the front doors of The Bonding were standing wide. Reynauld didn't like unpunctuality, especially on these nights. The purpose of the monthly meets was in part to maintain contact between the disparate individuals, to make sure instructions were passed on and to gather news, but primarily it was about Reynauld's authority. He summoned them because he could and they came because they didn't dare ignore him.

Wakefield was first; he arrived by taxicab. I watched him stalk up the long stairs – the entrance to The Bonding was a floor above the ground outside – and I checked on the security guards visible beyond him in the compound. They were all armed with tasers, which were in fact a good deal more effective against vampires than guns of any sort, should it ever come to that. Wakefield, his grizzled hair a dramatic frame to his elegant features, and dressed in a frayed Victorian frock-coat that quite possibly was one he'd worn when alive, brought me as usual a single dark-red rose from his garden, and he bowed as he presented it.

'Chatelaine.' His pale eyes seemed to apologise for the inadequacy of a gesture that I actually found perfectly charming.

'Thank you, sir.'

I'd always had a soft spot for Wakefield. Not because he was handsome – God, they're all beautiful, an evolutionary trick that helps with the hunting, I suppose – but because he was always so polite and so melancholy. Never any trouble to Reynauld, either. I invited him into the room beyond the foyer, where they would all be meeting. There were bottles of wine already uncorked upon the table, but no servants to pour: the only members of staff visible tonight would be myself and the security men.

'If you'll excuse me, sir.'

'Of course.'

The next arrival was Estelle, whom I did not like one bit. She was one of the ones it was wise to show that you feared. She drove up behind the wheel of a crimson Lamborghini convertible that growled like a tiger, and threw the keys at one of the guards. Her dress matched the arterial blood of the car's paintwork and was quite breathtaking: a silk cheongsam embroidered with chrysanthemum flowers, so tight that her lean body and full breasts seemed to have been vacuum-packed into it, ankle-length but slashed to the thigh to reveal her peerless legs. Her hair was cut short to her head but with a face and bone structure that beautiful she didn't seem to lack any ornament, and her earrings were complex chandeliers of ruby chips that hung low about her neck.

She didn't even look at me.

Ben was the third, and he arrived on the back of a motorbike driven by a girl in leathers, whom he kissed passionately before he sent her on her way. He swaggered up the steps like James Dean and I had to hide a smile.

'How's things, Amanda? He treating you well?'

'Very well, thank you, sir.'

'Don't forget, if you ever get bored of him you can always come and ride my face for a fortnight.'

Oh, dear, thought I – and yet he did it with such charm. 'I'll bear it in mind, sir. Would you care to step this way?'

Naylor cut it fine; at a minute to midnight there was no sign of him at the front door and I was scanning the CCTV images on the bank of monitors at the desk, looking over the shoulder of one of the security men at shots of the roof.

Vampires, unless they're very old or in a powerful hurry, show up on video as they do in mirrors.

'There,' Colin said, pointing at another view altogether: the old ramp leading down into the river. Something slim and pale was climbing the slipway, streaming water; something so pale it was obviously naked, though its features were a blur. 'That's him, isn't it?'

I took the microphone. 'Dafydd: guest number four is down there in the undercroft with you. Take three men and escort him up in the lift. No eye-contact, remember.'

'Wilco.'

We watched Naylor on CCTV and my mouth was dry every step of the way. Naylor was, of them all, the one I considered most dangerous. The staff were all under Reynauld's protection, of course, and very definitely off-limits, but Naylor was feral enough, in my opinion, to attack on instinct and not consider any consequences. When the door to the elevator opened my eyes went first to the three guards in there with him: all three were still on their feet, thank God, with face-visors pulled firmly down and tasers held across their chests.

Naylor, completely dry and dressed in soft trousers and shirt woven from shadows, smirked at me. I dropped my gaze from his wickedly narrowed eyes and indicated the door with my open hand.

'This way, please, sir.'

He paused. 'You think I'll have forgotten the way some time in the last twenty years?'

'No, sir.'

'Then why feel you have to tell me yet again?'

I set my jaw. He was actually no taller than I was, I reminded myself in an attempt not to give way to fear. At the periphery of my vision I could see the guys sidling out of the open lift and spreading out to get an angle. 'Would you care to go in, sir?' I said softly.

Naylor snorted down his nose. 'So why does he keep a dried-up old bitch like you?' he asked blithely. 'Does he like his donors wrinkly? Do you remind him of his mother?'

I felt a flush mount my neck. 'Follow me, please, sir,' I said, turning to walk away. It was a risky move: if Naylor took offence at my turned back he could move too fast for anyone to save me. My heels clicked on the quarry-tiled floor like ticks of a clock counting away my life.

'Nice tight ass though,' he whispered in my ear, making me shiver. 'I wouldn't mind getting my fist up that.'

God, he was a little shit.

The room they met in was windowless and nearly bare, dominated by a huge table whose chairs had been pushed back to the walls. It wasn't intended to set anyone at their ease. If this had been a meeting for humans it would have inevitably included dinner, but Reynauld drew the line at providing any of his employees for the entertainment of his kin. The three who had already arrived were standing about with glasses in hand, quite apart and as far as I could tell not speaking.

'Dahhhlings,' said Naylor, as if he were some stage lovey. Ben grinned, Estelle and Wakefield just looked at him.

I touched the electronic box looped over my ear and spoke into the microphone: 'They're here, sir.' Then I went back to close the door. By the time I'd done that and moved to the velvet-draped mirror that hung beside it, Reynauld had entered from the far side of the room.

Oh, thought I. He impressed me, even if it worked on none of the others. He paced across the room without any hurry, his brows knotted and his mouth set in a hard line, his gaze sweeping over the assembled guests. He looked handsome and grim in equal measure. There was no telling where his robe ended and the shadows began, and the air seemed to flow in his wake. One hand was curled into a loose fist. Even the most insensitive would've been able to tell he was in a black mood.

'Hey,' Ben said, deliberately nonchalant.

'Reynauld,' said Estelle, straightening even taller on her stacked heels. 'What a delight to be here again; we need to talk about the financing of the –'

He held up a finger, silencing them. 'Wait, please. We will talk later, Estelle.' His gaze fell on me. 'Amanda?'

Obediently I drew down the green velvet spread, revealing the huge mirror in its gilt frame. It was in fact the only ornamental mirror in that house. Spotted a little with age, the glass loaned a grey cast to all it reflected of that room and its occupants. I was pictured most clearly of all because I stood in front of it, but all five others showed up to some degree. Reynauld and Naylor looked blurred, their shapes warped and undefined and my employer little more than a shadowy smudge, but the younger vampires looked clear enough, staring from behind me.

'Roisin!' called Reynauld.

'Ro – ro – ro – sheen,' echoed Ben under his breath and I clenched my teeth, wondering what he thought he was doing, pushing it like that.

Inside the mirror her appearance was heralded by a flickering cloud of darkness that poured out from under the reflected chimney-breast: bats. Hundreds of bats. They swooped in a skein through the room's reflection, circling our heads. Out here in the real world we felt not a single brush of air against a cheek, saw no fluttering wing, yet in the mirror they whirled all around us. Three times they circled the room, and then headed straight for the glass – and out into the room, because the hard mirror yielded as easily as the surface of a pool. For a second the air was full of beating wings, and then the swarm furled itself into a clot over the table and coalesced quite suddenly into a human figure.

Roisin was enchanting, I had no qualms admitting that. She hung over the table with her bare feet not quite making contact, her delicate figure surrounded by a nimbus of translucent white veils, her hair afloat like her garments. That pointed, elfin little face was as inscrutable as ever. She stooped to offer a hand to Reynauld.

'Welcome, Roisin,' said he, taking her hand and kissing it. Then he turned it over and sank his teeth into the heel of her thumb, drawing deeply from her palm. Roisin trembled and if she'd been heavy enough she would have fallen to her knees; as it was she ended up in a crouch floating over the tabletop.

'No, don't beat about the bush,' muttered Ben. 'Out with it.'

Roisin's lips worked but she said nothing: it was years since I'd heard her voice. She just watched Reynauld's mouth at work on her hand as if it were the most mesmerising and terrible thing she could imagine.

I really should have been out of the room by that point, but I couldn't move now, not while such an intimate exchange was taking place and all eyes were fixed upon that.

After about a minute he lifted his face and let her go, dropping her hand with a nod of acknowledgement. She withdrew slowly, swimming over to perch on the back of one of the heavy chairs like the ghost of a bird of paradise. This, of course, was what it was all about: they each had to submit to Reynauld feeding from them.

'Well,' said Estelle with arch humour, 'since we're cutting to the chase tonight ...' And she sashayed forward to face Reynauld. She would have died rather than sound unwilling, I thought: nothing would make her admit she was doing this because she had no choice.

He looked down at her and licked the blood off his lips thoughtfully. There was a history between these two, I knew, and every glance between them was loaded. Her Chinese dress covered her torso and had a high collar, but it left bare her arms and a decorative panel over the upper slope of her cleavage, which her constrained breasts squashed up to fill. Reynauld took what was on offer by wrapping her in his embrace as if they were dancing the tango together, tipping her backward over his arm and sinking his teeth with very obvious relish into the exposed curve of her inner breast. Estelle, hanging almost upside down, made a noise as her eyes rolled up in her head, a noise I suspect she deeply regretted: a deep animalistic groan of pain and lust.

All the vampires stirred uneasily. I felt my own sex flutter, aching for the stab of his teeth and the thrust of his cock, without distinction. I really was trapped in my place now: moving would draw too much attention to me and all the vampires were strung out on tension and blood-lust. They hated letting Reynauld feed from them, but got horribly aroused watching it happen to each other.

'Wakefield,' said Reynauld in a low throaty voice, once Estelle had been finished with and had slunk off to the wall. Wakefield stood up, visibly trembling, unbuttoning his coat and shirt and pulling his cravat aside.

That was about as submissive a gesture as a vampire could make. It verged on the obsequious.

'For fuck's sake,' Ben muttered, embarrassed, but Reynauld shot him a glance that quelled him instantly. He fed from Wakefield's shoulder, holding him close, body to body, and they both gasped a little upon release. Wakefield's pale cheeks couldn't blush, but when he retreated to the side of the room he moved with a limp that suggested there was a surfeit of blood left in his groin at least.

'Ben.'

Ben shucked off his leather jacket to reveal a short-sleeved black T-shirt beneath. 'OK, OK.' He held out his arm. 'Here.'

His casual act was marred somewhat by the fact he'd worn a soft pair of jeans and his semi could be seen bulging against the stonewashed fabric. Nor did Reynauld take his attitude well. 'You're telling me what to do?' he asked softly, looming in over the shorter, sturdier man, right into his space, almost lip to lip. Ben swallowed, trying to shrink back but with his retreat blocked by the table.

'No. Of course not.'

'Good. I'm glad to hear that.' He lifted Ben's arm and bit down on the inside of the bicep. He could have gone for somewhere more humiliating – but mercy was part of Reynauld's repertoire too. Ben sucked his own lips hard and endured the feeding with wide eyes. What he couldn't help was his own free hand straying to his groin to cup the bulging erection there.

One to go. Ben slumped back against the wall. Reynauld wiped his mouth with his forearm and crooked a finger at the last of them. 'Naylor.'

'Whatever you say, Old Man.' Naylor hadn't spoken a word after Reynauld had entered the room. Now his eyes were cool with resentment and he approached with the staccato movements of a scorpion poised to strike.

Reynauld wasn't put off. 'That's right: whatever I say. In here and outside. My city. My rules.'

Naylor sneered a little. 'You and your rules, Old Man. It really gets you off, doesn't it? Always your fucking rules.'

Reynauld moved so fast then that I saw nothing but a blur: one moment both men were standing by the table, the next he had Naylor pinned on his back across the wood, his hand at his throat. 'You remember a single one of them, Naylor?' he hissed, and his fangs were bared. Naylor, wide-eyed, made a choking noise. 'The one about not killing anyone, for example?'

'What you talking about?' Naylor managed to rasp.

Reynauld bent low over him. 'I'm talking about a body found in the docks, you little shit. A pretty girl when she was alive – not that anyone could have told that when they found her, given how thoroughly she'd been mutilated.'

My heart sank. So that was what he'd been brooding over.

'So?'

'Not badly mutilated enough, though, to hide the fact she'd been bitten to death. The other wounds were all post-mortem. Do you think I don't keep an eye on the morgues for that sort of thing?'

'You assume it was me, do you?'

'Oh, yes.' Reynauld nearly spat. 'We do remember your previous exploits, Naylor. Even humans remember the mess you made in Whitechapel.'

'What can I say? I'm a victim of my own fame.'

'You'll be another sort of victim when I've finished with you. That girl was one of mine – she used to be one of my donors. Lillabet, her name was. Does that ring any bells, or didn't you bother to ask?'

I felt my insides clench. I remembered Lilla well: blonde

and busty, a music-college student he'd spotted at a concert. Her perky mischievous persona had hidden a heart obsessed and envious. '*Elitist*!' she'd screamed at Reynauld on their last meeting, like the word was some ultimate insult: '*Arrogant! Smug!*'

Well, *duh* ... as they say these days.

Poor girl.

Naylor on the other hand gave no sign of recognising the name.

'And what in the fuck makes you think I'd want your cast-offs,' he grunted, 'you – old – fart?' With the final words he got his legs up and kicked Reynauld away, striking out at his face as he rolled up on to his knees and rose to his feet in the centre of the table. Reynauld lurched back, lifting a hand to his cheek. Blood ran down from two parallel cuts just below his eye.

There was a collective hiss at that sight. Naylor grinned, happier than I'd ever seen him, and lifted his hand. His nails were now two-inch claws, black with Reynauld's blood, and he licked at them. 'Very tasty,' he growled, his voice thicker, his lips wet with drool that was gathering uncontrollably in his mouth. 'Better than any of your sycophant blood-bags, any day.'

The small wounds on Reynauld's face closed up, but the real damage I knew was much greater. They'd all just seen him bleed, and for vampires bleeding is not taken lightly. He'd bled, and Naylor had drunk his blood. Reynauld's expression was like stone. For the first time they'd had an excuse for doubting his dominance.

With one step he was three foot up, standing on the table.

'Oh, are you going to hurt me?' Naylor whined, somehow both craven and mocking. 'That's just mean of you, Old Man.

All I want to do is have a good time and mind my own –' He never finished the sentence. There was a blur and suddenly the two figures were one, moving at incredible speed as they struck at each other, shadows whirling and shredding about them. I blinked and suddenly Naylor was face down on the table with one arm twisted up between his shoulders, his nose and cheek mashed to the hard wood, and Reynauld's fist locked in his hair.

Naylor made a strange gasping noise, and I was disturbed to realise he was laughing.

'You just don't get it, do you?' Reynauld snarled, his weight on Naylor's arm and back. 'This matters! We leave them alone so they will leave us alone. Accommodation. Symbiosis. That's why there are rules!'

'I get it,' he hissed. 'You get off on being their daddy; I get that. Just like you get off on slamming me. I can feel your cock, Reynauld. You going to do something with that? I can feel it poking my asshole like a sweep trying to get his brush up the flue, you horny old fucker. Like a pig with its snout up my trough.'

Naylor wasn't lying: they'd both worn shadows rather than real clothes and now that these were reduced to whipping shreds both men's bodies were only too visible to those of us watching. Reynauld had a full erection and inevitably given their relative positions he was jabbing the man beneath him. I'll tell you something else: Naylor's cock was just as stiff. You could see it as he humped his butt up, heaving his hips from the table in an attempt to connect with the man behind him. His cock was slimmer and more curved than Reynauld's; it jutted beneath his belly like the share of a plough, and a strand of clear pre-cum was drooling from the tip, connecting flesh and tabletop. It was the blood, see. I knew the inevitable effect it had on them. Blood shed, blood drunk: they were both high on the taste, the smell, the violence.

'You pissant little crab-louse,' Reynauld snarled, wrenching Naylor's head to the side. Whoa, I thought – he's not going for the neck, is he?

'Go on,' Naylor gasped, wriggling frantically and pushing up on to his elbow, trying to impale his behind on the jut of Reynauld's tool. 'Go on, you cocksucker, you want it, you want to fuck me bad, you want to fuck my ass, you want to shove that big hard cock up my hole and make me your whore, you dirty fucking shit-shoveller, make me scream, there it is, yes, there, right up there where you want it –'

Then he roared, because Reynauld did exactly what he was begging for and rammed his cock deep into his anus. I saw three white pennants of ejaculate shoot out of Naylor's prick and spatter the polished oak. And I saw the look on Naylor's face.

Reynauld let go of his hammerlocked arm so he could get purchase on his hip: I was surprised the limb wasn't dislocated. 'Clean that up,' he said hoarsely, pulling him back on to his knees and jabbing deeper into his rear passage. 'You're not fit to leave a stain in my house: lick it all up.' He pushed Naylor face-down across the tabletop. What choice did Naylor have? Groaning, he put out his tongue and lapped the gobbets of his own cum off the wood until Reynauld heaved himself upright, his thighs straddling the younger man's ass, and began to fuck him.

I've never felt the slightest sympathy for Naylor, but my eyes watered on his behalf then. I'd had that cock up my own backside many a time, but not like that: Reynauld was always so careful with me. With Naylor he was merciless. He thrust like a machine, like he was trying to turn Naylor's insides to pulp, and Naylor soon gave up any idea of licking anything; eyes staring and fists clenched, he was simply trying to ride the waves of the invasion and not drown.

'Do let me know if this hurts,' snarled Reynauld, and Naylor groaned.

Oh, that cock, pounding away in that narrow ass; those hard thighs, braced like steel; the look of implacable retribution on his face. It scared the hell out of me, and it made my pussy run with juice.

But he was nearly finished: I could tell. This was going to be quick. Pausing in his rut, Reynauld caught Naylor's long hair and pulled him upright as he knelt back. Naylor, dazed, seemed to sag; it was only Reynauld's arms holding him in place. But the youth still – astonishingly – had an erection. His cock jerked as Reynauld bent to growl in his ear.

'You're not going to forget the rules again, are you?'

Then Reynauld bit him. In the neck. The vampires watching gasped and surged forward. Naylor's eyes flashed wide and then he came again – not hard, no jets, but frothy spunk spilling out down his cock on to his balls, blobbing in his pubic hair – as Reynauld rammed home and shot his own semen up that abused anal hole, drinking deep from his throat.

For a moment they held, shuddering, together. Then Reynauld thrust the other man off and dropped him on the table. Blood crawled down Naylor's neck and chest and the others shifted tensely. The room had a pulse now: I could feel it hammering at my skull. If Reynauld let them off the leash they would drain Naylor dry.

'Get out,' said Reynauld, standing. Jizz dripped from his cock on to the other man's buttocks. 'All of you, get out. Naylor: final warning. There won't be another.'

The vampires withdrew in silence, one at a time. Naylor, last of all, had to crawl off the table.

As soon as they were gone Reynauld stalked from the room, his robe of shadows gathering anew and swirling around him like spilled ink in water. I let out a ragged breath and sagged against the door frame, catching myself trembling. Under my suit I was wet with perspiration. Between my legs I was wet with something else, and though I was horribly ashamed at my response to the violence I couldn't deny it. I could feel my pulse at my throat and groin: I was lucky none of them had turned on me in the middle of all that and torn me open.

'Double the security detail this week, Colin,' I said, my voice unsteady, as I returned to the foyer. The man behind the desk stared at me, nervous but unable to ask. Fumbling a little, I bolted the front door and cast salt across the threshold, then went back to draw the velvet over Roisin's mirror.

'Amanda.'

Reynauld's voice, in my head. My heart thumped.

'The bathroom.'

Moving quickly, I walked through the house. The marble-clad master bathroom was warm with steam as I entered, and the lights low. He stood with his back to me behind the layered arms of the glass screens, his head bowed and shoulders set angrily, outstretched fingertips on the polished black marble and the water running full-blast at the back of his neck. I watched the water swirl around his dark feet, running into the drain between them and carrying away the grime and the tension and the lust. I saw the way he rolled his shoulders under the flow, working each stubborn muscle. Inside me something clenched with an exquisite, tender pain.

How could my heart not melt for a man who craved a long hot shower?

I didn't say anything. He knew I was there, and he would instruct me if he wished to. Instead I withdrew a fresh white towel from the cupboard and waited, watching him. I could follow the ebb of his anger by the way his shoulders slowly sagged, the way he finally moved to rub his neck and scalp, playing the water through his dark hair and then across his chest and down his torso. He soaped himself and I wished they were my hands massaging that body, my fingers chasing the suds cascading down his skin.

At last he turned off the water and stood there dripping, still facing the wall. I kicked off my heels and stepped between the arms of glass to hand him the towel, my eyes lingering on the water drops clinging to his skin, on the wet curls at the back of his head, on the runnels licking their way down his back and thighs. Reynauld wrapped the towel about his hips and tucked it in, then turned and set his back to the corner of the shower, leaning against the angled marble. His expression was haunted; he looked so weary and despairing that my heart felt like it would crack.

'I handled that badly, didn't I?'

What? I wanted to ask. You mean humiliating Naylor in front of everyone like that? Yes, I'd call that badly handled. I shrugged one shoulder.

'I shouldn't have lost my temper. He just makes me so angry. Why won't he listen? Is it so difficult to understand, what I'm trying to say?'

'I think you should have killed him, to be honest. He's a psychopath.'

Reynauld's mouth tugged into an unhappy smile as he admitted, 'He's a little short on empathy, certainly.' Then, with a sudden change of tack, he was ruefully defending the man he'd just beaten down. 'But that doesn't come naturally to haemivores. We have to learn it.'

Why couldn't Reynauld be as cynical as me? I had the distinct feeling that empathy was something the others had learned to fake. 'He's a killer.'

'We're all killers.' His voice was ragged.

That wasn't what I'd meant, but I couldn't argue with him. How can you possibly make a man twelve centuries older than you listen to a word you say? It's bad enough with ordinary men – can you imagine a forty-year-old taking advice from a teenager of sixteen? Now try and grasp the gap between Reynauld and me. If I were like him, if I were knit of strength and night and savage need, then he might hear me. But I wasn't, and never would be. I just looked at the water beaded on his bare chest and wanted in my frustration to strike him, to bruise him, to pin him to the wall and kiss him until he realised how much I loved him.

I think he saw the pain in my eyes, mirroring his own. With a curl of his fingers he gestured me closer and I dared to lay a hand on his bare chest. The feet of my stockings were soaked from the shower tray.

'Oh, Amanda,' he whispered. He took my face tenderly in both hands, brushing his knuckles across my cheek, using his thumbs to stroke the paths of my bones. His eyes narrowed, his lips parting. I trembled, knowing that he could sense my desire: he'd be able to feel the race of my blood beneath his fingertips, hear my painfully pounding heart – and to smell the heat of my sex.

Oh, to hell with it: why try to pretend? After all these years he still made me as wildly horny as an eighteen-year-old, as desperate as a smackhead craving a fix. Try as I might there was nothing I could do to hide it, not from him. Reynauld dipped his face to mine and I felt the brush of his lashes on my temple, the caress of his breath on my cheek as he nuzzled me. It was almost like he was searching for something. It was almost like he was scared to tell me what it was. How crazy was I, imagining that? But I could read something in his eyes as he lifted his face from mine: something wrong, something new and uncertain of itself, even as he acknowledged my lust. Gently he reached a hand down to the heat between my legs. My wraparound skirt was secured by a row of poppers angled across my right thigh – formal propriety combined with ease of access – and the serial click of their surrender sounded loud in the shower chamber. He had to stoop a little to reach between my legs in their dove-grey hold-up stockings. My knickers were grey gauze too, the shaved mound of my sex overlaid with appliquéd white lace flowers like a moonlit garden. Panties so beautiful I'd been almost nervous to put them on, wondering if I really deserved anything so lovely at my age.

As his fingers explored the garden a sigh escaped my lips and he caught it in his own. His eyes threatened to drown me in their darkness. Delicately he slipped the lace aside and I lifted my hips to grant him access to my sex, placing both hands on his ribs as I shifted my balance. He was hot from the shower and thrillingly wet. Pearls of water burst at my fingertips as he found my own wetness, my own pearl, and rolled his finger delicately around that tiny mound, finding it engorged.

I nearly fell to the floor.

'Oh, God,' I whispered, losing my all sense of danger, rubbing my hands over his flanks and arching my spine. My heart was racing. Lust and joy: I had him to myself for the moment, I had his complete attention. He threatened me with little biting kisses, on my face, my lips, my ear – his teeth never brought into play but every touch sending a jolt through me – yet he kept pulling away to try and look me in the face, watching the flow of my reactions as he fingered my clit, stealing my sex juices to roll it slippery between two fingers. I couldn't do it: I couldn't look him in the eye. I rubbed against him like a cat and writhed and then it became almost a game of chase, him trying to catch my gaze, kiss my lips, force me to acknowledge what he was doing to me as his fingers drove me further and further along the road of my arousal.

I could resist only so long, and then I surrendered.

I was almost dancing against him now, thrusting my hips and making dark damp patches on my top as I pressed my breasts against his wet chest. Abandoning caution I reached to his crotch, to the layers of thick soft towelling and the unmistakable bulge of his hardening cock beneath. As I grabbed it he vented a groan, stopped merely massaging my clit and began to flick with that staccato vibration that he knew worked so well for me. The towel began to slip from about his hips as I lost all self-control, all dignity: panting and blaspheming I fell against him and came on his hand, my legs nearly falling from under me, Reynauld catching me round the waist with his other arm to hold me up.

'Oh, God,' I mumbled into his skin. 'Oh, God.'

When I lifted my burning face from his chest, the towel was no longer wrapped around his bare hips but hung from the erect baton of his cock, held there by my tight right hand. We both looked down at it, and I gave it a slow hard squeeze through the heavy towelling before letting the fabric slip to the floor. That turgid flesh didn't yield at all. His cock was stiff once more, his balls riding high in a scrotum no longer soft and velvety but now tight and bulging. I brushed cock and balls with unsteady fingertips: he would take me now, before I had time to come down from the afterglow of my climax. He would take me and fuck me and bite me and that was exactly what I wanted.

'Amanda ...' His voice was a whisper. He bit his own lip. The ache in his voice persuaded me to meet his gaze. 'Would you ...?'

No completion to that question. No words for what he wanted. Just his glance tentatively indicating his cock. My eyes widened as I understood, my heart kicking against my breastbone. In 27 years he'd never asked this of me, and I'd never seen him ask or permit it of any woman. It wasn't even thinkable.

'Reynauld?'

He swallowed. 'Please.'

Slowly, without answering, I slid to my knees, pulling the damp towel under them for padding. My mouth brushed his flat stomach, the damp hollow of his navel, the thickening flare of his treasure-trail of hair. I licked my lips and his cock jerked. A big, blunt glans, glistening with pre-cum already. Slowly, savouring the thickness and heat of his meat, I took him in my mouth and sucked.

It was 26 years since I'd given head. Vampires ... Oh, God, for vampires there is no suggestion of submission or pleasure-giving in the act of going down. Just the opposite. The mouth is a weapon, the feeder dominant, the fellated a blood-sacrifice. They might accept it from another of their own kind: they would never submit to a mere human. What I was doing to Reynauld was, in vampire terms, grossly perverted and utterly shameful.

He groaned, a stifled desperate noise, and ran his fingers through my hair.

Get this: there I was on my knees, my lips wrapped about his cock, serving him with my mouth – all so very much what I wanted – and as far as he was concerned he was the one yielding, I was the one in control. And maybe in a way he was right. I swept my tongue in sweet circles over the head of his cock, penetrating the tiny mouth of his glans with the very tip, tasting his seeping eagerness. Then I changed, made my mouth all soft and accommodating as I engulfed him as deep as I could, swallowing him to the back of my throat. Reynauld pressed the root of his cock, angling it all the better for me to take, bracing his legs wider. His length was excessive for my mouth and his girth enough to stretch my jaw, but I slid up and down on that big cock and he responded to every change in pressure, every swirl of my tongue, every little slurp, as if I were plucking notes from his soul. For me it was extraordinary: for once I was calling the shots, I was in charge of the pace, I could give or deny. I felt like a goddess, encompassing this creature of night and dread, but at the same time I was a worshipper, most willing of slaves, his cock my idol on which I would pour out my life.

Why? Why did he want this?

He didn't thrust, not once. The more I sucked the more he pressed himself into that corner, his braced thighs stiff with strain, tiny trembles vibrating through his flesh. I couldn't see his face from this angle but something told me he had his head back, his throat stretched taut. His balls were so tight now; those big overcharged balls that were an unending source of semen and venery, full of seed that would never live, brimming and taut and ready to pump his sticky cream into any pussy or any ass. Or into my mouth:

he began to come, taking me by surprise.

'Amanda!' he gasped.

I pulled back a little, holding him on my tongue so that he could see, if he were looking, the gush of his spunk. That didn't last: I had to grab him and swallow as fast as I could because it was filling my mouth and spilling from my lips. The taste of him exploded in my head, wild and tangy and sweet. And cold. God – so cold. Spasm after spasm, his cock jumping against my tongue, until he'd emptied his balls down my throat and I was still sucking, still wanting more, wanting it never to end. Like a vampire.

Reynauld's legs gave way quite suddenly; he slid down the marble, stared at me wildly, then pulled me into his embrace. I thought he was going to bite me – and bite me hard – as I lay up against him, but he didn't. He just held me, stroking my hair, both of us huddled there on the floor of the shower like fools. Was it comfort he needed of me? I started to cry a little, out of shock I think; out of a sort of joyful terror. He held on to me the way a child alone in the dark clings to a soft toy, and I could only wonder.

(Reynauld)

And this is Reynauld, the Good Shepherd, whose authority over the other five is held by dint of careful planning and the minute application of brute force when necessary. He's not the oldest of them, because that distinction belongs to Roisin, but he's hardly young even by vampire standards. His name is French but he isn't, although should he choose to speak the language his grasp of it is perfect, and – just as in English – he has an aristocratic accent. He speaks Spanish too and Portuguese – Old World style, not American – as well as Arabic, Farsi, Old Syriac, Italian, Latin and Greek, all with equal fluency, along with many others on a less familiar basis. He always did have a facility with languages. He was 34 years old and a translator and scribe in the House of Wisdom in Baghdad when he died, in the year 218 after Hijra, which was the year AD 833 in the Roman reckoning. Both calendars were ones he was quite familiar with, being a man of sublime education.

His name then was not Reynauld, of course; it was Kerim ibn Zarad al-Razi, but he abandoned his Arabic name when he gave up his religion. There is no place in Islam for vampires, whose very sustenance is harram: *forbidden. The Faithful cannot drink blood. Yet, brought up in that world, he misses the strictures of faith. In 1907 he took up a bare-bones Buddhism and now meditation is as much a part of his nightly routine as feeding. Right speech; right action; right livelihood; right effort; right mindfulness; right meditation; right understanding; right resolve. The spiritual discipline appeals to him, as does its practicality: he carries no theological baggage along the Eightfold Path, no particular hope of reincarnation or redemption.*

He adopted a Greek name first, and others after that as he moved about from land to land. There have been so many names now that he hardly remembers them. 'Reynauld' came quite late on, when he posed as a French Huguenot immigrant in the sixteenth century. He has done well for himself in this, the latest of his adopted homes. His investments have been wise, his habit of building alliances among the living a key to his success. He is a broker in political games, seeking not power but stability and prosperity. Being in every way physically superior to the masses of the living, he sees it as his duty to care for them. He is benign, paternal and restrained in his dealings.

As Naylor says, if Reynauld were a farmer he would insist on keeping his livestock free-range, organic and in the most humane conditions possible. He would even give some of them names.

You'll have to be very, very lucky to meet Reynauld. To attract his attention, you'll have to move in the right circles, go the right parties, make your face known where he – or, more likely, those he entrusts with choosing for him – will find you. It's not that he's a snob about the social calibre of his paramours, but that he simply has no time to absent himself from the echelons of power. Even eternal life is not time enough.

So this is Reynauld's style of feeding: he lies in a bespoke handcrafted bed on an ocean of satin sheets, and there are six women with him. He likes to feel himself surrounded by feminine bodies, accommodating and delighted; to smother himself in soft curves, in warm flesh whose capillaries thrill with life. It's the giggles of pleasure that he appreciates, the soft appreciative moans as he takes a tender nibble, the tangle of smooth limbs which seems to have neither beginning or end, the wriggling press of bodies that seems ultimately to be not many individuals but one all-encompassing Female. He works vigorously at giving her satisfaction; he's not a lazy lover despite being hopelessly outnumbered. So his hard, dark body is in constant active motion in the middle of all that feminine flesh, his cock plunging into pussy after pussy.

The women often play together too, either from genuine desire or from the assumption that it will arouse him as it does other men. And it does arouse him, very much. In particular, watching living humans sucking at one another makes his cock harden and his balls clench. Provoked and rampant he will mount and ride them all, in turn.

You must understand that the women are all there voluntarily, in full knowledge of what he requires, and that not one of them will go away in the morning sexually unsatisfied, and that they are probably not the same ones who will grace his bed tomorrow. Reynauld does not have to hunt: there are more than enough women who are only too eager to follow up on the rumours of this wealthy, handsome man who's kinky for group sex and drinks a little blood, never more than a few mouthfuls from each of his paramours in a night, and in return is the most exquisite, prodigious lover. Most of them are young and every one of them is beautiful. Those that show unhealthy attitudes – too addicted to the bites, too clingy, too jealous – are coolly and firmly deposed from his favoured circle. It's easy enough to fill the gap with another model, another talented actress, another rising TV personality. Thus he keeps a list of select and discreet bedfellows on call, the cream of the City, and treats them with courtesy and generosity.

Not one of them is permitted any delusions of emotional intimacy.

You'll never find a man in that emperor-sized bed. Reynauld has no aversion to feeding from men, but he will not tolerate another cock among his hens. Ben calls them his harem, which Reynauld finds mildly offensive. But it's better than 'pets'.

Yet for all his authority and his confidence in the way he has chosen for his kin, Reynauld lives with a creeping fear. It looks him in the face every dawn, when he surges gasping from sleep like a man struggling from deep water. He does sleep now, whereas in the past he never needed to. He is growing older: not weakening, but drifting inexorably to the shadows. For decades he has struggled to remain conscious during daylight hours, even for as little as a few minutes, but these days he knows the battle is lost. As the sun rises he slides into a blackness so complete that even physical damage can't wake him, so he must be sure to be somewhere safe when the dawn strikes. 'Safe', in the old days, used to mean a shuttered room. These days it is a basement beneath The Bonding, behind a steel security door that would shame most bank vaults, with a lock that depends on fingerprint recognition and a manual seven-digit backup key known only to himself and Amanda. He trusts no one but her, and mistrusts his peers outright. If they knew how constrained he was it would make him terribly vulnerable.

For the first time he is beginning to feel anxious about the others.

Inside the vault is an airtight steel box with heavy bolts on the inside of the lid. It is, he recognises sourly, a sarcophagus in all but name. Reynauld despises the gothic accoutrements of the vampire condition. He doesn't even like the word 'vampire', so redolent of Technicolor B-movie kitsch – medieval/Victorian wenches in 70s makeup and cheesecake heroes strutting through faux Romanian villages – and he uses other synonyms instead, but practicality has led him to this pass: he must be safe while he rests. Worse still, he has found that he can no longer pass out painlessly upon even the softest of mattresses within. He must have newly-dug earth beneath him to make the transition bearable; something about the scent, he admits, is soothing. Again, no one but Amanda knows. She's the one in charge of ordering in bags of topsoil along with The Bonding's other supplies.

His worst nightmare is coming to pass: he is turning into something less than human, instead of more. Reynauld is following the same path that Roisin treads before him, and he dreads it. He will become in time as she is now: a thing of shadow and nightmare, an insubstantial haunting without true form or individuality. It is inevitable. And Reynauld, who has fought more than any other vampire to retain his humanity, rails with all his heart against this. He who has had so many names and homes now makes sure to hoard mementoes of each one. He takes out his souvenirs when he is alone – a broken cup, a lace handkerchief, a calling card, a hundred different pieces of inconsequential tat – and turns them over in his hands, reliving the memories, making sure that they are still strong.

He'd died in the spring, when the mountain crocuses were just opening …

He'd been sent out from the House of Wisdom to find a book. Such journeys were far from uncommon because the Caliph had ordered that a copy of every book of human knowledge, in whatsoever language it was written, be brought to the House and copied there into Arabic, to make the building an unequalled treasury of the understanding of man. Agents of the House were dispatched, so often as news came to them of a particularly valuable tome, as far as Constantinople and Alexandria and Ethiopia to make purchases. Kerim, as he had been called then, had been translating a torn scroll when he'd come across a reference to a heathen astronomer – a woman, to his surprise – who had been buried with her books in the Zagros Mountains to the east, many years ago. He'd made application to be allowed to search out these volumes, and had set out from Baghdad with an entourage of two trained warriors and three servants; they aimed to travel fast and provoke as little notice as possible.

High in the Zagros they'd found the little village indicated in the fragment, and heard that the cliff face at the head of the valley was known as Umm Hol, which had excited Kerim greatly because that was the name of the dead astronomer herself, or perhaps her title, since it meant Mother of Terror. They'd made their way to the cliff face and there, high over the valley floor, had spotted a slit-shaped opening in the bare rock that seemed to have been backfilled with rubble. Faint carvings suggested an inscription below that opening, but they were weathered beyond legibility. Constructing ladders of ropes pinned to the rock-face and working in turns, they'd unloaded the rock infill into the stream bed below, working quickly because the villagers had turned hostile and often came to throw stones at them. By the end of the first day they'd got inside the cave chiselled into the cliff, and in the middle of that night they'd uncovered a stone sarcophagus cut from the rock itself. It had taken three men to slide back the slab that covered it, and then Kerim had bent over to see what had been hidden beneath for untold years.

A hand, filthy and stick-thin, had shot out of that dark space and sliced into his neck. He'd fallen back on to the floor, and then seen another arm seize the servant from the other side of the tomb and drag him in, snapping his spine. Slumped against the cave wall and trying desperately to staunch the blood running from his throat, Kerim had watched the other men panic. The other two servants had blundered toward the exit; one fell out as the other pushed him. The torches had gone flying, shadows leaping wildly about the cave. The two soldiers had pulled their swords and struck at the creature, but it had done them no good; it had risen out of the tomb, striking swifter than an arrow flies from the bow: blackened, skeletal, mere rags of skin on bone, with blazing eyes and long yellow teeth. It had gorged itself on the living and slain them all, and finally made its way to Kerim, who'd been barely clinging to consciousness. Its cadaverous face looming over his was the last memory he had of his living years.

It had spared him death, he'd found out, because it was acute enough to realise it was centuries since it had last moved among men and it wanted a guide. Spared him death, but not torment. For the rest of the night and all the next day and night, as the changes had ripped through his tissues, he'd suffered the agonies of rebirth while Umm Hol hissed questions in archaic Persian and lapped the blood oozing from his throat. Luckily for him the tomb faced east: as the dawn sun lanced over a mountain ridge the creature had retreated hissing, wisps of smoke rising from its exposed skin, then crawled back into its sarcophagus and pulled the slab over itself. On the second night it had gone hunting and returned with a goat whose blood it had fed to him.

On the second morning Kerim had woken to find his neck healed. He'd risen, discovered himself unable to bear the dawn light in his eyes, and withdrawn into the shadows at the back of the cave. He had seen what the light did to his captor; he didn't imagine himself immune. Three men with poles had been needed to move the lid of the tomb the first time, but he did it himself now. Umm Hol, replete with the blood, lay within – no longer a leathery corpse but a slender woman with hair like a midnight sea. Her lips had been full and red, as moist as the crease between her legs, and her dark nipples had seemed to stare up at him. Without hesitation he'd plucked her body from the sarcophagus, embraced it in his arms and walked out on to the sunlit apron of rock.

Umm Hol had burned, screaming, to greasy ash and cinders

in his arms, but to Kerim's stunned dismay he himself had remained unharmed.

He hadn't even had a name for the thing he had become.

It's been a long road he's walked since that day, and everything he has learned he's discovered on his own, without guidance from vampire-kind. He has done things he's now ashamed of, and walked in the darkest of places. But somehow over the years he's finally managed to work out a peace with himself and his nature – a peace which still holds, for the moment.

So this is Reynauld, who sits in the dark before an old tin chest of junk, turning the pieces in his hands, gazing at the past but seeing with dread the future.

6: Five for the Symbols at Your Door

The man walked up to the shop window, scanned the name on the frontage and frowned. The line *Mind Body & Spirit* seemed to fill him with dismay. Cerri, standing behind the till, watched through the glass as his gaze dropped to the window display itself: witchcraft books and crystals and goddess statues and a jolly Ganesha figure that held lit incense in one outstretched hand. His expression, which had been tense up to this point, dropped like a failed soufflé and set into a stodgy solid of disapproval.

Cerri bit her lip thoughtfully. This was probably him. She was even surer when he looked around for the building number and checked a small piece of paper in his hand. Then his gaze fell on the lintel over the door, and she watched as he physically recoiled, taking a step back across the pavement and nearly backing into a passing mother and pram. Cerri continued to watch as he apologised. After that he looked around, walked away a few paces, hesitated and turned back to look at the shop.

Enough, she thought, reaching the door and opening it. His eyebrows shot up as she gestured to him with a crook of her fingers and a smile. He didn't look at all pleased, but he sidled back toward her.

'You're Doug?'

'Uh … Douglas.' He was younger than she'd been expecting, or perhaps just had an open youthful face. He looked like he'd grown that goatee in an ill-advised attempt to make up for eyelashes so long that they were almost feminine, but it had come out an unfortunate gingery shade despite his blond hair above. He was wearing a jacket and open shirt and chinos and she didn't think she'd ever seen a man look so ill at ease.

He was cute, she thought. Cute like a puppy. And nearly as helpless.

'And you're Cerri?'

'That's right. You want to come in?'

His gaze drifted up again, to the lintel where the iron pentagram was fixed. 'I don't think so.'

'You asked for help.'

'I'm sorry.' He started to back away. 'I won't waste any more of your time.'

'It symbolises the whole human being,' she said, more firmly. 'The five points represent earth, air, fire, water and spirit.' She smiled. 'Absolutely nothing to do with devil worship, I promise.'

His mouth opened a little, his eyes searching her. She waited, giving him the chance to take in her long corded braids, the blue and lilac hair weaves, the stud through her nose, the rather generous cleavage of her low-cut dress. This was his last chance.

'Um,' said he.

'Amanda said you were looking for help. Come on in.' Turning back into the shop interior, she didn't wait to see if he would obey. But she was pleased when he did. Once inside he looked around with undisguised suspicion at the bright and glittery New Age wares, as if he expected the walls to start running with blood.

'Drop the latch, will you? And turn the sign over so it says *Closed.*' He cleared his throat, but she carried on before he could question her: 'I'm assuming you'd like this to be confidential?'

'Yes,' he admitted faintly. 'That'd be good.'

'Right. Cup of tea?'

'Um ...'

'Camomile, or sage, or raspberry 'n' rose-petal? It won't be poisoned. Or spiked.'

He flushed. 'Raspberry then?'

'This way.'

She led him through the door at the rear of the small shop and up the stairs to her apartment. She was rather proud of her flat, as she was proud of her cleavage: she knew it made a favourable impression on most people. Everything was light and clean, the floors all bare pale wood, the walls cream, the furniture draped with white throws. She took him into the living room where a case of books was the only thing that clashed with the decor, and sat him down. He glanced at the pictures hung on the walls: framed collages of dead leaves and pressed flowers and natural *objets trouvés*. He brushed a large driftwood stump beside his chair with nervous fingers.

'The pictures are nice. Did you make them?'

Cerri nodded, pleased. 'I sell them online. Back in a sec.'

When she came back in with mugs of tea he was still perched in the armchair, his elbows on his knees, but she was fairly sure he'd been peering at the books on her shelf.

'You're a Wiccan,' he said, as if concluding an investigation.

'I'm a pagan,' she corrected. 'But not Wiccan. And not,' she added with a grin, 'any sort of Satanist. Promise.'

'OK.' He had a look that said he was reserving judgement, but willing to talk. She took the light out of his eyes with her next words though.

'So, what's your problem?'

He looked down into his fragrant tisane. 'I'm not sure that …' He let the sentence hang miserably.

'Let me make it easier. It was Amanda Grey who rang me and asked me to help you.'

'Amanda?'

'Silvery hair, expensive clothes, very respectable looking? You had an appointment with her at nine this morning.'

'Oh. Oh, yes … She didn't tell me her name. Amanda.'

'So it's something to do with vampires then?'

Doug's eyes narrowed. 'You know about them?'

'You'd be amazed how many people know.' She slipped her shoes off and tucked her feet up beneath her on the sofa. 'What's your story, Doug?'

He swallowed. 'I'm being threatened by one.'

'A vampire?'

He nodded.

'In what way?'

'Didn't Amanda tell you?'

'She hasn't told me anything except that you need help. Start at the beginning, Doug.'

'Right.' He wet his lips. 'Well, a week ago this man … came up to me. He started to make threats. He's been round my house and … waiting for me after work. He stands in the garden at night. He turns up out of the blue …' He shivered. 'You can't see him coming. He's just there. I went to the police, of course. I said I was being stalked and threatened. When I told them what he'd said they …' There was a moment's pause. 'They said it wasn't police business.'

'What had he said?'

Doug stared across the room at the window, a muscle in his jaw flexing. 'He said he was going to rip out my throat with his teeth and ... um ... make use of my still-warm body. And that, apparently, is not something the police see fit to take seriously.'

'I see.'

'But they gave me a number to call, said it was a special harassment helpline, and I was given an interview with this woman. Amanda. It didn't seem right to me. Little office, no nameplate on the door, barely any furniture. I didn't believe it was straight up. And she wasn't exactly sympathetic.'

'But she believed you?'

Doug snorted, bitterly. 'Oh, yes, she believed me. She took notes on everything and then told me to Lie Back and Think of England.'

'What?'

'Words to that effect anyway. She said the man was lying, that he wouldn't kill me or cause any permanent damage: that he was just trying to scare me. That was how he got his kicks. She said he'd only take a little blood – maybe a pint – and there wasn't any health risk, so that's all right then. Then she showed me the door.'

She's almost certainly right, Cerri thought, but didn't say it out loud: she could see he wouldn't take it well. 'OK. I'm going to have to ask: are you sure he's a real vampire?'

'Yes!' He was surprisingly vehement and he seemed to recognise that. 'I know ... I've seen one before. I know what they're like.' Abruptly he switched tone. 'And anyway I saw him; he walked into a shadow and just vanished. I mean that: he disappeared.'

'OK then. What does he look like?'

'Um. Shorter than me. About five-six, I think. Thin build. Dark, longish hair. Young: about eighteen, I'd guess. Quite striking features.'

Cerri nodded thoughtfully. 'Sounds like Naylor.'

'You're on first-name terms with them?'

She wanted to pat his ruffled feathers. 'I've seen some of them. Naylor's ... not nice, certainly. He likes to play rough. But he won't hurt you, not really: he can't kill you. You needn't panic. There are limits on them, you see, and they don't go beyond that.'

'But forcing me down and biting me is within those limits?'

She sucked the inside of her lip. 'It doesn't hurt that much. And afterwards it feels wonderful. Really great. Plenty of people seek it out, for the thrill.'

'And what about the rape?'

'Um.' She met his stony glare mildly. 'It won't be rape by that point, believe me. You'll want it. It's an effect of the bites.'

'I see.' His voice was clipped. 'So if you go to a club and someone spikes your drink with GHB and has sex with you when you're too wasted to care, you're saying you wouldn't count that as rape, would you? You're saying that's OK?'

Cerri winced. 'Fair point. It's not great. But it could be a lot worse. A *whole* lot worse. There are vampires out there and they're stronger than us and faster than us and they have these weird abilities ... They can mess with the way we see things. Like a sort of mental suggestion. And we are lucky they don't abuse that power more than they do. Believe me, they're holding back.'

'Lucky? To be treated like serfs or cattle?'

'Yeah, that's pretty much it. The fact is that we're not top of the food-chain. And it's painful to realise that, I do get it.'

He ground his teeth. 'Well, someone should do something.

Someone should stop them. If the police, the government know … They ought to do something!'

'Really?' Cerri sighed. 'D'you want to see a real fight between us and them, Doug? D'you want to see how much they could hurt us if they really tried?'

'I thought you were going to be on my side.'

'I am on your side. But I'm just being realistic.'

He put his mug down carefully on the low table, his face stiff. 'Thank you for the tea,' he said, standing. 'I can see you're not going to be able to help.'

'I didn't say that.' She looked up at him sympathetically. 'I can't kill him, if that's what you're after: I'm not bloody Buffy, you know. But I can show you how to protect yourself. How to put him off.'

He hung for a moment then hesitantly sat again. 'This isn't going to involve … magic, is it?' The way he said the word made it sound dirty.

'Why?'

'No magic.' His voice was hard. 'Absolutely not. I'd rather he bit me.'

That made her sit up, her cheeks flushing. 'Why not? If you believe in vampires, why not in magic?'

His glare was rather diminished in effect by the fact that she was finding him irresistibly cute. 'I'm a vicar.'

'Oh!' For a moment she struggled to think of anything she could say that was even close to polite. 'Well,' she mumbled at last, 'that explains why Naylor's picking on you. He'd find that even more amusing.'

'Well, it's one vicar joke I could live without,' he replied, and she wanted to give him a kiss for that. He did have a sense of humour after all.

'Um,' it was her turn to say, and she looked away as she

tried to sort her head out. She knew that plenty of her friends would jeer in his face and throw him out if they were in her position. Lots of pagans felt that they were an oppressed minority constantly under attack from a Christian-based Establishment. Funnily enough – she knew this because her sister was an evangelical – lots of Christians were convinced that *they* were the oppressed minority, constantly under attack from a secular society that had sold out wholeheartedly to sex, drugs and lunatic New Age individualism. 'Have you tried going to your Church? Naylor's pretty old: he might be vulnerable to Christian ritual.'

Doug shook his head. 'Sorry: I'm an Anglican. The Church of England "doesn't have an official standpoint on the existence or spiritual provenance of so-called vampires." That's what I was told. We sit on the fence on this – as on so many things. The Catholic Church ...' He rolled his eyes. 'They believe, all right. I've talked to some of my colleagues at ecumenical meetings. Tried to, anyway. The Catholic Church makes a great big noise about the reality of spiritual warfare, but they've got an absolute lockdown on any priest attempting to tackle vampires or discuss their existence. I can't work out whether it's siege mentality or ... well, in my Dan Brown moments I wonder if they're in some sort of pact.'

Cerri grimaced, and impulsively reached over to squeeze his hand. 'Don't worry, Doug. I'm on your side. We'll give it a go, eh?'

'No magic.' His hand was cool and firm and though he didn't respond he didn't shrug her off either.

'All right then, if that's what you want. Now. ...' She sat back, already starting a mental checklist. 'I'm going to have to get some stuff together. If you give me your address I'll meet you there in a couple of hours.'

* * *

The vicarage was out in a suburb, in what would once have been a village on the outskirts of the City; some of the oldest buildings were very large and would have been grand in their time. Then gradually every inch of green space had been filled in with more houses. The majority were 1930s semis but in the 70s someone had lined the whole of the high street with concrete blocks that looked like they were winners of an Ugly Competition and now hosted exhausted-looking discount tile emporia and charity shops, along with an international array of takeaways. Then the whole place had filled up with cars – cars parked nose to tail down every inch of kerb, creeping in single file down one-way streets barely wide enough to allow wing-mirrors to pass each other. The grand houses had been split up into flats that housed students for the nearby university college, and the air smelled of kebab fat and exhaust fumes. Tucked away behind the shops was a large brick church and in its shadow a double-fronted house which would have looked quite gracious if it had been given a newer coat of paint.

Over his door was one of those Ichthus fish symbols that Christians liked. Cerri wrinkled her nose at it.

Doug opened the door to her with a nod and a half-smile. He looked rumpled. One hand was thrust into the pocket of his loose trousers.

'Hi,' said she. 'Nice house.'

'Thanks. The diocese are selling it and moving me into a semi.' He waved her into the hall and added, 'We need the money.'

The place certainly had a spartan look despite its spaciousness: it was obvious he lived on his own. Cerri waited as he closed the front door and turned to stare at her, blinking.

'You OK, Doug?'

'Uh ... Yeah, I've just woken up, that's all. I haven't been sleeping at nights.' He rubbed his hand across his face; she noticed that his hair was sticking up untidily. 'I must have crashed out when I got back. Slept for an hour, I think.'

'You look like you need coffee.'

'Um. Yeah. In the kitchen.' He pointed down the hall. 'After you.' She started to head down there. 'What's in the rucksack?' he said to her back.

'Salt, mostly.' With a glance around the roomy but bare kitchen, Cerri shucked off the big rucksack to lay it on the dining table. Its straps tugged at the shoulders of her blouse and, aware that Doug was staring, she glanced down and saw that her emerald-green bra cup and the plump bulge of her right breast were both exposed, 'Sorry,' she said, more cheeky than sincere, smoothing the cloth back into place. He shook himself and turned away abruptly.

'Can I get you a drink? Coffee? Tea?'

'Black tea if you like, thanks.' She leaned one hip against the dining table. He was very seriously busying himself looking for mugs and spoons and though she waited he didn't turn round or speak again. 'Let's hope no one reports this to the tabloids,' she said with a grin. 'Can't you see the headline? "The Witch and the Vicar!"'

'Oh ... Please don't. That's all I need.' He tapped the top of the kettle in agitation as the heating element began to hum. Cerri wondered why he was so determinedly keeping his back to her, then realised with delight: he had a stiffy. He must have woken up with one when she knocked, and the poor guy was embarrassed. With a smile to herself she made a big, noisy show out of undoing the rucksack's buckles and straps, pulling out bag after bag of kosher salt and stacking them, until Doug felt safe enough to rejoin her.

'What do we need salt for?'

'Sealing the entrances to the house. You'll see.' She fished out a plastic bottle the size of a stick grenade and put it down in front of him. 'These are for you.'

'Garlic capsules?'

'One, four times a day at six-hour intervals, day and night. Garlic is your friend, Doug.' With a flourish she produced a glass bottle from one of the deep side pockets of the rucksack: "Garlic- and ginger-infused olive oil", said the label. 'I got this at the deli.'

Doug startled slightly and licked his lips. 'I assumed that sort of thing was just superstition.'

'Not exactly.' Cerri sat down and tried a cautious sip of her tea. 'Vampires are all different, you see. The older they are, the weirder they get, and the stronger – but the more things you can use against them. Like, a young vampire, a modern one: he could walk on consecrated ground. But an old one couldn't.' She had a sudden anxious thought. 'Naylor's not actually been into your church, has he?'

'No. He hangs out by the lich gate.' He grimaced sheepishly. 'I've actually spent the last few nights in the church: it seemed safer. Not exactly comfortable though.'

'Well, it's good news, in a way. Anyway, garlic's just about the one thing they none of them like; the taste turns their stomachs. Get it in your bloodstream, Doug.'

He popped the top and extracted a gelatine capsule; it glowed golden between his fingers, like a drop of amber. 'Well, that's simple enough.'

'Just remember: once you start down that road you're going to be taking it for the rest of your life. They've got long memories.' She smiled bleakly. 'And that's assuming you really are prepared to piss Naylor off. Everything I know about him tells me you'd be better off giving him what he wants.'

'No,' he said flatly, and swallowed the garlic capsule. 'Now what about this salt?'

'OK. Before it gets dark, you want to go round and lay a line of salt across every outer door and every window, and the fireplaces if you've got them.'

'Like he can't step over a line?'

'I'm hoping not.'

'That sounds ...' He spread his hands. 'Dodgy.'

'No. It's like – think of the Israelites being told to paint the door lintels with blood, in Exodus, so that the Angel of Death would pass on by their houses. That wasn't magic, was it? It's a mark of territory. Salt stands for blood, in this case. It says, "Private property: keep out." Like the consecrated ground thing. Vampires – old ones anyway – I think the world they live in is different to the one we see.'

'And it's got to be kosher salt?'

'No, but that underlines the point we're making. And before you ask, they can't go into mosques or gurdwaras or Hindu temples either.'

He didn't argue, just nodded. He looked tired and strung-out. Cerri felt the desire flex within her to kiss that unhappy mouth and give him something completely different to think about.

'You might as well start down here then.' She pushed a two-kilo plastic bag of salt toward him. 'Grab some scissors.'

'Are you going to show me first?'

'I'm not touching it. It's your house; your God. Make sure it's a good thick band, that's all.'

She stood at his shoulder and watched as he poured out

a line a handspan thick across the kitchen windowsill and smoothed it with his palm. 'Now you need to mark it.'

'With what?'

'The signs of your faith. A cross or whatever. The Lord's Prayer in Latin.'

'Do I look like a Catholic priest?' he wondered dryly. 'You'll be asking me for holy water and the Host next, will you?'

'It'd help.'

'Sorry. I could bless some bread, but it'd still just be bread as far as the Church is concerned.' He held his fingertip out to the salt, then hesitated and looked over his shoulder at her, his eyes narrowed. 'If you were doing this for yourself, what would you be drawing?'

'I'd be writing in hieroglyphs.'

'And what exactly would you write?'

'The invocation of my goddess, Bast.'

'The cat?'

'The goddess of joy and pleasure. That's my particular path, Doug.'

He exhaled down his nose, almost a snort but not quite. Then he drew in the salt with his fingertip: the Ichthus fish shape flanked by crosses. As he took up the bag and turned away from the window she failed to step back and he bumped into her hard enough to shower some of the salt over them both and on to the floor. 'Sorry,' he said automatically, looking down between them and then getting flustered by what he saw: the jut of her breasts in their tight blouse, the hitch of her hip.

Cerri didn't balk, just smiled. She saw his irises widen. The air between them felt thick.

'I am grateful,' he said, breaking the silence. 'For your

help. I mean, you're being very kind. You've got no reason to help me.'

'It's a favour for a friend. Besides,' she added, knowing she was being mischievous, 'I think you're cute.'

He laughed, uncomfortably. 'I rather wish the vampire wasn't of the same opinion. Um. So how come you know so much about them? What's your connection to all this?'

'Me? Didn't Amanda tell you?' She braced herself. 'I used to be a donor for one.'

'A donor?'

'Blood donor. A regular ... feed.'

He pulled away, suspicion tainting his expression. 'Naylor?'

'What? No!' She flushed, and was annoyed that she did. 'Amanda's employer. Reynauld.'

Doug swallowed. 'Doesn't that make you ...?'

'What?'

'A part-vampire?'

'No, it doesn't. If everyone they took a bite out of got turned into one of them, the whole world would be wall-to-wall bloodsuckers.'

'So it's him you're doing the favour for?'

She nodded.

'He's ... what? A nice-guy vampire?'

'Well, he's nicer than Naylor, certainly.' She was feeling defensive for the first time since they'd met. 'What about you, Doug? You said you've already met vampires. You were adamant you knew what they looked like.'

He didn't like that turn in the conversation. 'A long time ago. When I was a student.'

'Did he bite you? Or did *she*?'

He flinched. 'No.'

'But you got a good look? You were so sure?'

He jerked his chin. 'I need to get the windows done before dark.'

They had a few hours until nightfall at this time of the year, even on a grey day like this, but it was clear Doug didn't want to talk. Cerri hefted a spare bag of salt in each hand and followed him through the house. It gave her, after all, a chance to look round his place. Several of the rooms were, it turned out, shut up and unused, and the furnishings in the ones he did live in were modern and cheap-looking; Doug seemed to live simply. He had a big collection of books – not just theology but a whole load of historical novels – and from the photos framed on the wall of his living room it looked like he'd made several trips to the Far East and made a lot of church friends. He owned a computer – a Mac, she noted with tribal approval – but there was no TV in sight.

'You don't watch television?'

'I prefer the radio.'

The building was echo-haunted due to being so empty, and slightly creepy. All the bulbs were eco-fluorescents, which cast a dim yellow light that didn't seem to illuminate the high, shadowy ceilings. Cerri was glad she didn't live here. Outside the door of an upstairs room Doug hesitated.

'Perhaps you should wait outside. This is my bedroom.'

'You shy, Doug?' She grinned. 'Scared I'm going to see your big stash of porn mags?'

'Not exactly.'

'Or is it that, faced with a bed, you won't be able to resist having your wicked way with a poor innocent girl?'

Doug opened his mouth, paused, then shook his head. 'Well, if you find one of those in the house, send her home right away. And,' he added firmly, 'I'll see you downstairs.'

Cerri giggled to herself as she went back down.

With the whole house salted, they finished by sealing the front door, then Cerri led the way back into the kitchen. 'Phase two,' she announced, brandishing the big bottle of olive oil. 'For if he gets past the salt.'

'Yes?' He sounded like he knew something unpleasant was coming up. Clever boy, she thought.

'You're going to go have a shower. Then you're going to rub this stuff on. All over. Every inch, including your scalp. It may sting a bit.'

'Oh, no.'

'Oh, yes. If you want to make yourself unpalatable, then this is how you do it.'

'I'm going to make myself a pariah. How am I going to be able to go within a hundred yards of my parishioners?'

'Don't worry, you can wash it off in the morning. Go for it, Doug.' He took the bottle from her reluctantly, and she couldn't resist adding: 'Every inch, remember. Don't make me check.'

He set his jaw and left the room.

Naughty girl, she told herself, sitting down at the table and swirling the cool dregs of her tea in its mug. Teasing the poor vicar. The sound of the water running through pipes and the hum of a firing boiler came from overhead, and she glanced up at the ceiling, imagining Doug stripping his clothes off and soaping himself under the shower. The effect of that picture was more powerful than she'd anticipated; a flush of warmth made her shift in her hard chair. Biting the inside of her cheek she chided herself: So he really is cute – so what? He's not allowed to fuck. Show him some respect.

She held on while she made herself a fresh drink and explored the meagre contents of the fridge, stealing a bunch of grapes. She held on while the pipes hummed and then fell quiet. She held on while the clouds thickened outside and it began to rain. Then as the silence overhead lengthened she shook herself.

Respect be buggered: what respect did she owe the Christian Church? What respect did they show any of the old religions? She could feel the prickle of arousal all over her skin like cat-fur standing on end. The Path of Bast was not one of sensual denial.

She kicked off her shoes and made her way on bare feet through the shadowy house. 'Lady Bast, clear the path for me,' she prayed. The bathroom door was closed. Drumming her fingers on the wood in a token knock, she didn't wait for an answer but turned the handle. It wasn't locked. From within the room a wave of scented steam washed over her: pungent garlic and sharper, more fragrant ginger. Doug was fastening his trousers; he turned hurriedly at her entrance and stared. Shirtless, his skin glistened with oil; his hair was darkened into damp locks. His torso was neat and tight of line rather than broad or bulky. He looked horribly discomfited to see her there, and his hands bunched protectively over his groin.

Oh, yeah, thought Cerri: not bad at all. It was a good thing she liked the smell of garlic.

'Cerri – please!'

'You done? I came up to see if you needed any help.'

'I'm done. I managed fine.'

'Every inch?' She gave him a come-on grin. 'Back, sack and crack?'

He nodded, biting his lip.

'Bet you didn't manage between your shoulders. Turn around – let's have a look.'

He looked like he wanted to protest, but he obeyed without

another word, and she glanced over the smooth taut skin of his back.

'There. You did miss a bit. I'll sort it for you.' Silently she pulled her blouse off over her head and dropped it behind her. He'd plugged the handbasin and poured some of the oil out into that, a pool of gold in the white porcelain. Dipping one hand in, she laid it between his shoulder blades and felt him quiver as if she'd given him an electric shock, his spine arching. Her second hand joined the first and she smoothed her fingertips down his back, feeling the muscle and the frame of bone beneath. 'That's better.'

'Oh, dear God,' whispered Doug, which she thought not entirely appropriate for a vicar.

'Doesn't it feel nice?' She was massaging the oil into him now, kneading the flesh, feeling him push back into her. She watched a drop of oil gather and run down the defile of his spine, and she traced it all the way down until it disappeared under the waistband of his chinos. 'Oops,' she murmured, following the drop with a fingertip and nearly sending him into convulsions.

'Cerri, you mustn't.' His voice was hoarse. 'I can't. It's not right.'

'Why not? Your lot aren't celibate.'

'That just means I'm allowed to get married. I can't be having it off with anyone I like, you know.'

'So you like me?' She leaned into him, not caring that she was getting her bra messy, her hands exploring their way round his waist to his stomach, tracing paths through the line of oiled hair there. He felt lean and hard and good to hold.

'I ... I can't.' But he wasn't making any attempt to stop her. She found out why when she reached down to brush her fingers across the front of his trousers and encountered a rock-hard mass bulging against the cloth.

'Oh? Why not?' She worked the button of his fly with the other hand.

'Don't. Our bodies are not ours alone. They belong to God.'

'I can go with that.' He didn't seem to be wearing any underwear.

Doug sounded strained, almost ready to crack. 'We have to treat our own bodies and each other's as holy. I need to – oh, Christ!' That was the moment at which she got her hand around the erect shaft of his cock. The blasphemy startled her, but she held on tight as he shuddered violently against her, stretching his spine.

'Shush, lover,' she whispered, pressing her breasts against him, sliding her grip up and down his substantial length. She was more than prepared to respect his body when it was this big and hard. Hey – for a slim-looking guy he was a surprising handful. He'd oiled it too, as promised, and it slipped and slithered under her palm with luxurious ease, every ridge and contour a delight to her. Cerri pulled his trousers down over his hips, letting them slide to his calves, and laid her free hand on his ass-cheek, feeling the clench of his muscle. She licked at his shoulder and tasted the aromatic oil. 'How long since you had a good lay, Doug? The truth now.'

He rolled his head back, panting. 'Nearly – ah – not since Uni.'

'Do you jerk off?'

'Huh?'

'Do you masturbate, Doug? Do you make yourself come?'

'Yes. Oh, God ... I try ... not to do it too much.'

'Why not, lover?' Her hand was moving up and down in a slick inexorable dance.

'It's disrespectful ... to those I'm thinking about.'

Without letting go of his erect cock she slithered round in front of him, looking up into his flushed, stricken face. 'Don't you respect me, Doug?' she asked with a gentle smile, her hand never ceasing its work but moving slower now, firmer. She was worried that he would explode far too fast if she let him. His stomach muscles were tight, his shoulders tense. He looked down into the depths of her cleavage as if into an abyss.

'Cerri ...'

'Take my bra off.'

His hands shook as he smoothed down the emerald straps from her shoulders and released her breasts from their confines. Her nipples were big to match the generous orbs and they pointed at him, beading visibly in accusation. She wondered if she would be able to get him to suck them. She wanted him to suck them. She wanted him to lick her pussy: she had a feeling he'd be very good at that. She wanted him to suck her clit while she straddled him and gobbled his cock.

'Oh, you're beautiful,' he said, like something inside him had broken, and she smiled.

'It's OK. It's fine. You can think about me every time you come. I'd like that.'

Without warning he caught her face up in his hands and kissed her. It was clumsy but that hardly mattered; it was also hungry and desperate and staggeringly sweet. It was as if he were trying to breathe her in. Cerri felt a quite unexpected rush of warmth flash between them.

'Whoa,' she said, her eyes shining, as they drew apart.

'Cerri, please ...' His eyes were losing focus.

She liked being in charge, at least most of the time. She always had done; that was why Reynauld had been no more than a passing phase for her. Gently but firmly she pushed Doug back against the bathroom sink, and he grabbed the ceramic with both hands. 'Spread your legs,' she murmured, kissing him, and as he did so she cupped his oiled balls in her other hand.

His head went back straightaway, his mouth and eyes round. She played with his scrotal sac, rolling the balls within and tickling his perineum. That made him gasp. His cock, already massively solid, seemed to swell in her hand. He was going to come real soon, she could tell; he was going to erupt all over her wicked fingers. She stopped looking up at his face and focused on his crotch, noting each tightening muscle, each subliminal quiver. And the more she played between his thighs, the closer he seemed to get. There were beads of sweat springing out through the sheen of oil now.

Is this what you like, lover?

Without a by-your-leave she slid her fingers right along his oiled crease and found the pucker of his asshole. Panic flared in Doug's eyes: for a second she thought he was going to throw her off. But his cry was 'Please! Oh, please!' and then, as she worked his cock with one hand and slid the invading finger of the other into him, he came with a shocking series of spurts, gush after gush of semen crossing the gap between them. She felt its soft rain fall on her breasts and her belly, and the last few pulses slopped over her wrist.

When he stopped shaking Doug slid forward from the hand basin and slumped to his knees on the bathroom rug. Biting her lip, Cerri knelt before him, rather cautiously. This was the moment when it could all go wrong, of course. This was when he might decide it was all her fault and he hadn't wanted it at all, not him. She wanted to ask him how he was feeling, but she held her tongue.

Then he reached out. There was a slop of semen melting on the warm slope of her breast, she realised, easing slowly down toward her nipple. He touched the gluey ooze with his fingers, watching as if hypnotised by the glisten as he rubbed it into her skin, massaging it in circles about her areola, making Cerri catch her breath as unsatisfied desire roiled inside her.

'Are you OK?' she asked.

'The summer after my first year at university,' he said as if he hadn't heard her, 'I had a job in my Aunt Maria's shop. My Uncle Dave had married out in Italy and brought her back, and they had these big plans for starting an import business and a chain of Italian delis. They brought me in to help in the shop for the summer because she was having her first baby. I had to clean the place and stock the shelves and unload the van; that sort of stuff. And serve behind the counter.'

Cerri put her hand on his leg and squeezed gently, not sure where all this was coming from.

'They kept funny hours. We were open really really late at night, and because I was family and I was staying with them I was expected to work late too. There was a private club on the opposite side of the road – I think it had a casino – and the odd person would come in late and want a sandwich made up or something. Most of them were Italian, they knew my aunt and would ask after her. I was fairly pissed off: I was nineteen and had much better things to do than hang round selling cheese and stuff. But, you know ... it was a student job. Then one night Aunt Maria was taken into hospital because there were signs there was something up with the baby, I don't know what, but they left me to look after the deli on my own. So I had to stay up well past midnight. And I was wondering if they'd forgotten me, because nobody rang to say what was going on or whether I could lock up. I didn't know what to do with the till so I was sort of nervous.

'About 1 a.m. this man came in. I assumed he was one of the Italian crowd. He had that sort of look, the fancy suit and everything. Slicked-back hair. Very ... handsome. The sort of person even I knew you didn't ask questions about. He was interested in buying some olive oil. This was before it was really easy to get in supermarkets, you understand; we had big tins of different varieties and I had to draw off a saucerful of each and let him taste them. Well, not all of them. He wasn't interested in the garlic-infused one.'

Doug smiled, a twisted smile.

'I see,' said Cerri.

'You don't see.' Doug swallowed and cleared his throat. 'You got to understand, I'd had plenty of girlfriends at university. I'd never even thought about another guy like that. But when this man looked at me ... it was like he reached down through my body and grabbed me by the cock. I was ... shaking. I watching him dip his finger in the oils and suck the tip, and all I could think about was ... oh, God. And when he'd finally chosen the oil he wanted, he picked up a bottle and pointed through into the back room and said, "Shall we?" and I took him in there. There was a big table where we unpacked all the boxes. He just looked at me and I took my clothes off there and then, and he put me face down over the table and he poured the oil on me. All down my spine and my backside and between my legs, so it ran off my balls down on to the sawdust on the floor. Then he used the oil ... on his fingers. To get them inside me. Then his penis. He took plenty of time, because I wasn't used to that sort of thing at all. He had sex with me. It was ... so scary, and ... extraordinarily pleasurable. I mean, physically. I came all over the floor under the table, and he came in my ass. Then he did it again. I think I sort of blacked out – it seemed to go on for ever, and I was woozy as hell. Hours, it must have been.'

Cerri put both her hands over her mouth, wide-eyed. Understanding all sorts of things.

'I know that because by the time he finished it was getting light. It was the middle of summer, so maybe three in the morning or whatever. He opened the door and looked out and he went ... he went grey – really sick looking. He said, "Have you got a cellar?" and he made me take him down into the basement where they kept the wine. And all the time he was looking more and more sick, like he was dying. He said, "You tell nobody that I'm here. You let nobody in. You say nothing until Monday." It was a Saturday night, see ... well, Sunday morning really. Then he died. I mean it. Hanging on to my shoulder in the cellar. I put him down on the floor and he was just a cold grey corpse except for these ... his lips were all drawn back and he had these, uh ... *teeth*.' He grimaced. 'I ran upstairs and threw up in the sink.'

'Oh, shit,' Cerri whispered.

'I didn't tell anyone. It was a Sunday, and we didn't open on Sundays, so I locked the shop and ran away. I went back to Aunt Maria's but she was in hospital and Uncle Dave was with her, so I spent the day on my own. I was ... bricking it, as we used to say in those days. But I thought I knew better than to tell the police or anyone. I didn't know what to do, and everything seemed so mixed up in my head I didn't even know whether it was real or I'd dreamed it or what. But I thought I had to be sure before Uncle Dave came in to open up on Monday morning and found a body. I had to clean up, I thought ... the oil and stuff. So I went back that night. Just after it got dark. I walked past the shop front and it looked normal. I walked back ... and he was coming out. The man. Straightening his shirt cuffs.

'He looked fine. He'd been dead, and now he wasn't. And he'd opened a door I knew I'd locked. He just looked at me, and nodded, and walked away.' He fell silent.

'Well,' said Cerri, 'no wonder Reynauld asked me to help you out.'

'Reynauld?' Doug blinked. 'Your ...?'

'Tall, dark and handsome,' she said dryly. 'Fangs. Nice suit. Might pass for Italian. That was him.'

'Oh.'

'Did he bite you?'

'No. I guess my aunt had been feeding me too much garlic. He just ... fucked me.' Doug scrubbed his fingers across his oily scalp, spiking his hair. 'He messed me up, Cerri. He messed me up so bad. I got buggered by a dead man! I didn't know how to deal with that.'

'Oh, Doug. Is that how you ended up in the Church?'

'I thought that if anyone knew about these things, if anyone had the answers, it had to be them.'

Unable to comfort him, she leaned in and kissed his lips softly. She was surprised and gratified when he took her hand and guided it to his groin, back to his erect cock.

'Cerri,' he mumbled, kissing her deeper. His hard-on jumped under her fingers, giving no sign of flagging, no sign that he'd already emptied all chambers. Uneasiness stirred in the back of her mind even as she ached to pull him into her. He'd stayed stiff as a pole all the way through his story.

The nasty suspicion, once formed, grew to monstrous

proportions. Cerri pushed him back and bent for a closer look. And there it was: yes. On the underside of his cock, near the base: two dints in the flesh, one a little higher than the other. Puncture-marks. 'Fuck,' she said hoarsely. 'You've been bitten.'

'What? No, I –'

'You've been bitten already.' She stared into Doug's uncomprehending eyes, her voice rising. 'He's already had a piece of you!'

'But I haven't – I don't – when?'

'This afternoon,' said a silky voice behind them. 'Funnily enough, I don't usually feel hungry during the day, but you were just so fucking sweet and irresistible. And the look on your face ...' Cerri scrambled round and saw the speaker, the vampire Naylor: beautiful, glittering and jagged as razor-wire. He was nested in the angle of the landing ceiling, arms spread like a blasphemous crucifix, clinging to the plaster by a network of dark tendrils that emerged from his flesh like cobweb, melding him with the shadows. 'Rather like that look now,' he finished with a ghastly smirk.

She knew she hadn't seen him until that moment. She knew they'd been through every room of the house and if he'd been there he couldn't have remained hidden. Not if he were human, anyway. 'You were in the house all the time,' she said, feeling sick. 'We didn't seal you out. You were already here.'

'Uh-huh. I've been here since last night. Not as clever as you think, are you, girly?' He slithered down from his impossible perch and landed on the carpet lightly, the shadow-tendrils hissing as they dissolved. Doug scrambled to his feet, yanked up his trousers and held them with one hand. The other one sketched a cross in the air.

'In Jesus' name –'

'Didn't work last time, won't work this. You've too many doubts, little God-botherer. Plus,' he added acidly, 'I think the fact you've just hosed your scuzz all over your witch girlfriend's tits might count against you. Pretty impressive, by the way – the spunk-show, I mean. And,' he admitted with a long hard glance at Cerri, 'the tits. I'd like to bite them off.'

'Don't you touch her!' Doug barked. Cerri came up behind him and put her hand on the small of his back.

'You should go, Naylor. You'll only be making trouble for yourself.'

He tilted his head, an odd smile dancing in his eyes. 'I should be angry with you, witch-bitch. You get in my way. You've gone and spoiled my *dinner*.' His eyes, green as poison, narrowed as they flicked back to Doug. 'But you know what? I'm not angry. You two just went and told me a lovely story. The most interesting story I've heard in years. And that's why I'm going to play Mr Nice.'

* * *

Cerri woke in Doug's bed, on torn sheets, as the line of sunlight crawling across the wall reached the pillows. She squirmed against the unfamiliar mass of Doug's arm, then blinked herself awake. Doug, flat on his back, didn't move, even when Cerri raised herself up from prone and slid out of the bed. She was muzzy-headed with dehydration, almost as if she had a hangover. The bedroom refused to come into focus. Naked, she stumbled slowly downstairs into the kitchen, sought the refrigerator and found, to her relief, a litre bottle of fruit-flavoured water.

Only when she'd quenched her parched throat did she

remember what had brought her to the house and think to check the line of salt across the windowsill. It looked undisturbed.

'Hmm,' she grunted, wiping the sleep from her eyes. Then she padded back up the stairs to the bedroom, the plastic bottle in her hand.

Doug lay much as she had left him, breathing slowly and only half-covered by the sheet, which had managed to get pushed down to his hips. Cerri climbed on to the bed, expecting him to stir, but he only took a deeper breath and slumbered on.

Damn, but the man was a heavy sleeper, she thought, smiling to herself. He looked pretty cute too, half-naked like that. The sparse hairs on his chest gleamed gold in the sunlight and his nipples were flat dimples that invited the brush of a tongue-tip. Oh, how she liked the sweet vulnerability of a sleeping man. And under that sheet – well, it looked like he had a morning hard-on, a ridge of solidity beneath the rucked cotton.

She found that just irresistible.

Stealing a hand out, she ran her palm over the hidden shaft, finding warmth beneath the cool cloth and a confirmation of her suspicions. He was thick and full and more than half-hard already. The brush of her hand, soft and slow, completed the job in moments. A thrill tickled down through her nerves all the way to her sex, which clenched unexpectedly, greedy for that good stiff length. Cerri shaped an O with her lips, slightly surprised but not at all displeased to find herself feeling so horny even after a night of hot action. 'Come on, my beautiful boy,' she breathed, her fingertips measuring his cock and caressing its hardness.

Doug's eyes opened suddenly. 'You're still here,' he said. 'It wasn't all a dream.'

Cerri withdrew her hand a few inches. 'Hello, lover. Sleep well?'

'I …' He stopped abruptly and then looked all round the room, eyes wide. 'Ah. Ah … I guess it worked. He didn't show.'

'Yes.' Cerri frowned. Memories of the previous night were finally coming back to her, and she searched them carefully. She found no sign of any vampire. Sure, some of the scenes were a bit vague, but wasn't that the way with sex the first time with a new bloke? The high of arousal tended to smudge the details. And good grief, there had been a *lot* of it to commit to memory. They'd been at it half the night. 'It worked,' she agreed, glancing over at the windowsill where the salt lay like a miniature levee against a flood. 'That's good.'

'Thanks.' Doug then looked abashed. 'I mean, for helping. And …'

She grinned fondly. 'That's all right. My pleasure.' She watched him blush and look away. 'Want some water?'

'Oh, yes, please.' He hitched himself up to sit back against the headboard, pulling the sheet up with him to preserve his modesty. But as he took his first swig from the bottle and his attention lapsed, Cerri seized her moment. Twitching the sheet away, she wrapped her fingers firmly about his erect member.

Doug nearly choked. The bottle lurched in his hand, splashing fruit-scented water over his bare chest. His wide eyes met hers.

'Is this for me?' she asked, grinning.

'It's – it's just because I've woken up, you know, Cerri? It's not a real, uh …'

'It feels pretty real to me.' She threw one knee over his

hips, straddling him. Pushing the swollen head of his cock into her wet slit, she slid it up and down and fed it to the mouth of the slick passage within. 'Does this feel real to you?'

'Oh, fuck,' he groaned. He dropped the open bottle over the side of the bed and clutched the sheets beneath him. His hips kicked beneath her, pushing his cock inside. Cerri felt the jolt of pleasure as she was stretched open. She began to work herself down over his shaft, biting her lips in concentration, sliding one hand up to cup her left breast and tug at the nipple.

'You,' said Doug in a thick voice, 'are really bad at taking no for an answer.'

'Am I?' She felt shivery all over, as horny as a nun who'd just discovered a dirty magazine. 'Are you saying, "No", Doug?' She lifted herself up, her thighs tense, until she held only the tip of his glans within her; threatening to withdraw the hot embrace of her sex from the stiff cock between her legs. 'Are you?'

'Oh, God.'

'I don't think you should be saying that, Doug.' She licked her lips, sliding down on him once more, then up again. 'You're a vicar. I. Am. Fucking. A. Vicar.'

He didn't answer that, except with another groan. He just grabbed her hips with his hands, his thumbs sinking into her pubic mound, and jammed her down right to the hilt on his cock. The shock knocked the breath out of her. Then, setting his heels in the mattress, he slammed rapidly into her, over and over, lifting her right up on his pelvis and making her breasts bounce wildly. Cerri cried out, her voice vibrating. By the time he paused they were both gasping. She looked down at his tense face with its parted lips and its half-grin. Even now, he looked incredulous. He was still finding it hard to believe this was happening to him, she thought. And feeling guilty.

Well, bollocks to his stupid guilt.

'Tell you what,' she smirked, shaking out her braids. 'I'll make it easy for you, shall I?' She pushed his hands away and slid off him, sideways. 'Just say, "No", Doug. You can do that, can't you? I'll even turn my back.' She rolled away on to hands and knees, presenting her curvy ass-cheeks and open split to him with a wiggle, and looked back over her shoulder to wink broadly. 'You can say, "No", hey, Doug?'

She barely had time to get the words out before he was on her from behind, grasping her hips and ramming his cock deep inside her. She barely had time to wonder what had gotten into them both, making them act like a couple of crazed teenagers, before he knocked all philosophising out of her with a thrusting action that sent shocks all the way up her spine to the deepest darkest pleasure centres of her brain and took her breath away.

'Doesn't look like it,' he said through gritted teeth. 'Oh. Yes.'

Yes, she thought: yes yes yes. Very soon after that there was no thought in her head at all but the sensation of his riding her, no words on her lips but only her escalating groans and squeals of excitement. She dropped her shoulder and cheek to the bedclothes and thrust her hand back between her spread thighs. She could feel the heavy pouch of his balls slapping against her with every thrust. She brushed it with her fingertips, then found the wetness leaking from about his pistoning shaft and used it to slick her clit.

That was when Doug chose to wet his thumbs in his mouth – first the right one, then the left one – and work them one after another into the whorl of her asshole. That was way too much for her to bear. She had to bury her face in the sheets to muffle her screams as she came, loud and long. She was still coming as Doug pounded to his own climax and unloaded deep inside her.

Then he fell forward over her, his sweating chest pressed to her back. 'Oh, Cerri,' he groaned, nuzzling his lips against her lips and ear. 'Are you OK?'

A giggle bubbled up in her breast. He was just too sweet. 'I'm good, lover.' She slid her knees down the bed, relaxing beneath him. He eased carefully to the side so as not to crush her.

'You're beautiful. So beautiful.'

'You think?' She hitched round to plant an appreciative kiss on his lips, and smiled at him. For a moment they looked into each other's eyes, and then he rolled away on to his back and stared at the ceiling.

Funny, she thought, sobering. That moment just before she'd come – when he stuck his digits into her ass – she'd had the sudden sensation that she was about to remember something. Something important. Then her climax had overwhelmed everything else, and now she had no idea what that memory could be. It was gone from her head without leaving so much as a footprint.

Hey, it couldn't be that important then. She reached out and stroked the softening length of his cock fondly, and Doug sighed.

'The tabloid headlines would have been right then,' he murmured, scratching at his chest. '"Vicar In Pagan Sex Romp With Witch Shock".'

'"Romp"?' she wondered. 'It was more like a Rut, I reckon. You were impressively enthusiastic.'

He laughed, embarrassed.

'And an incredibly good fuck, lover,' she added. He was going to hear it, even if he refused to listen.

'Right. That'll be a help as I start looking for a new career.'

Ow. She looked down at her hand. 'I'm sorry.'

'So, anyway.' His voice was soft. He sat up, brushing her off gently, and rubbed at his thighs with a certain awkwardness. 'I've got hospital visits to make this morning.'

'Uh-huh?' He was *so* the wrong sort of person for her to fall for, she told herself.

'So … I'd better go have a shower. I don't smell all that fresh.' Doug stood, and she looked up at him regretfully, wanting her last memory of his naked body to be a good one.

'OK.'

He bit his lip. 'Want to join me?'

Tentatively, she smiled. 'Yeah. I'd like that.' As he held out his hand and pulled her up into what turned into an embrace, she decided she'd like that very much.

(Naylor)

And this is Naylor, as sweet and cruel as a wasp hidden under a windfall plum. It's a curious fact that of all the vampires in the City, he's the only one that was born here; though he often leaves for protracted periods, he's always drawn back. This is his home. Matthew Naylor – Little Matty the apothecary's son – grew up on the banks of the Fleet River long before it was paved over, while it was still an open drain carrying the ordure and rubbish of the streets away down to the river confluence. There were a lot of dead rats in the Fleet the year he died, their bedraggled bodies so swollen by gas that it looked like they had perished from over-eating. And perhaps they had. They certainly had plenty to dine upon that year.

It was 1665, the year of the Great Plague.

That summer, he remembers, was unusually hot and humid – and the bonfires burning all day and night at street corners, by order of the parish, only added to the filthiness of the atmosphere. In that hothouse air strange flowers blossomed: swollen buds of livid flesh that burst to reveal red and sticky hearts, their perfume unbearable. Upon boarded doors and window-shutters the daubed crosses began to appear.

He remembers being told that the King and all his court had fled the City for the healthier environs of Oxfordshire, and, though he'd never seen the King, it had felt like they'd been abandoned by Providence. He ran wild through the streets that summer, defying the edicts to stay indoors, to stay away from other people. Adolescent fury burned in his veins. He led a pack of youths in hunting down the dogs and cats that were blamed for spreading the Sickness, and rejoiced in every kill.

He remembers when the men of the watch came to secure his father's house with the whole family still inside; his father and stepmother semi-conscious in their bed upstairs, their faces swollen beyond recognition, sweating and groaning from the fever and the pain. Matthew sat in the half-dark and the suffocating heat behind the rough new boards, with his little sister Anne in his arms, watching the chinks of light. Sometimes a parcel of food would be pushed through the gap under the door, but if he didn't get to it fast the rats would have it before he did. Anne wasn't much interested in eating. He sang her nursery rhymes and told her stories, whispering because his throat was parched and sore. Often he'd forget where he was in the tale, but Anne didn't notice. She just liked the sound of his voice.

Ring a ring o' roses …

He remembers half waking in the middle of the night, his back and arse numb from the hard boards, and looking up to see the glimmering Lady hovering over them. She was as beautiful as an angel, as light as mist, and she held Anne in her arms, stooping to kiss her. Matthew watched, smiling in wonder at the cloudy drift of her red hair, the shimmer of her bare limbs. Even when she let Anne's limp little body slide to the floor and advanced on him, he still smiled. She slipped her arm about his neck, tipping his head back as she straddled his thighs. He remembers that her up-tilted breasts brushed up against his chest, and against his feverish skin she felt as delicious as cool water. Tenderly her fingers sliced open the rough linen of his clothes and furled about his lobcock. He was young: even in the midst of this drifting delirium it stirred and stood. His mouth fell open as she slid his member into the cool depths of her puss. He remembers that moment of pure gratitude at the undeserved grace, as her pelvis writhed upon his and she bent to kiss his lips and nuzzle down to his throat. He remembers that her mouth did not taste as sweet as he had expected.

Then he felt the teeth pierce his shoulder, and the sudden jagged pain. The rush of rapture was almost instantaneous – but not so swift as his own response. Matthew Naylor, the despair of his father and the terror of the parish, the young man they'd prophesied would swing from the gallows if he didn't mend his ways, lashed out the only way he could – twisting his neck and sinking his own teeth into that slim throat. He remembers the skin parting reluctantly under the grind of his blunt incisors, and as the ecstasy exploded in his head her blood flooded his mouth, fiery as brandy. After that he could neither let go nor fight further: he passed out in seconds as she tore his throat open.

He remembers them throwing him into the burial pit. He lay there upon the heap of the dead with his eyes open, though withered as figs, unable to stir as the carters dropped body after body down on to the mound of cold flesh. He wanted to shout at them that he was still alive, but his mouth wouldn't move and there was no breath in his lungs. He wanted to thrust the stinking meat aside and rise up to strike them, he wanted to hold his hands up to protect his face as they shovelled a sprinkling of slaked lime over this newest layer in the cadaver-pudding, but he couldn't lift a finger. He wanted to call for his mother, but she couldn't hear him. The lime burned his lips and eyeballs. The bodies piled higher, cutting out the light.

After three days he clawed his way out through the corpses, into the free air.

Naylor is dangerous, anyone will tell you that. Brought up in an era where empathy and compassion were stunted values, he took to the unlife of the vampire without the faintest distaste. Every warning he'd been given about death and Judgement had been exposed for a lie, and he made the most of his new freedom. He has a yen for the hunt, a taste for the adrenaline and cortisol shot in a circulation charged with terror; that effervescence of fear. Left to himself, he would kill almost every time.

Pray you don't run into Naylor. He is not gentle in his feeding or his fucking. If you meet him, it will most likely be the old-fashioned way – he is, after all, old, despite his looks – down a dark alley in the depths of night. He wants you to run. He wants you to try and scream, though his hand will close over your throat and stop your breath before you get the chance. Or, worse, he will stalk you in the places you cannot avoid, closing slowly, letting you know the full hopelessness of the fate that awaits you. He wants your fear and your despair. He wants your death.

But luckily for the inhabitants of the City, Naylor is not left to make that decision on his own. After Naylor's notorious spree among the whores in 1888, indulged shortly after he had returned from the Belgian Congo, Reynauld took it upon himself to tame him and make the parameters clear. This training involved inflicting a great deal of pain, and it took Naylor several months to regenerate certain body-parts. He got the point though, in the end.

That point being that Reynauld owned the City and was stronger than he was.

There are no two ways about it: Naylor hates Reynauld. It's possible to argue that he doesn't even see the other vampires of the City, not really. Wrapped up in his own interests, Naylor's opinion of the others is scathing, his understanding shallow. Ben is his little buddy, his satellite, his gofer. Roisin is an irrelevancy: she wrenched him into this new world without meaning to and has avoided him ever since. She's weak: The Alzheimer's Vampire, he calls her with that sneering grin of his. Estelle is a bit of a hard bitch, but far too young to worry about. Maybe he'll take her down a peg or two one day; she could certainly do with it, and he'd like to shaft that fine caramel ass of hers. As for Wakefield – fuck, he's a joke, a tofu-munching piss-take of everything a vampire should be. Naylor doesn't hang round this city for the pleasure of their company, that's for sure.

He's not without his less predatory side, though. His interest in art is genuine: he craves the new in music and sculpture and painting. Apart from blood, creativity is all he values in human beings. Their flashes of inspiration, their ephemeral and unpredictable moments of innovation, utterly fascinate him. He likes to hang out with interesting people and lead them in a dance on that vertiginous edge between vision and chaos. All too often their contact with him leads to a self-destructive spiral that ends in alcohol-induced brain damage or an overdose, but the symbiosis is genuine while it lasts. His own art is derivative, though he tries his best; he's an extraordinary artistic mimic who can recreate almost any style with those wickedly clever hands. But he never feels satisfied by anything he makes himself. Everything he does is old, and he craves novelty.

Naylor would leave if he wanted to; there are countless places where he'd be freer to indulge himself. But somehow he always comes back, drawn to his home. The water of the subterranean Fleet runs in his veins and his bones are packed with the ash and grime and soot of this city. He feels its pulse and it makes his own flesh quicken with arousal; he breathes deep the dark secret smell belched from the vents of the Underground, a scent so pervasive that the living do not register it, and to him it tastes of an eternal promise. Though its buildings fall and rise with the years, and the faces on the streets change, this is his place.

Yet he's restless, like any young man. He chafes at Reynauld's rule, and when his feet itch he burns up the miles. In this last century he has taken the increasingly easy opportunities to travel, a tourist of particular tastes. He goes where the mess he makes will pass unnoticed, where bodies fall unexamined. He was in Ethiopia after the Italian invasion and South Africa during the Second Boer War. He stalked the trenches of Ypres and the Somme, took enthusiastic though perfectly bipartisan part in the Spanish Civil War, and favoured the Eastern Front throughout the upheaval of World War II. His accent went unremarked in Korea and Vietnam though he was forced to be more cautious there: he has huge advantages of stealth and evasion but he's not invulnerable. He spent a chunk of the 1970s and 80s in South America under various regimes, was annoyed to miss the First Gulf War but made up for the loss in the Balkans at his leisure, and Sarajevo is still a place he remembers with nostalgia. When the invasion of Iraq took place he made sure he was embedded with the American ground troops: he disliked the weather but appreciated the many opportunities presented to him after dark.

He's back home now, the wildness out of his system for the moment, his feral hunger temporarily assuaged. Under grey skies his behaviour is more restrained – in this he's no different from any young man of the City who jets off to Ibiza or Ayia Napa and goes a bit crazy, the heat and the copious drink and the easy sex going to his head. After his frenetic vacation he wants to kick back a bit and relax, hanging out with friends like Ben. Just chill.

But this latest run-in with Reynauld has fired him up. The girl's death didn't have anything to do with him, for fuck's sake – he'd never touched or even met her. He's been blamed purely out of habit.

Aggrieved, he casts around for release or for vengeance. And with the innocent recounting of an old story, he thinks he just might have found the way to it.

7: Four for the Gospel Makers

Last night it was wet and slick on the streets and the puddles were red with neon. I went underground instead. Word was there was something on the Circle Line, something that hunted along the platforms late at night when there were hardly any travellers left – just the lost. Something that slithered out of the dark tunnel mouth like a snake and left fang marks in its prey.

Mind the gap.

I caught up with it deep in the AM. Not saying which station, but we were three flights of escalators below street-level and the air smelled stale and burnt like all of the day's hopes gone up in smoke. I lurked about on the northbound platform, doing my Lone Female thing on a bench with head bowed like my bloke had just dumped me, ignoring the drunks and the clubbers, hoping that no one with a pulse was going to try anything on because I always feel a bit bad when I hurt a live one. Not too bad, but a bit. Call me sentimental.

With the third tube train pulling out I found myself alone. Suddenly it was quiet, only the growl of an unseen engine on another line to keep me company. I felt the hair on the back of my neck stir. My senses are honed to the presence of vamps. I knew there was one there even before I raised my face and saw him ooze from behind a pillar.

He looked like he lived in the Underground, did this one: bald as a rat's tail and pale as a slug. Shabby-looking parka coat. Lips all black and cracked with hunger: typical Bloodkind. As he closed on me I stood, pulled a stake from under my own coat with a slick movement and had it heading for his ribcage before the sudden flash of alarm in his red eyes had time to work its way through to his forebrain. It was only instinct that enabled him to twist aside from the stake, and the wooden point scored his ribs beneath his arm, catching on the cloth and jerking out of my hand. Bastard. I followed my strike up with a tae kwon do kick to the solar plexus and he folded over my New Rock boot like wet newspaper. But he didn't go down. He just staggered back down the platform, shaking his head and staring like his chicken nuggets had just stood up and pecked at his face. His mouth was suddenly full of jagged teeth.

I slipped another stake from my belt-holster and reached into an inside pocket of my coat for the bottle there.

'Bitch,' he said. He'd have been wasting breath if he had any: insults don't hurt me. Especially insults from a corpse who hadn't realised yet that he was supposed to be lying down for the rest of eternity. Well, it was going to be a steep learning curve for this guy.

'Watch your language, Potty-mouth,' I sneered. As he came in swinging I ducked and smashed the bottle right into that ugly face of his. Holy water. Works a treat on the undead. The vamp threw his hands up to his face, screaming, and fell back – right over the platform edge. Down he went on to the live rail. There was a crack and a spark and then he exploded into dust, just as a gust of wind muscled out of the

tunnel mouth to announce the arrival of the next train. My vamp blew away like someone had just emptied a bagless vacuum cleaner out into the wheelie bin. The driver never even saw him. Which is cool as far as I'm concerned.

A good night's work. I'll be back on the streets tomorrow.
XOXOXO
StakeGirl

I click on Publish and the text vanishes as the page reformats itself. *Your blog post has published successfully!* it tells me. *View Blog? In a new window?*

Click. I always like to make sure: goddamn paragraph breaks seem to appear and disappear at random. I scan the finished product with a sense of satisfaction. It looks good, from the StakeGirl logo in blood-red lettering at the top to the visitor counter at the bottom of the page, which is ticking up even as I watch. No comments, of course: I don't allow comments, it just turns into a brawl and there's no dignity in that. StakeGirl has to keep her dignity. The picture at the head of today's post is one of a tube train shooting past that I snagged from the Net and Photoshopped to add a bit more atmosphere. I'm thinking that tomorrow or the day after I'll do something set in Kew Gardens – I like the Victorian glasshouses full of tropical trees and I've got a nice picture of a strangler fig.

Kerchunk. Damn – that's the sound of the front door. He's home early – if this is what you call his home. He doesn't usually bother with the front door either.

Quickly I fold the little notebook, stuff it into my rucksack and slip that under the bed. Naylor's a stupid git for all his cockiness: he never bothered searching my bag and doesn't know I've got the laptop. I'd like to keep it that way. Can't have him interfering with the blog. Moving quietly, I arrange myself on the mattress, curling up on my side. The chain that attaches to the iron bedstead has caught on something out of sight and tugs at my ankle uncomfortably. I fix my eyes on the back of the door, feeling my stomach knot with anticipation. There's not much light in the room, even though there's a streetlamp bang outside, because the windows are pasted over with newspaper. Enough, though, to show the drifts of takeaway food cartons and the few sticks of crappy old furniture that the house owners couldn't be bothered to take with them when they moved out.

The door opens, and in walks Naylor. A flick of the light-switch and the single bare bulb comes on, making me blink and throwing into focus the dingy room with its broken detritus and its peeling rose-patterned 1970s wallpaper, and me on the bed that sits in the middle of the room, curled up, waiting for him. I once saw him nest there during the day, in a top corner behind that wallpaper; spinning shadows until he faded away into the plaster, emerging at dusk like a bubble of damp bulging out through the rose print. The place is a real pit, irredeemably seedy. I've got no idea who's paying the electricity bill, though I'm pretty sure it's the neighbours' wireless broadband I've been riding. I hitch myself up on one arm. My skin is doing all sorts of horrible things at the sight of him: burning and crawling, moisture leaking into every pore. My insides are tying themselves in knots.

'Hi, honey,' he says with a cold smirk. 'I'm home.'

He's not alone. Shit. What's going on? I've been kept here over a week and this is the first time he's brought anyone back with him. Two men. One look assures me that they're not vampires, whatever they are: they're just not good-looking enough. Both have close-shaven heads and beat-up faces, one is black and youngish with scarred cheeks, the other's white and starting to get grizzled. They've a thuggish, bored look about them. Their eyes widen as they spot me but they don't say anything, just stare and then glance at Naylor speculatively.

'This is Joanne,' he says, like he's introducing someone at the office. 'Jo, meet Luke and Mark. They're doing a little job for me.' Luke's the younger one, it turns out. Naylor dumps a white plastic bag on the small table and I catch a whiff of hot food. Smells like Chinese tonight. He usually lets me eat after he's finished with me.

'Help me,' I whisper, widening my eyes pleadingly at the two strangers. I'm real interested in what their response will be. Luke snorts incredulously with a brief but expressive cast of the eye at Naylor. Mark grins, amused.

So that's the way it's going to be. My stomach clenches and I lose all appetite, though it's twenty-four hours since I last ate.

'Business first,' says Naylor, going into the table's single drawer. He finds a couple of envelopes which he passes to Mark. 'Two passports. Two Eurostar tickets to Brussels, first thing tomorrow morning.'

'Brussels?' says Luke. 'I've never been there.'

'You're going to be disappointed: it's the most boring shitehole in Europe. Office-central for Boring. On that bit of paper there's the address for a Timothy Grey and a copy of his ID photo. You two are going to go to his flat and secure him; he's one of those Eurocrats, so don't expect any interesting conversation. Grey by name, grey by nature, I guess. Make sure he's out of sight; I don't want another soul involved and I don't want him damaged. Then call me. That's all. Keep it low-profile. And if anyone else finds out …' There's an odd emphasis to the 'anyone'.

'They won't, boss,' says Mark. The guy's clearly old-school gangster.

'They'd better not. Fuck me over, and there won't be enough left of you to send home in a shoebox.'

'No worries.'

'If you get this right …' Naylor's eyes narrow and his face suddenly looks as sharp as an axe-blade. 'It's the high life for us all. Anything you want. Jet-ski up the fucking river to work if you like; snort coke off the tits of supermodels. I can be very generous with my office bonuses.' He turns his head and looks at me, and a chill like a Jurassic centipede crawls up my spine as I note the speculation in his eyes. 'You fancy a bit of that, say?'

'No,' I whisper, appalled.

'She ain't no supermodel,' says Luke.

Mark sniggers and agrees: 'Bit on the porky side, isn't she? Not that there's anything wrong with curves, mind. Gives you something to hold on to.'

'You know what she is?' Naylor swaggers slowly toward me, reaching to seize my jaw and draw me upright on my knees for their inspection. I'm wearing the same black leggings and grey lycra sports-top that I came here in. Stained now, and none too clean. 'She's a vampire hunter.'

'No kidding.' They snigger like schoolboys.

'She came here to stake me. Instead I staked her – right up that fat ass.'

Yeah. I came here to slay him. After he dared me. After he gave me his goddamn address. I remember only too clearly that night in the club when I first saw that beautiful, delicate face, as he leaned in so that it was nearly touching mine. I remember the lurch of my heart, smitten by the impossible promise of his green eyes – and the flutter of my pussy. I remember wondering why someone that fabulous had taken notice of me. I'd been about to find out: 'You're StakeGirl,' he'd said.

Hell, I'd thought. How did he know? Yes, I'd used some indistinct photos of myself on the blog, but not raw ones. I never show my face and besides, StakeGirl is a good forty pounds lighter than I am. Not that I have any problem with my curves – they've always stood me in good stead – but I know that people expect a vampire hunter to look like a cross between an Olympic athlete and a swimwear model. Suddenly I'd found myself nervous as hell.

'You smell just like your blog,' he'd said, as if answering my unspoken question. 'And both like bullshit.' As I'd opened my mouth to protest, he'd added, 'Have you ever even seen a *real* vampire?'

'I don't know what you're talking about,' I'd said huffily. The way I'd recoiled from him must have telegraphed my discomfort because my friend Elliot had spoken up from behind me. Elliot had been keeping an eye on me that night.

'Everything all right, Jo?'

'If you want to slay a vampire, you fake, you come and find me.' Naylor had drawn back his lips, running the tip of his tongue over his upper incisors – and I'd watched wide-eyed as two cruel fangs slid down into place over his human teeth.

'Jo?' Elliot had become insistent. He was right behind the stranger. 'Hey you: hands off her.'

'Bet you don't dare,' he'd whispered to me, ignoring the big guy. Mocking. Then he'd told me his address and, as Elliot dropped a hand on his shoulder, had turned and stared at him. Elliot is six-five and a bodybuilder but one look from those green eyes had made him quail. He'd shrunk back and let the wiry little man disappear into the crowd. And I'd sat there quivering with shock.

So I'd come here to find him, just like he wanted. I'd thought hard about it of course. I'm not actually a tae kwon do master in real life. I mean, I did some lessons for about six months a while back, but I pulled something in my knee and never got back into it after taking time off. So OK, I don't really kill vampires. But StakeGirl does, and in some ways she's more real than Joanne. How many people know or care about Joanne, compared to her? I just thought I had to give StakeGirl her chance. It was my shot at living in her shoes for real.

And maybe it had something to do with the way he made me feel, when those contemptuous green eyes fixed on me. The wet burn that flooded my core. I couldn't just forget that. He needed teaching that I wasn't to be despised. That I was tough enough to take what he had to dish out.

So I whittled myself some stakes and bought myself a mallet from a camping shop and came to this house one sunny afternoon. Just an ordinary terraced house in a run-down part of town. From the outside it looked abandoned, its windows milky and blind with the pasted newspaper. I got in through the tiny walled back yard, finding a kitchen window cracked ajar. I probably made far too much noise clambering over the sink, but I reckoned he'd be unconscious during the day, probably down in the cellar. I was wrong, of course. He was here, in this shadowy back room, this creaky old bed. He lay with his hands folded across his stomach, perfectly still. Not breathing or anything. I felt sort of sick, getting my stake and mallet out. I was suddenly unsure I had the strength to drive it through a real-life ribcage, and I didn't really want to, even if he was a vampire. I'm not the sort of girl who goes round on a Friday night picking fights. I don't like hurting people. I'm scared of the police. All of a sudden this didn't look like such a good idea at all. And as I lowered the point of the stake toward his breastbone in its faded old Stones T-shirt, watching it tremble, he opened his eyes and grabbed my wrist and, grinning, broke my grasp on the wood with a single twist of his hand.

After that he did things to me that it makes me sweat to recall.

And now he's here with two leery-looking blokes in tow and they're all eyeing me up. The two goons are shifting their hips slightly, probably wondering if Naylor's just taking the piss, whether they're going to be made fools of or whether they should play along. And probably wondering what I'll be like if they do get a go. Luke wets his lips.

'Please, no,' I beg, widening my eyes. There are snakes of terror crawling up and down my back. I don't know these guys and I don't know what they might do to me.

'Shit. She going to bleat all the time?' Luke asks, pulling a face. He's definitely the less cool of the two: Mark just grins at the sound of my plea.

'I could gag her,' Naylor concedes. 'But then you wouldn't be able to get your cock in that big mouth.' He licks my cheek and I cringe away from him. 'That'd be a waste, wouldn't it? She's got real cocksucker lips, don't you think?'

'There's more than one way to gag a woman,' Mark agrees, hefting thoughtfully at the bulge at his crotch. I'd swear it's looking bigger already.

Luke grins, catching up. 'Just got to keep her mouth busy, haven't we?'

Oh, God. I need to hold out for more time. 'Wait – I need the toilet,' I blurt. 'Honestly, Naylor, I've been chained up all day: I'm bursting for a pee.'

He grabs the single braid at the back of my scalp and tugs my head back, jerking it from side to side just enough to hurt. 'Tsk. Poor little girl.' He puts on a sing-song voice, mocking me: 'Poor lickle Jo want to go wee-wee?'

'Please!' The pain of his hair-tugging is making my eyes tear up.

'What if I don't let you? What if one of my nice gentlemen-friends here fucks you till you piss all over yourself?'

That's a horrible thought: I burst into a flush of sweat. 'Please, no!'

'Huh. All right then.' Letting me go, he passes his hand over the padlock at my ankle and the metal half-loop jumps free. As I stumble off the bed he swats at my ass; not playfully, but with the intent to humiliate me. There's a burst of general laughter.

'Wooh! See the jiggle on that!'

I don't look at any of them. I just hurry through the kitchen, my bare feet making sticky noises on the filthy lino, to the tiny bathroom. It was obviously built as an extension to the house when the outside toilet in the yard became no longer acceptable. It contains a white-tiled shower corner and a separate toilet cubicle; everything's cobwebbed and grubby but I have it to myself as Naylor doesn't seem to have need of the facilities. I hurry into the inner box and shut the door. There's a tiny frosted window with a latch and a lever arm. Outside is the yard gate and freedom. I jerk the latch but it's too stiff to move. I'm still pushing hopelessly at the frame of the window when the door opens and Naylor is standing there, grinning that cruel grin of his.

'Thought you were having a slash?' he asks. 'Don't worry; there's enough fresh air if you keep the door open.' Behind him his two thugs drift nonchalantly into view. I don't try to look innocent; I just stare wide-eyed at the three of them as the pit of my stomach plunges inside me. 'Go on,' he says. 'Have a piss, girl. Drop the pants.'

Silently I shake my head.

'Fucking do it.' His voice is soft and implacable.

So I pull down my leggings and panties in one quick motion and sit down hard on the wobbly plastic seat.

'Pants right off. Open your legs.'

I obey, though my face is burning with shame. My hands make furtive, clumsy attempts to cover my fleece.

'Hands on your knees.'

Squirming with horror, I reveal to the three men lounging in the doorway my pubic mound, with its dark hair and its pink cleft. Cool air licks my moist tissues.

'I like a nice bit of bush,' Mark comments.

'Hell, yes.'

'Good girl. You can piss now.'

If it wasn't that I really am desperate for a pee I might not be able to unclench my muscles. As it is I have no choice; my body takes over. *Hiss* goes the porcelain and they grin and hoot and mock me. It's the most exquisite humiliation, passing water in front of those men. I've never done anything like it and it rattles me to the core. I'm shaking with shame by the time my bladder is empty.

'Now look: she's all dirty,' Naylor chides. 'You'd better clean her up, you two.'

They take me by the arms and put me in the shower cubicle, still clothed from the waist up and naked from the waist down. The showerhead's missing and there's just a hose. Mark spins the handle and water jets out in my face, and I shriek instinctively and throw my hands up. It's a good job it's a warm night because the water is cold – not bone-chilling but bad enough to shock my skin. I try to shield my face and he directs it at my crotch; I try to protect that and he shoots it all over my breasts, making me leap about. When I turn my face to the wall he directs the jet up under the overhang of my buttocks right into my pussy and my crack. I can't stop screaming, my cries punctuated by pleas of 'No!' The two blokes pass the hose between them, laughing, until they've thoroughly soaked me and my remaining garments, until they've reduced me to shock and near-collapse, sitting helpless on the floor with my back to the tiles, my knees splayed, the jet splashing on my split.

'Get that shirt up, bitch,' Luke orders, bolder now. 'Let's see those tits of yours.'

I pull the wet cloth up to my armpits, revealing my bare breasts and their sunken bite-marks. After the assault of the cold water my nipples are standing out like bullets.

'Killer tits,' is Mark's opinion.

'Yeah. Fat birds've got it going. Tits and ass.' Luke moves the flow up, targetting the bull's-eyes of my nipples as he plays it from side to side, making my breasts wobble. They laugh harshly.

'Please,' I gasp weakly.

'Jeez,' Naylor complains, moving to stand behind the two men, clasping their shoulders, all very matey. 'Do you never shut up? Gentlemen, turn the water off; I think it's time we gave this bitch a bone to keep her quiet.'

The funny thing is that in a whole week Naylor hasn't once demanded a blowjob off me. Yet he seems eager to see me service his two stud dogs. Is this a vampire thing? I wonder blearily. He stands there between them and watches the look on my face as flies are unzipped and belts uncinched and the two cocks come out, one white and one black, both already stiffly angled. They're both big too; thick and uncouth, blind eyes weeping with eagerness. I wonder if Naylor picked them both for their size, or whether it's just pure luck.

'Get here.'

So I crawl forward and take them one in each hand, knowing it's pointless to protest. Slabs of meat, slightly sticky from their body-heat and confinement. My fingers are cold and those dicks seem to burn. The scents of the two crotches are distinctive but both torridly masculine, and I remember that Naylor has no body odour at all.

Mark, I notice, has twin puncture marks on his shaft.

They have to take it in turns. First one plunders my mouth, then the other. Big. God, they're big: they stretch my throat. And salty. I work to fill my mouth with moisture and keep breathing as they thrust their hips and grab me by the hair to push me deeper. I make messy desperate gobbling noises as they pull out and shove back, slurping on their bulging heads, turning from one to another to snatch a moment's respite from the pressure.

'God, you love it, don't you, girly?'

'Damn, that's good. That's good, bitch.'

I know I'm good.

'You're a proper little cocksucker, aren't you? A proper little slut?'

I moan deep in my throat, unable to make any more articulate protest around the dick fucking my mouth.

'Glad you like her, gentlemen. It's always the feisty feminist ones that make the best cocksuckers,' Naylor observes. 'Once you've broken them to it.'

'I want to fuck that big ass,' says Mark. My hand is working his boner as my lips see to the other man.

'You'll get your chance. We all will. Like the sound of that, Jo?'

I flash Naylor an agonised look over Luke's prodigious length. The vampire's long teeth are fully exposed now: I know he's got a hard-on.

'I'm going to shoot,' says Luke urgently. He's young; it's not surprising he hasn't Mark's endurance. His balls are clenched so hard his scrotum has a bluish hue.

'Feel free.' Naylor grabs me by the hair and pulls me off Luke's cock, holding me there as the man starts to come. My mouth is open, gasping for air, but I receive such a gush of semen that I nearly choke. The rest is directed over my face and on my breasts, Luke jerking his length with his hand to wring out every last drop.

'Shit – shit – shit!' he cries.

'Swallow,' Naylor orders, letting me collapse from my aching knees to my butt, and I know better than to disobey. Luke's ejaculate is tangy and sharp.

Mark grits his teeth in a grin and turns away, his cock ruddy with frustration.

'Now clean your face, you dirty cow,' Naylor admonishes mildly. 'You're not finished yet. You two: bring her along.' He walks out of the bathroom.

Luke's cum is looped in sticky strands on my cold skin. I pull my wet top off over my head and wipe my face with it as best I can. Luke is smirking and pleased with himself, but Mark, still nursing his stiffy, is less relaxed. He reaches down to help me to my feet and catches my eye, frowning at the tears welling there. 'You're all right, girl,' he says gruffly. 'You've not been hurt.'

Well, that one takes me by surprise.

Together they frogmarch me out through the kitchen,

back to the downstairs back room and that creaky old bed. When we enter the room Naylor is sitting on the stained yellow nylon quilt, naked. I don't know where his clothes have gone; there's no sign of them. His cock is fully erect, elegant in comparison to the two heavies flanking me. He smiles a vampire smile, cruel as razors.

'Lift her up,' he says, gesturing. 'Spread her.'

With a quick glance at each other they take hold under my arms, grabbing my legs to lift me horizontal, holding my sex wide open for Naylor's pleasure; though I twist my hips reflexively I can't hide what's between my legs. My feet dangle in mid-air: they're both big boys and have no difficulty holding me between them. I feel weightless, for once, and hopelessly weak; my struggles are tokens only, ineffective against their immensely superior strength. Standing, Naylor approaches and buries his hand in my pussy, sliding fingers inside me. I squeal and buck in vain, making my breasts slam up and down.

'You like that, don't you?' he asks.

'Nooo!'

'Cunt doesn't lie, Jo. Wet cunt says you're a dirty slut. That you like being used by three big bastards at once.'

I count two big bastards and a pretty-boy, myself, but I'm in no position to argue. His hand is moving in and out and twisting round, measuring the limits my hole will stretch to. Then he pulls it out and slides those fingers, slippery with my juices, to the puckered iris below. I feel my muscles resist him only for a moment, and then he's past my last defence and sending hot flashes through my whole body as he invades my tender anus. His free hand takes over duties in my pussy – and now he's inside me with both hands, playing me like a glove puppet, making me shudder and sweat and keen loudly.

'Bite her,' Luke urges under his breath.

'Hm?' Intent on his work, Naylor only raises an eyebrow.

'Why don't you bite her?' His voice is husky. I know his type. Vampire wannabe, not vampire groupie. Sees himself as a Top.

'I can't bite her: she'll only end up enjoying herself.' Naylor's teeth – they're hollow, I've worked out, and they inject something just like a snake does, when he bites – are all out on display though, now, and his irises are narrow green rims around depthless black pits. The need for blood is rising with his arousal. They're hypnotic, those eyes, and I can't look away. I see myself mirrored in them, his slave. 'That would never do, would it Jo? I mean,' he adds, rolling my clit with his thumb as he ruthlessly plunders both my holes, 'imagine how humiliating that would be, to be held down and fucked by three men, screaming "Yes!" and coming – over and over again – because you can't get enough of being treated like the dirty little slut you are ...'

And his words are drowned as I do come, screaming, just like he wants me to. Then I burst into tears of shame. The tears keep on coming as he pulls out his hand and replaces the sudden void in my bottom with his cock, driving it home with ruthless thrusts and squirting me full of his cold semen as he climaxes. I feel utterly violated.

He doesn't go soft afterwards, of course. He's only just getting started. He pulls out of my butt and plants his stake straight back in the softer ground of my pussy. Dirty bastard. What does he care? He plucks me out of the cradle of arms and walks over to the bed, holding me impaled on his cock. My head falls back and my braided hair swings like the rope of a gallows victim. I feel him swing me round and then he settles himself back flat on the bed and pulls me down on top of him, legs sprawled astride his hips. 'My filthy little whore,' he whispers. 'Tonight you're going to ho for all three of us.'

He's as cold as a corpse, still. Even his cock, inside me. It feels like glass. My pussy's still clenching around it.

'Come on, gentlemen. Let's get stuck in; there's room for a couple more up top. Luke, take her ass; I've lubed her up for you. Mark, get up here in her mouth.'

The two grunts strip off, with clumsy eagerness. Luke gets down to naked, his chest muscular and gleaming. 'I'm going to use a rubber,' he says, extracting a crushed packet from his jeans pocket. 'Don't know where the dirty bitch has been.'

'Suit yourself,' says Naylor. I don't suppose STDs apply to the undead.

Mark keeps his T-shirt on, white with a sports logo; maybe he's a bit ashamed of his faint paunch. But as he climbs up on the bed and straddles Naylor's head I see vampire track-marks all over his legs and groin. He's an old hand, it seems. His cock is a little softer than last time I had it in my mouth, but a couple of strokes of his palm buff it up good as new. He slaps my cheeks with it, like he's challenging me to a duel. I turn my face away, still trying to catch my breath; this time he slaps me with his open hand – not hard enough to hurt, but hard enough to shock and make his humiliating point clear. I gasp and look contrite.

'Come on: be a good girl.'

Naylor sniggers and stabs me deep. I don't resist when Mark grabs the hair on the top of my head, tilts my head back so my mouth falls open, and aims his rod at the back of my throat. Beneath me, Naylor gets a ringside view of that cock sinking into between my lips. There's that oral fixation again. He can't resist any longer: he starts to bite Mark lightly, up the insides of the thighs. For a second the cock goes soft in my mouth, then Mark grunts and there's a surge of solidity in the column of flesh gagging me. His breathing starts to come quick and shallow, his thrusts little more than quivers as he pushes my head up and down on him, both hands wrapped in my hair.

So I'm back to giving Mark a blowjob, my attentions undivided this time, while Luke mounts up behind me and sticks his thick fingers up my sorely used bum-hole. Naylor's come has got me greased up, making entry easy. I'm glad of that: Luke's girth is going to be a burden as it is. He's taking his time impaling me though, working his fingers in and out, sometimes pressing his hot cock to my dilated aperture, but never rampaging home. He's not hard enough, I'm dimly aware, though most of my attention is on my frenzied sucking and on Naylor's feeding going on below.

Then Naylor reaches Mark's balls and takes a greedy bite, and the big man explodes in my mouth like a salt-sea breaker and I have to swallow it all down or choke. Mark is moaning and swearing and coughing like he's been punched in the stomach, his cock throbbing on my tongue.

'For fuck's sake, Luke,' Naylor complains, detaching his bloody mouth from Mark's scrotum. 'What's taking you? You going to spit-roast the hog or not?'

'Give us a chance,' Luke mumbles.

'What?'

'Shut up, Luke,' Mark coughs, hoarse. 'I'll do it, Naylor. Let her suck him for a while ...'

His cock, I notice, is still rock. Like a vampire's.

Naylor's voice hardens. 'I want Luke to do it.'

'I've already come once. I need a minute ...'

With a grunt of irritation Naylor rolls me off on to the

mattress and sits up, staring at Luke. The young man looks defensive.

'Give it here,' says Naylor impatiently, reaching for Luke's cock like it's a TV remote that needs new batteries.

Luke's hands get in the way. 'Oi!' he protests.

From that I'd know, even if I hadn't seen his smooth, unpunctured skin, that he's a vampire virgin. He's never messed with one before. Stupid fool, I think, as Naylor's eyes narrow and he stretches out his hand again.

Luke yells: 'Get off it, you fucking qu–'

But Naylor throws him backwards off the bed and on to the floor before he can even finish the word. Then he picks him up, one hand to that broad throat, and slams him against the wall at the full stretch of his arm. I can see Luke's feet kicking, trying to make contact with the floorboards. His eyes bulge. His bulk's no match for that slim inhuman strength.

Just for a second there's no one holding me or watching me and I nearly panic, wondering what I should do. Should I try to escape? Then Mark's fingers knot in my hair from behind and he pushes my wrist up behind my back, and I relax.

'Shut up. Stay still,' he whispers in my ear.

Luke's face is darkening with congestion. He tries to push Naylor away, and that doesn't work. As he runs out of air he starts to freak out and hit and kick in earnest; his blows bounce off the willowy vampire without the slightest effect. I'm not sure that Naylor even feels them. He keeps Luke pinned there until the struggles cease and then drops him contemptuously. Luke rolls on his side, choking and clutching his throat. Naylor kicks him over on to his back then kneels and wrenches those big dark thighs open, before yanking off the condom and sinking his teeth brutally into the man's cock.

Luke can't scream; his throat is too bruised. He makes a

horrible breathy squeaking noise in which terror and pain are mixed. Then he inhales and does it again, but this time the sound has changed. His back arches, his hips buck, his hands drum and clutch at the boards. He's coming; I know he's coming; his orgasm is being wrenched out of him by a force stronger than anything imaginable as Naylor feeds, slurping down without distinction his seed and his blood.

When Naylor finally sits back, Luke touches his genitals like he's amazed to find them still there. His cock looks bloated and turgid, and his balls are drawn up tight to his groin. And he's crying with shock: tears stand in his eyes and run down over his scarred cheeks. But he doesn't make a sound.

'Get up,' grunts Naylor, standing. And Luke obeys, abashed and shaking.

Like the beam of a lighthouse, the vampire's attention switches back to me. 'Enjoy the show, Jo? I hope you took the opportunity to rest.'

I'm going to need every second of my brief respite, I realise. Luke's hand is already moving over his swollen prick, trying to soothe an itch of sexual desperation that's building in his poisoned flesh. Mark is stabbing at my ass from behind, panting with impatience. And Naylor's cock is standing as proud as ever. He's as beautiful and virile as a pagan god on a museum postcard. Three men, all with rock-hard cocks, all able to go for hours. And all now looking at me.

* * *

When I wake up, underneath that horrid quilt, it's daylight and they've all gone. I open gummed-up eyes and lie there for a while without thinking and then, when I dare, I start cautiously to take stock. My whole body aches; every muscle, every orifice. My jaw feels like I've been chewing through industrial rubber. My mouth is dry and tastes of cum, and my hands smell of it too – as well as of my own pussy. That particular part of my body feels bloated and tender, and my thighs are stuck together with semi-dry spunk. My ass twinges, raw, as I clench my bottom; now that the effects of Naylor's bite have worn off I can feel the abused tissues again.

Naylor didn't manage to resist, of course. He bit me almost straightaway and drank deep: all over my tits and on my pussy and right on my asshole. And just as he'd predicted I spent the rest of the night begging them frantically to fuck me, to fuck me now, to fuck me harder. They hardly needed encouraging.

Mark and Luke must be as sore now as if they'd run a marathon. In sandpaper underwear.

My stomach growls, gnawing at me. I roll out from under the quilt and shuffle gingerly over to the table, right at the limit of my chain, and find the takeaway food still untouched – cold and greasy now, naturally, but a blessing in my ravenous belly. I shovel the contents of the foil boxes into my mouth with my fingers, mixing body-salt with the fragrant sauces. As I eat, memories of last night surface: visions of them fucking me in every imaginable position, all at once or one at a time. Mark kneeling on the edge of the bed riding my ass, slapping my cheeks like I'm a mule, as I hang upside down with my face on the floor. Luke shafting the ravine between my tightly-squeezed breasts. Naylor fucking Luke from behind even as the man nails me hard with my ankles pinned over my head; he's howling and weeping and coming all at once.

Halfway through the carton of beef in black bean sauce I pause and wipe my lips. I need a drink of water and I need to use the toilet, really desperately. And oh, God, do I need a wash. With a promise to the egg fried rice that I'll be back, I return to the bed, grasp the iron frame and pull. One metal leg lifts a couple of inches and I slip the loop of the chain out from underneath. Carrying my bonds, I pad through to the back rooms.

Naylor's a fucking idiot, really. The chains achieve nothing. If I wanted to escape I'd be lost for choice – I wouldn't even have to bother climbing out of this bathroom window with the links wrapped around me. My blog connects me to the outside world still. I've got e-mail. My bloody cell phone is in my rucksack, for fuck's sake; I rang in sick to work after the first night, hoping they'd not dump me from my job, not right away anyhow. Not that I give a shit about my job, but a girl can't live on takeaways and semen for ever.

Don't get me wrong: it's not the bites that keep me here, any more than it's the padlocks. I've heard that for some people it's the sexual high and the all-night orgasms that turn them into vampire-junkies. Now, I've got nothing against orgasms. But that's not what I stay for.

It's the humiliation.

Did Naylor realise, when he confronted me in the cellar of the BDSM club that night? He should have, of course, but he's so bloody self-centred it's actually possible he didn't work it out. He might well think that the degradation, the shame and the sleaze are something he's inflicting on me; a fate worse than death.

Idiot.

My name's Joanne and I'm not real. I'm a plump bird with a crap job retrieving shelved goods in a catalogue-shop, and no one knows who I am. I'm not pretty or chirpy enough to get noticed. If I don't ever go back to work I don't suppose anyone outside of the admin office will even realise that I'm missing. No one remembers Joanne. She's not real.

These two are real, though. StakeGirl is real. StakeGirl matters to people. And Jo. Jo-Jo-Jugs they call her, in the public clubs and the darker underground places. The sort of place where Naylor found me, kneeling on the floor with a vibrator between my open legs, playing with my tits and my pussy while a ring of men round me watched and jacked off. No touching, goes the rules, but anyone – anyone at all – can come in and beat their meat and squirt their jizz all over my big bare tits and on my face. They know me in the clubs. They look for me. They treat me like a goddess; their own tawdry filthy idol. They gather to make their votive offerings, week after week, in awe at my sluttishness.

That's real.

Naylor, the stupid bastard – now he makes me feel real too. I'm not daft; of course there's a certain amount of risk. He's a fucking vampire. But it's got to be worth it, to be real. Worth the fear – the genuine fear – and the discomfort.

Two men. He brought two men last night. Two total strangers to fuck me. What'll he do next time? Five? Six? A football team? No, better: a rugby team. I'd like that: big, strong, ugly, frightening men with smashed-up faces; men that'll make me feel tiny and helpless and debased. I put my hand between my legs as the mere thought makes my sore pussy quiver and grow moist again. The prospect terrifies me. I'm not at all sure my body can take that sort of punishment – but I want to know. I want to try.

I slip back into the bedroom, grabbing another mouthful of Chinese food in passing, and retrieve my laptop from under the bed.

Time to blog.

8: Three, Three the Rivals

Rosa 'Peace': yellow-pink blend, hybrid tea rose

Reynauld settles himself down into his casket, just as he does every morning before dawn. There's no point in struggling to eke out the last few moments of consciousness; the process is unpleasant enough even when he's relaxed. Already he can feel the chill taint in his flesh. He could stand in an Arctic blizzard and not feel cold, but he's clammy now. Reaching up, he grasps the handle on the underside of the steel lid and slides it into place, the rim settling with a clunk into its airtight seal. That last sliver of light shows the outline of his hands, and then for a moment darkness is total before the interior lights flicker on – so faint that a cat would be blind, but he can see clearly enough. His fingers feel clumsy as he slides the interior bolts into place over his head. Then he lies back and relaxes his muscles. The earth beneath him smells rich and Amanda has seen to it that it's been dug over well to make him a soft bed. It's so quiet in here that he can hear the worms burrowing through the damp particles of soil. No other sound impinges on his hearing: not even the tick of his pulse. That stopped some time in the fourteenth century, a redundant function of a body that no longer needed such habits.

Death comes quickly. It's all over in a minute or two if he doesn't fight it, so he deliberately empties his mind just as if kneeling in his shrine to meditate. Cold creeps from his fingertips and toes toward his chest, the flesh growing flaccid and numb. Despite himself he does feel it; an indefinable shrivelling within, a cessation of effort on the minutest level. Not for his body the stuttering continuation of biological processes that outlasts human death, the biochemical factories that carry on burning and building hours or days after higher functions have ended. His body has been dead for centuries and knows that only too well. It's not biology that makes him feel nauseous as the paralysis surges up his torso. It's not hormones that fuel the guttering flicker of despair. It cannot be his heart that clenches in agony, somewhere in the darkness in a body that he can no longer feel: his heart hasn't beat in years.

Reynauld spasms, a reflex action that jerks his chin up and exposes bared fangs, but his consciousness is already snuffed out like a candle, no longer existent.

He's dead.

* * *

Rosa 'Special Friend': pink-apricot blend, hybrid tea rose

Amanda is stripping the sheets in the master bedroom when her cell phone rings. She turns and looks out of the window as she lifts it to her ear: the first thing she did at dawn was throw open the shutters and the glass to let in light and air. Outside, there are barges plying up and down the river, and traffic is building on the bridge downstream. The City is coming to life.

In here, as she listens to the voice dancing gleefully down the aether, something inside her dies.

* * *

Rosa 'Intrigue': reddish-purple, floribunda rose

They arrive within a half-hour. Naylor she knew would be there, and she's not surprised to see Estelle too – she never trusted that woman. But she's hurt despite herself at the sight of Ben. She'd liked Ben. What, she wonders in despair, is his problem with Reynauld? And how long have they been conspiring against him? It's another tooth in the horror that's gnawing away at her insides, another ingot on the pile of her guilt.

Hunched under hoods and blankets the three vampires stalk up the ramp from their boat and glance around warily at The Bonding's undercroft, not quite hiding their relief at being in shade again. Behind them shuffle three human men, but they're irrelevant as far as Amanda's concerned. Sunlight shines on the water, turning them all to black silhouettes.

Her mouth feels like it's full of sand.

'I know an old lady,' Naylor sings, grinning crookedly, 'who sold out her guy. I don't know why she sold out her guy. I guess she'll die.'

Fuck you, she wants to say. Fuck you, you sneering little piece of shit. I hope one day someone rips off your eyelids and cuts off your head and stakes it on a ten-foot pole so you can watch the sun come up. When she opens her mouth, though, it's to address Estelle. She wishes her voice weren't shaking. 'Funny. Of all of them, you're the last one I'd have called stupid. But you're trying to put *him* in charge?'

Too fast for her to see, Naylor is round behind her, pinning her in his arms, pulling her jaw back. His nails puncture her skin and there's no euphoria as with the bite, just a jagged pain. 'I know an old lady,' he croons, licking at the trickles, 'who wants to die. She wants to die 'cos she sold out her guy. I'll drink her dry.'

Shaking, sweating, Amanda wishes he would. She clenches her teeth, but it still shocks her when Naylor throws her to the ground – hard enough to bounce her head off the stone floor – then wrenches her up again. The pain makes her want to vomit.

'I'm not in charge,' he announces, barely audible through the ringing in her skull. 'I'm not *gauleiter* Reynauld. I'm setting us all free.' Then he tosses her across the room, into Ben's arms. 'Less chat, more action. Lead on.'

* * *

Rosa 'Champagne Moment': apricot, floribunda rose

Amanda punches in the numbers to the combination lock and then stands aside as Naylor pulls the door open. She feels sick and unreal. Even the pain throbbing in her wrenched muscles and bruised flesh seems distant now. This has happened so fast. She's made decisions in moments that she couldn't imagine ever taking. And now, with this door, she's betrayed Reynauld irrevocably.

The room within is silent, and completely bare but for the metal casket. Naylor glances at her. 'You first, darling.'

Damn. The faint hope she'd entertained of trapping them inside until sunset withers up, as one of the three humans that Naylor's brought with him gives her a firm shove between the shoulder blades, propelling her inside. She staggers and has to catch herself on the sarcophagus. It feels cold beneath her fingers and she pictures her body-heat sinking through the metal to warm Reynauld. If he could hear her, if he could wake …

But he can't. He's helpless.

She can see her blurred reflection in the metal. 'Roisin,' she whispers. Roisin is the only one old enough to help, if she cares to. Then Naylor struts in like he owns the place, a smirk on his lips that makes that ripe mouth quite ugly. Ben brings up the rear.

'Beautiful,' Naylor says, eyeing the coffin as Estelle runs her hands across it, feeling for the crack of the lid. 'Just beautiful. He's like a tin of Spam, isn't he?' He lifts clenched fists in triumph. 'Fuckin' awesome!'

'Please,' Amanda says, addressing Ben. There's no point in begging Naylor, and there's no use in being surreptitious either. 'You mustn't let him do this.'

Ben smiles uncomfortably and shrugs. He's had an expression on since they got here like he's playing a game and he's very proud about how clever they've been, but he's not sure how it's going to finish. 'It's the way it goes, Amanda,' he mutters. 'Old guard and all that. It's gotta happen some time.'

'He was always fair with you!'

'Shut it,' says one of the men unwisely, reaching out to her.

Ben's hand intercepts his wrist and twists. 'Don't touch her.' The eighteen-stone man gasps with pain.

'Girls,' interrupts Naylor testily. 'Save it for the playground. You – Wrinkly. Get this open.'

'I can't,' she answers. 'It's bolted from the inside.' She wonders if Naylor's going to kill her right now, the way his green eyes turn on her, blank as emeralds. She thinks she'd be glad if he killed her straightaway; she can't bear to see the consequences of her treachery.

'Really.' He's not perturbed. It's late summer and they have hours of daylight yet: he knows time is on his side. 'Then Daz here had better go get some cutting equipment.

You know where to find it, don't you?'

Daz is the one with the cracked wrist. He nods, white-faced.

'It's specially reinforced,' Amanda says, desperate.

'Well, you'd better hope it's not too special,' says Naylor, taking out his phone and tapping it meaningfully against the casket lid. 'Because if it starts to look like this'll take too long, your little Timmy's going to be filling out forms in triplicate for Saint fucking Peter.'

* * *

Rosa 'Breath of Life': pink-apricot blend, large-flowered climbing rose

Reynauld wakes, and it's nearly as frightening as dying. He feels the blood in his veins turning back to liquid, the burn of air in his lungs as he takes that first gasp, and the surge of hunger in his empty belly just as he does every night at sundown. And then this new thing: the pain. The sensation of blistering rawness across his chest and thighs is entirely overwhelmed by the agony in his wrists and hocks: for a moment it's so terrible that he can't think straight. His eyes fly open but the light's too bright and he screws them shut, howling.

Someone laughs.

The First Noble Truth of Buddhism: all is suffering.

With an effort of will Reynauld seizes the pain and shoves it deep deep down, at the furthest extent of his reach. This is not entirely a Buddhist thing: vampires are tolerant of physical damage – they can if necessary walk on broken bones and crawl away from their own severed limbs. The pain remains at the back of his mind, but as he regains control of his will he begins to properly grasp his situation. His head is hanging back – right back, nearly upside-down, stretching his throat. His arms and legs are spread wide, and the pain is concentrated there at his extremities. Reynauld forces his head up and his eyes open. Blackened patches of skin dance before his blurred vision as he fights to focus. He's been burned. He's naked and he's been exposed to sunlight while he lay dead. That's not the worst, though. He's suspended from wrists and ankles, spread wide, hanging off steel cables that attach to girders that arch overhead. The cables don't just loop round his limbs; they've been punched through them – behind his wrists and his Achilles tendons and grinding up against the bones. He's starting to bleed now that he's revivified.

Panting, Reynauld lets his head fall back and looks at the world upside down as he tries to make sense of it. More girders out there, painted white. Glass panes between them, and beyond that a blue twilight. He's not entirely hanging; there's another metal beam, horizontal this time, that runs across from side to side at the small of his back and stops him folding in half. But he can't move, and he can't reach any of the bolts holding the cable loops. He could rip his fetters out – he's strong enough to do that – but he'd be completely crippled. And he'd fall. How far would he fall?

Another blink, another moment to sort the images. He can see scaffolding, and wooden planks. Many beams, curved like ribs. He's suspended under an immense glass roof, just over a scaffolding platform. He's still gasping, and each breath seems to clear his head a little.

Then Naylor walks into his field of view.

* * *

Rosa 'Red Rascal': medium red, shrub rose

'Wakey wakey, Reynauld. Rise and shine.'

Reynauld doesn't answer: quipping with Naylor isn't a priority right now. He rolls his head, still trying to fix his bearings. It's a railway station, he thinks. One of those big glass roofs over the platforms, all Victorian ironwork and pigeon-shit. He can smell that and some sort of industrial grease and diesel fumes. And, more faintly, perfume. But there's no sound of engines or commuters. He's not really familiar with the public transport system. Aren't they restoring the roof at one of the big central stations at the moment? Is that where he is?

If he was Roisin, he'd just take his body apart and escape the cables. That's the irony: he's old enough that he should be able to escape any prison. But he's spent centuries clinging to human form. He's never let go, whatever the temptation. He doesn't know how.

'Looking for your breakfast?' Naylor asks. He grabs Reynauld's hair and twists his head savagely the other way. 'There she is.'

It's Amanda. She hangs almost limp in Ben's grasp, where he stands balanced casually on a beam. The makeshift planking platforms don't extend that far beneath them; she's dangling over empty space. Her clothing is dishevelled and Reynauld can see a couple of obvious bite marks on her bared shoulders. Black rage wells up to join the red and gnawing hunger in his belly.

'Pass her here.' Naylor crooks a finger. Ben makes a face as if – just for a moment – he's thinking of refusing, then takes a deep breath and jumps the eight-foot gap to the platform, with Amanda tucked under his arm. Naylor takes charge of the woman and drops to his knees with her, right next to Reynauld so that even from his position he can see her torn skirt, the tops of those hold-up stockings he likes her to wear and the puncture marks on her exposed breasts. Her eyes are glazed; she's in a bite trance. He can smell her warmth and hear the swift stumble of her pulse, and his dry mouth is suddenly running wet.

'She did it,' Naylor confides. 'She let us into the house, sent the guards away, opened the crypt. She sold you out, Old Man.'

Amanda slowly shuts her eyes and turns her bruised face away from her employer. The movement exposes her throat. Like a chained dog, the ravenous appetite in his gut surges forward. Suddenly he can't hide his teeth.

'Hungry?' Naylor whispers.

Every evening when Reynauld awakes he feeds a little from Amanda, just enough to blunt the crueller edge of his craving, to allow him to concentrate on other matters. He'd normally think nothing of it but now it fills him with shame, a curdling addition to his brew of desperation and anger. Shame, because he can see how she's been abused – and yet he writhes with longing to bite her. His stomach is empty but feels like it's full of knives. He can smell the trickles of blood carelessly spilt down her skin and the rich aroma is sending him crazy. Blood is what he desperately needs right now. Blood would solve all his problems. Blood is healing and strength – and revenge.

* * *

Rosa 'Crimson Cascade': dark red, large-flowered climbing rose

Helpless, he watches Naylor twist to sink his teeth into

her throat and hears Amanda gasp. There are no words in Reynauld's head, only rage. Vampire etiquette is clear: you don't go for the neck unless you mean to kill. Or don't care if you do.

When Naylor lifts his face his mouth is full and overflowing. He holds the woman away at arm's length – she sags like a doll – and turns back to hover over Reynauld, knotting a fist in his prisoner's loose hair to prevent him from snapping up and taking a piece out of his face. Very deliberately he lets a crimson stream dribble over his lower lip, down on Reynauld's chin and cheeks. Red drips spatter olive skin. It's sticky on his lips.

Reynauld's body nearly turns itself inside out with the effort of not opening his mouth and licking at the flecks, but he retains control.

'Not even a kiss for me? You're such a prude,' Naylor admonishes mockingly.

Through gritted teeth Reynauld says, 'I'm impressed.'

'He speaks! The Great One deigns to speak!' Naylor tosses Amanda aside so he can sit down hard at Reynauld's head, and props it up on one hand as if listening to the whispers of an oracle, looking down the length of his torso. 'Tell us why you're impressed, O Great One.'

'I didn't think you'd have the balls.'

Despite himself, Naylor's spine stiffens. Reynauld feels the shift of tension, though he can't look at the man at his shoulder. 'You're about to find out what I have the balls to do,' the younger vampire hisses, drawing a sharp nail along the line of the other man's throat.

'Oh, I knew you resented me. I understood that. You're a malformed little child hating his daddy for not buying him a bag of crisps. I just didn't expect you'd have the balls to do anything about it. Or the brains.'

Naylor's voice is gloating: 'Yet here we are. I discovered your weakness.'

'Yes. You did. And you persuaded Ben and Estelle to back you up.' He twists his head as if staring at Estelle. He can't actually see her – he thinks she's somewhere down by his left flank, though his leg's in the way and he can't lift his head far enough – but he can smell Chanel. She likes to bed down on sheets that have been rinsed in *eau de toilette*. Old-fashioned in some ways, but then it's easy for a vampire to slip into a habit that lasts decades. 'Smart move. You must have really thought it through. I assume you've given as much consideration to the consequences?'

Naylor leans in to lick his cheek and temple. 'Oh, believe me: I've thought about it.'

* * *

Rosa 'American Beauty': deep pink, hybrid rose

From the shadows Estelle emerges, stretching indolently, to position herself between Reynauld's feet. She's wearing a black dress that's more strategic holes than fabric and her hair is moussed metallic gold. Her position grants her the best possible view up his body. For once she's willing to overlook the fact that he's not as beefy as she prefers her men; his pain and his fetters make up for that. And he's no weakling, even she admits. Now every inch of the scorched piebald skin stretched over his taut muscles is shiny with a clear plasma that the sunset's rays squeezed from his pores, and streaked with ash – his own ash. She could count every muscle if she chose. He's a work of art. Everything about his hard frame screams of strength, but his cock and ball-sac are rendered completely vulnerable by the roping apart of his legs and his chest is inflated with the pain he's bottling up. Strength and submission in one; she finds him all but irresistible. She's itching to touch him and to touch herself. Her mouth and pussy are both running wet.

He really does have a beautiful cock.

And oh, God, the smell of his blood ...

Reynauld strains to raise his head higher. 'Estelle. Why?'

What a fool he is. She only lifts an eyebrow and Naylor answers for her: 'When you're ash, Old Man, we'll all be free. A free-for-all. As it should be. It's what I've wanted all these years: just to live my own life. Don't I deserve that? You and your pathetic rules – there *are* no rules for us: don't you get it? We can do anything we like!'

'How do you think the humans will react to that?' He's forcing himself to stay rational, she observes. Why's he trying? Naylor isn't a rational adversary.

'Will I give a shit?'

'You will when they come for you. They're not stupid. They'll fight back if you start to kill.'

'Let them. We're the apex predators here.'

'Oh, yes. Like tigers. And sharks. And grizzly bears. You see any other apex predator they haven't brought to the edge of extinction?'

'You're boring me, Reynauld. As usual.'

'They've got weapons and they far outnumber us.'

'Not for long.'

'That's what you're after? A war?' He grabs Estelle's gaze. 'You planning to do business in the rubble, Estelle? Is this your vision too? Is that why you jumped on the bandwagon?'

She reaches between his legs and runs a fingertip from his thigh up to his pierced ankle, tracing a runnel of blood.

Vampire blood is much darker than the human variety, almost black. Poking the wound elicits a pleasing tremor from him. She licks her fingertip – it tastes as savoury and rich as raw chocolate – then runs both hands lovingly down the insides of his thighs, all the way to his crotch. She can feel her lips are swollen, her mouth watering. 'I jumped,' she answers, her voice a purr, devouring his pinned and naked body with her gaze, 'because I had to see this, Reynauld. I'd give anything to see this.'

And though he tries, he can't quite hide the look in his eyes: his hurt at her betrayal.

She finds that most amusing.

* * *

Rosa 'Mixed Feelings': red-pink stripes, miniature rose

The planks are splinter-coarse and white with the dust of old limewash. Amanda's hands look nearly as white and her pristine nails are ragged. She broke them while they were playing with her, him and Naylor. For some reason this irrelevant detail wakes a creep of guilt in Ben's gut. She always takes such pains about her appearance, and now they've really messed her up

With infinite effort Amanda pushes herself up and starts to crawl away on her belly, away from Naylor and Reynauld. Ben doesn't know what she's thinking of but she's aiming for the platform edge so he intercepts her and she crawls right up to his shins. 'What are you doing?' he hisses, stooping.

'Stop him, Ben,' she whispers as he scoops her upright. She feels light and frail in his embrace. Her lips tremble against the whorl of his ear; she doesn't seem to care that he's taken as much blood from her as Naylor has. 'Stop him. You can't let him do this.'

He forces himself to resist the lure of her warm throat, so close to his lips and already ruptured by Naylor's teeth. 'I can't, Amanda ...'

'What are you playing at, Ben?' demands Naylor, momentarily distracted from taunting Reynauld.

'Nothing.'

'Put her down. Put her fucking down. She's not yours.'

He lets her slide back to her knees. Naylor has the knack of making him feel inadequate. 'Well,' he mumbles. 'I thought ...'

'You thought what?'

'She could ... I could have her.'

'Really? What's the attraction? She tastes like Old Man's jizz, she's so well used.'

Ben shakes his head, feeling hopelessly inarticulate, his eyes not meeting Naylor's. 'She's not a problem. I mean ... I'd quite like ... There's no need to ...'

'Fuck me, Ben. You getting sentimental? You like the old biddy?'

He shrugs. How could he explain that sort of thing – especially to someone like Naylor?

'Or are you hedging your bets?' Naylor casts a narrow glance at Reynauld. 'Having second thoughts, are you?'

That makes him jump. 'No!'

'You'd better not. It's a bit late for that. You'd better put her down, Ben. I mean, right down. Drop her.'

He doesn't want Naylor turning on him. The guy can be a bit of a nutter sometimes. 'OK, I ...'

'I mean enter her into the indoor skydiving championships. Now.'

He freezes, dismayed. 'That isn't fair.'

'Fair?' The concept sounds ludicrous, the way Naylor says it. 'What sort of hippy shit are you on? Why should it be fair?' His face is barred with teeth. 'Now throw her away.' His voice becomes a growl that reverberates through the roofspace. 'I mean it.'

It's best not to think, just to act. Ben makes a funny noise in his chest, then with a convulsive movement jerks Amanda's body sideways out over the empty space, shakes off her clinging hands, and lets her fall.

Reynauld howls with rage, the cry echoing under the glass.

* * *

Rosa 'Angel Face': mauve, floribunda rose

Amanda, who wants to die, still screams as she plummets. Scaffolding poles blur past her; there's ninety foot of drop between the platform and the tracks below.

But before she hits, something snatches her from the fall, nearly snapping her neck. She stares up into Roisin's colourless eyes. The vampire woman is standing in mid-air, solid as rock although her garments flare to white mist around her, her slender wrists supporting Amanda's weight without effort. The expression on her face is one of intense concentration, as if she's trying to remember who Amanda is.

'Oh, please,' Amanda mouths.

Then Roisin lets go, and she hits concrete. But it's only a six-foot drop this time, though it knocks all the wind out of her and for a moment she can do nothing but lie there. Her neck feels numb; she's glad about that. Most of her is numb and heavy. If she were lying in a comfortable bed she'd even describe the lassitude as blissful, but in this context it's anything but.

When she opens her eyes and manages to focus through the gloom, she's staring at the cracked leather of a pair of narrow boots, right in front of her nose.

'Chatelaine?' says a voice.

Wakefield's.

* * *

Rosa 'White Spray': clear white, floribunda rose

The moment Amanda drops out of sight Naylor forgets her. The prospect of Reynauld's helpless body is just too much to be distracted from. He's wanted to do this so long. He's fantasised about this moment for decades, almost from the first time they met – when he was just newly blooded and Reynauld was clearing the ground for his domain.

What a hypocrite. This shit-bag systematically wiped out every vampire in the City after he first got here, sparing only Roisin and Naylor because he thought they were harmless. Scorched earth: literally. He burned the last of them out. You wouldn't know that from the way he talks now. You wouldn't think from his fine words that he'd burned down a city to lay claim to the ashes.

Well, now it's time for the Good fucking Shepherd to get what's coming to him from the wolves. He hangs there, spread-eagled and trembling with the strain and the pain. His skin is charred in patches from when they unwrapped him to hang him up, making him even more naked; he reminds Naylor of the skinned carcasses down at Smithfield market. His hands have flexed into claws. It's a pity he doesn't have a heartbeat – Naylor would dearly love to hear the fear in his racing pulse. But he's breathing hard, and his pupils are so dilated they look like obsidian, and the sinews in his neck stand out like wires.

Naylor's going to enjoy this. He's got a triumphant hard-on already. Which, he figures, he might as well make use of. Springing up on to Reynauld's chest, he drops to a squat, relishing the heave that tells him his prisoner is fighting the pain his extra weight inflicts. 'There are times I really miss being able to take a piss,' he remarks, cutting the shadow-fabric of his clothes with his nails and stroking his cock. 'Still, this'll do. Open wide.'

He starts to tug on his stiff shaft. He's so fucking hard he feels it throbbing like a wound, and the surge begins almost at once. This is the revenge he's dreamed of; the first of a hundred lovingly crafted humiliations. He wants Reynauld to curse and protest, but the older man goes quiet; having vented a howl when Amanda fell, he now sets his jaw. He twists his face away, though, in a most satisfactory manner, and Naylor enjoys clamping him in place as he spurts all over his face in fluid dollops. The physical thrill is almost an irrelevancy; it's an act of contempt, not lust. But there's a lot of pleasure in seeing his pale spill painted on that sallow skin.

'Was it good for you?' he asks, straddling Reynauld's chest before dropping back to the boards. He intends to get a lot more use out of his dick before the night's over, but he's denied himself the main reward for too long. Besides, he's hungry.

* * *

Rosa 'First Kiss': light-pink, floribunda rose

'Give us a kiss, darling,' he mocks. 'I always like a kiss and cuddle afterwards.' Taking hold of that thick hair he pulls Reynauld's head right back and sinks his teeth hard into his throat.

* * *

Rosa 'Euphoria': yellow-orange blend, ground cover rose

It barely has time to hurt. That's the worst thing about it: the physical shock is breathtaking but it's followed by a surge of intense euphoria that nearly knocks Reynauld out. It's like the rush of morphine, it's like sex and death dancing together through his veins, it's like the distillation of surrender. It goes on and on. He can feel Naylor's teeth grinding against the gristle of his Adam's apple and it *doesn't hurt*. He hates that: he'd rather have the pain. He wants to be able to scream but his body is no longer under his control. He can feel his limbs spasming, feel the whole scaffolding edifice shake.

For the first time, in the eye of that hurricane rush, he despairs.

Then Naylor pulls away, sucking his teeth, and Reynauld realises blearily that the shaking is still going on. That someone else is making the tower tremble. Someone climbing up. He lets his head hang loose, feeling the wound in his throat leaking, blood trickling down toward his ears. He sees hands appear on the platform's edge.

It's Wakefield. And beyond him, rising through the darkening vault of the station like a spectre, hovers Roisin with her arms outstretched and brows knotted in anger.

* * *

Rosa 'Blue for You': mauve, floribunda rose

'Stop this,' says Wakefield, eyes wide, taking in the sacrificial scene laid out before them. Naylor is rising from Reynauld's throat. Estelle stands beyond, between the victim's legs. Ben is lurking to one side, looking nervous. 'God in Heaven, Naylor, you've got to stop.'

Naylor wipes his mouth, positioning himself between so that they can't see Reynauld's face. The blood smear looks as black as pitch. 'I don't remember inviting either of you to the party.'

'Stop,' echoes Roisin – and it is like an echo – it's a voice without substance, without a source: her lips are parted but do not move. It crawls through the air like the breath of death itself and makes the gloom seethe. Paint flakes off the girders in rusty patches; the brittle skeletons of pigeons rise from their resting-places on the joists and strut about; a swarm of dead flies buzzes around them.

Some of them can't remember ever hearing her speak before. Now they wish they never had. Ben actually cringes and even Estelle looks shocked. Only Naylor manages to mask his consternation. 'Of course,' he adds with a ghastly grin, 'you're welcome anywhere, Lady.'

'You don't really want to do this,' Wakefield tells him.

'Oh, I think I do.'

'Naylor. Please.' Wakefield spreads his hands in revulsion. 'Look at yourself! What the hell are we?'

'Last time I looked ... I was a vampire. What about you, Wakefield?' His voice becomes silky as he switches his attention to Roisin. 'What about you, Lady?' He steps aside, deliberately revealing Reynauld's hanging body – and the damage to his throat – as if drawing back a theatre curtain. 'What,' he asks, 'are you?'

Brushing past Wakefield, Roisin floats closer, her face thrust forward, as she takes in the sight of Reynauld's head hanging back below his shoulders, his throat exposed, the trickles of black blood working their way into his beard and down into his dark and dangling hair to drip on the boards. He's still conscious: his eyes are open, but they seem unfocused.

'Oh,' she says, and everyone there feels the hair stir on their arms as the air vibrates. Then she moves forward to kneel before him, cupping his inverted face in her hands, kissing his lips and pressing her cheek against his: a *pieta* as cold as any carved in marble.

'That's right: kiss the poor thing better.'

Wakefield feels his stomach lurch, the skin crawling on his spine.

With horror but no surprise he watches as she leans in and nuzzles closer, her kisses becoming sucks, her tongue joining her lips. Lapping at the ooze of blood.

'Thought so,' says Naylor softly.

'You bastard,' Wakefield says weakly. He knows he's no match for Naylor on his own.

'Don't you want to try it?' Naylor moves in close, slipping a hand behind Wakefield's head as if drawing him in for a kiss. Nose to nose, skin brushing. 'After all those years of abstinence, think how good it'd taste.' Even his voice is soft and full of promise. Wakefield can smell the blood smeared on his lips. It's far richer than anything from an animal or human, a scent that claws at his throat and makes every inch of his skin catch light. Suddenly he knows famine in each bone of his body. He can hear himself starting to pant, hear the little whimpers bursting out of his chest, feel the clutch of his scrotum contracting as arousal surges through his extremities.

'Let me go,' he gasps, his stomach knotting with hunger, his teeth sliding to sharp points. Even as he says it, he's straining to lick at the blood.

Naylor takes a step back, but his eyes have a surer grasp even than his hands. He directs Wakefield's own gaze down. 'Look.'

There's blood on his feet. Naylor is clothed but his feet are bare, and Reynauld's blood has splashed on the tops of his feet.

'Oh, my good God ...'

'Lick it,' he says, and his voice is like velvet and iron and the implacable press of a hundred million years of black silt, pushing Wakefield to his knees. 'You want his blood. Lick it up.'

Limbs buckling, Wakefield goes down and presses his mouth to Naylor's feet, tasting heaven.

* * *

Rosa 'Burning Desire': bright-red, hybrid tea rose

Dimly, Reynauld hears Naylor's voice – 'Come on then. This is what you all really want, isn't it?' – as at the same time lines of fire are scored down his ribs. Naylor's cutting him, he realises; using his nails to make the blood run. And of course the younger vampire is right in what he says. They're all pressing in now, mesmerised by the sanguine flow. The temptation is too alluring. Even with his eyes shut Reynauld can see them all around him, glowing violet against the darkness inside his head. They can't resist. No matter their personalities or their loyalties, whether they prefer him to Naylor or the other way round, they need by their nature to feed. They are, at core, predators. And in the end blood is the only thing that counts.

The Second Noble Truth of Buddhism: all suffering arises out of craving.

He can feel Roisin at his throat, gentle as a leech, offering no succour. Naylor sits astride his waist and bites into his chest. Then come more bites – Wakefield on the inside of his upper right arm and Ben on his left armpit, gnawing at the tears Naylor's nails have made. Bliss storms through his body, an invading army, taking the pain and turning it to arousal, taking the weakness and dressing it as euphoria. All the defences of his body, all the instincts that would make him struggle or flee, are subverted. Every nerve turns collaborator. He can't fight, any more than a human pinned by a single vampire can fight. He doesn't want to. He wants ...

Estelle moves on him last of all, taking his cock in her mouth and biting that. It takes seconds for him to hit his first orgasm. He comes blood and semen, and it doesn't stop. He thinks he might be screaming, but he can't tell.

They will empty him of every last drop.

* * *

Rosa 'Heartbreaker': cream-pink blend, miniature rose

'Whoa whoa whoa!' Naylor is suddenly annoyed. 'Somebody is enjoying this far too much. That won't do at all.' Sitting up, he strikes at Wakefield and Ben and they release their bites, backing away to lick their chops, looking dazed and angry. Wakefield even lifts a hand in frustration, but thinks better of it as he recognises the look in Naylor's eye.

'That's right,' Naylor hisses. Twisting, the slender man lashes out back-handed at Estelle, smacking her across the face. She jerks away from Reynaud's bloody flesh and bares her teeth in a silent snarl. In less than a second Naylor is on his feet between Reynauld's spread legs with her, face to face since they are almost the same height – Estelle a few inches taller. For a moment they glare at each other, and it looks as if Estelle is going to spit. Then she drops her eyes in submission. Naylor smirks, cups her jaw in his hand and reaches up to lick the blood and semen from her lips. He smears it over her cheek with his wet tongue.

Estelle holds herself motionless, as stiff as a board. Even when he reaches down and gropes her pubic mound through her dress, his fingers pinching cruelly hard.

'Good girl,' sneers Naylor. Then he turns back to face Reynauld. Estelle can wait for later. Roisin he leaves to her own thing, though, and she continues lapping at the pinned man's throat.

'Can't have you enjoying yourself, can we, Old Man?' he croons. Blood has run down his chin and is streaking his bare chest.

Reynauld responds with a groan. Naylor doesn't think he's dying, not quite yet. It's an interesting question though: can a vampire die of blood-loss? Naylor suspects not. He thinks if he goes too far Reynauld will just pass into some sort of coma. Which would mean he'd miss all the vengeance Naylor has planned for him.

'You know what? Change of plan: I'm going to flay you raw and lick you like a popsicle until the sun comes up. I'm sure you'd like to stay awake to see that. The weatherman says it's going to be a beautiful day, Reynauld.'

The glass will provide no protection, he knows. The bastard's going to burn to ashes.

'But first,' Naylor adds, 'I'm think I'm going to tear your knob off. Then I'm going to cut you a hole and fuck it.'

He reaches in. His attention is on his victim's face though; he's relishing the anguish he's about to cause. So he doesn't notice Estelle's shift of stance, the fluid movement that brings her up at his shoulder. He doesn't notice until the blow hits him from behind and by then it's too late, far too late; he looks down in shock at his own bare chest and sees the ribs heave, forced up by the pressure from within. He opens his mouth but the gush of black blood chokes his words.

And then Naylor burns. His body turns black, the tissues disintegrating into charred wet flakes like wadded paper that's been thrown on the fire, his face peeling into a myriad fissures. Tiny blue flames erupt from those cracks and dance down to the splayed tips of his fingers. Shock registers in his eyes. He screams, a thin noise like steam venting. There's a crack as his jaw falls off and bounces off Reynauld's chest and away across the boards, spitting chemical sparks.

Then quite suddenly Naylor is gone, his body crumbling apart into flakes of ash as if it had never been a living thing but rather one of his sculptures, a papier-mâché parody of human form. There aren't even any bones. Reynauld is deluged in black flakes. From the smouldering debris a plume of smoke rises to lick the glass overhead.

That's when Roisin lifts her head, as intent as a greyhound spotting a hare, and launches herself straight up at the roof. There's no light source here where they are except for the last of the pale and guttering flames; it's hard to say for sure what is reflected in the glass. But she vanishes into the mirror-world without hesitation.

'What just happened?' Ben asks, as he and Wakefield back away.

* * *

Rosa 'The Dark Lady': dark-red, shrub rose

And that's when Estelle, who's had her arm thrust to the

elbow inside the cavity of his chest like a ventriloquist with a dummy, unclenches her hand enough to reveal Naylor's bloody heart still grasped there. It's the only thing left of his body: a potato-sized knot of blackened muscle. She brings it to her lips and licks it, openly luxuriating in the taste, her whole body shuddering as she arches her back, pressing her pubic mound against Reynauld's pelvis, barely able to keep herself upright. Her fingers grind into his flesh.

She's *coming*, Reynauld realises: she's just torn Naylor's heart out and she's climaxing.

In other circumstances he'd be horrified, but he's too weak with shock right now to feel any emotion. He can only watch as her face twists and she moans with triumph.

When Estelle's eyes open again, they're red from lid to lid. She peels her lips back to show her extended teeth in a grin that looks like it would like to devour the world. 'Well,' she says, her voice bubbling and thick. 'He wasn't expecting that.'

'Oh, shit,' says Ben faintly – and then he bolts, right over the edge of the platform, not even bothering to climb down. Reynauld hears the thump as he hits the concrete below and then the sound of his pounding feet fading into the distance.

'What about you?' she asks Wakefield, who looks like a man facing a firing squad.

'Me? M-madam, I am delighted, believe me.'

'I think you should leave too. *Right now*.'

Wakefield isn't the least inclined to argue. His departure is swift and soundless.

Then they are alone. Reynauld looks up at Estelle and tries to moisten his throat to speak, but nothing happens. His last ember of hope flares up into life again.

Then it dies for good as she drapes herself down full-length on his torso and sinks her teeth into his neck.

* * *

Rosa 'Times Past': pink, climbing rose

'It's nothing personal.' She's had to slap him back into consciousness. She spits his own blood into his mouth to moisten his lips. 'I never had any objection to your regime, Reynauld. It had the great advantage of stability. I just want to be the one on top.'

He's still pinned, still in agony. He's not even capable of lifting his hanging head now, but when he closes his eyes he can see her propped up on his chest, Naylor's heart tucked under her chin like a clutch purse. The damned object glows in his inner vision, white hot. With effort he manages to whisper, 'You always did prefer it that way.'

She smiles. 'And as I remember, you love it.'

He can't string together a cogent riposte, only the ghost of a moan.

'Do you remember Leysin, Reynauld? The Rhone Valley spread out below us? The sun setting over the Alps, turning the high slopes gold? No, of course you don't. I watched that alone, didn't I? – all bundled up on my couch on the terrace, coughing blood into my handkerchief. I remember, even then, thinking that it was a weakness of yours: this fear of the light. When someone is so strong, it's best to be aware of their weaknesses. I've kept a list of yours, over the years. Perhaps I should have warned you how dangerous they were. The way you trusted that Amanda, for example. Not wise. But I imagine you realise that now.'

'Estelle ...'

'Does it hurt, lover?' With lingering voluptuousness, she licks the sweat from his blistered skin. 'I can fix that, you know.'

He tries to draw a deeper breath, but there's no strength in his lungs. 'Don't leave me to burn,' he whispers.

'Actually, I think I'm going to let you go.'

Reynauld opens his eyes. He can't see her from this angle, just an upside-down view of girders and glass, and the sullen orange urban night beyond.

'Call it sentiment,' she muses. 'For old times' sake. You gave me my second chance, remember? But if you're still within the city limits when I come looking for you at dawn, I will kill you. Do you understand?'

'Oh, yes.'

'They all drank your blood. You're finished here.'

'I know.'

* * *

Rosa 'Gift of Life': yellow-pink blend, hybrid tea rose

Dismounting from him, she lays her free hand on the steel cable supporting his left leg, and watches with interest as the strands turn to rust and disintegrate. 'New tricks from old dogs,' she says with a smirk, giving Naylor's heart a little squeeze.

When his leg drops the pain is horrible; when the second falls it feels like his back is breaking. Estelle leaves him lying there, walks round to his right arm and frees that too.

'Let yourself out, Reynauld.'

He doesn't watch her go. It takes him a long time to gather himself and roll on the crossbeam, hauling his body by pulling down on his pierced wrist. He has to grope his way up to the bolt and for a nasty moment he thinks it isn't going to let go of the cable end. After that the cable has to be pulled out through the wound, inch by agonising inch.

The first thing that happens when he's free is that he falls on to the boards and lies there winded.

He licks splashes of his own spilt blood from the rough wood.

He can't climb down; he's too weak. He simply crawls to the edge of the boards and drops into the darkness, landing on the tracks. Fortunately falls don't injure him, but it takes nearly ten minutes for him to get up on his feet and climb up on to the concrete passenger platform. It's quite dark down here now, quite silent. Human senses would be nearly useless, but his inner vision is sharpened by desperation. Naked, filthy and injured, his first need is blood. Hunger is the only thing keeping him conscious now. Hunger is his strength, and it doesn't fail him. He can sense rats out there in the darkness, little flickering bulbs in the blackness, their rapid heartbeats like the twinkle of red stars. But there's something else too; close by. Something much bigger and warmer. Reynauld grinds his knuckles against the concrete and starts to crawl toward it.

There: huddled in the dark against a tiled wall. Bleeding a little, but still aglow with life despite everything. He's close enough to smell her.

'Amanda,' he rasps. Relief claws the inside of his throat. His voice doesn't sound like his own, but she recognises him.

'Reynauld? You're all right?'

She's nearly blind in this light; she reaches out toward his voice, her hands shaking. He takes them and presses them to his face, lets her feel her way down his chest and arms. She weeps, repeating his name. Inside him, the hunger roars.

* * *

Rosa 'Mother's Love': yellow-pink blend, miniature rose

'Oh, God, Reynauld. I'm so sorry!' The words sound utterly pathetic to her, though she means them with all her heart. Her tears are falling on his raw and bleeding body as if remorse itself could heal him. She wants to hold him tight, but she's scared of hurting him more. She wants to break her heart open and pour out her guilt and her anguish until he sees only the love.

'You let them in to take me.' His grip, descending on her shoulders, is far from gentle: he might be weakened but he's still strong enough to make her gasp. 'Why?' he demands. 'Why did you do it?'

'I didn't want to!'

'But you did it anyway.' His voice has dropped to a growl. Anyone else would recoil from the threat in it, but Amanda is not afraid. Now that Reynauld is somehow, miraculously, safe again, nothing in the world can make her afraid.

'They have Tim,' she says hoarsely. 'I heard him on the phone – they've taken him hostage. Oh, God, Reynauld. They threatened to kill him unless I gave you up!'

Reynauld's voice is a barely human snarl now. 'And you chose him over me?'

'Reynauld –'

'You don't even see him!'

'He's my son!' Her cry is full of pain. Reynauld knows all about the broken, distant relationship between Tim and her. He knows, but he doesn't understand how much it has hurt her, or how inexorable are her instincts. He can't feel what she felt, and despair makes her cry out, 'How could *you* understand? – you don't have children. You're immortal!'

He grips her jaw like he's going to break her neck, but she manages to lift a hand and lays it on his cheek. She knows what he's going to do.

* * *

Rosa 'Forever Yours': dark-red, hybrid tea rose

For Reynauld, rage and hunger are now indistinguishable.

'Just drink,' she gasps. 'Take it all. I love you.'

And Reynauld wrenches her head to one side, baring her throat, and bites down savagely.

* * *

But here in the City, all the roses grow red.

9: Two, two the Lily-White Boys, clothed all in green-O

Once upon a time there was a girl who fell into a fairytale.

Her name was Shanella and she came from a poor family; her father was a sailor on a merchant ship and she hadn't seen him since she was a little baby, and her mother needed help to keep food on the table. So Shanella went out to work, and because she was a brave girl and not scared of anything she ended up working in the house of a witch.

The witch was named Estelle. Despite being very beautiful she had a reputation for wickedness, but she wasn't cruel to Shanella herself: perhaps she was too busy thinking up bigger badder mischief to notice a servant girl. Oh, the witch certainly made her work hard: up at dawn making the beds and cleaning and fetching the shopping and serving at table, all the way through to midnight when she fed the six Siamese cats and crept to her own bed in the attic. But Shanella did not complain. Shanella wasn't the sort of girl who complained or worried. She was glad to have somewhere to live and plenty to eat, and when she had a moment's free time she would just sit and admire all the pretty things in the witch's house, all the jewellery and the paintings and the furniture; and with a smile on her face she would dream of the day when she owned a house of her own and beautiful ornaments and perhaps one little Siamese kitten. When her father came back from the sea, she told herself, he would bring all the money with him he had made over the years, and make her and her mother rich and comfortable for the rest of their lives.

One night Shanella was just getting ready for bed in her room at the very top of the house when she was called by the Housekeeper: 'Quick as you can, Shanella – go to Madame's bedroom, find the black lacquered box by her bed, and take it to the Green Room.'

'But I've taken off my dress and I'm all in my petticoat,' protested Shanella.

'I don't care if you're naked, girl! Madame wants that black lacquered box right now, and don't you keep her waiting. Trip-trap!'

So Shanella, all in her petticoat and with her feet bare and not even her stockings on, ran trip-trap down the stairs to the witch's bedroom to fetch the box for her. Estelle liked to have this particular box at her side most of the time when she was at home: while she ate or entertained guests she wanted to keep it to hand, and would often stare at it. Nobody in the household knew what was inside, Shanella least of all. But she knew better than to keep the witch waiting.

There was a man lying on the bedroom floor when she went in, but he didn't have any clothes on so Shanella was careful not to look at him. He must be asleep, she thought. She went straight to the dresser where the black lacquer box rested and took it up so that she could run back, trip-trap, all the way to the Green Room. But as she picked it up she felt something inside the box give a leap and a thump, and it startled her so much that she dropped the whole thing on the carpet.

For a while she just looked at the box, lying there, but it made no more noises. She wondered if there was some small animal alive inside the box, and she felt worried that she might have hurt it by dropping it. What could it be, she asked herself, that the witch prized it so much? Carefully, though she knew she ought not to, Shanella opened the lid.

Inside, nested on rose petals as red as blood, was a blackened human heart. And as she watched, it clenched itself in a single beat, spitting a little gore.

Now Shanella was afraid, because she guessed that this must be the witch's own heart, kept out of her breast for safekeeping. She'd heard stories of such things. It meant that Estelle was a very wicked witch indeed. Quickly she closed the lid and picked up the box – but it was already too late, because there was a black splash of witch's blood on her white petticoat now that she could not hide.

Trembling, Shanella rode in the elevator all the way up to the Green Room, which was high in one of the towers. It was a very beautiful room because the witch had filled it with trees and plants and flowers, all growing in big tubs, and there were birds and butterflies flying loose so that it was like a garden indoors. When the yellow lamps were lit it looked like a forest by daylight, and when the lamps were dark it looked like a forest at night, but today the lamps had green shades and the whole room looked as mysterious as the realm of Old Dame Circe, who was the first witch of all and lived under the sea. Among the leaves crept the six Siamese cats, watching. Shanella stole in quietly, hoping not to be noticed as she put the box by the witch's favourite chair – but it was too late. Estelle was already there and waiting, her long nails clicking on the armrest.

'What is your name, girl?' she asked.

'Shanella, Madame.'

'Why is it that you are all in your petticoat and with no shoes, Shanella?'

'I was in such a hurry, Madame, to bring you your box, that I had no time to dress.'

'And what is that stain on your skirt, Shanella?'

'I spilt some ink upon it, Madame,' she lied, because she was afraid to confess that she had looked inside the box.

Estelle nodded to herself. 'You had better go downstairs, Shanella. There are two men there that I have summoned to attend on me. Bring them up, and don't delay. Trip-trap!'

Back down the stairs Shanella ran, trip-trap, all in her petticoat and her bare feet, right to the lobby of the witch's house. There were two men waiting there, just as she'd been told. One was as golden as the sun, with yellow hair and brown eyes, and he was pacing up and down, looking nervous. The other was as pale and silvery as the moon, with grey hair and blue eyes, and he sat with his head in his hands as if in despair.

'You must come with me, to see Madame Estelle,' Shanella told them. The two men stared at her all in her petticoat and her bare feet, but they followed her into the elevator. They appeared so miserable that Shanella felt sorry for them.

'Are you afraid?' she asked, as they ascended.

'We are,' the man of gold told her.

'We are afraid that Estelle will hold us prisoners here,' added the man of silver, 'and never let us go.'

Shanella nodded sadly. 'You should be afraid,' she confided, 'because Madame is a very wicked witch, who keeps her heart in a box of black lacquer. I've seen it,' she added, as the two men looked at each other. 'But I will try and help you if I can.'

'What can you do?' wondered the man of silver. 'You're only a servant girl.'

'Hush,' said the man of gold, who was even more handsome than his friend. 'Don't say that. We may be grateful for her help yet.'

Shanella led them both into the Green Room where they found the witch sat waiting for them, a knife in her hand and a bowl of salt on the table next to it. The black lacquer box was in her lap and, as they approached, Shanella heard the lid snap back into place, and she saw the witch lick her lips.

'Take off your clothes,' she said to the two men.

'Estelle ...'

'I never give instructions twice.'

So they obeyed, and Shanella didn't know where to look. The green light made their bodies look all sea-shaded and glimmery, but made the witch look as dark and deadly as an eel lurking among the weeds.

'Now take up these chains and bind their hands,' said the witch, and Shanella obeyed, binding the wrists of the two men behind their backs. She did not do it very tight, though, because she felt sorry for them. It made her feel strange, holding their arms and seeing their bodies, without a stitch of clothing on but still so handsome. She was too busy concentrating on her task to listen to what the men were saying to the witch, and their protestations were of no use anyway because Estelle had no mercy. She dipped the knife in the salt and took the man of silver by the hair, pulling his head back and bending him right over until he was almost falling.

'Make no sound, or it will be the worse for you,' she warned him.

Then she began to cut his chest, drawing her wicked sigil there with the tip of the knife. The man of silver made no cry, not then, though his face twisted with the pain. Not until she had finished, and the blood was running in little lines all the way down to his thighs, and she took up a handful of salt and rubbed it into his wounds: then he made a small noise of pain.

'What was that noise?' the witch asked.

'Madame,' said Shanella, wringing her hands, 'it was only the mew of a cat.'

'Is that so? Then you keep silent too.'

The witch turned to the man of gold next, warning him also: 'Make no sound, or it will be the worse for you.' So he was silent while she cut his chest, making the same signature there on his breast as on the other man's, only this time his chest was all rough with golden hair and the blood did not run so freely down to his belly and thighs. But when she rubbed salt into the open wounds, he too could not help crying out a little.

'What was that noise?' the witch asked.

'Truly, Madame,' said Shanella again, 'it was only the mew of a cat.'

'Is that so? Then sit yourself down, girl, and you keep silent too.'

Shanella obeyed, as she had to. She saw that by this time the pain was making the pintles of those two men swell up stiff and proud, all sticking out and getting in the way. Their eyes were strange and dark too, from the blood. The witch laid hands on both men and rubbed their pricks cruelly, making them writhe with shame. They could not stop her because their hands were tied at their backs, you see. She licked the blood on their chests and kissed their lips and though they tried to pull away from her she had them both firmly in hand and they were as helpless as kittens. Then she pulled them both so they were facing each other and their two pintles bumped up together, fip-fap, one springing from a nest of gold and one from a nest of silver, but both big and fine and eager.

'No,' said the man of silver, whose name – Shanella had gathered – was Wakefield. He tried to pull away, but his prick was still pointing at the other man.

'A prize to the rider,' laughed the witch, rubbing their lengths together between her palms. 'Which one of you will it be?'

The man of gold, whose name was Ben, did not try to pull away. His mouth had gone a very strange shape, like he was trying to hold himself together, and he was breathing hard as he pushed his hips forward, rubbing up against Estelle's hands and Wakefield's cockalorum. He kept staring at the blood on Wakefield's chest, and Wakefield kept staring at the blood on his, and both men were panting and looked so angry and strange that Shanella didn't know what to think.

Even when the witch stepped away altogether and left them to it, the two men did not break apart. Ben pressed in closer to his friend, nuzzling his lips to the man's cheek and jaw like he was smelling something good to eat. Two hard pricks fenced against each other like parrying swords, and two velvety ball-sacs brushed and bumped together.

Shanella thought she had never seen anything so disconcerting as those two pricks a-rubbing each other. It made her feel all sweet and sticky, like honey running out of a comb.

'Come on,' said Ben, with a voice thick as batter.

'I am not her toy –' Wakefield gasped.

With a wrench Ben got his hands free of the chains. He

lost the skin off them doing it, but he got both hands out and seized Wakefield's face between them, and to Shanella it looked for a moment like they were kissing, before she saw the flash of teeth and the blood on both pairs of lips. In the green light the blood looked black.

Shanella was glad, though she was shocked. She had wanted the man of gold to kiss her, not the man of silver, so she was glad he was only biting. She was glad when he wrenched the man of silver over on to the rug, pinned him flat on his back by the jaw, and bent his head to the slashes on his chest to suck and gnaw at the wounds there. When the salt made him spit he fastened on the man of silver's dark nipples instead, piercing them both in turn. Wakefield howled and arched his back and writhed from side to side, tearing his own hands from his bonds. Their stiff pricks bobbed and stabbed at each other. As Wakefield got his hands on Ben's head it looked for a moment as if he would break his neck. The man of silver's throat corded with strain and he threw back his head, his lips peeling back from teeth like daggers.

Then Shanella saw which way he was pushing: down. Down toward his own belly, which Ben bit avidly. Down toward his crotch and his full prick, all shiny with its being swollen, and bursting with the need to be sheathed – even if that sheathing meant being bitten. Perhaps especially if it meant being bitten. Both men spasmed as Ben's teeth fastened in the flesh offered to them, and Wakefield cried out. There was a moment of stillness. Then the man of gold swung himself in a circle, right over the man of silver, straddling his head, prick to mouth, and with a groan sank down into the waiting throat and jaws below.

Gold and silver, they made a perfect match, two halves of a circle without beginning or end. Gold and silver together, they kicked and humped and wriggled on the rug; two pricks in two mouths and both men ravenous, both almost choking each other, rolling from side to side and heaving their bodies one upon the other. The pounding of their hips became frantic, but their groans could only be heard coming muffled from their chests, as each man's throat was crammed with meat. Hips pumped. Muscles locked like stone. Wakefield's hands clawed muscle – drawing more blood – and then, as Ben stretched out quivering legs and thrust to his triumphant conclusion, those hands suddenly dropped limply.

Both men fell away from each other after that, revealing bloodstained lips and turgid, bloody cocks as they rolled on to their backs.

That was when the witch stepped in, taking the man of silver by the hair and pulling him across the floor until the two men were hip to hip. Wakefield hissed protest once, baring his teeth with instinctive fury, but Estelle slapped his face and he swallowed his indignation. The witch knelt over them both. She took their crimsoned pricks in her hands and bent to suck from each in turn, swallowing hard. Her dark head bobbed from pintle to pintle, and neither man put up any fight when she bit them, or offered to bite her in return. They simply submitted, bucking and arching their backs and groaning, as she fed deep and long. Two pricks emerged and disappeared between her dark lips, shiny with spit and blood. She took them both up to a climax – first Ben, then Wakefield – and each time pulled her head away so that their seed spurted out in great gushes over their bellies, white as salt.

Shanella could only stare in terror; at their red flesh kneaded in the witch's grasp, at the glaze pooling on their beautiful bodies. She clutched herself between the legs for comfort.

The witch did not stop. The witch did it again, hounding them to crisis after crisis. She kept drinking until they were gasping in fear and torment as much as in pleasure. Only when she was replete did she let them go. Their eyes were black and blank with hunger.

'My poor boys,' said she. 'You must be parched.'

Swaggering to her feet, she lunged to snatch up Shanella, who thought she had never seen anything so awful as those empty witch eyes or those full, black-stained lips. Her heart was racing so hard, trip-trap, that she thought she would faint.

'Here,' the witch said; 'take this one.' So saying, she tossed Shanella into the outstretched arms of the two men. Shanella shrieked once.

'Those noisy cats,' said the witch, shaking her head.

And Shanella lived happily ever after to the end of her days.

10: One is one, and all alone

So I quit nursing altogether, after he turned up. There are some things no one should have to put up with – and I've put up with a fair fistful in my time, let me tell you. Drunks and loonies every night when I was in the public sector: knife-fights in Casualty and people who'd spit on you even while you were trying to staunch their bleeding wounds; hysterical mobs of girlfriends and dirty old bastards who'd stick their hands up your skirt. Not to mention halfwit young doctors who knew less than I did, and consultants who treated us like dog-dirt.

I thought that things would be easier when I made the jump into private practice. I thought it would all be ingrowing toenails and breast enhancements – and to be fair it was easier, and there was plenty of that. We did a lot of cosmetic surgery at Nine Elms Hospital, a lot of hip replacements, a lot of scans and biopsies – you know: the sort of problem that isn't immediately life-threatening but you wish could be done faster than on the Health Service, and in more comfort. If you were standing outside the place now, in its wooded garden, you'd think you were looking at a country house hotel. Inside, it looks more a luxury spa, all plush carpets and fresh flowers and guests – we aren't allowed to call them 'patients' – in complimentary white dressing-gowns. I'm not saying the guests were all sweetness and light, that they always treated us with gratitude. But no one ever tried to punch me, and they were at least sober. And young. You know, relatively. In public healthcare so much of the work is in Geriatrics, and that's a soul-crushing business. At least the patients at Nine Elms stand a good chance of getting better after admission.

It was a good job, I had. But I'm not going back.

The night *he* turned up I'd finished my 2 a.m. round of the rooms and was down in the lobby, killing time with Stefan, the night orderly. Stefan came from Poland originally and has a big bony face and big bony hands and gappy teeth. It sounds ugly but somehow it worked and he had a certain way about him, the horny beggar. He liked to drag me into a supply cupboard and shaft me from behind, up against the rattling shelves of drip tubes and dressings. He liked to push my boobs together and stick his face down into the cleft between, snuffling and slurping. He was a bit of fun, was Stefan. We'd go at it most nights when our shifts coincided.

So I was sitting on his lap, behind the desk with its ranks of CCTV monitors, with the skirt of my nurse's uniform rucked up to my hips to give his tickling fingers access to my undercarriage, and his big Polish *kaszanka* sticking up between us, hot in my hand. We weren't doing anything heavy yet, just a bit of mutual teasing, and I was just popping his plum out to say Hello when a taxi pulled up outside the front door. I twisted to see it in the monitor; it was a black cab from the City. I was surprised to see one out this far, and at this time of night. The rear door opened and a figure got out, hunched and bulky, blurred by the camera into a shadowy mass.

Stefan eased me off his lap as he frowned at the screen and thumbed the intercom. 'Attention. This is private property. No public access permitted at this time of night.'

The figure didn't pause. The security doors, all modern smoked glass under that Georgian portico, were electronically locked, of course, because any hospital can be targeted by thieves looking for drugs. I could see the red 'locked' light glowing over the lintel. That didn't stop them sweeping aside with a faint pneumatic hiss, and the man striding straight into the lobby.

The electrics must have been playing up.

'Hell,' said Stefan, struggling to get his cock back into his trousers before leaping into action.

'Sir,' I said, jerking my skirt straight and hurrying out from behind the counter. I could see straightaway that he was carrying a limp figure in his arms, and there was the familiar hue of blood all over her torn clothes. 'This is a private hospital; we don't have a casualty department. You need to ring an ambulance.'

'She needs a transfusion. Now.' His voice was rasping and deep. I took in little of his appearance other than that he was dark-haired: my attention was all on the woman in his arms, who looked so pale and slack that I couldn't be at all sure she was alive.

'We haven't got a casualty department,' I repeated, louder and firmer. 'We don't have the facilities to deal with injuries. I'll ring the proper emergency services for you, sir.'

'Blood,' he said. 'O negative. Now. Page Dr Hogg.'

My hand paused over the telephone. Dr Hogg was on our staff and he was actually on call tonight, if one of the guests required a doctor. I wondered how the man knew that, and looked at him sharply, wondering if it were someone I ought to recognise. But he was a stranger to me; dark-eyed and dishevelled. So dark-eyed, in fact, that I got the disconcerting impression that he had no sclera at all, just blackness behind those narrowed slits.

'Keep calm, sir, please,' said Stefan, finally stepping out from behind the shelter of the desk. 'The nurse will ring emergency services for you; the ambulance will be here very soo–'

'*Call Dr Hogg*. Now.' His voice was extraordinary; I felt the force of it strike my breastbone. Something cold gripped my heart and squeezed – and that is no metaphor: the sensation was entirely physical and utterly terrifying. And then it was gone and both Stefan and I were gasping and clutching at our chests.

'Jesus, Jesus, Jesus,' Stefan muttered, crossing himself. 'Holy Mother of God.'

'Call Dr Hogg,' I ordered, my voice faint. 'I'll get plasma.' I wanted the excuse to get out of there. But I did go for the blood-plasma, and I did hurry. I grabbed a wheeled stretcher from the waystation and jogged back with it. When I got into the lobby the man was standing there exactly as I'd left him, looking down at the woman in his arms. He must have been pretty strong, thinking about it afterwards; he didn't show any sign of strain, supporting her weight. Stefan was hunched behind the desk, ringing through to the surgical team, and Dr Hogg stumbled out of the lift with his bed-hair still sticking up in all directions just as we laid the woman down on the gurney and I started to punch the cannula needle into her arm.

'Oh, hell,' said Dr Hogg. He knew the strange man; from the look of dismay on his face there was no doubting that.

Mobster, I concluded, setting my jaw and puncturing the ashen skin. She had dried and blackened blood all over the lower part of her face and neck. I'd thought my days dealing with this sort of mess were over.

And that was how they checked into the hospital, those two. She ended up in one of the luxury guest rooms, and he installed himself in the family room adjoining it. 'Mr and Mrs Smith' they were signed in as, as if they were a shameful adulterous couple in a 1960s bed-and-breakfast. 'Smith', my ass: 'Singh' I might have believed, given the midnight darkness of his eyes and hair. Whether they were actually a couple I couldn't guess, at first: she was certainly a bit older than him.

We pumped her full of blood, but she didn't regain consciousness that night. To be honest I was surprised she wasn't dead, given how much she'd lost. Scans showed brain activity at an absolute minimum. There were multiple shallow stab wounds in her throat and more, along with grazes and cuts, all over her skinny, dirty body, as if she'd been dragged down the street. Her clothes were torn, her shoes missing. It took me about thirty seconds to wonder if Mr Smith were the perpetrator.

You know how you sometimes like someone on sight, before you even get to know them? Well, I disliked that man on sight. He gave me the creeps. It wasn't just that weird thing he'd done with his voice either. He was one of those guys who just oozed money and privilege. He was used to having people do exactly what he told them, and everyone who wasn't doing something for him was beneath his notice. You could see it in his every glance: he didn't throw himself on the doctor's expertise or look for reassurance from the nursing staff. He didn't beg us to tell him if his girlfriend would be all right. He just looked straight through us all, as if we hardly existed.

He seemed genuinely concerned for the woman, that much

I admit. Then again, abusers often are. He sat up with her for the rest of the night, refusing food and drink, holding her hand and sometimes pressing it to his cheek. But he didn't cry or try to talk to her; he just stared. Like I said, creepy. If she was his girlfriend, I thought, I didn't envy her: I'd just bet he was one of those psychotically jealous, possessive types.

Just before my shift ended he gave up and locked himself in his room to sleep.

* * *

When I came in on duty the following evening I was surprised to find them both still there. More surprised still, when I looked through the clipboard of her medical notes. The human body can do some weird stuff, but in the ordinary run of things there shouldn't have been any way Mrs Smith was alive. She'd lost so much blood that her brain and heart should have shut down, and I couldn't see what had been sustaining her, even unconscious. I cornered one of the day doctors on his way out and asked, 'Shouldn't Mrs Smith have been transferred to an intensive care unit by now?'

'Um,' said Dr Bellingham. 'It's been decided that we're her primary medical caregivers.'

'But we haven't really got the facilities to look after coma patients, have we?'

He puffed out his chest. 'Mrs Smith is our guest, and we've been requested to keep her here.'

'By Mr Smith?'

He blinked like a mouse in a trap. 'Yes. By Mr Smith. As you say.'

I didn't question any further. It was clear that Mr Smith had influence and had been throwing it around. I went round to her room out of sheer nosiness and didn't bother knocking – a calculated impoliteness, I admit. He was sitting back by the bed, his elbows on the mattress, his bowed head in his hands and his eyes closed, which is why he didn't notice me entering, not at first. I had a chance to take in the scene; the woman lying still and silent against her pillows, the man hunched over her, a picture of misery. He dropped one hand to clasp hers and I heard a whisper: '… so sorry, Amanda, so sorry I can't start …'

That was when he realised I was standing there and he lifted his face. He was a bit of a looker, that guy, if you like the Middle Eastern thing. But his face was a mess now: drawn in lines of wretched despair, and deeply haggard – even more so than I remembered from last night. He blinked at me; he must have been momentarily blind, because there was black stuff oozing out from his eyes, black runnels already tracked down his cheeks. I thought it was mascara at first, crazy though that sounds. Then I just didn't know what to think. I mean, you can't cry blood, can you? And if you did it wouldn't be black, would it?

It was so freaky that the only thing I could do was pretend I hadn't noticed.

I'll give him credit: he didn't try to hide his face and he didn't get defensive. Indifferent to my witness, he just looked at me with those terrible, bleeding eyes, like all his pain had been distilled into material form and could no longer be contained. For a moment I felt a reluctant sympathy for him, despite my skin crawling. But I buried both under a businesslike manner, bustling forward to the bed.

'Just going to turn her on her side,' I announced, running an appraising eye over the banks of machines monitoring her every function. 'We don't want bedsores, do we?' They'd put her on a medical ventilator, just to be on the safe side, and you could hardly see her thin, rather refined face under the mask. She was rather pretty, I thought – or at least she had been, a few years back. She made me think me of some *grande dame* of the theatre, all fine bones and faded beauty. Her silvery hair was still matted with dried blood in parts and I made a note on her details board that she needed a wash tomorrow when the dayshift came on.

'Will you give me a hand, please?' I asked, but I was speaking to myself. The room was empty; somehow he'd slipped away without me seeing a thing.

* * *

The third night was when it got really crazy. I was making up a bed in an unused room ...

OK: I was with Stefan. I had been making up the bed when he snuck into the room behind me, tossed me forward on to the mattress and pulled my skirt up and my panties down. I responded by spreading my legs and wriggling my ass at him, of course, and his reaction was to sink to his knees behind me and bury his face between my cheeks, pushing them apart with his hands so he could get his tongue right to the tight hole of my bottom. God: that one took me by surprise, I can tell you. I kicked and wriggled in outrage, but he pinned me down effortlessly and licked at my pucker with his hot wet tongue until all my reserve exploded out through the top of my skull and I was giggling and sighing like a teenager getting her first oral. Shocked that he'd do it, and astonished how good it felt to be teased there on my most sensitive and intimate flesh. My muscles fluttered and clenched, while hot and cold flashes danced over my skin.

When he straightened his tongue to a point and began probing, I began to moan breathily: 'Oh, yes. I want your cock, you dirty bastard. I want your big cock in my asshole.' He stuck his finger in me instead and I muffled my squeal in the top sheet as he wriggled it around. It felt so wrong and so right, both at the same time, and the wrongness was what made it right. My hips danced, impatient. 'Oh, go on, yes, go on!'

He laughed and nipped at my bum cheek with his teeth. 'I think you are a dirty girl, a bad nurse.'

'Oh, God, Stefan! I'll be good, I promise – if you fuck me.'

'Promise?'

'I promise! Just give it to me, in the ass – please.'

There was the sound of a zipper being pulled down, of a condom packet crinkling, of his breath coming in constricted snorts against my bouncing flesh. Then he stood and as I wriggled my hand under me on the bed, feeling for my clit, I felt the thick tip of his cock rake through my wet gash and nudge up against my bum-hole, clumsy but determined. He stooped over me, his breath coming in hot gusts against my ear

That's when the pager at my belt went off.

Swearing, I wriggled the little electronic tyrant from beneath me and brought it up under my nose to see who'd pushed their Nurse button. 'Oh, hell. You'd better stop, Stefan. It's Mrs Freeman.'

'Fuck her,' he suggested with a grunt, trying his best to do just that to me. His cock was already embedded in the airtight seal of my ring. It was with reluctance – and some effort – that I elbowed him in the ribs and rolled out from beneath him.

'She's got a heart condition. I'll get back to you.' I yanked up my panties and hurried out, with only a reluctant grimace for poor Stefan, stiff as a flagpole but with no flag to run up it. I'm not a bad nurse, see. I put the patients first, even under duress.

I reached Mrs Freeman's room and found her gasping and flapping her hands about.

I jumped to the heart-rate monitor, interpreting the numbers. 'What's up, Mrs Freeman?'

'Oh, my dear, my dear – there was a man in my room!'

'A man? Are you sure?'

'Yes! I just woke up and he was there, leaning over me!'

My concerns blew away at once: she'd been having a nightmare and carried it through into waking. I had to force myself not to snap at her. I mean, she wasn't to know she'd interrupted my roll with Stefan – but *honestly* – how dumb can you get? There was no sign of any trouble on her monitor, though she was clutching at her chest and throat. I looked round the room to check there was no other occupant, but the pristine chamber was empty of course.

'Well, there's nobody here now. Are you sure, Mrs Freeman? Are you sure you weren't just having a dream?'

'Of course I'm sure! He pulled down my nightie!'

Frankly I couldn't imagine anyone wanting to pull down Mrs Freeman's polka-dotted nightdress and expose that big freckle-painted chest, leathery from years of ill-advised sunbathing. But I looked anyway, dutifully. To my surprise her gown was actually ripped; her gold crucifix gleamed up at me from her exposed breastbone. Mrs Freeman was a good Catholic and had had the priest in to see her on her first day of admission.

I frowned. Presumably she'd done it herself, in her sleep.

After helping her get changed into a new gown and

reassuring her that there was absolutely no one there and that I'd check in all the adjacent rooms and set Stefan to watch over the corridor, I went to find the orderly in question. We had unfinished business, after all. I couldn't find him, to my irritation. He wasn't waiting in the unoccupied bedroom and he wasn't at his post in the front lobby. I paced through the corridors, wondering what he was playing at, until I reached the men's toilet at the end of the wing. The lights were off but I pushed open the door and flicked the switch and blinked as the strip bulb flickered into life.

'Stefan?'

And there he was, lying against the wall, under the towel roll. He stirred groggily as I approached him, mumbling my name and trying to shield his eyes from the light.

'Stefan? Are you OK? What happened?' I'm used to dealing with trouble, but my voice sounded too loud and too anxious in this echoing room. Stefan was my first backup if anything went wrong or needed dealing with: it rattled me to see him down like that. Kneeling over him I checked for wounds, sliding my hand round the back of his head in case he'd injured it in falling.

'Joyce.' He gazed up at me, his pupils wildly dilated, his lips slack. My groping hand found no injury. Drugs, was my immediate suspicion – but he'd been fine a quarter of an hour ago. What had happened to him? With clumsy hands he fumbled at my breasts. 'Joyce ... Gi's a blowjob.'

He sounded drunk, he looked stoned, and there was a bulge in his pants that he was trying to get me to grab on to. But when I pulled my hand from his head, despite not having detected any swelling I found blood on my palm – two little smears. Knocking his groping hands aside impatiently I rolled him enough to get a look at the nape of his neck.

There: two small shallow wounds, barely bloody. Just like the ones Mrs Smith had been inflicted with.

I took a deep breath. If I rang for backup now, Stefan would get the sack: this looked too much like getting wasted on duty. And I didn't think he'd been taking anything illicit. My suspicions were focused on someone else entirely. I was sure I knew who was involved.

You've no idea how hard this was for me. I'm a dyed-in-the-wool sceptic: I don't believe in any of this nonsense. Yet the dark certainty roiled in my gut, propelling me to my feet. Certainty, and anger. Fury that anyone had brought this madness into my ward, on my shift.

I left Stefan. Yes, I know it sounds callous, but I didn't think he was in danger any more. I walked back down the corridor to the guest rooms and threw open the door into Mrs Smith's and marched straight in.

Mr Smith was sitting on the bed with her, cradling her against his chest. Her oxygen mask was off; I would have protested, automatically, except that one fundamental thing had changed: she was conscious. I could see that because she was holding his forearm to her face, and her lips were pressed to his wrist. My mouth fell open and no sound came out.

Slowly, he turned his face up and locked his gaze on mine. That look was enough to douse all my hot indignation and turn my insides to ice instead.

'Oh,' I managed to say. Then I turned and headed for the door.

He was there in front of me. I've no idea how. He was standing in the doorway, his fingers resting lightly on the frame either side, and from the wound in his wrist the black blood oozed down toward his fingertips. He smiled, very faintly, and with no warmth.

I cast a terrified glance over my shoulder; Mrs Smith was kneeling up in bed, bereft and groping blindly. Her mouth was smeared with the dark blood.

'I am sorry.' His voice was smooth; it held none of the broken and desperate sincerity of his earlier plea for forgiveness, the one I'd overheard him whispering to her. 'Normally I'd try not to be so brusque. But she needs to feed.' He caught the front of my uniform in one hand and pulled me up against him.

All the air left my lungs – I mean, Christ, I hadn't fully realised until now how much he *loomed* over me, how physically dominant he was. My brain went completely blank. I'd always prided myself on being able to think and act fast in threat situations, but right now his eyes seemed to drain all the volition out of my limbs. All I could think of was the incredible hardness of his body, the way mine had squashed against it as our frames collided. The speed and the strength in him.

He showed that strength by taking the front of my uniform in both fists and tearing it open to my waist, without the slightest discernable effort. Only the fabric protested. He looked down at me, pleased: my breasts are big and firm, full of bounce. Stefan loves them, the poor guy, and this man seemed equally appreciative. His mouth hooked up at the corner. I said before he was handsome, didn't I? Handsome like Satan. My insides were turning to butter and it was running out down between my thighs.

He snapped the front of my bra and let my breasts tumble out. My nipples ripened from soft berries to hard nuts at the touch of the air, tingling.

'No,' I said weakly: the first word I'd managed to utter. It didn't seem to come from anywhere – certainly not my conscious mind, which had melted into a soup of unbelief. It was a leftover; a reflex protest.

'Shush.' One cool finger brushed my lips gently, sealing them. He reached behind him to close the door, but his gaze never left me.

Tears welled into my eyes

'The thing is,' he said as if confiding in me, his hands gripping my waist, 'her new teeth have not come in yet. So I think you'd prefer it if I took the lead.' Then he lifted me bodily – right up, to bring my breasts to his face. And he took my right nipple full into his mouth, and bit me.

There was pain. Then it was gone, and something else was there in its place. Goddamn – I've been on a diamorphine infusion once, when I broke my leg: I'll tell you now, that had nothing on this. That bite turned my nipple into a clit and my whole body into one giant sexual organ, wet and trembling and receptive. I was aware of my hands grabbing his head and of being carried over to the bed, but my concentration was all on the pleasure; the almost unbearable pleasure of his sucking mouth. It was overwhelming and irresistible and so wrong I have no words for it.

I hated him so fucking much, even as I writhed in his embrace.

He laid me out across the bottom of the bed, and his woman came crawling down to me, brushing the tubes and the monitors off her as if they were grass-seeds. When he released my nipple from his mouth I could see there was blood welling up and running down my breast, into my cleavage, toward my throat. I tried to shut my eyes, but I couldn't. I seemed to have no will left, no power over my own body.

'Amanda,' he murmured, cupping her head in one hand and guiding her down to me. Her eyes were as empty as an animal's, betraying only hunger. My hips bucked and my thighs parted as she settled, kneeling as if at prayer, sucking my flesh between her black-stained lips. Pleasure burst and danced in my nipple all over again as she slurped at me. Her pale hair flooded my breastbone.

I looked up at his face from where I lay. He was smiling, but at her not at me. Proud, like a new father. And fearful: I saw it lurking in the corners of his eyes. I tried to lift my hands – to pull at her hair, to push him away or perhaps to pull him closer – but he intercepted my clumsy movements. To soothe my fretting he pulled up the skirt of my uniform and slipped his hand between my thighs. My panties were soaked through, and when he pressed the heel of his hand against them and began to rub with small circular movements, well, then I nearly left the planet. I could feel myself dilating under his fingers, the fabric being stretched as his fingers nearly pushed my gusset inside me. My hips lurched, pushing my mons up into his hand, showing him how open I was. He could have had me, easily, but he didn't want me. Not that way, anyway. Sliding down on the bed, never losing his hold on my sex, he took my other breast in his mouth and began to feed.

That was when I started to come, over and over and over, like waves falling on a beach. As they both squeezed and tugged at my breasts I could feel the bright orgasmic surges rolling up from my pussy to my nipples and streaming out of me, like light, into them. It didn't stop. I couldn't breathe. I started to black out between peaks, waking only to another tumbling spasm.

And then he released me. I blinked my eyes into focus just as he prised Mrs Smith – well, Amanda – from my right breast. 'That's enough now.'

She didn't like that at all. She hissed at him like a cat defending its kill, baring red teeth and grabbing at his forearm to sink her nails in.

'Amanda! That's enough!' I heard in his voice a rumble of that inexorable command he'd used on me and Stefan, and her eyes flashed wide. Then he touched her cheek in a caress and his voice softened. 'All right, come on, talk to me, Amanda. Can you hear me?'

I'd almost say he sounded afraid.

She blinked, her expression crumpling. Face to face they stared at each other over my bare breasts, their mouths sticky, their eyes full of unfathomable emotion. She sat back first, wiping the blood off her lips with her fingers, glancing helplessly at them and frowning at him as if finally waking into consciousness.

'Reynauld?' she whispered.

He blinked, biting his lip, and bowed his head. His shoulders sagged.

'Reynauld,' she said again, more forcefully. 'Where's Naylor?'

'He's gone. Dead.'

'You're safe?' she asked. Not "we" but "you", I noted – and wondered blearily what sort of messed-up world they came from where he was the one in danger.

'Yes. We're safe.' In his averted, uncertain eyes I read a strange dread. Then her hand stole out and clasped his face, wonderingly, as if to reassure herself he was really there. I saw his lips part; black tears glittered on his lower lids.

She didn't say anything else. She leaned in and kissed him, her smudged mouth trembling on his. For a moment he did not respond; I think he was still holding his breath in fear. Then his lips moved, seeking hers: quick, hard, hungry. I've never found desperation an attractive quality in a man; these were kisses of burning need and terror. He clasped her face in both hands like he was eating her breath. Then he pulled her to him across the bed – and across me as I lay supine, but I think they'd both forgotten I was even there – and rose to his feet so he could embrace the whole of her body and draw it tight against his. Pressing her face to his chest he buried his own face in her hair, and then he pulled away from her again so that he could hold her cheek in his hand and look into her eyes.

And all the time I was lying there, too weak to move, black roses blossoming behind my eyes as unconsciousness loomed; drowning in the heavy golden afterglow of their kisses.

'I took your life,' he groaned.

Her arms slipped about his neck. 'I gave it to you.' Her voice was weak and husky – but then she had no right to be talking at all, or standing up, after coming out of a three-day coma. She had bright-blue eyes, and they were wet with human-looking tears. 'Do you not know love when you see it, Reynauld?'

He grimaced. 'Love? I do, now. It's come closer to destroying me than Naylor ever did.' His fingers were infinitely tender on her face, in her hair, but his face was full of anguish. 'Amanda ... Oh, God ...'

'Shush. It's all right.'

'But, you understand ... you're going to be ...'

'It's OK, Reynauld. I can live with that.'

He laughed, bitterly. 'For ever.'

The tears spilled over her lashes and ran down her cheeks, but she smiled. 'Yes.'

'I'll help you. If you'll stay with me.'

'If I stay ...?' she wondered.

'I need you,' he said, his jaw clenched. 'With me.'

'Oh. Yes. Yes – of course.'

He hugged her fiercely to him, then kissed her again, his passion swelling into arousal. 'I need you,' he growled.

'Yes,' she breathed, pressing up against him. No exposition was necessary; the upwelling hunger in her expression was enough. His hands took possession of her bottom, hefting her whole weight up so she could wrap her slender legs about his hips. She responded by knotting her fingers in his hair to kiss him. Turning, he crossed the room in two strides and shoved her up against the wall. I heard the rasp of his breath as he tugged her flimsy hospital gown up from where it was trapped between them. From my place on the bed I could see little of her but her limbs – knees crooked up, hands clawing at his back – and the pale blur of her hair, but I could hear the soft eager noises she was making. I didn't see him make any adjustments to his own clothes, but then there was something strange about his clothes anyway; they were shredding and dissolving under the clutch of her fingers, falling away to reveal his bare back and legs.

'Amanda,' he groaned, his voice thick.

I knew the moment he entered her, from the push of his hips and her gasp of shock. Shameless, they were, doing that in front of me. But I didn't exist, so far as they were concerned. I was nothing.

And oh, God, his body was beautiful: long, hard muscles, golden-dark skin and black hair. Shreds of clothing, as dark and insubstantial as paper-ashes, flickered and floated and fell away from under her hands and heels.

'Reynauld!' she whimpered, her head thumping back against the wall. The play of his muscles was terrifying: the woman had only just recovered consciousness and he took her deep and strong, not gentle at all, his pelvis thrusting between her splayed thighs and his breath coming short and hard. Her gasps and half-articulated moans – 'Oh, yes, oh, just – go on – oh, you're – oh, my sweet god, yes oh yes oh yes' – only spurred him to greater efforts.

Judging by her cries, she was coming at the exact moment I went – out and down, into unconsciousness.

* * *

I quit my job because, when they found me the next morning, they weren't surprised. They just offered me a bonus to keep quiet. I mean – they knew. *All* the doctors. They *knew*.

The scars around my nipples are fading quickly. Last night I jabbed myself with a skewer-point just to keep them fresh. Because there should be a mark on the outside to show what's underneath.

I don't know how to express my rage.

Do you understand me? Do you understand why I quit? Why should I have to put up with that? With being used like a goddamn *ready-meal*? With what he did to me? With the way he's fucked up sex for me? – because no matter what I do it's never, ever, going to feel that good again.

Why should we put up with their sort existing at all?

11: And ever more shall be so

In the end she'd had to go to Kyle. There wasn't any choice. It wasn't like she could concentrate on anything else – her lectures, the multi-media project for the end of term, the shallow chatter of her friends in her hall of residence. The words in her books just blew across the page, like they'd already been burnt to ashes, and nothing went into her memory even when she tried to concentrate. Everyone irritated her: Ali and her whiney griping, Jay's goofing about. None of it mattered. None of it was real, as real as what she was feeling inside. All she wanted to do was go back to her room and curl up with her phone, flicking through her photos of Kyle until it was time to ring him again at 7 p.m. And afterwards, to cry to herself until she dozed off.

It hurt. It hurt beyond anything she could have imagined, just being separated from him. It was like they were two halves of a single being that had been torn in two, and the raw patch ran right up the centre of her body from crotch to throat and refused to heal. Every time she pictured his face the pain performed an exquisite twist in her belly. She wanted him so badly that she couldn't sleep at night, or escape from her dreams during the day. She wanted to wrap her limbs around his and lick the scent of cigarettes from his smooth skin. She wanted to lie and watch him clean his teeth and play on the Xbox. She wanted to straddle his slim hips and ride his cock in front of her open dorm window, the sun on her breasts, squealing with each orgasm so everybody knew how much pleasure he gave her. She wanted sex, all the time – but just to be in the same room with him, and alone, would have been enough. Keeping him company while he worked on his French translations; making him coffee; running out on errands for him while he was busy.

She loved him. She knew she'd never love anybody as much as she loved Kyle right now. She couldn't even imagine wanting somebody else. And despite her pain she felt sorry for the rest of the world, because they didn't have what she and Kyle did.

Her own college course was insignificant in comparison, withering before the furnace-blast of her desire. And at eighteen, wasn't she old enough to know what she wanted?

So she left campus one morning and set off for Paris.

And she was old enough to look after herself. She didn't need her parents' disapproval or her friends' bitchery, so she left no note and told no one. She figured she could phone from France. Sure, the lorry-driver she'd hitched a lift with on to the cross-Channel ferry had been a bit too interested, the old creep – and he'd had greasy hair and BO too, stinking of cigarettes – but she'd known how to handle it and had given him the slip when drivers were summoned back to their vehicles. She'd disembarked and gone through passport control on foot, her knapsack over her shoulder, pleased with herself for not leaving it in his cab like he'd suggested.

She hadn't figured on her phone not working on French soil. It pissed her off. Typical of the French, she thought, wondering again what Kyle saw in them, why he wanted to study abroad when he could do it just as well at home somewhere. But he was smart. He liked to throw himself into everything he did, and do it to perfection. It was one of the reasons she loved him.

She knew he'd be over the moon when she turned up. She wanted it to be a wonderful surprise, the best surprise ever, so she hadn't told him she was coming. Although, to be honest, she slightly regretted that now: it would have been nice to ring him from the port here, to make sure he was in when she reached his flat. Especially now that dusk was falling, and her excitement was wearing thin and turning to loneliness. She wished she was there already, that she didn't have the overland miles to cover. Or that she knew which bus to catch. Kyle would have been able to help her with that, if she'd been able to phone him.

Still, she could hitch again, now that the lorries had all driven off. There must be plenty of people going to Paris.

Wanting to save her meagre euros from being wasted on a taxi, she was one of the few people to leave the harbour area on foot, and it had started to rain by the time she crossed the last car park and started up the exit road. The town ahead looked distinctly industrial, a bank of warehouses and swift roads. And there was no pavement here where she walked down the length of the chain-link fence. She wondered if she'd missed the proper pedestrian exit. There weren't many cars headed out this way either, and none stopped at the jerk of her thumb. Hunched under her cagoule and rucksack, she plodded toward the streetlights. She'd have better luck hitching somewhere well-lit, she thought: if they could see she was a girl they'd be more likely to take pity on her.

Bugger the rain. Her jeans were getting colder, as they

grew sodden across the front of her thighs.

The daylight was really gone and the world was turning to a confusion of glimmering neon reflections in the wet asphalt, when a car pulled up at the kerb in front of her. It was a big, black, old-fashioned-looking vehicle of a make she didn't recognise, and the windows were smoked glass. She approached with due wariness, pushing back her hood from her face.

The driver's window slid down and a woman looked out. She was one of those well-preserved beauties, slightly reminiscent of Michelle Pfeiffer, or maybe that puppet from that old *Thunderbirds* DVD Kyle liked so much. Her platinum-blonde hair hung in a bob and she wore a grey dress that looked a bit like a uniform.

Despite everything, she almost laughed; it looked for all the world like Lady Penelope had decided to give her chauffeur the night off and drive the car herself.

'*Bonsoir, mademoiselle*,' said the woman.

'*Bonsoir*,' she answered, the word clumsy in her mouth. 'I'm sorry – do you speak English?'

'Oh, you're English.' The woman's eyes crinkled up. She had a lovely soft voice and an accent that sounded a bit posh and definitely English. 'Are you looking for a lift? This isn't a good place to be walking out on your own.'

'I'm trying to get to Paris. My boyfriend's at the university there.'

Those perfectly sculpted eyebrows lifted. 'Well, we're driving to Paris tonight. Do you want a lift?'

The word 'we' registered and the girl's eyes flicked to the darkened glass of the rear window. As if anticipating her question, the kerbside window rolled down and the interior light came on, a faint, pleasant scent of leather wafting from within. There was a man there, sitting towards the far door and looking out at her with interest. Like the driver, he was sort of middle-aged, but sort of hot-looking too. She wondered if she should recognise him: was he someone famous?

He opened his hand in a gesture of invitation and the door unlatched itself with a faint *thunk*.

For a fraction of a moment she hesitated. But there wasn't anything to fear, was there, with another woman in the car? Anyway, he looked nice. And ever so slightly unfocused, as if he'd just woken from a doze. He smoothed back his hair apologetically and moved up to give her plenty of space on the seat.

A trickle of rain found its way down the back of her neck and she shivered. 'Thanks,' she said. 'That'd be great. Really great.'

'You probably want to sit in the back,' the woman said. 'Front seatbelt's broken, I'm afraid. It's an old car.'

She ducked into the back and the man took her bag from her and dropped it through on to the front passenger seat.

'Hello there,' he said with a pleasant smile. 'My name's Reynauld.' He indicated the driver. 'This is Amanda.'

'Hi,' she said, settling into the leather. The upholstery seemed to embrace her. 'I'm Rose.'

'It's a pleasure to meet you, Rose. But you picked a dangerous place to try hitching: you never know who might stop for a young woman in this sort of area.'

'It worked out though, didn't it?'

'Didn't it just.' He nodded thoughtfully. 'We'd better make sure your luck holds.'

Amanda was already watching the traffic in the side-mirror and indicating to pull out. The Bentley slipped smoothly away from the pavement, its engine sound hardly rising above a purr.

'Are you sure it's not taking you out of your way?'

'Not in the least,' he answered. 'We have a hotel room booked in Paris tonight.'

She noted the singular 'room'. A couple then. Why he should be in the back and she should be driving, she couldn't guess, but rich people did weird things. Maybe he was seasick from the ferry crossing.

'Well, I'm really glad, you know. Thanks. This is nicer than my last ride.'

His answering glance evoked in her a warmth she was used to only feeling with Kyle, and she felt a brief twinge of confused guilt which was gone in a moment.

'I think we can promise that.'

The drizzle on the outside of the windows seemed to belong to another world. Rose settled her shoulders back into the seat, delighted, as the car bore her away down the empty, rain-slick roads, into the night.

* * *

There is a City. There are many cities, and in each one of them there are vampires. In your city too. They go unseen, but they are there. Perhaps they have chosen to rule benignly, or perhaps to be ruthless. But make no mistake – they are there, using us as they see fit.

Fear them.

Pity them.

For them, unlike for us, there is no escape.

www.ingramcontent.com/pod-product-compliance
Ingram Content Group UK Ltd.
Pitfield, Milton Keynes, MK11 3LW, UK
UKHW022247180325
456436UK00001B/42